STILL
AMONG
THE
LIVING

STILL AMONG THE LIVING

A NOVEL OF SUSPENSE

ZACHARY KLEIN

1817

HARPER & ROW, PUBLISHERS, New York
Grand Rapids, Philadelphia, St. Louis, San Francisco,
London, Singapore, Sydney, Tokyo, Toronto

FIRST EDITION

Designed by Kathryn Parise

LIBRARY OF CONGRESS CATALOGING-IN-PUBLICATION DATA

Klein, Zachary, 1948–
    Still among the living / Zachary Klein.—1st ed.
        p.   cm.
    ISBN 0-06-016411-5
    I. Title.
PS3561.L3768S7   1990
813'.54—dc20   89-46227

90 91 92 93 94   NK/HC   10 9 8 7 6 5 4 3 2 1

For Sue

Who is, happily, very much alive.
And who has been, in no small measure, the reason
I'm still among the living.

ACKNOWLEDGMENTS

Lots of gratitude to Herb and Nancy Katz for their regard, commitment, and effort on behalf of my novel. Their work turned a manuscript into a book and a dream into a reality. Thank you. And a special thanks to Herb, who turned *Miles to Go* into *Still Among the Living*.

I learned much of my writing craft from Susan Goodman and Sharon Singer Salinger. Without their generous time and teaching, *Still Among the Living* would be still inside my head.

Thanks also to Bill and Bonnie, Ron, Dr. J., Jeff, Pav, Eddie, Eric and Nancy and Anji-san. Your support and enthusiasm eased many a blank and anxious moment.

And thank you Larry and Eamon for a wonderful welcome to the business of book writing.

STILL
AMONG
THE
LIVING

—1—

My eyes opened half an hour before the alarm was supposed to sound. Something had sliced through my sweaty tossing. I reached for the glass on the floor and swallowed through a dry mouth, hot with leftover grass and tobacco. The harsh, grating blare of the back-door buzzer eliminated the remnants of my indeterminate dreams and dragged at my dread tight stomach. I almost spilled the water. It wouldn't have mattered; only the plants liked the lead taste. I forced my eyes closed and wrapped a pillow around my head. The buzzer kept insisting and I finally stood up. I could outwait the telephone, but lost every time to the doorbell. I held onto the dresser but avoided looking into the mirror on the way to the kitchen. I wobbled across the room, fumbled with the chain, yanked the door open, and stood gridlocked in my underwear in front of my shrink.

I stole a glance down the front of my shorts to see if my fly was open, then worried about whether Dr. James had to pick her way through sleeping drunks in the alley. My apartment was in a mixed area of the city—ranging from students and musicians to the rich and famous. I lived closer to the musicians. When I lived here years ago the alley housed a solid percentage of the city's alkies. Since this was a neighborhood the pols used to broaden the tax base, most, but not all, of my old neighbors were gone by the time I returned.

After the accident my father-in-law, Lou, bought the building and

1

put me in charge. He assured me his cash flow dictated a real-estate investment and his banker had gold-starred my city. We both knew this was bullshit since Lou didn't like the building, and hated the neighborhood the moment he saw a couple of men kissing under a streetlight. Also, Lou lived twelve hundred miles away and I had a hunch there were other hot towns closer by.

But Lou wouldn't listen and I didn't care enough to argue. I needed a cave to hibernate in and he felt guilty that he still had some family and I didn't. There was no reason for him to feel that way. He didn't lose much less in the accident than I.

The building was one of two six-flats set back like garages from the large, absentee-landlord apartment buildings that dominated the block. Between the money I got for selling the suburban house, and the salary I'd get for caretaking, I didn't have to get a job. Truth be told I wanted to be a janitor. Cleaning made me feel productive.

Lou was indirectly responsible for Dr. James as well. I had stared at the bronze dedication silhouettes in the hospital's private, plastic-paneled waiting room for so long they had begun to resemble my long-lost parents. It must have been the eighth or ninth day of the wait, when we were sitting there alone, that he said, "Boychik, you haven't said a word for two days."

I looked at him.

"I'm not exaggerating. I've been watching. Your friends come into the waiting room and you disappear into the wall. Nobody wants to bother you right now, but people are worried. I'm worried. Even if they come out of it okay"—he jerked his head toward the closed green sliding doors as his eyes fixed firmly down on his own feet—"You gotta get help. They are going to need you."

"They're not coming out of this okay." I looked away. "I appreciate your concern."

"This isn't just concern."

"Lou, let it alone. I'm experienced at watching my life disintegrate."

Well, experience is no substitute for smarts and right then I wasn't very smart. But Lou's words pulled at my skin six months later when Simon, my lawyer friend, sat impatiently explaining, "Look, I can get you a year suspended if you see a shrink. Not a bad deal for assault and battery on a bartender. All he did was say no. Shit, Matt, the witnesses said you lost your fucking *mind*."

He tried unsuccessfully to flatten his upturned jacket collar. "Jesus, I suppose it was lucky that you did go off. Otherwise it would have been suicide. He was twice your size."

"What kind of time do I get if I don't take the deal?"

Simon sat there furiously inhaling his cigar. "You *are* crazy. Listen to yourself. It's one thing to drink yourself to death, or even leave a bartender in a puddle, but jail? You know what happens to soft Jews? Prison doesn't give the kind of help that you need."

"I don't feel soft right now."

"By the time you're out you won't feel anything."

"Sounds good to me."

He kept tugging on his coat, "Well it shouldn't. I've been watching you crawl deeper and deeper into a hole and I don't much blame you. But bottom is bottom. Going to jail rather than seeing a psychologist just doesn't cut it. Damn, how afraid can you be of them? You're a fucking social worker."

"I'm not a social worker anymore, Simon."

"Whatever the hell you are isn't going to be helped by the can, Matt. Take the deal."

"Will this stick to my record?"

"I think we can do something about that."

"Simon, is there anything 'we' can't do something about?"

A small grin softened the irritability in his face. "You'll take the deal?"

I thought about the interminable hours under the stark fluorescent light of the waiting room. "Get it off my record and I'll take the deal. Hell, Lou doesn't have anyone else to look after his damn investment."

It was four years later, and every Thursday I still fought with myself about showing up at her office. I often didn't make it, and hadn't last week, but standing humiliated in my skivvies seemed like a tough cure.

—2—

I peered over Dr. James' shoulder for Brown Shirts but all I saw was the vaguely familiar face of the grocery store checkout girl. She was staring queerly at me from behind the chain-link fence of the store's parking lot. I quickly looked back to Dr. James and felt a tingle of satisfaction when I saw her pawing at the dirt with her feet.

Her words came in a rush. "I'm sorry to have caught you so off-guard. Perhaps we could move inside?"

Still unwilling to trust my voice, I nodded and backed through the open door. I closed my eyes for a second to make her disappear, but she just followed me inside. The morning chill had finally cracked my numbness and I felt like reaching for a robe, only I didn't have one. I tried talking around the lump in my throat. "Look, I have to get dressed. I haven't made coffee yet either. I'll get it in a minute."

She was looking around the kitchen with a quick nervous intensity. "Please don't go to any trouble on my account."

Although lack of use kept this room the neatest of any in the apartment, everything out of place crowded into my sight. I waved toward the kitchen table. "Look, why don't you sit down? Make yourself comfortable. Don't worry, I won't slip out the back window." I walked into the bedroom and caught a glimpse of her face in the mirror. She looked confused, as if she didn't understand what I was talking about.

I fumbled through my dresser trying to find something clean or unwrinkled. I gave up and grabbed yesterday's clothes off the chair by the bed. When I returned to the kitchen she was sitting at the table eyeing the black deco design baked into its brown enamel top.

She pointed to the table. "Why is it signed, Mr. Jacob?"

"It was a way for artists to work during the thirties." I paused behind a chair. "Listen, Dr. James, you can call me Mr. Jacob in your office but here I don't like to be called 'Mister.' There was no reason for you to come and get me. I was going to turn up." I aimed my finger at the clock. "Probably on time."

She looked startled, then jerked her hand up over her open mouth. I had trouble watching her. In her office she always seemed so implacable.

I threw up my hands. "Dr. James, I'm sorry. I didn't mean to upset you."

She gasped for air, then suddenly burst out laughing. Her shoulders trembled and her eyes filled. She was laughing out loud, while I felt like a fool. I grasped the back of the chair and felt my legs grow weak.

She rummaged through her oversized pocketbook and pulled out a man's blue handkerchief and wiped her eyes. "You thought I came to get you for our appointment. I'm sorry, Mr. . . ." She stopped and caught her breath. "What would you like me to call you?"

"I don't care. Matt, Matthew. It doesn't matter."

She placed her purse down by her feet. "Matthew seems best."

The way she said "Matthew" reminded me of my mother. I tried to hold my annoyance in check. "And you?"

"What do you mean?"

"What am I supposed to call you?"

My tone drove the laughter from her voice. "I don't mind Dr. James." She was staring at me and pressing her lips together in a tight line.

I turned away and walked over to the stove and shook the espresso pot. I thought about making fresh, but just turned on the flame under last night's leftover. I could hear her twist in the chair behind me. "This is really a wonderful kitchen. It feels so comfortable. Like my . . ."

"Grandmother's." I turned and faced her. "Dr. James, it's too early in the morning to feel like a fool. If you're not here to harass me about attendance, what the hell are you doing here? A survey of client artifacts?"

Her eyes narrowed and she spoke without a hint of amusement. "I'm not used to your sharp tongue."

"And I'm not used to having my shrink laugh at me in the middle of my kitchen."

The stand-off gave us both a moment to regroup. She ran her hand through her short brown hair. "I'm sorry for this intrusion, especially if my laughter disturbed you. I've been so anxious that it was a relief to be misunderstood." She shook her head. "The days have been such a blur that I even forgot that we meet today."

I imagined myself banging on the door to her empty office—an image that left an unwelcome taste of my own medicine in my mouth. I took two cups from the cabinet, poured some black sludge, and returned to the table. I didn't ask if she took cream or sugar.

From where I sat I could see her entire body. Her legs were crossed and her skirt pulled tight across her thighs. I grew anxious as I felt a slight movement between my legs. When we regularly met she was behind a desk, so all I usually saw was a jacket or sweater. I kept my eyes on her face. "Dr. James, what exactly are you doing here?"

She lifted the cup to her lips and drank warily. I was surprised by the maroon color of her nail polish. I was seeing things I'd never before noticed. Someone once said that paranoia was just a form of heightened awareness. I think it was Charlie Manson.

Her face was cloudy and her finger ran a trace around her eyes. "Mostly I'm here on instinct." She smiled automatically but her face continued to droop. "I'm not in the habit of visiting unannounced, and never a client's home, but I've tried to call you for two days and thought you might be keeping the phone off the hook. I took the chance of dropping by. Now that I'm here," her hand swept over the apartment like a benediction, "I keep wondering if I made a mistake?"

"Something you find disturbing about the decor?"

She spoke earnestly. "No, not at all. I like your taste. When you've talked about junk stores you made it sound like Goodwill."

"Some of this stuff is from Goodwill."

She took another tentative sip of coffee, grimaced, and ignored my remark. My anger was disappearing and in its place something like curiosity started to nibble. I guess I'm a softie when it comes to my shrink in distress.

"Look, I guessed wrong about why you came. You were right about the phone. Something seems to be bothering you, so why don't you tell me what it is." It was disconcerting to be the one doing the reassuring. I took out my cigarettes, lit one, and threw the pack on the table. What I really wanted was a joint.

She started to reach for the pack, hesitated, then pulled one out with her fingertips and looked at me. I nodded, surprised. Smoking during our hour had been an early point of contention that I had lost. I handed her my lighter and watched as she lit the cigarette, inhaled, and kept the smoke in her cheeks. It might have been funny but I felt impatient. Despite the wrestling match with the cigarette, worry never left her face.

"Dr. James, I think it would make it easier for both of us if you told me why you're here."

She tilted her head. "That's what I'm wondering about. Seeing you this angry makes me realize how complicated talking to you really is." She looked off into the living room. "Of course Eban would laugh at my discomfort. Tell me that I was acting like an uptight, traditional psychologist. Maybe he's right. Or perhaps that's just my personality." She turned back toward me and took a few rapid puffs on her cigarette. I pushed the ashtray toward her and noticed a roach half hidden among the stubbed-out butts. "Of course if Eban knew I was here because of him, he would be the one who was uptight."

Her musings only added to my hazy discomfort. "Dr. James, what are you talking about? Who is Eban? And why is anyone other than me uptight?"

She met my eyes. "For days I've thought about nothing except hiring you and now that I'm here I think it will destroy our therapeutic relationship."

At that moment I could guarantee it. "What do you want to hire me to do? I don't want to manage another building."

She shook her head impatiently. "No, not janitorial. Detective work."

I looked at her and felt helplessness sit on the neck of my frustration.

"Dr. James, I've never done any psychological research. Just legal. You know that. Graduate students are a dime a dozen around here. What do you want with me?"

She looked up from the table. "I wasn't thinking of research. I need a detective, a private investigator."

I couldn't believe what I was hearing. I felt like I was chasing the White Rabbit. "What are you trying to pull? I don't do detective work, you know that. I take care of this building and do occasional legal research for a friend. All I do with the license is hang it on the wall when I clean my gun."

"Well, I thought this might be an opportunity for you to do something else with it."

I recognized the look and tone and didn't like either. Never had. "Goddamnit, lady, it's one thing to sit in your office and push me to get more active with my life, another to create work therapy. I appreciate your good intentions, but isn't this a little much?"

Dr. James pushed her cigarette into the ashtray and pulled out the roach. "I didn't think you were still using drugs."

I shrugged and lied. "Just sometimes."

She pulled up her bag, rose to her feet, and began to stuff the handkerchief back in. "This was a terrible idea. I don't know what got into me." She finished tugging the bag closed and looked at her watch. "Believe it or not, I came here for me, not you. Please, let's meet next week at our regular time, so we can discuss all of this. I'm sorry I've upset you, but believe me there was no sub rosa therapeutic agenda for my visit. None."

Her choice of words broke through my anger. I began to laugh, and some of the tension eased. "Sub rosa agenda? Does that mean you're inviting me out for Italian subs?"

She looked flustered but I didn't care. "I'll tell you the truth; it's hard to make promises about next week. If this isn't about therapy, I can't fathom why you're here. I've never detected anything that moved on its own accord, and you know that. How will we be able to discuss anything if all I keep asking is why were you here?"

She began to fiddle with the clasp on the bag but didn't move. I stayed seated. After a moment she sat back down. She put the purse back down on the floor and placed her hands in her usual prayer position. She looked familiar and my kitchen looked familiar, but the combination of the two seemed awfully strange.

She took a deep breath. "I think I'm only compounding a mistake, but I'm sure what you say about next week is true. I know how stubborn you are. It was one of the reasons I thought of you." She paused and I pondered my bullheadedness. When she continued her voice dropped an octave; she kept her eyes on the table and I felt myself grow tense. "Eban Holmes is a therapist and friend I care strongly about. He is considered a renegade by most local psychologists. His beliefs, his politics, fall outside establishment norms and values. In fact, he wouldn't even like that I called him a therapist."

She looked up from the table and searched my face for a reaction. I forced a blank look and tone despite my uneasiness.

"What does he call himself?"

She shrugged. "It depends on the week. Consistency is not one of his virtues."

Something about her last remark left me wondering if she was referring to his work. I kept my tone neutral. "I don't quite see the problem?" There wasn't anything unusual about an oddball shrink. There sometimes seemed more charlatans hovering around the mental health field than clients. "He doesn't sound terrible," I added.

She seemed relieved by my remark. "He's not at all terrible. Quite the opposite. He even gets grudging respect for his ability to work with people who wouldn't go near a psychiatrist or psychologist." There was a moment of quiet. I had a hunch we both were thinking of the same example.

She tossed her head as if she were shaking hair from her face. "It's his writings that cause the stir. Since *The Radical Therapist* folded, no one will publish him. The journals won't print his attacks on what he calls the 'helping industry.' Eban believes that the industrialization of a professional helping hierarchy is one way the culture maintains the status quo. He is brilliant but they won't publish a word! Worse, they hate him for his assault on what he sees as their self-serving professional greed."

I was surprised and embarrassed by the bitterness and passion in her voice. The delicate therapeutic relationship we had constructed over the past four years creaked under the weight of the morning.

Still, I was aware of a hint of relief mixed in with my discomfort. Also, Eban Holmes sounded interesting. An antitherapy therapist. My kind of shrink. But I didn't think Dr. James was offering me a referral.

I lit another cigarette and offered her one but she shook her head and frowned. "I have a complicated relationship with Eban. We often disagree but he is a longtime friend and teacher." She hesitated. "And sometimes therapist." She stopped momentarily, as if considering whether to answer the question that shot into my head. She took another cigarette out of the pack, rolled it in her fingers, then flicked it onto the table. "I've tried to return his help as best I can. Since he is so far out of the mainstream he has difficulty getting referrals. I've helped him with that and other things."

"Other things?" My curiosity outmuscled my discomfort.

"An office in Number 290 opened, and with a little help he was able to rent it at a cost he could afford." Her voice faded.

"What sort of help?"

"One of my clients was related to the landlord."

I shook my head. "I don't see much harm in that."

"I don't want you to think I routinely make it a practice of asking favors of my clients."

I smiled. "I can't imagine you asking many favors of anyone. What you did sounds like a nice thing."

She clenched her fist and a note of panic crept into her voice. "Maybe, but last weekend the building was ransacked. One of the offices broken into was his, and I feel responsible. I am indebted to Eban, and, if something horrible should come of this, I'll never forgive myself."

I realized that I didn't want her to continue. Every answer brought me closer to Alice's rabbit hole, but I heard myself say, "Dr. James, I can understand your feeling responsible, even though it seems like reaching, but so what? Won't insurance cover any damage?"

She ran her hand back through her hair. "It's not damage that I'm worried about. I'm afraid Eban is vulnerable to blackmail."

I suppose a real P.I. might salivate at the mention of blackmail, but I wasn't a real P.I. What kept me rooted to my seat was the tone of Dr. James' voice, the explosiveness of her anxiety, *her* vulnerability. But vulnerability to what?

—3—

My curiosity about Dr. James jumped to more personal territory. "Why me?"

"At the time I thought it simple—you are a detective."

"I'm a janitor. You know what the detective stuff is about."

She tight-lipped a smile and shook her head. "I know what you think your license is about, and I know what I think it's about. Perhaps if I had kept the difference straight I wouldn't be here."

"What are you saying?"

"Nothing that I haven't said before. You are honest and smart and loyal. When you latch on to something you see it through—despite yourself. Your therapy is a good example. Also, you're not very talkative."

"Sounds like you got your client list confused."

She looked exasperated. "My mind has been so full of Eban since the break-in that I began to think like him. I don't know how many times he has talked about 'clinical distance interfering with honest intuition and real human interaction.' " She shook her head. "When the offices were burgled I thought of you." Her sarcasm wasn't heavily disguised. It seemed like Holmes' theories were dissipating in the face of reality. I was off the hook. All I had to do was sit there.

"Dr. James, are you and Eban Holmes lovers? Is he married? Is that why he's so vulnerable to blackmail? Is that why you are so upset?"

Her head snapped back. I wanted to choke myself. Her eyes flashed and she began to speak, then jammed the words back down her throat, and pulled herself to her feet. "This was a lousy idea"—she pointed to the dope on the table—"for many reasons." As she leaned over to pick up her purse from the floor, I watched the rear of her black skirt ride up her calves.

I knew enough to keep quiet, but I had to take my mind off her body. "Look, don't steam out of here angry. I wasn't accusing you of anything. I'm sorry if I insulted you but I just asked the obvious." I told myself to shut up, but I wouldn't listen. "What is it you actually want me to do?"

"Right now I don't want you to do anything. It will be difficult enough to continue our therapy."

"Dr. James, right now continuing our therapy is impossible. I doubt if I'll be able to help, but I can't see you go without knowing what the hell you're worried about."

She moved back toward the chair and sat on its edge. I fought a battle to take my eyes off her legs. I wondered if I was losing all self-control: I'd just urged her to tell a story I didn't want to hear, held out a hint of help I didn't want to give, and felt myself grow heated toward a lady I thought of as a friendly teacher. Like the one I had in grammar school—the one who liked me mostly out of pity.

It was too late to stop. "What about the cops? What are they saying?"

"The police are calling it a simple case of someone breaking and entering random offices."

"Offices?"

"Yes. There were two other offices that were broken into."

"If the police aren't attaching anything significant to the robbery, why is Dr. Holmes? Also, why didn't he at least come here with you?"

"Dr. Holmes isn't attaching any significance to it, I am. He doesn't know that I'm here." She smiled ruefully. "While he would not approve of my coming, he would applaud my attempted spontaneity." A frown crossed her face. "Certainly more than I do. Anyway, the building houses medical doctors and none of their offices were disturbed. If you were a thief wouldn't you at least check for drugs?"

Did Dashiell Hammett drink? "What did the cops say about that?"

"They told me not to worry. That's one of the things I had hoped you might find out."

"But somehow you don't think the police are doing a good job?"

"No, I don't. Their attitude seems totally laissez-faire."

"Well, I don't feel very active myself."

"You never do; but it doesn't keep you from getting things accomplished. Look, Mr. Jacob . . . I'm sorry, Matthew. I think this was one of those 'good ideas at the time.' It's best to forget it and work through the feelings, don't you think?"

Unfortunately, no, I didn't think. And if she had she wouldn't have been here. But she hadn't thought and now it was too late. I couldn't just forget she came, even if I did talk about the feelings.

"I'll look into it." I held up my hand as she started to talk. "Don't say anything. I won't be able to learn more than you already have, but I'll try."

A look of relief crossed her face despite her ambivalence. Part of me felt pleased and another part of me got more angry.

I questioned her about the nature of Holmes' vulnerability but I didn't get very far. He was married, but she wasn't worried about her relationship with him. She wasn't as self-assured when I asked her about his clinical practice. I dropped it when it became clear that she didn't wish to speculate. All she would say was she wanted no harm to befall Eban Holmes. I wasn't surprised by her close-mouthedness. It was one thing to ask me to nose around, another to take me into her confidence. Throughout the course of our relationship, while Dr. James had seemed personally involved, she always gently but firmly declined to offer information about herself despite my sporadic interest. Although I now felt able to ask whatever I liked, I really didn't want many answers.

"I have very mixed feelings about this, Matthew."

"So do I, Dr. James."

She reached into her purse and pulled out a checkbook.

"No, no, Doctor. I wouldn't know how to go about charging for this and I certainly don't want money from you."

"That's out of the question. I expect to pay for the work I ask someone to do."

I shook my head, "Look, you came here for a favor. Let me check around and we'll talk money when I see you next week."

At the mention of our appointment another look of relief crossed her face. She stood. "It pleases me that you feel all right about continuing therapy."

I didn't think I said that but I didn't want to start another conversation. I got up and both of us stood awkwardly for a moment before she shook her head ruefully, smiled, and walked toward the door. She turned back to me, "Thank you, Matthew."

I shrugged. She turned her back and I could make out the faint ridge of her underwear beneath her skirt. I was relieved when she finally left.

It wouldn't take a weatherman to know which way the wind was going to blow. I went into the bedroom and pulled the stash out of my drug drawer. I felt angry, anxious, and depressed. Dr. James' visit had seriously disrupted my morning routine. I swallowed a Valium and lit the offending roach. I went back into the kitchen, brewed a fresh pot of coffee, and when the pot began to perk I walked into the alley for the newspaper. Since the delivery service expects no tip, finding the paper usually doubled as my morning exercise. When I returned I relit the joint, poured the coffee, and struggled to decide between the sports and TV sections.

I started with sports but when I felt the drugs come on I switched. Despite its hectic start I still had a chance to massage the edge off the day. But reading wasn't going to get Dr. James out of my head. I gathered the roach, cigarettes, and coffee and headed toward the living room when Mrs. Sullivan's light flashed.

When Lou first bought the building I decided to become a responsible caretaker, and installed intercoms from all the apartments to mine. As time passed and I got sick of hearing the damn things go off I removed them, but changed Mrs. Sullivan's to a flashing light. She really was too old to leave unattended. Although she talked about having a son somewhere in the Midwest, I'd never met him, and for all I knew he had forgotten she existed. It made me angry and guilty. It also made for more work.

I called to get the sentence and it wasn't bad. A leaky faucet. I promised to get the plumber upstairs before the end of the day; she always liked my little jokes.

I finally made it to the couch. I lit a cigarette, leaned my head back, and watched the plumes of smoke. I *rc'd* the TV and spun the dial. It seemed only proper to celebrate my new job by watching Harry O. A boring dead man resurrected as a detective, and I enjoyed the joke until I remembered the phone.

To turn on or not to turn on? I chuckled out loud as a touch of drug hubris coursed through my veins. I walked over and turned the damn thing on, and I was surprised that punishment was as swift as it was. The fucker began to ring.

"Well, would you believe this, Mr. Alienation is up for air," Simon's voice growled into the earpiece. "Where the fuck have you been? I've been trying to contact you for two long days."

I felt lightheaded. "Good things come to those that wait, my friend."

"Yeah, well, this is important, Matt."

"What isn't important to a big shot like yourself?"

"I'm not joking around. Why don't you at least buy an answering machine so people wouldn't have to wonder whether you're lying in that basement being eaten by rats?"

"Don't insult my housekeeping. If I had a machine I'd have to return calls."

"You don't get enough calls to make that a worry." Simon's tone changed to business. "We need to meet right away."

"What's the matter, wheeling and dealing not leaving you much free time?"

"Stop the jokes. I have a problem that I want you to look into."

" 'Why is this night different' and so on. Just send me the material and I'll do the research. My schedule isn't exactly bursting at the seams."

An unfamiliar tension crept into Simon's voice. "It's not a regular job. Look, I don't want to talk over the phone. Do you remember the El Rancho, the place under the highway where we used to go for quahogs?"

I felt a touch of alarm at the mention of El Rancho. "Jesus, isn't that a little out of the way?"

"That's why I'm suggesting it. How soon can you be there?"

"Are you okay?"

There was a long pause on the other end of the line. "No."

"I'll be there in a half-hour."

I heard a muffled thanks before the line went dead. Simon never thanked me for anything. I shook my head, stuffed a cigarette into my mouth and wandered around the apartment organizing myself to venture out. It wasn't something that came easy, but today nothing had. I guess it was my day for strange.

—4—

I was driving around the dead-end ramp of the terminally unfinished highway when my past reached out to grab me. I edged onto the raw concrete overpass and caught sight of the rundown Irish tavern where Simon and I first met. The Astro-Phillies playoff game had been on the box but we were the only two interested. Most of El Rancho's clientele were impatiently waiting for the hockey season to begin, since the hometown ball club had been dead in the water for months. Still, I loved baseball, and if there was something on the line, I didn't care who was playing. Simon, I quickly discovered, was a loyal ex-Philadelphian.

By the time the game ended we realized we had more in common than baseball. Both of us lived in the adjoining gray landmark neighborhood, and both of us were in the bar to escape the sinkholes of our marriages. There was still shine on our first rings, but we were both already shellshocked from soured fantasies. Although he was on the road to importance and I was listing toward anonymity, the similarity of our present lives put us at ease with each other. Our childhoods were remarkably similar as well, though neither of us talked that trash until well into our friendship.

Before I pulled off the overpass I looked toward my old turf and reconfirmed my reasons for avoiding this side of town. The bleak three-deckers and the new rehabs—all overwhelmed by the hulking granite local monument—brought on the same grinding stomach ache I had most of the time I lived here. Neither the sight of El Rancho nor the chemicals in my bloodstream offered solace from the unhappy feelings I associated with the neighborhood. Almost two decades, a second marriage, a disaster, and drugs dented the quantity, but not the quality.

I didn't notice much difference in El Rancho's gloomy interior, maybe another layer of city grit and tears on the walls, a few more brown cigarette burns on the oval formica bar. Simon was seated at one of the few rear tables. Since he was usually late and I had arrived early, my stomach knotted even more.

I thought about ordering a drink at the bar but walked directly to his table. "I don't get it. You're important people, but in the middle of a work day you decide to roust me out to reminisce? Is this the anniversary of your divorce? Or mine?"

He looked at me from underneath his mop of unruly sand-colored hair that threatened to obscure the turned-up collar on his camel sportcoat. Whether he wore corduroy, the way he did when I first met him, or cashmere like he did now, some piece of his clothing was always out of whack. How anyone could look like he just ran out of a *shvitz* and still be an important lawyer in this town was testimony to how smart and hard Simon really was. His second marriage also helped. Hey, he was smart enough to marry her, and I was glad he was a friend.

"Your beer is on the way." Despite the fat cigar stuffed in the corner of his mouth, his words were clear and clipped. He looked at me balefully from tired, bloodshot eyes. "It's not too early for you to drink, is it?"

"Not unless they legalized narcotics." I twisted around to see what was keeping the waitress. Something about his mood was making me thirsty.

"Are you high now? Jesus, between cigarettes and dope your lungs only see gray. And I don't understand why you won't get a fucking answering machine. Getting in touch with you is tougher than reaching the Pope."

He chewed on his unlit cigar. I noticed a bottle of imported water in front of him. I suppose a regulation of success is staying healthy.

"Come on, Simon, I'm more flexible about sex than the Pope."

"Again with the damn jokes. I'm serious." His tone took on an imperious quality and he unplugged the cork from his mouth. "When I need to get in touch with you I don't want to wait until it crosses your mind to answer the fucking phone."

He was pissing me off. "You know where I live. If it's so damn important, drive over. I'm not pining away for your calls."

It was a good thing we were interrupted by the waitress. She didn't ask who got the beer. I couldn't swear, but she looked like the same lady who used to work here—just a serious twenty years older. Simon reached for the check and I started to complain. He pushed it back and told her to keep it running. I liked that; it was going to be more than a one-drink meet. I was already half through my beer and the waitress was barely gone.

I looked at Simon and grinned, my annoyance easing as the alcohol said hello. "I don't know about you, but this neighborhood gives me the creeps. What are we doing here?"

He shook his head. "Instinct." The coldness in his voice had changed to resignation; it wasn't a tone I associated with him. "I figured Fran wouldn't see us here, then I realized it wouldn't matter if she did." He kept popping the cigar in and out of his mouth. I wished he would light the damn thing. I dug into my pocket for my own smokes, lit one, and drained the rest of the beer. I stifled my immediate desire to find the waitress and forced myself to pay attention.

Simon had his glasses up over his forehead and was rubbing his eyes. "I'm in trouble. I think my marriage is going down the toilet so I picked the place where it happened before. Sue me."

I couldn't stop myself from twisting around in my seat. I needed the waitress. I turned back to Simon but he was too caught in his own thoughts to have noticed. At least that's what I thought until I saw him raise his arm. I mouthed my thanks.

He said carefully, "You just finished the beer and you need another."

"Simon, we've both kissed floor enough times in this bar that it's tough for me to feel guilty by your granola conversion. Leave it alone. Now what the fuck are we doing here?"

He pulled his glasses back down and looked at me intently. "I want you to follow Fran and I don't want her to know about it."

I sat back in my chair and looked around for a place to put my eyes. Thankfully, the beer arrived, and I killed time fiddling with the glass. This was the second time today that reality seemed to slip out of focus. But I couldn't deny a worm of satisfaction buried at the bottom of my disorientation. I must have looked embarrassed.

"You think that I want photos," he rushed to reassure me. "It's not like that at all." He smiled, "I always knew you had the head to be a P.I."

"Is that a compliment or an insult? I got enough on my mind without starring in your fantasies."

Simon looked at me with sudden concern. "Damn, man, I've been so mired in my own shit that I just got angry with the no-answers. Was the phone off the hook for some specific reason?"

I couldn't help smiling. It was impossible for Simon to imagine life without a telephone; I struggled to live with one. "I'm okay, but this is the second time today that someone is trying to turn a janitor into a detective. I never thought I looked like Eliza Dolittle."

Simon looked confused, "What are you talking about?"

"Nothing, except I'm not a fucking detective."

He said adamantly, "I don't ever want my personal life linked with a regular detective firm. In this town confidentiality lasts as long as the next happy hour." I started to protest but he waved me off, "Quiet a second. Hear me out."

I didn't want to hear him out, but fighting would only postpone the inevitable.

"After we got back from Nantucket Fran began having nightmares. Alex was there as well, and I thought the nightmares had to do with conversations that took place among the three of us. Alex was feeling his mortality and talked a great deal about his 'arrangements.' Given how close they are, the subject naturally disturbed her."

Fran's father, Alex, owned a large piece of the Island and a good chunk of Maine so I was sure the arrangements were complicated. I had been invited to both places but something always seemed to come up. Mostly my own reluctance.

"Is Alex sick? Dying?"

Simon shrugged. "He says not."

"But you don't believe him?"

He shook his head, "I don't think about it much. It makes me too uncomfortable. I like the guy a lot. Also, I have my hands full at home. It's been a couple of months but the dreams won't go away. Worse, they're creating an enormous amount of tension between us."

I interrupted, "Why are you telling this to me and not a shrink?"

He looked at me strangely, started to speak, stopped, and began again. "Fran sees a shrink." He stopped again as if inviting me to talk. I had nothing to say except, "I don't want to hear anymore."

His eyes narrowed but he spoke softly, "You know, it wasn't so long ago that we used to sit here and listen to each other talk about everything."

"You're mistaken, Esquire. It was a long time ago and both of us hated our wives. Also, neither of us asked the other one to do something about it. I can't spy on your wife."

He pulled the cigar out of his mouth. "You still got your mind in the gutter. I love the woman. I'm not trying to spy on her. The fucking dreams don't disappear, she doesn't sleep, I don't sleep, the shrink helps, but everything keeps getting worse." He paused momentarily and looked down at my glass. I quickly nodded and finished what was left. I needed to slow down, sip the next one before I said something stupid.

"Simon, we both know you love your wife. I just don't want to get involved."

It looked like he was going to say something about the edge in my voice, but instead he signaled the waitress. I braced myself for another shove down memory lane. I looked at the waitress intently when she brought the drinks, until I was sure she *was* the same lady. I felt oddly satisfied when I returned my attention to Simon. I had found someone else who aged as badly as me.

Simon ignored what I had said. "I want you to look after her. She's starting to have trouble functioning during the day. Misplaced car keys, forgotten errands, that sort of thing. When Fran blows appointments the shit is deep in the fan."

"Simon, no, I don't want to do this. I'm not a detective, I'm not a day-care worker. Hell, Simon, I can barely take care of myself."

I thought he would get angry but he just sat there and shook his head slowly. "You confuse taking care of yourself with not doing anything. I'll tell you, watching her be frightened of sleep tears me up. And not knowing what the hell the dreams are makes it worse."

"Why don't you know what she's dreaming about?"

He shrugged. "First she can't remember, then it's too hard to talk about. Finally she comes into the den and tells me that she doesn't really want to talk but generally the dreams are about someone watching her, then picking her up, and taking her someplace that she fears but can't see. She says it makes her feel like a scared kid."

"Did you ask for more details?"

"Well, I didn't keep staring at the television."

"Did you turn it off?"

His eyes darted from the table to my face and he started to react, but after a second said, "You asshole, someday someone who doesn't know the decent side of you is going to do some real damage."

"It's nice that you think I have a decent side."

A small grin flickered across his face. "I can't help myself. Anyway, that was all she said, but I have to tell you I was relieved. I was afraid the dreams were somehow about us, something that would kill our marriage. Hell, I'm living with a woman who can't sleep, then she starts feeling guilty about keeping me awake. Before I know it I'm sleeping in the guest room. More tension. It's making me a little crazy.

"Then something she said caught my attention. That lately she has that feeling of being watched during the day as well. At first I didn't think much of it. When you are doing nights like she's been doing, some of it has to flop over into the day. But a day or so later it starts to nag at me. I mean, what if we've got it all reversed? What if someone is somehow fucking with her? Maybe someone is provoking all of this. She's rich, and hell, I've pissed off a fair share of people. And who knows what Alex has been involved with? I know it sounds far-fetched. But I've heard of enough weird things happening that I couldn't just throw the idea away."

He stuffed the cigar back into his mouth and spoke around it. "That's where you come in. You could keep an eye on her and at the same time see if something really is going on."

I lit another cigarette and stopped nursing the beer. "I think you've been sleeping alone for too long. What does Fran think of your idea?"

"I've no intention of telling her. She has enough on her mind, don't you think?"

"I think your idea about the dreams spilling into the day makes more sense."

"Sense or not, I want you to follow Fran and make sure that my idea is crazy."

I felt like I was drowning. Again. "Roth, the only reason you want me to do this is because you can't stand sitting still any longer. If something is happening around you, you can't leave it alone. Never could. You know what kind of detective I am. We're not talking Lew Archer here. I may not be a friend of Fran's, but I know her well enough to feel damn stupid traipsing around after her. Hell, if she catches me I'll never get off her shit list."

"How many times do I have to tell you that you're not on any list." He sighed, "Neither of you gives each other much of a chance."

"There will be no chance at all if she spots me. This is crazy. Let me pick up the check and you go home and take a nap."

He looked at me and raised his bushy eyebrows. "It wasn't crazy when you wanted the detective license, was it? Damn, Matt man, if you were someone else I'd tighten the screws. Christ, you owe me enough, but that's not what this is about. I don't have anyone else I can ask. Or *want* to ask. When I first had the idea I went to Alex to see if he had any suggestions . . ."

"I can't believe Alex would suggest me."

Another smile crossed his face. "No, he didn't."

"So listen to your father-in-law."

His tone was final. "If Fran bumps into you I'll take the weight. But I think you can do a decent job. Christ, you watch enough TV and read enough of those hard-boiled books. I didn't bust my balls getting you that license so you could browse the library."

"There's not going to be anyone out there," I said futilely.

It was going to come out the way Simon wanted, no matter what.

"I know the odds. I just want you to make sure of it." He reached across the table and grabbed my hand. "It relieves me that you'll keep an eye on her."

We sat talking for another fifteen minutes or so and I got a sense of how deeply upset and helpless he felt. Welcome to the club. It should have pleased me to help him out, but all I felt was depressed. As we walked through the dreary tavern toward the door the waitress thanked us and hoped we'd come again. This time I felt no satisfaction; all she looked was old. When I got to the car I rummaged through the ashtray looking for a discarded roach. I needed to get away from this side of town.

—5—

In my rush to leave the area I flooded the engine. I pounded my hand on the steering wheel. It was still too early for the afternoon movie; if I went home I would mope and wind up playing plumber. By the time the dope burned my finger the El Rancho and the Monument sat squarely in my rearview mirror. That relaxed me enough to head across town to the discount lumber yard to price materials for a deck that Charles and Richard wanted me to build. Richard was a high-priced architect who cared enough about the porch to work out an inventive design. Although it would cut into the small area where I fantasized laying cement for a basketball court, that was a minor objection. I had imagined the court since I moved in, but doing something or doing nothing always got in the way.

Since I was on Dorchester Avenue anyhow, I nosed around a row of secondhand stores. There was a '40s radio; unfortunately old plastic was in but the price was out and I was in no mood to haggle. My earlier depression was beginning to reappear, so I stopped at the market and bought a couple of bags of junk food. A man has to do something besides smoke when he's flat on a couch.

I had used up most of the day's light by the time I returned to the building. I parked in the alley but walked to the front to pick up the mail. I pushed through the front door cradling my groceries, and nearly tripped over Charles and Richard sitting on the interior steps with an oversized suitcase at their feet.

"Another fight?"

Charles smiled and took Richard's hand. Rich said seriously, "Business. The firm is sending me to Detroit to save a building the locals are butchering."

"Well, no doubt you'll kick ass. How long will you be gone?"

"Too long," Charles wailed, letting go of Richard and reaching for his own head.

"Two days to two weeks."

The grocery bags were getting heavy but I delayed moving. "I priced the deck today."

"OH-FUCKING-KAY!," Charles suddenly hollered, threw his hands toward the ceiling, and began to dance and sing. "We're gonna have a deck tonight, we're gonna have a deck tonight. We're really gonna rumble . . ."

I nodded, "What's he on?"

Richard smiled. "Show tunes. A bad habit he picked up from his mother. He sings them in times of stress."

"*West Side Story*, right?"

Just as suddenly Charles stopped dancing around the hall. "Who's been teaching you, Matt? Could it be that little fireplug who rattled our nice tranquil home at some ungodly hour this morning?"

Calling Dr. James a fireplug was more than I could bear. "You better take care of that man before you leave, Rich. He's a basket case already, and I gave up social work a long time ago."

Richard started to reply but I cut him off. "As for you, Charles, you're in real trouble if you have nothing better to do than play Peeping Tom with me."

Charles raised his eyebrows and leered, "I like to watch."

I shook my head and started toward the back of the building, then remembered why I had used the front door in the first place. The two of them watched while I cleaned Ed McMahon out of my box. I was almost to the back stairs when I heard Richard call.

"Before you buy anything I'll take another look at the plans and see if we can steal a little more space for your basketball court."

I nodded my thanks as I went through the door to the basement. I got to the apartment and managed to put the bags down and the mail in the garbage before Mrs. S.' light began to flash. She probably stood at her windows waiting for me. I felt guilty about my wave of annoyance and telephoned upstairs. But it wasn't her leaky faucet; she wanted me to come to dinner. As unappealing as another solitary supper of Taylor Pork Roll on an English seemed, talking to someone was worse. I thanked her, declined, and promised to get to the faucet within the next couple of days.

I searched futilely through the *TV Guide*, but turned the tube on anyway. I was starting to roll a joint when I heard Julie's patterned knock. If it had been anyone else I'd lock myself in the bathroom, but Julie was different; you don't ignore your dealer. I started to speak, then, appreciating quality work, I stood silent and listened to him pick the lock. It was a game. I changed the lock a couple of times a year but neither of us ever mentioned it. This one was going to be a piece of cake. Second time in a week, the same lock.

When he saw me watch him enter, he shook his head and jerked his thumb back toward the door. "You're a smart fellow, but you spend hundreds of dollars a year betting a losing hand. If I didn't get in you would be morose."

"Tradition doesn't count for much today, huh?"

"What?"

"Nothing. You're not supposed to talk about the locks. Not only would I be morose, I wouldn't get my dope."

"I heard your psychologist visited today. I thought it wise to check it out."

I rubbed my face. He was a sweet guy. "How'd you find out she was my shrink?"

"I like to ascertain my surroundings. People keep me informed."

I wasn't going to push. This wasn't the first time I'd wondered about what lay behind his gentle face and close-cropped gray hair. It was strange, though, to think of myself as someone other people kept an eye on. The whole damn day continued to surprise.

"Well, she was here all right but it wasn't about me. She wants to hire me to do detective work."

"You look none too cheerful, slumlord."

"I'm not. You ever been caught in your shorts in front of your shrink?"

"I thought seeing a psychologist meant taking your underwear off."

I grimaced. Julius was another tenant I inherited when Lou bought the place. A powerfully built, medium-height, fifty-five-year-old black man. For almost a year he had barely acknowledged my presence. Just a check, right as rain, in my box. One day I came home and found him sitting at my kitchen table with a large beige canvas bag.

"Sit down now, boy."

His voice was deep, quiet, and commanded attention. Not unlike God in *The Ten Commandments*. "I've been observing you for a while and I like what I see. Respectful to the tenants and the building. I like that. I am also impressed with your concern for Mrs. Sullivan. She's getting on but no one cared to acknowledge it. I know about you and I know you got a cop license that don't move. If you prefer this to rent money, tell me."

He pushed the bag over to me and I pulled out a large ziploc full of dope. You wouldn't need a hookah to realize this was some fine stuff. All buds. Gold.

He looked at me. "I know you don't intend a citizen's arrest. Would you care to partake?"

I grinned at him. "Partake? Hell yes. This shit looks terrific. Let me get my pipe."

"Sit," he commanded and produced a joint. He lit it and, while he smoked, took out a molded silver flask and placed it on the table. I reached for the silver, opened it, and drank. Julius' face remained impassive but his head moved in a small nod. He passed the joint, took the flask, and swallowed. I smoked the dope and it was every bit as good as it looked.

We spent two hours talking. I should say I talked, Julie punctuated. Since that night, every month he would let himself into my apartment after knocking, and wait with his canvas bag. He never mentioned working so I assumed he made his money dealing. By now I realized he had fingers in more than one pot, though I never asked and he never volunteered.

But he did know what I meant about opening the door in my drawers because his eyes, usually the stillest part of his body, began to widen as he pictured the scene. He started to laugh and little by little so did I. Maybe I was making too much out of nothing.

—6—

Another night of drugs and drink brought another morning of grogginess and dehydration. Last night's laughter with Julius was today's joke, but alone in the morning's dreariness I couldn't crack a smile. I had two detective jobs that hit me worse than the hammer whacking at my brain. I stumbled to the kitchen where water and coffee began to put the world back on its feet. The dope stash sang from my bedside drawer but I tried to exercise instead. About half a workout later the singing grew too loud and I silenced it with a small pipeful of grass. I pictured myself stretched out in front of the television with my Fritos and beer, but I shook off the desire. Between Dr. James and Simon a couple of outstanding markers had been called, and I had no choice but to pay.

I walked into the bedroom and pulled the locked box out from under the bed, sat on the floor, fiddled with the combination, and stared at the .38 in its stiff leather holster. It had been a while since I last played with it and I was mildly surprised by how much pleasure the gun still gave me. I took the holster out and strapped it around my shoulder. Here I was, the naked detective. All I needed was a pair of thick and thins with a stocking cap, and I'd be set.

I took off the holster, got dressed, and returned to the kitchen for more coffee and nicotine. I brought the box and holster with me and let my hands fondle the gun while I tried to figure out where to start. There was a difference between owing and paying.

After the accident I had asked Simon to help me get a P.I. license and he reluctantly obliged. I had ideas about actually working at it, though they evaporated after Lou bought the building and I lost my taste for generalized revenge. Who should pay for a life yanked out from under you? Especially since the last ones who did the yanking were the ones you loved and they were already dead.

Still, sitting at the table caressing the cold black metal, recalled the pleasure of learning to use it—when the smell of gunpowder and cordite, and the explosions in my ears, were able for the moment to push the hate and hurt from my head.

Sitting at my kitchen table cleaning the gun, my hands moving automatically, brushing, wiping, reloading, while my mind was drawing a blank, didn't bolster my confidence. Licensed or not, I felt illegitimate. Not legal. Somehow I didn't think the police would fawn over my ticket. Which was a drag; if I could check the official report, I could probably get out from under Dr. James.

I found the turn of phrase disturbing and snapped the gun's chamber shut. I jammed the gun back into the holster and strapped it around my shoulder. Despite the unsettling circumstances of both cases, and my own reluctance to get involved, there was, I had to admit, a germ of excitement about trying something new. I was a detective today.

Now, if I could just think of something to do.

———

The wet-looking, oversized granite steps reflected the impersonal institutions libraries had become over the course of my life. When I was a kid, old-fashioned bookstores and libraries had been a refuge from the fierce storms at home. For years I was disappointed whenever I walked into either one and missed the smell of musty wood with paper and leather. Now I was adjusted. I no longer expected malls or mottled concrete to smell.

The newspapers were useless. Small story, big town. Even the local weekly ignored it. It seemed odd there was no mention, but Dr. James' neighborhood was a well-known stomping ground for junkie b&e's. I guessed that familiarity breeds acceptance. I did discover, however, that the hot local issue was a tug of war between an expansionist university and a tenacious organization of residents. I'd always felt as if I were walking through a battleground when I went to my appointments; now I had something other than my own interior life to attribute it to.

I was luckier when it came to Eban Holmes. Although my research confirmed Dr. James' statement that contemporary journals were unwilling to publish him, he had been a prolific contributor to the defunct *Radical Therapist*. His essays were an enjoyable read. His was a no-holds-barred attack on the psychiatric Holy Trinity—fee structure, clinical distance, and therapeutic objectivity. He had little patience for what he termed the "helping industry," arguing that social services reinforced modern society's political and cultural status quo. I could imagine any number of shrinks I knew from my social work days squirming under Holmes' attack. It was a pleasant daydream but not one that offered much of a clue to Holmes' vulnerability: straight psychiatrists, psychologists, or social workers didn't have the balls to blackmail.

It wasn't difficult, however, to imagine clinical situations involving Holmes that might leave him vulnerable. He believed in getting actively involved in clients' lives and trashing professional boundaries. He assailed traditional distinctions between friend and client, teacher and student, even doctor and patient. Although he never came right out and said it, he also hinted around the edges of therapist and lover.

Still, it had been a long time since the *Radical Therapist* had stopped publishing and plenty of political blood had flowed under the bridge. Some of it mine. I wondered whether time had done to Holmes what it had done to so many radicals of that era. It would be disappointing to discover he drove a BMW.

The morning passed more quickly than usual. Research had often made me feel like I was in school; today it seemed almost fun. My headache was gone and, despite the lateness of the morning, I wasn't dope-starved. I thought about switching cases and trying to locate Fran, but I wasn't ready for cloak-and-dagger. As much as I hated the idea, I decided to go to Charley's Place and see if anyone I knew still ate there.

Charley's Place was really Charley and Phil's. Charley did the cooking, Phil the cleaning. Charley was an ex-social worker, Phil an ex-cop. Since it was located between Police Headquarters and the Department of Social Services, the luncheonette was a perfect place to establish informal contacts. At least it used to be; I didn't know whether the restaurant had survived gentrification, or whether there was still informal business to conduct. It had been a long time since I wanted contacts with anyone.

I was lucky. Although the block was gussied up and bore little resemblance to my memories, Charley's was still standing. The swells probably liked the Forties feel of the place. Despite the changes I felt the stirring of a time I'd rather not remember, but I forced myself to walk inside. I realized I enjoyed the rub of the holster under my arm. In the past I'd always felt a little naked meeting with fully armed cops.

Although the counter was filled, I was taken aback by how few people were scattered around the different tables. Lunch was a time this place used to jump. I ignored the empty tables, stood behind the counter seats, and waited for the man working the grill to turn around. When the broad back bending over the stove straightened and turned it was Phil, fatter, balder, and older than the picture in my mind. He stared, recognizing though not remembering.

"Matt Jacob, Phil."

"Well I'll be damned." A look of surprise creased his face. "I thought you left town." He suddenly looked somber. "There was some sort of accident, wasn't there? I remember. Your family . . ."

Sometimes a big town is never big enough. "Yeah. That's all history now. Don't sweat it."

Phil shifted uncomfortably, trying to find something to say. A look of relief crossed his face as he glanced over my shoulder. "Wait a second, I got to get this order together."

He turned back to the grill, and his hands began to fly. I looked around at the storefront-cum-diner and, for the thousandth time, wished it wasn't a storefront but the real thing. While all the accoutrements seemed out of a film noir, the actual storefront itself didn't quite make it into the right atmosphere. Probably just as well for Charley. You didn't see much money serving food in a railroad car, though the uniforms might have felt more at home.

"Where's Charley, Phil?"

Without turning or missing a cooking beat, he said, "Dead."

"I'm sorry, man."

"What for? He got outta his cancer and I got a business. Nothing to be sorry for."

A skinny customer with a protruding Adam's apple finished his sandwich, stood, and reached for his wallet. "You guys don't make it easy to enjoy lunch. Accidents, death. Friendly place you got here."

Phil grabbed the money from the man's hand. "A fried egg and coffee don't buy you friendly."

I sat in the vacated seat. After looking at the prices on the board I knew nothing was going to buy me friendly so what the hell. "That guy's sandwich looked pretty good. Could you add some bacon?"

"I can add anything you want, it'll just cost you."

"That's fine."

Again he turned toward the grill, pulling the disparate pieces of someone's lunch onto a plate and slamming the plate down on the waitress' section of the counter.

"Anybody work here anymore?" he growled. A tall redhead got up from the table where she had been smoking and talking with someone who looked like a traffic cop.

"Whatcha bitching about, Phil?" the traffic cop said. "You didn't hire her to pour coffee when she first got here."

The few uniforms in the place liked the joke. The redhead even winked. Phil just cursed. Cop humor. The more things changed the more they stayed the same.

When he set my coffee down he apologized. "I don't remember what you take."

"Black. Why should you? Do the welfare people still come here? I don't recognize anybody."

"It's been a long time."

"You'd think someone would keep their job."

"Did you?"

"No."

"See. The pols figure the only people around here now who need social workers are regular working people and no one gives a shit about them. They give the broken people social workers and they give the rich money. Everybody else gets a lotta shit. Were you looking for someone in particular?"

"Not really."

"Don't tell me you're looking for work?" A bell rang behind him and he turned back to attend to the food; somehow he managed to get a slew of lunches cooked and organized without seeming to move very fast.

He went on with his back to me, "I'm tired of hearing about good men not being able to find a job. Used to be just the broads and blacks. Now it don't matter, the whole thing stinks."

I agreed with the last part. "No, I'm not looking for work, just a little information."

He looked back over his shoulder. "What for?"

"Believe it or not, I'm a private cop."

He shrugged. "Why not. Everybody's got to do something. I didn't know you were a vet."

Vets and ex-cops had a monopoly on licenses. "Jesus," he added, "I didn't think you could make a living on divorce work anymore. I thought nobody cared who plugged who. Men take their own wives and give 'em away for a night. Then they get the other guy's. Hell, I'm surprised you can still make a buck keyholing. Lousy job, but in a way it's good to hear about it. It means there are still people who give a shit."

"I guess."

"You don't seem the sniffing type."

"Yeah. I'm pretty new at this and it's not that easy to begin. I thought that some sw's might know someone inside who could help, so I came here looking."

"It really don't sound like you been at this very long."

"Long enough to know I need some help." The memories of the old Charley's kept intruding, so when Phil focused his attention on his cooking, I drank my coffee and forced myself back into today. I looked around and saw the redhead back at the table with the cop. He kept his left hand under the table and every once in a while would lean portside as though he was reaching for something. I imagined he was. There were occasional murmurings of conversations from the other tables, but nothing distinct. El Rancho's yesterday and Charley's today. My new job was leading me back to the haunts of my old life. Whatever excitement had existed this morning was gone.

Phil delivered my lunch, refilled my coffee, and stood around. I bit into the sandwich and nodded appreciatively. "This is good. Better than I remember."

"Why do you think Charley never let me cook?" Phil growled. "He never could have gone back to cooking once anyone tasted my stuff. No way he was gonna let me. He didn't want to bus."

I smiled. "Well at least you're cooking now."

"Yeah, right. I'm cooking with gas. The way the world is going I should be glad I'm not being gassed. What information did you say you were looking for?"

"There was a break-in about a week ago at 290 Commonwealth. The police tagged it as a junkie do, but I got a client who wants to be sure. I said I'd check the report. Do any caseworkers still come in?"

"You got Welfare on the brain? You're not gonna find anything talking to them."

I shrugged.

"Well, Matt, it sounds harmless enough. You sure you're telling the truth?"

"Of course. Why?"

" 'Cause I might be able to get a copy of the report, but I don't want to stick my ass in the air."

I shrugged. "I don't want you to either. I'm telling you what I know."

Phil suddenly leaned to his left and muttered something unintelligible behind me. The redhead jumped up and stood waiting at the station.

"What did you call me for if you wasn't ready?"

Phil didn't bother to reply. He loaded a tray and placed it in front of her. "Less mouth, more work, okay?"

She stuck out her tongue though she looked too old for the gesture.

He turned and walked back to where I was finishing the last of my sandwich. He reached back and pulled my order form off the wall. "Three seventy, including the Governor's."

I stood and pulled a ten from my wallet. He looked at it and took out some bills from his apron pocket.

"No, Phil, keep it."

"You're overpaying."

"Nah, I haven't been here for a long time."

"Why don't you come back in a couple of days and I'll see what I can do?"

"Hey, that's not what the tip was about."

"Bullshit it wasn't." He waved the hand with the money and started toward the cash register. "You might be a better sniff than I thought."

— 7 —

I returned home emotionally exhausted. Too much history stuffed in between the bread of my fried egg sandwich. There was no flashing light and I didn't know whether to be relieved or worried. I picked relieved. There was no need for the stash to call since I was rolling before I had my coat off: I wanted to get high and go to sleep. My headache had returned. I just wanted to disappear, but the telephone rang and without thinking I grabbed it.

"Well?" Simon's voice was impatient.

"Well what?"

"What happened?"

"Nothing happened."

"I don't understand. Where did she go today?"

"Simon, I don't know." I started to feel numb. "I don't spy on Fridays."

"Goddamnit, we went through that yesterday. I'm not talking about spying."

"That's right, you're talking about me spying."

"Look, I don't care what you call it. Are you going to do the job or what? I thought we had an understanding."

I was too tired to argue. "We have an understanding; I will follow Fran as per your request. Okay?"

Simon's voice was grudging. "The words are fine, it's your attitude that concerns me. The words were okay yesterday too!"

"Lighten up. I said I'd do it."

"You said that yesterday, but you still haven't done shit. I understand it makes you uncomfortable, but right now my life is miserable and I need your help. Not your mouth."

I was almost too exhausted to feel guilty. Almost. "Look, Simon, I told you I was working on something. I'll start covering Fran tomorrow. I promise."

"What are you doing for the rest of the day? It's only three."

He wasn't going to let up. I started rummaging around my pocket for the lighter. "Look, Simon, I have to take care of something in the building. I'll get on the case tomorrow."

I glanced across the room to Mrs. Sullivan's light: where are you when I need you? "I have to go. Mrs. S.'s light is flashing and you know how she gets if I don't respond right away."

"Me too, Matt man, me too. I don't like it when people don't respond."

"Jesus, man, I'll pretend you didn't say that. I have too much to think about without threats from my best friend."

"Look, I don't mean to threaten. I'm sorry. But please don't be gone too far or too long. Try to stay straight, okay? Also, while we're doing this, will you please leave your phone on?"

"Sure, and I will check things out tomorrow. If you know where I might be able to locate her without camping in front of your house it would help."

"I know she has a ten-thirty at the faigeleh hairdressers' on Newbury Street. I think the address is 119."

"Simon, what the fuck's the matter with you? Faigelehs, for Christ sake?"

"I'm sorry, really. I don't know what I'm saying. This has me by the short hairs, and I've been spending too much time with businessmen, I suppose."

"Well, go wheel and deal. It will use up some energy."

There was a pause and I suddenly felt uncomfortable. "Simon."

"What?"

"I'll stick out like a sore thumb on Newbury Street."

"According to you, you stick out like a sore thumb everywhere. Just remember to keep your phone turned on. I'll get back to you."

I filled a shot glass with bourbon and swallowed it in a gulp. The phone began to ring again, but this time I knew better. After the ringing stopped I turned it off. I wasn't going to stay awake anyhow.

—8—

Sixteen hours of sleep and I still crawled out of bed tired. My skin's clammy texture was evidence of dreams, but what you don't remember won't hurt you. Mrs. Sullivan's flashing light forced me to dress, grab my toolbox, and go upstairs. Two coffees, four homemade oatmeal cookies, and an earful later, I had the washer replaced and was ready to sleaze behind Fran's back looking for ghosts.

Misplaced keys, then forgotten cigarettes—I had trouble getting out of the house and on my way. The city looked dirty and battered from another long, cold winter. In bright summer light there were days when even the parks appeared as elegant as Frederick Olmsted envisioned, but mostly the town looked like a working woman: too tired to be attractive most of the time.

I drove to Newbury Street and set up shop. It was a warm pre-spring day so I opened the salt-stained window. In contrast to most of the drive, this street glistened with wood, glass, and gold facades; an inclusive shopping experience for the rich. Between the haute couture department stores and high fashion European boutiques stood fancy salons and distinctive art galleries.

I wondered whether my parking spot provided enough cover, but felt reassured as traffic on the street began to pick up. My gun rested quietly and comfortably under my arm. I turned the radio on, then changed my mind. It distracted from the hum of the morning.

Years ago I drove a cab and parked in different spots throughout town to view the sunrise. After a while I became enamored of the rhythm of the city's awakening, watching as the pace gently accelerated to a full urban trot. It became an intrusion if someone hired the cab. I had forgotten how pleasant it was to sit and watch the world go about its business.

Fran's red Mercedes swung around the block twice before she found a spot. A smooth park and she was out of the car striding toward the hairdresser. She might be afflicted with horrid nightmares but you couldn't tell it from the way she looked. Ann Taylor derrière with attitude to match. Tall, blonde, and leggy—not your typical Jewish look. She was spoiled, but given the delight her father took in her, it was no surprise. Alex Hirsh was a self-made millionaire who had elbowed his way into the town's inner sanctum. Although he was Russian, Jews who didn't know him believed he was German. Too classy to be a Litvak.

He always seemed like a nice guy to me. Nothing but kindness and generosity toward Fran and Simon. It would have been easy to be hostile toward their marriage. Hell, Simon was already growing shark teeth when they met. To Alex's credit he recognized Simon's devotion. In fact, Alex took him under his wing. If he couldn't refuse Fran Simon, I couldn't imagine him refusing her anything.

It was a few minutes before I was sure Fran was safely ensconced in the barber's chair. I reached under my seat for the baggie and carefully lit and cupped a joint with my right hand and watched for police or anything else suspicious. Nothing caught my attention.

Time drifted quickly as the street began to groan under the weight of consumer madness. I was getting around to chastising myself for too much smoking when Fran strolled through the door. I ducked, started the car, and peeked out the window as she walked toward her parking spot. She rummaged around in her purse and put money in the meter before I realized she wasn't driving anywhere.

It's funny how some things strike you. I didn't feel like a detective at the library. Or at Charley's. But following Fran down Newbury

Street sent an adrenaline bolt through me, pushing the joint's high into the background, and brightening my vision. I stayed about half a block behind on the other side of the street, and kept her in my line of sight. Window shopping kept her busy and oblivious to her surroundings. It dawned on me that Fran wasn't my quarry. First order of detecting is to remember the job.

I dropped back and put more distance between us. I hoped she would enter a store and give me an opportunity to spot someone lingering. Instead she swung over to Commonwealth. She stopped for a moment and I ducked behind a parked car. She checked her watch, then started briskly down the avenue. I crossed over to the island that ran the length of the boulevard and matched her pace. The more we walked the more familiar the neighborhood became. Without hesitation she walked up the steps and in the door of 290.

For a moment I stood transfixed, then dodged the oncoming traffic, and raced up the steps. I walked into the entrance hall, looking nervously at the stained oak wainscoting, then remembered the glass directory high on the wall. I pored over the names and notations and figured the odds were seriously against her being here to see Dr. James. My unease lasted until I was back outside; then it exploded into a stomach ache as I realized most of the doctors on the list were Ob/Gyns. It opened a disquieting vein of thought about Fran's nightmares.

I jogged to my car and drove back to Commonwealth, and luckily found a spot where I could see the building. Suddenly it felt like I was being watched, and my anxiety broke into a full sweat. I joined the growing crowd of pedestrians, walked a quarter-block to a sub shop, and surveyed the area in an attempt to determine if my paranoia was based on anything real.

By the time I returned with a large sausage I decided it wasn't. I remembered the time I was notified for jury duty and wound up thinking I was going to be the defendant, reminding myself as I reentered the car that I was the one doing the watching.

I unwrapped the sandwich and noticed that the pork fat was beginning to congeal but ate it anyway. When Fran finally came out the door I gave her a head start and followed well out of sight. Her pace was considerably slower than it had been on the way to the building. It gave me too much time to think. Her step quickened as she approached her car, and I stopped daydreaming. Checking whether someone was following her, I didn't notice anything unusual though I still felt uneasy after she drove away.

At least I could honestly tell Simon that I had kept my eye on Fran and, with luck, after I spoke to Phil, clear the deck with Dr. James as well. I fumbled through my pockets looking for my keys and cigarettes and remembered the trouble I had leaving the house in the morning: I didn't want any piece of this.

———

If there had been a lunchtime crowd it was already gone with no early dinner arrivals. The black and white floor tiles seemed to breathe silent relief for the company as I walked through the door. Phil and Red were sitting at a corner table smoking. He nodded and she turned around to look. The way she quickly turned back compelled me to look down my front for sausage. None showed. I went to the same seat at the counter and debated whether I could get away with just ordering a large coffee. I heard Phil get up and slowly walk to the swinging counter section and watched as he pushed his bulk through sideways. He faced his arsenal of short-order equipment and looked back over his shoulder.

"You're a man of habits, right." He wasn't asking so I just nodded.

"Good, saves us both time." He turned toward the grill and began an egg and bacon sandwich. At minimum, I was going to pay for information with my digestion.

He wasn't talking so I just sat there feeling my belly roll until he brought my order, then returned to his table while I forced myself to eat. I wondered if he'd forgotten yesterday's conversation, but then I figured he dealt with considerably more food orders than requests for police reports.

I was pushing the last bite of sandwich into my mouth when he tapped my back with an envelope. "I did some checking yesterday and you come out pretty good. Why didn't you tell me you know Julius?"

"It didn't occur to me. How do you know Julius?"

"Are you kidding? In this city every storekeep knows Julie. He always has a deal working."

I didn't understand what he was talking about so I smiled. "He's a good guy."

He looked like he was going to say something but changed his mind. He walked behind the counter across from me, leaned forward, and slid the envelope over. "This was harder than I expected."

I looked at him. Was I supposed to offer something?

His face darkened. "Don't look at me that way. I'm not asking for anything."

"Look, Phil, you have to understand. I don't know much about doing this business. I'm sorry if I insulted you."

He rubbed his face and grunted. Red stood up and called from the table, "Phil, I want to go out for a while, okay?"

He didn't stop rubbing. "Every day you go out."

"So what, you don't own me."

He lifted his head and stared hard at her. "You want out without pay?"

She sank back down into the booth and pushed herself into the far corner, draping her legs over the edge closest to the counter. Her uniform rode high on the tops of her thighs. "Never mind."

I turned away from her legs toward Phil who was staring at her. "Damn it, go on."

She was up and out in an instant. She didn't bother to say thanks.

"This is the shit I was talking about yesterday. She goes out damn near every day. She says shopping. I figure I'm paying her to get laid."

I shrugged sympathetically. He shook his head and changed subjects. He must have decided that I was the better topic. "Julius said you were a cherry."

"Not the way I'd put it, but true."

"The reason I mentioned the difficulty was 'cause it usually isn't. Everybody seemed tighter than a plugged asshole on this one."

"Does that mean anything?"

"Maybe, maybe not."

"I hope not."

He didn't say anything, but took his hand off the envelope. I reached out and brushed it toward me. Since the entire day felt like a movie

I ought to do my best. I lifted the envelope off the formica and slid it into my inside pocket opposite the holster.

"I appreciate this. I uh . . ."

"Just eat here more than every few years. You were all right back then and Julius says you're all right now."

I laughed as I stood. "I can't refuse that sort of invitation. It's money in the bank."

—9—

Saturday nights never were drumbeaters and this one began worse than usual. Once again I'd surrendered to primitive socialization and answered the phone.

". . . and I've put up with your idiosyncrasies, bullshit really, for years. I'm no fool. I didn't expect you to turn chickenshit into chicken salad, but I did expect more than twenty minutes of work. That just doesn't cut it, Matt man. I just want a little peace of mind. I can afford it, you know."

"Simon, you think you can afford anything. Including me."

"No, with you I don't think 'buy.' "

"Just 'owe.' "

"You are fucking hopeless. I don't just think 'owe,' shmuck, I think 'friend.' "

No way to get that hook out so I reeled myself back in. Simon started talking about 'round the clock, but we quickly settled that. Getting out of Sunday surveillance was more difficult. A couple of lies did the trick, and we finally agreed that I'd pick her up early Monday morning. By the time the conversation ended I was depleted. All the discomfort of the morning piled on top of my guilt. I flashed on my earlier unease, and pushed away the growing suspicions I had about Fran and her nightmares. I tried to convince myself that my general antipathy toward her was coloring my judgment. I took the envelope with the bills. I'd saved it to read with dessert but now there wasn't going to be any dinner. No dinner, no dessert.

I stretched out on the bed, found someone on the radio complaining about the Governor, and balanced a glass of bourbon on my chest. It proved too taxing so I sat up and drank it. By the time I heard my lock being picked I had finished three and fallen asleep. My mouth felt like the Sahara so while I waited for Julie I got up, poured a glass of orange juice, and turned on some light. The door swung open and he stood half hidden in the shadows of its frame.

"Are you moving in?" I asked.

He didn't bother to answer, just shut the door and walked into the kitchen. He was carrying his medicine bag so I poured another o.j. It was going to be a long night.

"Got some coffee?" he growled.

I thought about the time, then Phil's comments this afternoon. I offered him the second glass of juice while I worked the coffee. Julie sat at the kitchen table and unpacked his bag.

"Here's your regular stuff, though I truly do not understand Valium or codeine. If you want to do downs why not 'ludes?"

"I like to stand."

"A new and different you, my man."

I looked over from the counter where I'd been willing the coffee to drip faster. I don't know why I bothered to pour the juice since neither of us was going to drink any.

"What's that supposed to mean?" I glanced at the dope on the table. "Isn't it a little early in the month for this?"

"From what I hear, I'd say I'm right on time." He didn't lift his eyes from the table where he was lighting a chunk of hash, patting out the flame and crumbling the burnt hash into a cigarette paper. I waited and watched his fingers fly as he pulled a couple of buds from the bag, crushed and added them to the paper. He worked a joint like Ozawa worked a baton. The only thing he did better was chop and dice cocaine, but there were probably other reasons I enjoyed that. He lit the concoction and passed it. It went back and forth for a while with neither of us talking. The coffee filled the room with a wonderful smell and the lamplight played off the green marbled front of my Depression-era stove. It felt good to be awake.

Julie's voice cut through my reverie. "The java's done, slumlord."

I got the mugs from the cabinet, poured, brought them to the table and sat back down. I motioned for the joint, relit it, passed it back and lit a cigarette. The coffee tasted as good as it smelled and I was getting easy.

"Every time you call me slumlord, you like something I've done around here. What's it this time?"

"Not here, my man, out there." He nodded toward the back door.

I didn't think he meant the alley. "How so?"

"I had a citizen inquire about you yesterday." He stopped talking long enough to suck on the reefer and sip some coffee. Julie referred to everyone he did business with as a citizen. It hadn't occurred to me before but I was probably a citizen too.

"This citizen has ears that dip heavily into the constabulary of our town. I've worked with this gentleman as his business occasionally has use of one or two items I often possess."

"Phil pushes dope?"

Julie looked at me with disappointment on his face. He let me get a real good look at it too. I felt terrible, but wasn't sure why.

"Matthew Jacob. Do you really think I survive by dealing drugs?"

"Damn if I know, Julie." I waved at the stuff on the table between us.

"Not an entirely unreasonable assumption, but an ignoble line of work." He stared at me balefully. "I don't know how you got Phil willing to check for you if you think like this."

"Come on man, I was straight when I talked to him."

"Don't be silly, slumlord, it would take a year off dope for you to be straight."

He might be right but I didn't like hearing it. "Hey, lighten up. I'm sorry if I offended you."

He looked at me carefully. "Likewise."

I nodded as the moment of tension passed, took the cups, and reloaded.

"I occasionally broker goods. Dope I do with whom I smoke."

"You don't have to explain to me." I grinned and lit another cigarette. "What kind of goods?"

He looked at me and laughed. "I work with lost semis and their insurers."

"Stolen stuff?"

"All sorts of misplaced items."

It made sense. It also explained his ability to straddle many worlds.

"So Citizen Phil was useful, I would imagine?"

I stood up, passed the joint to Julie, and went to the desk to get the report. "Yeah, whatever you said helped." I returned to the table, envelope in hand. "He said it was difficult to get. He seemed surprised by that."

Julie looked at the envelope. "Allow me a glance, will you?"

I tossed him the envelope and played with a cigarette while he looked the report over.

"Things are odd here."

"What things?"

"That our citizen had any trouble getting this."

"Why? Is Phil that wired into the Department?"

Julius lifted his eyes. "Like I say, the man oughtn't have had any difficulty getting this."

"So what does that mean?"

"I have yet to determine its meaning. One other thing is odd as well."

"What's that?"

"I don't know who did the break-in."

I lit the cigarette and passed it over. "Is that unusual?"

"If I want to find out, it's unusual. Not unheard of, but unusual."

My head was beginning to hurt. I rummaged through the pharmacy on the table for Valium. Julie saw what I was doing and shook his head. "Why do you want to ruin a good high like that?"

I pointed to the report. "I don't want any complications with this shit, damn it. I'm a superintendent, not a detective. All of a sudden you're telling me I have a mystery on my hands?"

"Maybe."

"Maybe is more than I want to deal with."

"Your problem, slumlord, is you don't know your own talents. For the citizen to check you out, much less get you the report, speaks well of your innate abilities."

I stood and leaned on the sink and was reminded of my conversation with Dr. James. I went back to the table, though I remained standing. "I'm unaware of any abilities."

"To be sure. That allows for a great deal of inactivity."

I let myself show a flash of anger. "Damn it, man, I don't want to do anything, and now I'm a fucking detective out on the street!"

"You're lying to yourself, slumlord." He said it quietly, stood and prepared to leave. "Whether you know it or not."

I sat back down, the anger suddenly gone. "Maybe. Anyhow, thanks for the recommendation. And the dope. Should I be concerned about this mystery?"

Julie shrugged. "It would be wise. Something is not aligned. I would stay alert."

"Terrific. No sleep for the weary."

"Slumlord, you ain't alive enough to be tired."

10

Sunday was divided among newspapers, a couple of handyman house specials, *Murder, She Wrote*, and growing apprehension about my detective work. The feeling I had the other day, the transformation from hunter to hunted, was still fresh and I almost looked forward to talking about it in therapy. Only therapy was no longer therapy—it was a case. The police report indicated a straightforward burglary, but Julie's warning and Phil's difficulty in obtaining the report made it impossible to tell Dr. James there were no loose ends. Dope and alcohol numbed my nervousness but didn't change the fact. The best I could do was try to put the burglary out of my mind until Tuesday.

I awoke early Monday morning and, despite my headache and misgivings, arrived with time to kill before Fran left her large mock-Tudor home. It made me nervous sitting in a parked car on a tree-lined, quiet suburban street. I kept imagining that someone would report my presence to the police. Since I was carrying, I couldn't afford a search.

Luckily her departure beat my arrest. As I watched her gracefully enter her car I was struck with a mixture of respect and annoyance: she always looked so damned elegant, so in control. It was hard to picture her thrashing around in her bed in the throes of a nightmare. It was hard to imagine her thrashing around in bed, period. I was glad when her car pulled out of the driveway and I was able to concentrate on following her.

Without city traffic the game was tough. I had to remain far enough behind not to be recognized, but close enough to keep her in view. It was almost fun until I realized that once again I wasn't watching for anyone else. Eventually we turned onto a busier road where I tried to keep one eye on the cherry-red Mercedes and another on our surroundings. I was lucky I didn't drive off the road.

We cut a slow zigzag through suburbia toward the city. After two shopping plazas, one dry cleaner, and a croissant shop, we finally landed on Commonwealth Avenue. Although I never left my car it seemed like I had just played the great American sport of "shop 'til you drop." With a mixture of relief and revival of earlier worries I saw Fran pull into a space directly in front of 290. It took me a few minutes before I found parking on a nearby cross street, and by the time I returned Fran was nowhere to be seen. I would just have to take it on faith she was here to see a doctor.

For a moment, insanely, I thought about doing some shopping of my own but this wasn't an area I could afford. Instead I stooped it, smoking and watching as people busied by. Despite my resolution to ignore the burglary, sitting across the street from Dr. James' building made it impossible. I had believed her when she said she wasn't having an affair with Holmes, but I wouldn't make book on her student/ mentor explanation. It disturbed me to imagine my therapist blatantly lying. That she might be unaware of her feelings didn't leave me dancing either.

I looked up and down the street at the ornate oak front doors on many of the block's brownstones. For a moment, scenes of my last family vacation in Aix-en-Provence and its famous portals stirred, and with it the longing for a life that no longer existed. I felt a familiar rush of angry helplessness and ground my cigarette under my heel. I looked at my watch, and, unable to stand still, crossed the street to reconnoiter the burglarized offices.

As I entered the building the feeling of being watched returned in force. I looked out the lobby window, saw nothing suspicious, waited, and glanced again. No one seemed interested in 290. I didn't want to chance into Fran, so I took the stairs to the floor where the b&e's occurred. The offices were laid out around the outside of the hallway.

You could follow the hall around a square, ending where you started. I recalled the numbers of the offices that were entered, and Dr. James' suspicions began to sink in. The offices weren't adjacent to each other and there were medical offices in between those hit. A detail unmentioned in the police report.

It was time to reclaim my perch across the street. I loped down the stairs, but before plowing through the front door took a moment to peek out the window to see if anyone was watching the building. I saw no one, though my paranoia got stronger when I walked outside. I felt breathless and stopped at the top of the steps. I didn't hear the front door open behind me and grabbed the wrought iron railing to keep from losing my balance when I felt a hand tap me on the shoulder.

I turned and stood eyeball to eyeball with Fran. She found her voice a lot quicker than I found mine.

"Matt, what a nice surprise." She looked at my hand that was still glued to the rail. "Though by the look of it more pleasant for me than you. I'm sorry if I startled you."

"It's good to see you, Fran," I croaked. I tore my hand from the iron, turned and leaned against the metal. It quivered and, for an instant, I had visions of falling to the ground. Fortunately everything held.

"Where have you been? I haven't seen you in ages."

I shrugged. "Busy, I guess."

A look of displeasure crossed her face. "Well, you've been too much of a stranger and if you don't start visiting soon, I'll start to believe that you're fighting with Simon. Or with me."

I began to apologize but she interrupted. "Also, I don't remember seeing your r.s.v.p. for Wednesday." A sardonic glint crept into her eyes. "Of course you might have told Simon and he could have forgotten to tell me."

I frantically rummaged through my head trying to remember what she was talking about. I couldn't and she knew it. I'll give her credit; she could maintain civility.

"Our anniversary party. You absolutely must show and stay longer than ten minutes. Simon says you're the only person coming he can relax with."

"He exaggerates."

"Whether he does or not, you have to come." Her face was set, her feet planted. She wore her polite smile like a summons. She wasn't going to leave until she got what she wanted.

I couldn't hide the reluctance in my voice. "I'll be there but I might be a little late with a gift."

Her smile grew wider; it almost looked as if she meant it. "Oh Matt, no one expects a gift. You said the same thing at the wedding."

It was my turn to smile though it didn't quite match the smoothness of hers. I wasn't as adept at maintaining civility. "Well, at least I'll be there. What time?" Fuck her if I didn't remember her anniversary.

She passed me on the steps. "People are arriving after dinner but you come whenever you want. There's always enough food. Remember, it's at Alex's."

I mumbled my thanks to her back, and watched as she walked to her car and drove away. For a moment I wondered why she hadn't asked me what I was doing there, but then remembered myself and rushed down the steps toward my car. I noticed a skinny, straggly bearded kid sitting in a luxurious cream-colored Lincoln looking at me. He seemed out of place and I must have slowed, because he immediately started the Lincoln and pulled away. I wondered if he had stolen it, or whether he worked for the guru who lived in Oregon and collected limos.

When I finally got to my car I had no idea where to go. Before I could decide whether I felt relieved or foolish, Fran's car flashed by in my rearview mirror. I sped out of the parking spot, ignoring the blasts of angry horns, hurried down a block, swung a right, and waited for the light to change. Damn, Rockford made this look easy.

The light finally turned and I kicked the engine; if I didn't make the green on Boylston I'd have no chance of finding her. The horses complained but obeyed. I was in luck. It's funny, when you're hauling ass down a crowded city street, worries disappear. All I could think about was catching Fran and not killing anyone doing it. It was exhilarating.

Until I lost her. I got stuck behind a bus and didn't have the balls to blindly hurl myself across the center yellow line, an intelligent but humiliating decision. I was cursing and aimlessly circling the neighborhood when I had another rear-window vision. Damned if the cherry red wasn't climbing up my back. I pulled to the side as if to double-park and kept my face down. I didn't think she'd recognize my car. I was back in business and it felt great.

We drove to the wharf where she pulled into a multi-storied parking garage close to the Aquarium. I followed her in, and kept driving up and around the structure until I passed her car. She had her back to me and was heading for the elevator. The place was quiet, so I pulled into a vacant spot, stayed in the car, and waited for the elevator to whisk her away. I jumped out of my car and started for the stairwell until I noticed the 6TH FLOOR sign. I turned, lit a cigarette, and walked back to the elevator. There were limits to industriousness.

When I was gung ho about detecting I used to pick out strangers and follow them. Women had a better sense about being watched. For good reason. I managed to find Fran again, though, as soon as I got to the street. The bushy electric blonde hair made it simpler. I stayed a reasonable distance behind and was surprised to see her turn toward the Aquarium's entrance booth. I didn't want to follow.

I hadn't been in the Aquarium since the accident. The three of us used to go there on Friday mornings. We even had a fish tank at home. When I moved I left all the equipment behind; I didn't even eat whole fish anymore.

I stood by the outdoor harbor seals and smoked. I wanted dope and considered returning to the car, but before I could decide Fran came streaming back out the door and I had to turn quickly to avoid being seen. A great deal of my relief was smashed by her intent walk to the dolphin boat: she wasn't leaving, she was going to the show.

I glanced at the sign on the admission kiosk. Along with shock at the cost of a ticket, I noticed show time was an hour away. My curiosity overcame my inertia. I saw her enter the main door but when I pulled quietly on the handle it was locked. I trotted back to the booth and bought a ticket. If I was going to nose around a locked ship I wanted to have a stub to make the lying easier.

When I went back to the boat I didn't bother with the main entrance, but walked around the deck to see if there was another entry. A door toward the back was wedged open with a rock. I listened carefully for voices, then slipped in without making much noise.

The inside was dark and humid; and my nose was attacked by the stench of chlorine. In the distance I could hear the sounds of splashing water. I saw a crack of light, waited for my eyes to adjust, and walked carefully toward it. I made it without falling into anything, and looked out the door onto the main show arena. There were a couple of dolphins swimming in the pool and two trainers chatting amiably on the stage. I stood there feeling like an intruder, momentarily caught in memories of better times. I could even remember the dolphins' names. Unless they too were dead, and these were new ones. I was getting set to leave when I noticed movement in the dark shadows of the audience seats. I stared at the intermittent motion until I was sure. It was Fran and someone else, but the room was too gloomy to see the person beside her.

I wanted a closer look. The unlit corridor wrapped around the pool and auditorium, so I began a slow careful journey to where I could see them. It took an eternity but I finally got to a doorway that I thought would work. It was closed, so I pulled a handkerchief from my pocket and smothered the latch as I edged the door ajar.

Simon was wrong; it wasn't blackmail. The ugly suspicions I'd had when I connected Fran with the gynecologists in 290 were becoming all too solid. I was close enough to watch Fran's friend's hand disappear under her jacket, and it was nowhere near her pocket. I was close enough to watch her lean her head forward, close enough to watch her lips open and lick his. I was close enough to feel my stomach tighten with disgust and rage.

—11—

Home didn't help. No matter how high I got I couldn't get the smell of chlorine out of my nose or the knot out of my stomach. When I first started social work I had counseled a young couple, and in the course of a conversation about sex I asked the woman something about what she enjoyed. She told me that she liked to insert hairbrush handles. I sat there dumbfounded. Later the supervisor suggested that I not ask questions if I wasn't prepared for the answers.

I wished I had just lost Fran after her doctor's appointment. And I fucking well wished my friend hadn't gotten me involved to begin with. I felt like calling and telling him, but odds were he'd ask why, and I didn't feel like letting him know that his wife had nightmares because she was either diseased or pregnant.

It was too early to go to sleep. Too early to watch TV. Too early to do much of anything.

I got more dope from the stash and sat at the kitchen table. The gun didn't feel comfortable anymore so off it went. I spent the next forty-five minutes furiously smoking and cleaning the weapon. I didn't even bother to turn on the radio, just sat there and worked up a sweat. Finished, I reholstered it and hung the whole damn thing over the chair. I changed into shorts, got down on the floor, and started to work out. My lungs needed a breather so I stopped and smoked a cigarette. After the smoke I felt drained so I popped a Valium, showered, and lay down. I don't know how long I slept or what time it was; I only knew it was dark when I woke to the banging at my door.

For a wild moment I thought it was Simon coming to kill me for what I had seen. I stayed tucked and groggy in my bed hoping for the commotion to stop. Only the hammering continued. Finally a strange voice began hollering my name. I didn't want to move, but it would be only a matter of moments before Mrs. Sullivan's light began to flash. I padded over to the door, calling "Wait a minute," and had just unlocked it when it was pushed hard into me and knocked me backwards.

I stood there confused as two large men filled the entrance. One was a fat white man with silver hair and a bulbous red-veined nose that looked as if it had been pickled in boilermakers. The other was black, with hard eyes and a body built by Gold's Gym. Both wore suits and looked like they just walked out of a barber shop—Lenny Bruce's tell on cops. I got sweaty thinking about my stash.

"What do you guys want?" It wasn't snappy, but neither was I.

The Nose growled something unintelligible. I hoped his friend had brought a leash.

"Do either of you speak English?"

The black man smiled though his eyes never softened. A part of me began to hope they were cops.

The black turned to his friend. "We have a smartass here."

The fat man's jowls began to shake and his mouth opened in what seemed to pass for a smile. He took a step forward. I tried to figure out how to get to my gun.

"Wait, Connolly, if you start now he won't be able to talk."

"What are you doing here? Do you have a warrant?"

"Listen to the man, Connolly, he wants to know if we have a warrant. I told you he was smart. He guessed we were police."

My admirer walked over to me and slapped me hard across the face. I kept my head still but the blow brought tears to my eyes.

"You like our warrant?"

I didn't say anything. I hoped they found that agreeable. Connolly began to wander around the room while his partner stood and stared at me.

"We have some questions."

I kept quiet.

"I hope I didn't knock your tongue out. I'd hate to feed you to Connolly here." Body-by-Gold never took his eyes off me.

"What do you want?" It wasn't easy to talk, my cheek and jaw still throbbed.

"We want to know about your sudden interest in 290 Commonwealth."

"What interest?"

Connolly started to walk toward me, but the black guy moved between us. Just as I began to relax, he slammed me across the other side of my face.

"I just did you another favor." He nodded toward Connolly. "Now we can do this hard or we can do it easy?"

Something told me that easy wasn't going to be easy. "I don't know what you want. That's my shrink's building."

This time he let the dog through. I picked myself off the floor after he hit my stomach.

"Shamus, you are being foolish. It's really a simple thing here. What does a shrink in the building have to do with a bad stakeout?"

Any doubts about their being police vanished in the face of calling me shamus. I hadn't spent enough time watching 290 for someone to have identified me without the help of a government computer.

"Who hired you?"

"No one hired me. I felt fucked up and thought about seeing her. Just didn't want to when I got there."

"And I didn't want to do this when I got here." He nodded toward the Nose and I thought about running, only there was nowhere to go. When I opened my eyes I was on the floor again with a black boot headed in my direction. It seemed to be moving in slow motion and I figured I'd have no trouble avoiding it, but I was wrong. All I could do was inch my face out of the way. My neck didn't appreciate it.

"That's enough," the hard body ordered.

Connolly didn't think so. He bent over and grabbed me by the front of the shirt, pulled me up and held me while he punched me in the belly with a hand that looked as big as his foot.

"Damn, Connolly, I can't take you anywhere. Let him go."

When he did I crumpled to the floor and tried to find a way to breathe.

"Now look Jacobs, I guess you've watched too much TV and think that you're supposed to protect your client's identity at all costs. But I don't think you were at that building for your head. Now I don't like too much blood so I'm going to be a nice guy and suggest that, if you have a shrink appointment, you do it in the office. If I find out you're around that place, and don't have an appointment, I'm going to let Connolly have some real fun. You see how he likes to have fun, don't you?"

I looked up from the floor to see an open toothy gap under the white man's nose, his eyes lit with pleasure. The black guy was shaking his head at me with pity.

"We don't see too many of your type, Jacobs, degree boy with no smarts."

"It's Jacob, without the s."

This time the black man lifted me up. "Jacob, without the s. I'll remember. And you remember this."

He held me with one hand and pummeled me with the rock-hard other. I tried to move away but my body wouldn't respond to my begging. I closed my eyes and waited for the beating to stop. He finally let go.and I slumped back to the floor. I kept my eyes closed and hoped they'd think I passed out.

"Now you play 'possum all you like, Jacobs, but listen good. Stay away from 290. Go to your shrink and go home. And tell whoever hired you that you're off the case."

I opened my eyes a slit and watched as four blurry feet walked out the door. At least, I thought it was the door. I could see a small pool of blood gather by my face and somehow knowing it was mine threw my stomach into overdrive and I began to dry-heave. I heard someone whisper my name and I was afraid they had changed their minds.

But the voice sounded familiar, so I forced myself to look. All I could see was a pair of purple Converse high-tops. I looked up to see Charles standing by the door in a plaid three-quarter-length nightshirt, looking horrified. The clash of green plaid and purple kept my stomach rolling but I managed not to throw up.

"God, Matthew, I thought you were dead."

I couldn't talk. Someone had stuffed a grapefruit in my mouth.

"I'm going to call an ambulance."

I shook my head and brought tears to my eyes.

"Why not, Matthew?" Charles whispered.

I didn't know why not so I tried to get up. Charles scurried over and tried to help but I was too much dead weight. He set me lightly back down on the floor and went into the bathroom and emerged with a washcloth. He sat down on the floor next to me, cradled my head, and began to gently wipe my face. I couldn't stomach the plaid so I kept my eyes closed.

"I don't know why you won't let me call an ambulance. You might have internal bleeding. They may have broken your ribs."

I shook my head again.

"I saw them, Matthew. They just trashed you."

His shock was comforting. He was comforting. He opened my shirt and we both looked at angry red splotches on my belly and chest.

"This is outrageous. Two . . . two *animals*. Just trying to hurt you. I don't understand it at all!"

His voice was getting shrill. I closed my eyes and prayed for the room to stop spinning.

"Damn it, Matthew, you can't just lie there. At least let me call the police?"

I opened my eyes and stared into his face to stop the whirlies. I tried to speak around the grapefruit.

"Charles, they were the police."

—12—

I don't know how long we stayed there, Charles holding my head and me moaning, but from where I lay Mrs. Sullivan's light grew more and more insistent until I tried to get up. Charles demanded a hospital visit which I refused, though parts of my body cursed my attitude. I thought about my storehouse of pills but decided on a hot bath first. Charles helped and, other than a momentary flash of homophobia when he slipped my pants off, we negotiated the change from floor to tub without much additional pain. I asked him to go upstairs and reassure Mrs. Sullivan, and I promised to call if I changed my mind about the emergency room. Despite his tender care, I felt relieved to be alone and up to my chest in hot water. I didn't want to look at his nightshirt anymore. I was starting to relax when I was hit with another wave of pain. It almost changed my mind about the hospital, but after a few moments the hurt subsided and left me lusting for a cigarette.

I crawled out of the tub and inched into the bedroom where I took the Kools, matches, and ashtray and returned to the bathroom. I needed more soaking so I added hot water, swallowed a couple of pills, and groaned my way back in. My cheeks were still smarting, and the crook between my shoulder and neck felt as if a knife had slit it apart. The blotches on my chest seemed to dance and I wondered whether I could see the bruises turn color. I couldn't, but wasn't sure if my blurred vision was brought on by the waves of pain or the overwhelming loneliness I suddenly felt while I lay there doing inventory on my body. I felt like crying.

I was onto my third cigarette, and the tub water was turning cool. I was beginning to become impatient for my chemical white knights when the anger finally hit. It was one thing to be beaten up, another to have the damn thing happen in my home. My fucking home.

I dragged my body from the bath and forced myself to look in the mirror. My cheeks were okay but my eyes looked like Hearns' after the Hagler fight. They must have broken my nose but I couldn't remember when. I could breathe, so the hell with it. I didn't want doctors sticking Q-tips up anything. I went through the torture of pulling on my undershirt before I realized there was nowhere to go and no one to see. It was the middle of the night and I would have to wait until the morning before I could do anything. I stood there too sore to move, but frustrated, and reluctant to go to bed.

I spent the next hours smoking, dozing, and hurting. During the moments of awareness, images from the afternoon and night flashed across my throbbing eyes until I began to wonder where the dreams began. For a while I thought I was in a coffin, staring up into the hard, cold eyes of my black visitor and the sadistic face of his bloated friend. I would try to turn my head, and when I couldn't, look back and gaze at the concerned faces of Simon and Fran. Seeing them was worse, but they refused to leave when I blinked. I almost prayed for the cop's image to return. When I awoke from that one, I worried about having overdosed.

I hadn't and, as long as I lay there and remembered that the beating wasn't a punishment for what I saw in the afternoon, I was okay. More than okay; I was enraged. Two fucking cops had trashed me in my own home and I didn't even know why.

13

The call to arms had lessened considerably by the time Charles found me late in the morning drinking coffee and eating toast. My body felt like it had been left in a washing machine stuck on agitate. My head was drugged-over and my mouth fuzzy—the usual down side of using chemical solutions to approximate normalcy. I must have appeared presentable in my sunglasses though, because he sat down and didn't say a word about my face. He was probably being polite.

"Do you want some?" I pointed to my cup and plate.

"Just coffee. Have to watch my weight, you know."

I began to get up when he reached over and put his hand on my shoulder. "You stay. I can get it myself."

He stood and fixed himself a cup, his head turning like a pigeon's. "Bakelite appliances, Depression-era cookware, 1940s toasters," he swung his arm and followed it with the rest of his body. "You have a gay gene, Matthew."

"You forgot to mention the radios."

A look of exaggerated horror crossed his face. "How could I have forgotten the best part?"

I grinned, though it hurt. "Then I'll take this all as a compliment, and thanks for last night. I appreciate the care, though the nightshirt should go to Goodwill."

Charles stopped looking around the room. He hadn't heard a word.

"What's going on, Matthew? I made up some crazy story to Mrs. Sullivan about you being drunk and fighting with yourself on the stairs, but she didn't believe a word of it. I think she saw those animals come in, although she wouldn't say."

"Is she all right?"

"She's okay. Same as me, scared but okay."

"You haven't anything to be afraid of. This has nothing to do with the building."

"Well, I'm somewhat relieved to hear that, but it isn't really the building that concerns me. Or Mrs. Sullivan."

I felt embarrassed and looked away. "I don't know what to tell you. I'm involved in something I don't entirely understand. I am going to try to get some answers."

"I spoke to Richard this morning and he wants to know whether you would like him to return early. Is there something you might need him for?"

My discomfort just grew worse. "Nah. But I could use your help around here while I find out what this is all about. I need someone to look after the building and Mrs. Sullivan."

Charles looked at me quizzically. "Are you going to have to travel?"

I started to shake my head but stopped when it felt like something was going to break. "Nothing so drastic. I just want to focus my attention."

I started to get up to refill my cup but it didn't take more than a moment before I thought better of it. "Would you mind?"

Charles took my mug and turned toward the pot. I lit another cigarette. My ribs ached. I thought about taking more Demerol but decided on codeine instead. I didn't want to be any more stupid than I already was. I thought about asking Charles to get it from the bathroom, but it was difficult to keep asking for help. Charles handed me the mug, steam rising from the black.

"You take it black, don't you?"

I nodded. It surprised me that he knew my coffee habits; maybe he should do the detective work and I take care of the building.

"Matthew, I know that you're a detective and all, but do you know what you're doing?"

I couldn't think of a rousing response. "How do you know that I'm a detective?"

"Matthew, really." Charles sounded exasperated. "Everyone in the building knows about your detective license." He looked at me slyly. "Before last night it was somewhat reassuring."

"What else does everyone in the building know?" It was my turn to sound exasperated.

Charles looked at me and smiled. "You're a strange man. Everyone is interested in a person with two first names."

It was my turn to smile. "Not technically two."

"Matthew, seriously, do you know what you're doing? Last night you said it was the police who had done the, the . . ."

"Beating."

"Yes, the beating. Are you sure? Why would the police do this? If they wanted they certainly could have arrested you. On drugs, if nothing else."

"More common knowledge?"

Charles looked annoyed. "What does it matter? No one holds it against you."

I liked that least of all. But he was right. What did it matter? Today wasn't going to be the first day of the rest of my life. "You're right, Charles. It doesn't matter. I have a pretty good idea they were cops. If they weren't, I don't think they'd have left me in one piece."

Charles seemed dubious. "I don't know. Usually police just abuse blacks and gays."

"That's institutional. This was private."

"What do you mean?"

"I'm not sure myself. That's why I have to do some work." Some of my anger returned. "I'll find out what's going on."

"I suppose. But how can you do anything? I'm not even sure you should be moving."

"I'll be fine. I just have to loosen up."

"Richard said you're a stubborn fuck."

"What else did Richard say?"

"To just let you do what you want."

"Thank Richard for me. Will you keep an eye on things around here?"

"Of course."

I started to get up again. Charles pointedly didn't help. The prick. It took a while but I was finally vertical.

"I'll go up and talk to Mrs. Sullivan."

A look of horror crossed his face and he quickly stood up as if to block my way. He didn't have to worry. I wasn't ready to climb stairs.

"Don't be silly. One look at you and she'll have a seizure. I'll make something up." He started to let himself out the door, then turned and said in a neutral tone, "Also, Matthew, if you are going to go outside, please wear something other than mirrored glasses. You look like you work at McDonald's."

I took his advice and tried to loosen my body by wandering around the house until I found a pair of regular sunglasses. For my money they didn't look much better. Upwardly mobile to Burger King. Despite moving around, my body felt no better and was going to refuse to twist into the car. It was a good time to organize my drugs. I pulled out the pills I could cover with scripts and put them into the medicine chest. The rest I sorted into different containers, then placed the entire stash into my hide-hole. If the police returned to arrest me they would have to work for it. I returned to the bathroom and took the codeine. Compared to the Demerol it was light but, after I home-brewed a taping job on my ribs, I felt a little better and somewhat more mobile. I went back into the kitchen and had more coffee. I wanted to stay awake.

It took about forty-five minutes for everything to kick in; finally I felt like I could get into my car. I got up to call Dr. James. Today I wasn't going to wait outside.

14

The telephone conversation got me angry all over again. She was busy, couldn't it wait until our regular appointment, why today, and a reluctant okày if I arrived in an hour. I steamed around the house and stormed to the car, then realized it was a helluva lot better feeling angry than awkward or anxious. Anger also helped reduce the fear I had of going anywhere near 290. When I pulled up in front of the building I thought I noticed the same cream Lincoln parked up the block. I couldn't tell if anyone was inside, and wondered if my cold feet were making something out of nothing. There were plenty of luxury cars in this neighborhood and, frankly, that kid hadn't looked like he worked for the police.

The drugs were keeping me reasonably loose, so I managed the steps without looking too much like an invalid. If my nocturnal visitors were watching I hoped they thought I had miraculous recovery powers, but I wasn't going to linger outside to impress. I didn't bother to look out the lobby window either, but went right to the inside stairway. If I kept moving it would take longer before my body began to tighten.

Dr. James' waiting room was empty, so I sat down and fell into my client routine. Unfortunately *The New York Review of Books* was a Chomsky handout, so I put it down. I wasn't interested in an etymological chronicle of the world's plight: I had my own to worry about. Too late I heard the door to the inner sanctum open, and found myself caught off-guard as Dr. James called my name.

She sounded like she did every Thursday and, for a moment, my usual weekly nervousness and resentment reappeared. Until I began to walk. Then my body reminded me why I was here.

"Come in, Mr. Jacob." She closed the door behind us.

"It was Matthew on Thursday." I walked past the shelves of books that lined the walls. Over the course of visits I had grown familiar with most of the titles; you had to look pretty close to find fiction interspersed with the rows of books on psychology. Though Proust and Mann were hardly easy reading.

"I know," she said, responding to my unspoken complaint. "Despite my initial reluctance to see you today, I'm rather glad you're here. I want to talk about Thursday. Why don't you sit down?" She finished her apology and suddenly saw me. "What happened to your face?" Some of her formality began to slip.

I creaked over the plain gray rug and wedged behind the muted floral couch by the window. I looked down at the street for what happened to my face, but as usual saw nothing. Even the Lincoln had been replaced by a silver Toyota van. I kept my eyes outside, but leaned on the back of the couch toward the center of the room. She seemed to understand that I wasn't going to sit.

"What happened to you? Why do you keep staring out the window?"

"You talk about Thursday first." I had trouble keeping the harshness out of my voice.

She walked to the rear of her desk as if to take her seat, changed her mind, and leaned up against the side. She was wearing a pair of white jeans and a bright pink corduroy shirt. It seemed a sharp contrast to her dull office and it was certainly different from what I was used to seeing her wear. I wondered whether she dressed in different styles according to her day's clients; it bothered me to find her appealing.

She made up for her clothes with the chill in her voice. "Since we last met I've done a great deal of thinking and decided I was too impetuous in requesting your services. Especially without talking to Dr. Holmes."

"And this time when Holmes reassured you, you believed him?"

"Exactly."

"And now you want me to forget about it and resume our regular work."

Her face relaxed and, for a moment, a look of genuine relief shone from her eyes. "Yes. That's right. I know we'll have to work through my visit to your home, but I'm sure we can do that."

"Crap." This time I didn't try to disguise my tone.

A look of confusion crossed her face and her body yanked upright. "I don't understand. You didn't indicate that my visit would end our therapeutic relationship."

"Right now I don't care about our therapeutic relationship. I care about the case. You are the second person to warn me off the burglaries." I stopped and pointed to my face. "Though you are more polite about it."

She stood with her hand over her mouth. "You mean someone actually hit you?"

I just looked at her.

She started to walk toward me, but stopped. "Have you seen a doctor? Of course I'll pay for whatever this costs you. I am completely responsible. I'm *really* sorry."

"I don't want your money and you're not responsible for anything. You didn't do the beating."

She looked around the room like she was going to move but couldn't find a destination worth the effort. "I don't understand. Eban swore to me that there was nothing to worry about."

"He might be telling the truth. We'll find out soon enough."

She frowned. "What do you mean?"

"I mean exactly that. I intend to find out what my beating was about. I don't know whether your friend Holmes is involved or not, but I do know that the police are fucking with the report and want me out."

"I still don't understand."

"The police did this."

A look of disbelief crept into her eyes. "Why would the police beat you up?" She shook her head. "Are you certain?"

"I intend to get certain." I sounded more confident than I felt but then, I wasn't here to talk about my feelings.

She looked at me, a slight smile beginning to tug at the corners of her mouth. "You know, Mr. Jacob . . ."

"Matt."

"Okay, Matthew. The reason I originally asked you for help was the attitude you are displaying today. Now I'm concerned about it. I mean, how much of your stubbornness is self-destructive?"

"I don't give a damn, Gloria." I leaned on her first name. "I'm not here to inspect my stubbornness. You can save that shit for my fifty-minute hours."

She shook her head and walked over to one of the easy chairs and sat down. "This *sucks*."

I started to laugh.

"What are you laughing at?"

I felt as if someone had buried a knife inside my ribs. It made it easy to stop laughing. "I'm sorry. I wasn't laughing at you. It's just that for a moment there you sounded human."

She looked angry, then she started to laugh. If I hadn't still been recovering from the first one I would have joined her.

"I feel torn," she said. "I've waited years to see you act like this, but it wasn't supposed to happen this way. And I am concerned about your safety. I mean, if they were police, you have no one to get help from." Another worried look crossed her face. I wondered if it was for me.

"Also, Eban was adamant. He didn't want anyone nosing around his business."

"Well, it's too late for that. You don't have to worry. I'll tell him myself."

Her eyes narrowed and she looked like a lioness protecting a cub. This time I didn't wonder if the look was for me.

"You can't just go barging into Dr. Holmes' life looking for infor-mation," she said. "I won't let you."

"You can't stop me." The words hung in the air and I realized how childish they sounded. I walked to the front of the couch and dropped down. The morning's pills were wearing off and I began to remember how bad I really felt. "Look, this isn't a fight between us. I can't let the police, or anyone, stroll into my house and beat the hell out of me, then pretend that nothing happened. I don't plan to browbeat your friend. You can see for yourself."

"Meaning what?"

"Get him over here now."

"Just like that?"

"Why not?" Just like Rockford, I was thinking on my feet.

Dr. James looked uncertain. "I don't know if that's a good idea. I don't know if he's in today, much less free."

"Why don't we find out?" I moved as though to rise. I hoped she would say something to stop me.

She did. "I'll call and see what he says." She stood, walked over to her desk, and knelt down behind it. My first thought was she had a special knock on the floor to contact him. My second was how well she filled the seat of her pants. I tried to shake my head clear. The pain in my body was starting to affect me.

"I had to plug in the phone," she said as she stood up and read the look on my face. She dialed a number, impulsively hung up the receiver, then dialed again. This time she waited. I could hear the murmuring of her voice but my body hurt enough that I didn't pay attention. I didn't know whether I was up to meeting Holmes. The next time I practiced thinking on my feet I'd make sure I was able to stand.

She finished her conversation and turned to me. "He'll be here in a minute. He seems quite interested in meeting you." Almost absently she said, "You look really uncomfortable; do you want anything?"

The words slipped out before I could stop them. "Morphine would be fine."

It got her attention though she didn't see the humor. "Don't be ridiculous. If you're hurt badly enough for morphine you belong in a hospital." She looked angry. "With your drug problems morphine would push you into an early grave. It's something we're going to have to talk about, you know? You can't keep hiding your dependency."

I waved my hand. "Relax, I was only joking."

"Well, I don't think your chemical use is as funny as you do."

"Well, can I have some H_2O?"

15

I was drinking the last of the Poland Spring when Eban Holmes bounced through the door. I had expected Basil Rathbone and found myself wordless after I struggled to my feet and extended my arm downward to grasp his short stubby hand. His grip was firm and his fingers acted as a conduit for the air of electricity that accompanied him. It felt like shaking hands with a cattle prod.

"So this is our sleuth." It wasn't quite a question, but it wasn't all that obnoxious either. He released his grip, took a step back, and looked me up and down, his bright eyes sparkling deep within a forest of red hair.

"My clothes aren't for sale, Dr. Holmes."

A quick grin and a look into my eyes as he continued to inspect. "You do seem a little the worse for wear," he said affably. Dr. Holmes wasn't leading with a hard sell.

"Your building seems to house some forceful mysteries."

An even larger smile stretched across the naked section of his face while his head bobbed up and down. If it weren't for his remarkable aura, he could be mistaken for a leprechaun. "How could it be otherwise? A building that houses doctors of the mind and body would certainly harbor mysteries."

"That's not exactly what I meant, Dr. Holmes."

"I didn't think so, Mr. Jacobs."

Dr. James' voice and mine rang out simultaneously. "Without an s."

Everyone chuckled and, for a few seconds, the tension in the room eased.

"Please call me Eban. It's Matthew, isn't it?"

"Or Matt. How did you know?"

"Dr., uh, Gloria told me."

I looked sideways toward Dr. James. "What else has Gloria told you?" It was awkward to use her first name but I'd get used to it.

"Whatever she wanted, Matt. We have very few secrets between us." He waved his arm around the room. "Perhaps if we all sat down and made ourselves a bit more comfortable, this conversation might become easier." Although part of me minded his assumption of host, another part, my body actually, was grateful. I couldn't stifle the grunt as I sat down.

Holmes' eyes were all over my face. "You are in pain, aren't you?" He didn't wait for an answer but turned to Dr. James. "Do you have something for him?"

"I don't want to give him drugs, Eban. You understand, don't you?"

He looked at her kindly. "I understand, Gloria, but this man is in a dreadful amount of discomfort."

While I grew hopeful Dr. James became defensive. "He didn't say he was in that much pain."

"I'm not surprised." Holmes looked at me, then his voice became businesslike. "Glo, do you have any painkillers here?"

Gloria stood by her desk and hesitated while she made up her mind. It bewildered me to think of her doing what he said.

She went into the bathroom and returned with two pills. I started to get up but she frowned me back into my seat and took the glass from my hand. I looked at the pills. They were fat with a 3 on one side. Tylenol with codeine; I could feel my body start to relax. I nodded my gratitude when she returned with the water.

Dr. James, Gloria, shook her head brusquely, "Thank him. I'm reluctant to give you aspirin."

As she sat back down Holmes resumed talking. "Gloria and I go back a long way and we truly don't keep many things secret," he paused, then continued, "personal or professional."

"I thought there was a question of ethics involved?"

He raised his eyebrows and shrugged. "Perhaps. But in the larger scheme of ethics, precise confidentiality seems somewhat trivial."

"Well, it sounds like some things remain unchanged. What kind of car do you drive?"

"What?" He looked puzzled.

"That rap sounded like your essays in the *Radical Therapist*. Come on, what kind of car do you drive?"

He started to look annoyed while Dr. James twisted uncomfortably in her seat. Holmes coughed and smoothed away the annoyance. "A Volvo. I don't know whether to be flattered or suspicious by your research."

"I understand. I feel the same way about your conversations with Gloria."

Holmes burst out laughing. The sound boomed across the office. "Gloria has spoken so highly of you that I was predisposed to like you, but I hadn't imagined how much."

"Eban!" Gloria's face was turning pink.

He shook his head at her. "Now listen, Glo, you can't turn back the clock. You asked this man to help us out. The fact that I don't need any help is quite beside the point. You can't expect us to play games now. Matt knows perfectly well that we have talked about him. I don't intend to pretend otherwise. And you know, as well as I, that he would know immediately if I lied. I can't tell you what to do for yourself, so if you want us to talk somewhere else we will."

Dr. James' hands were balled up into fists. It bothered me to see her so unhappy so I said, "I know this is tough for you 'cause it ain't a walk in the woods for me. But you keep acting like you're letting me down by not being my shrink right now, but that's not true. Now I don't know what I think about Dr. Holmes', Eban's, philosophy but right now I don't care. First things first."

I felt my temper rising and heard it seep out into my voice. "Someone wants me out of their way and was willing to use muscle to get it done. Well, they should have asked politely."

I didn't think she felt settled, but her hands did unclench and she tried a weak smile. "I suppose you're both right but I keep getting in deeper than I want." She looked at Holmes and a sharpness returned to her face. "I'm not used to this, Eban."

"I know you're not." He nodded toward me. "But it seems as if you picked a decent enough person to try with."

"I'm not sure I want to try. It certainly wasn't the reason I began," she finished glumly.

I interjected, "Why did you begin?"

"I told you the reasons when I was at your house." She spoke as if she were remembering a trip to the emergency room.

"Well, you didn't tell me enough. Some vague notion of protecting him," I jerked my arm, "just doesn't cut it. That was fine if your concerns were groundless, but they aren't. My face and body are proof of that." Right then nothing hurt and I even felt a little light-headed. Thank you Dr. Gloria.

Holmes' eyes were glittering. "You mean your face is connected to this?"

"My face, my body and, because of other information, my mind."

"Other information?"

"My contact found it difficult to get the police report on the break-ins."

"Should it have been easy?" His voice had grown quiet but there was no mistaking his interest.

"Easier than it was."

"What else?"

"Not much more than what Dr., I mean, Gloria suggested. The police wrote it up as a typical junkie crime, but it doesn't look that way to me. Anyhow, if there was any doubt that something strange is happening, it should be laid to rest with this." I gestured toward my bruises.

Dr. James spoke from behind her desk. "He thinks it was the police who beat him up."

"What? Can you be certain?"

"Same question everyone is asking. They didn't leave a card."

"Let's accept your hypothesis. What did they want?"

I was getting tired of the interview. "They wanted to be friends. All I needed to do was stay away from here. Now I'm hearing the same thing from her."

The image of the two cops filling my doorway flooded my mind. "Look, I'm sick of this shit." I looked at the two of them deliberately.

"I want to know why Dr. James thought the break-ins had something to do with you."

Holmes sighed and pushed his body to the back of the chair. He tugged at his beard and stared vacantly past my shoulder. Finally he looked at Dr. James and nodded his head. "I think you need to talk, Gloria. What he wants to know has more to do with you than me."

"Eban, I can't. I've been treating Mr. Jacob for four years. I can't just talk."

I looked from one to the other. "I don't give a shit who talks. Lie down on the couch if you have to." I struggled to my feet while both of them looked at me oddly. "As far as my treatment is concerned, Gloria, consider it complete. Over." My own surprise at my words calmed me down a little. "Successful."

There was a moment of shocked silence. I had suddenly found myself adding another breakup to a lifetime of dissolutions. And like I had before, I almost wished I hadn't said anything. And, like I had before, I felt almost giddy with relief.

"Bullshit! Bullshit, bullshit, bullshit!" She stood and grabbed at the corners of her desk. Her voice was shrill and her mouth looked distorted as the words came tumbling. "Regardless of any mistake I may have made, I deserve better than this. I've worked week after week, month after month to get you back on your feet. I've struggled to see through your passive hostility, your cynicism, your resistance. I know I'm not the warmest therapist alive but I think I've worked with compassion and belief in your capabilities, your potential. Surely you have some sense of that?" She turned toward Holmes. "Goddamn you!" She turned right back toward me. "You can't walk out. You're getting better. We've worked too hard, too many hours for you to leave now. I just won't let you."

By the time she finished her voice had choked and tears were edging down her face. I felt myself pale under my black-and-blues. It was hard to look at her. My own throat was tight and I felt a ball of sadness well up behind my eyes. "Of course I know what you think of me. I certainly know how hard you've worked, how difficult I am. I don't think I could have stayed with therapy as long as I have without knowing those things. But maybe you've been more successful than you realize. If it were only looking into the burglaries I could stop.

Hell, I didn't want to start; I still don't cotton myself a fucking detective."

I flashed on the scene in the Aquarium, then shook my head. "The beatings make it different. I can easily imagine a time when someone could have trashed me and I would have believed that I deserved it. I'm different now. I don't want to just let it go. I can't."

Holmes was sitting quietly, watching, his face a mask. Slowly he got off the chair and walked across the room toward Gloria. I felt foolish just standing there and sat back down. Gloria had her face covered with her hands and pulled her arm away when he touched her elbow. He held his ground. "Glo. Listen to me. There are many ways to understand what's happening here, but we're not going to get anywhere if you don't pay atttention to yourself. You can hear what you're saying. You have a lot of deep feelings for Matthew and you really deserve to understand them."

His voice was soft, almost a whisper. I could feel my own shock begin to drain, and I could see Dr. James begin to relax. But now that I was out of treatment why was I thinking of her as Dr. James?

Holmes kept talking. "All three of us understand that the two of you have some talking to do before any final decisions about working together should be made. But Gloria, we also know that consciousness is the last stop for information, not the first. When you decided to visit him at his home . . . no, let me finish . . . you were trying to tell yourself something. Now you need some time to sort things out, and so does he. Both of you seem to have arrived here somewhat accidentally."

Dr. James had stopped crying and was looking at him, but he looked at me. "You seem intent on following through with this investigation?"

He didn't wait for my answer. "Why don't we agree that for the duration of this work both of you will try to cooperate as peers and both of you will give more thought to your professional relationship." His voice grew absolutely neutral. "Perhaps to your relationship in general. When your investigation is complete there will be plenty of time to talk."

Dr. James began to say something but Holmes wasn't finished. "What sort of business arrangements did the two of you discuss when you met?"

I shrugged. Gloria found her voice. "None, really."

"Well, I would think something more formal might be useful."

I stared at him, "So why don't you hire me?" I couldn't believe it. I was asking for a job.

"I have no reason to hire you."

"She thought you did."

"She was wrong."

"Eban, then what are you saying?" She had regained her composure and was looking at Holmes who was still standing beside her. "If you don't need to hire him neither do I."

He walked back to his chair but didn't sit down. "First of all, Matt needs it. He is going to stay involved and, since you got him into this, some legitimacy would probably help. Also, Glo, I think you need to work with him in a way that doesn't simply reinforce your perception of him as a patient. Since you both seem uncomfortable with 'neither fish nor fowl,' I think some pasta might help."

I understood what he meant, and she certainly did. The room grew quiet while she sat thinking. Eban reached into his pocket and withdrew a pipe. The sight of it reminded me of how badly I wanted a cigarette. I reached into my coat, pulled out my pack, and lit one. Another taboo broken. Dr. James read my mind. "I almost told you not to smoke during a session." She smiled wryly past her tear-stained face.

"That's okay, I was almost too afraid to light it."

16

The reasons that originally drove Gloria to my apartment produced an undercurrent of sadness that threatened to escalate into full-scale depression as Holmes traced the history of their relationship. A teacher/student love affair fragmented with bouts of guilt, recriminations, and self-doubt. Although they maintained contact after Dr. James graduated, they apparently hadn't resumed their friendship until after he married. His wife seemed to protect them from themselves. At least Holmes thought so.

After Holmes stopped talking, Gloria, her throat tight, continued, "What Eban says about our relationship is true. While I was with him I felt loved and taken care of. A part of me never felt better. But I had no need of Yvonne's protection. Once we finished that part of our relationship," she looked at both of us defiantly, "it was over."

Undertones of a deeper, more complicated conflict punctured their differing perceptions, but I'd had enough of Dr. James without her professional clothes. "You don't have to tell me all this."

"I know." She closed her eyes. "Please, this is difficult enough without interruptions. You see, Eban is a genius in my field." She stopped, opened her eyes, bit her lower lip and continued in a soft even voice. "I care a great deal about my work. For as long as I can remember, work has been a source of pride and identity. If he and I were together, *my* work, *my* ambitions, would necessarily take a back seat." She closed her eyes and shook her head. "As wonderful as our relationship made me feel, there was too great a sacrifice."

The three of us sat there; they with their memories, me with my own history of four-card flushes. It was one thing to fire my therapist, another to be confronted with her shattered dreams.

"So you were afraid Holmes graduated from fucking students to fucking clients."

The hostility shredded the atmosphere. I stood, grateful for my sunglasses. "Look, I gotta go. If there were any doubt," I opened my hands toward the two of them, "that last remark clinches it."

I walked toward Dr. James and tried to make up. "Dr. Holmes is right about my needing some protection. Why don't you give me a dollar like they do on television. You know, then I'll have a client." I smiled but she was still stung by my big mouth.

"I wouldn't give you a quarter. Your body may hurt but I think I've taken a fair beating myself today. There was no need for you to act like a shit."

I took off the glasses. "You're absolutely right. And so was he," I jerked my thumb toward Holmes, "before. I think it's probably the right thing, but changing our relationship is harder than it looks." I stared directly at her. "I am going to keep looking into this with or without your dollar. Tell you the truth, I'm not sure whether I'm better off with or without a client."

"Which raises another question, Matt." Holmes was stroking his beard thoughtfully, but his eyes were hard and filled with something I couldn't recognize. There was a side to him that I hadn't yet met. "Your intent is clear, but you might be in over your head." He couldn't resist, "I suspect the other fellow won the fight."

Who could blame him? None of us had had it easy today. He'd just done a busman's holiday, stuck his ass on a clothesline, and had his fantasy about his and Gloria's relationship slapped. But I wasn't going to back off now.

"I was in over my head the minute I said I'd get involved. It's a consensus. But now that I'm in, I'm staying. It's not a feeling I often have and," I bowed stiffly, very stiffly, toward Dr. James, "thanks to her help, a feeling I don't intend to ignore." I looked back toward

Holmes and was surprised to see him struggling to rid his face of a twisted, hostile expression. "The other fellow only won the round," I said starting for the door.

"Wait."

I was glad it was her voice. She was opening her desk drawer. "Here's a couple of dollars. We will discuss real payment some other time."

There was no accounting for the sense of exhilaration I felt when I pocketed the singles. I shook hands with Eban, who had bounced up from his chair and was trying to generate his earlier warmth and friendliness. After his look of a moment ago it didn't square, but he didn't dampen my enthusiasm. I had trouble walking out the door, but by the time the elevator deposited me in the lobby I was admitting the obvious: I liked what I was doing.

The weather outside was beautiful. One of those days when the sun and blue of the sky reach out and cradle you, insulate you from the people and activities which surround you. For a moment even my body, though in need of a hot bath, felt like mine and not some alien graft to contend with. Although I needed to make sense out of all that had occurred I wasn't going to do it now. There weren't too many days when I noticed the weather, and even fewer that I liked. Sometimes you just had to smell the flowers.

I decided on a long ride home. As I drove around the city I found myself thinking of the family without the usual gravel-in-my-face sensation. I felt badly that they were buried in Chicago; I wanted to visit their graves. Instead I drove to Author's Ridge, a cemetery in an outlying town where a number of famous literary figures lay. I walked to the point where you could see both Emerson's and Thoreau's graves; Emerson's was marked with a large round monument, Thoreau's a small modest plaque. As they lived so they will be remembered. It bode well for the memories of those who were mine.

The drive back was quiet. A slight drop in the temperature gave early warning to the onset of evening. I was amazed at how quickly the day had winged by. I thought about talking to Phil, but time had lightened my ambition and I didn't want an injection of cynicism. It was time to put things in perspective, comfortably, at home.

Only there was more left to the day. I noticed the door leading to the basement was slightly ajar. The calm I'd felt since leaving Dr.

James' office evaporated in the face of another potential visit from last night's friends. I forced my body to walk the hall quietly to my apartment. The sound of the television drifted out from behind the closed door. I thought about leaving and returning later but there seemed no point. Whoever it was, was making himself right at home. I bunched my body into a tight, painful ball, grabbed and simultaneously twisted the handle of the door, thrust my way in, and scared the shit out of Lou who was lounging on the recliner watching the tube. He jumped to his feet and looked wildly around the room. I just stood there panting with fear and pain. Neither of us said anything for a moment.

"Jesus Christ, boychik, do you always come home that way? What the hell happened to you? I thought your days of picking on bartenders were over." He stood with his hands shaking.

I finally caught my breath. "Lou, how are you? Why didn't you let me know you were coming? What are you doing in town? How is Martha?"

"Slow down, Matty." He lowered his bulk onto the chair though he kept the back upright. "Sit down, will you? You're acting crazy." He looked at me carefully. "Why are you wearing sunglasses? Are you high on something? Are you drinking again?"

I walked over to the couch. "Now you slow down. I'm not drinking and I'm not high. I've had some trouble lately and I'm jumpy about it."

"What sort of trouble?"

I waved my arm. "I'll tell you later, first things first." I took off my glasses and looked him over. "You're looking fat and sassy."

He grimaced. "Fat yes, sassy I'm not so sure about. What the hell happened to your face?"

"Broken nose, no big deal. I promise you we'll get to it. What brings you to town?"

"Got to check on my investments, right?" He smiled. So did I.

"Right."

"The mayor sent me to feel out whether it makes sense for him to initiate a national campaign."

"You mean you want to find out whether it makes sense to run the mayor, don't you."

"You've always thought I was more of a kingmaker than is true."

I nodded and smiled. Here was the last relic of Chicago's Daley years, a guy who managed to land in a new era with his local clout intact, and he was still pretending to be a political hack. We both knew that the high point of his life had been handing Illinois to Kennedy in '60. Every time a national election rolled around Lou looked to repeat the experience.

"How long are you in for?"

"Just 'til the morning."

"Lou." I was disappointed.

His face set. "I can't leave Martha alone too long these days."

"Is she sick?"

His hands tightened on the arms of the chair. "Not really. She's having trouble remembering things. The whitecoats have some fancy name for it but I call it age."

"What do you mean by whitecoats? Is she hospitalized?"

"Not now. She has to go once in a while."

"When did this begin?"

"Oh, it's not recent." He didn't want to talk but my silence seemed to push him into it. "It's been coming on for a long time. Hey, it was even pretty funny for a while. We sometimes would sit around and laugh about some of the shenanigans she used to pull."

"When did it stop being funny?"

He looked at me sharply. "Still not one for tact, are you?"

"I guess not." He was one of the very few people who could still make me feel sheepish.

"It got bad about a year ago."

"Jesus, Lou, I didn't know."

"How could you? I didn't tell you. You've got enough *tsouris* of your own."

"Sure."

"Look, don't sure me. All telling you would do is worry another person. It seemed like a dumb idea."

"Do you stay home with her?"

"Most nights. I got steady help in the day."

He pushed himself to his feet with his large powerful arms. "Enough with this. By the looks of it you got some problems yourself. Anyhow, I don't want to talk about mine or even hear about yours. I want to eat. Then I'll want to listen."

I felt relieved about not talking. I also felt hungry.

"Sounds like a great idea. Name your fancy, my treat."

He shook his large head and grumbled, "I'll name the place but you leave your money home."

"We'll work it out. Where do you want to go?"

"Where I always go. The joint that doesn't have a name. The one by the ocean."

17

Wednesday morning brought a return to physical normalcy: my head hurt worse than the rest of my body. I think it was light when Lou left but I wasn't sure. He has the capacity to drink through the night and wake up friendly and energetic. An early career as precinct captain trained him well. I couldn't have gotten up even if I hadn't matched him drink for drink. For the first time since the accident we had talked about the family. I had felt comfortable during the conversation, but my sleep was less benign. Lou's goodbye awakened me from standing hunched over and picking through the splattered remains of a Volkswagen camper, and the sound of his voice filled me with an almost uncontrollable sadness. My goodbye grunt came with my teeth clenched on the pillowcase.

I forced myself out of bed and walked over to the mirror above the dresser. The shades in the room were drawn but even in the shadows some of the facial swelling seemed down. I knew there was some reason to continue inspecting my face, but it wasn't until I was at the bathroom mirror, looking at the pale green circles under my eyes, that I remembered why. Tonight was Simon and Fran's anniversary party.

I headed back to bed with a pit stop in the kitchen to put up coffee. I felt thrust into a tempo I used only in emergencies and disasters. I grabbed my head and felt my right temple pounding. I heard Star

Trek's Scotty shouting, "She canna take much more, Captain, she's gonna blow."

Everything was coming at me too fast. Snippets from the last six days danced in my mind as I tried to create order out of chaos, but the confusion just grew worse. I couldn't push the sinister sense of Holmes' twisted face from my memory. If Holmes authored the beating, it was possible that my unwillingness to back off the case might invite worse. On the other hand, I was probably taking my antipathy to his Volvo much too far.

If they were police. The coffee was perking so I got back out of bed and plodded into the kitchen. My range and comfort of movement had increased since yesterday. I nodded to my reflection in the coffee pot. Welcome back to the land of the ambulatory.

If they were police. It made sense to talk to Phil, and see if he could provide more information, but the idea of seeing Simon and Fran after my Aquarium visit, layered on top of an uncomfortable social situation, made any additional work unthinkable. During my second cup and third cigarette I considered blowing off the party, but knew I hadn't recently heard from Simon because he expected to see me tonight. I could never answer the phone again if I didn't show.

I thought I'd sleep the five or so hours before getting ready, but sleep came in snatches or not at all. That the world I had so carefully constructed over the past four years was in shambles clearly contributed to my restlessness. And I didn't have a shrink to talk with about it.

The time crawled while I fought about whether to get out of bed. I felt guilty about not seeing Phil and promised myself I would visit tomorrow. If I stopped investigating I'd end up adding the past week to my refuse bin of unfinished business; only there wasn't much room left.

I reached under the bed where I picked up an unfinished roach and smoked, then I got up and blasted myself with a shower. The hot water felt good as I stood there with closed eyes. The grass didn't hurt either. As usual, there were limits to my ability to tolerate a good thing. I dried off and walked to the closet, pleased with the way my body felt. I turned on the light, opened the closet door, and thought about calling Simon or Fran to find out what to wear, but I doubted whether I could be anything but underdressed anyway. My

cummerbund. The man's tone had been polite but he was only looking for one answer. I nodded and opened the door and slowly began to exit. I felt better than I had yesterday, but maneuvering my body in and out of a car was still tricky business. The man watched while I grabbed onto the top of the door and pulled myself up. He made no offer to help, but stood there and ran his eyes up and down my body. I was glad I hadn't brought my gun. My car, clothes, and sunglasses were enough.

"Your business, sir?"

I stood and watched as a stretch limo slowly drove past and headed in the direction of its parked relatives. No one waved it over to the side. It struck me that I wasn't dealing with a servant, but with security. If this joker pegged me for garbage, what were the guests going to think?

"No business. I'm invited."

"If you wouldn't mind waiting for a moment?" He reached inside his jacket pocket and produced a folded piece of paper. I decided I didn't want to watch him read with his lips so I started walking toward the house. "Jacob. Without an s."

I guess he managed to find my name because no one tackled me from behind, and the Oddjob standing at the huge doorway with a hand-held intercom just grimaced when I walked by. At least he didn't hold his nose.

The directly lit exterior segued into an indirectly lit grand foyer replete with a grand stairway that brought you to a grand greenhouse that usually served as the grand gathering place for intimate social occasions. Tonight, however, guests were politely funneled into a great ballroom off to the left of the hall. I had never been in this room before and stood mesmerized by the scene in front of me.

The floor of the room was set three steps down from the doorway. From my perch I could see a huge fireplace at one end of the hall, groups of people socializing throughout the room, with waitresses scurrying around and offering food and wine. No tiny hotdogs wrapped in Bisquick here. There must have been three hundred people, and this was a Wednesday night. There were also a few large tuxedoed men with black cummerbunds and chiseled smiles interspersed among the crowd.

I was able to hear Simon before I saw him. His laugh, actually. It always reminded me of Celtic great Bill Russell. More of a cackle, really, than a laugh. I found its source in the center of a group of people about two o'clock from where I stood. I didn't think I'd be around too long so I left the steps and walked over to his group. He saw me approach, nodded a welcome, and finished his story. I was close enough to listen, but instead chose the cacophony of indistinguishable voices that filled the room. I must have gotten lost in the motion and sound of the place because the next time I saw Simon he was pulling at my sleeve as he slowly began to lead me toward the steps.

"Have you seen Fran?"

"What?" I had to lean closer to him.

"Tonight. Have you seen Fran tonight?" Some man—about fifty, silver-haired and very expensively dressed—grabbed Simon's arm and began to extoll the pleasures and virtues of marriage. I wondered whether his mistress was in the crowd. After he left Simon turned toward me. "Do you always have to be so fucking hostile?"

"What are you talking about? I didn't say a word."

"You didn't have to." He smiled as a jeweled middle-aged lady planted a bright red kiss on his cheek. I handed him my handkerchief.

"See, I'm not hostile."

"Right. I forgot that you wear sunglasses to all the parties you attend."

I grabbed Simon's arm and pulled him to the side of the steps where we had some measure of privacy.

"Look." I took off the glasses, gave him a few seconds to catch the green, and put them back on.

"What the hell happened?"

"I fell off a bike."

"Bullshit!"

"Right as usual, Simon. Why did you ask if I had seen Fran?"

"We had a bet."

I didn't have to ask what it was. "Well, you won this one, but I hope you aren't in a pool about how long I'll stay."

He grinned. "I'm not stupid, Matt man. Let's try to find her upstairs. I want to know what happened to you. No one will notice if we're gone for a few minutes."

"They sure as hell won't miss me."

"Nor you them." I recognized the voice, turned and looked up the stairs.

"Boots, it's been a long time."

She pointed toward my face and started down the stairs. "Working for the mob these days?" She landed alongside Simon and was holding back a smile. "No, no, it must be a fashion statement, to go with the rest of your dazzling wardrobe."

I shook my head. "Time hasn't lowered your nose, doll."

She burst out laughing. During the period we hung out together I think I enjoyed her laugh the most. It was strong but not overpowering, ringing with ease and a lack of self-consciousness. She was Fran's best friend but, unlike many a best friend/husband chill, she and Simon had a warm, independent relationship.

My friends, the matchmakers, were patient before they set us up. But two years to them was just the blur of a sleepwalk to me. Boots worked as a vice president for the phone company and had to have been hard as nails to chew her way past her male competition. I always suspected I gave her a chance to play Nightingale. I was drinking pretty heavily in those days and couldn't have been easy. Still, I was surprised when she stopped seeing me without much of an explanation, but I was too drunk most of the time to realize I'd lost something. Hearing her laughter next to me now, I knew that I had.

She pointed to the glass of bourbon in my hand. "Well, the alcohol didn't ruin your fast mouth."

"It did for a while but hard work, perseverance, and chemicals returned the gift."

Simon was giving up hope of dragging me off to Fran. If needed he could always get Boots to substantiate my presence and win his bet. He turned to me and grabbed my arm. He looked meaningfully toward my face, "I want to talk with you soon. Meet me in the solarium, okay?"

I nodded. Solarium, not greenhouse. I had forgotten.

Boots and I stood aside as Simon glad-handed his way up the stairs and out the door. It was fun to watch him work. Each person Simon chatted with seemed to walk away pleased by the encounter.

"I'm the only one he ever bashes," I muttered.

"What did you say? I couldn't hear you."

I wasn't going to repeat something that was stupid the first time.

"Nothing." The noise in the room had grown louder and I almost had to shout to be heard. Boots frowned, then grabbed my hand and pulled me around and up the stairs. Her hand was warm and looked very dark against my palm. Going up the stairs was a helluva lot more fun than it had been coming down.

We got to the hallway and paused. There were fewer people but I still caught a fair number of surreptitious looks. What was that long-hair doing with such a lovely lady? And, she was lovely. Olive-skinned, high-cheekboned, and slender, with green eyes and black, thick hair, she looked like an aristocrat from Northern Italy. In the old days I figured she was slumming, but I used to tell myself it didn't matter, sometimes she made my nightmares disappear.

She kept holding my hand—she always did like to shock—and pulled me toward the butler's pantry. It had been commandeered by an expanded kitchen staff to serve as the waitresses' pickup station. It was almost more boisterous than the ballroom. Someone with a chef's hat raised his head and began to protest our presence, saw Boots, smiled, and waved us over to a protected alcove.

"You always had a way with men, doll."

"Don't 'doll' me. That's Andrei. I've been eating here for years. What is this 'doll' shit—to go with your glasses? What are you doing now?"

I didn't want it to sound like nothing had changed in the past couple of years. "I'm working as a detective."

She raised her eyebrows in surprise. "So you wear sunglasses?"

"Jesus, Boots, stop with the glasses already." I took them off and pushed my face in front of hers. She squinted and said, "Put the glasses back on. Your face looks terrible."

"Shoulda seen it a couple of days ago."

"What happened?"

"Got it working on a case." I grimaced as I heard the words. It didn't matter that it was true; it still rang like a B movie.

"It's pretty ugly. What happened to the other guy?"

"Maybe he was hit by a car. I was laying on the floor when they left."

It was her turn to grimace. "Are you sure you're in the right kind of work?"

I laughed. "That's what everyone asks." I had forgotten how pleasant it felt to be around her. "And you? Still clawing your way toward a bathroom key?"

"You're still so tactful. No, I already have it." She had a mischievous and satisfied look on her face. "They had to build a whole new loo."

I laughed again. Ma Bell without an executive bathroom for women. "They can't fire you now. Too much invested."

We stood quietly and watched as platters of food kept replenishing the long wooden table that ran the length of the room. It seemed as if Boots and I had run out of things to say. I wasn't in a rush to separate but I didn't want her to feel stuck.

"Listen, I've got to see Fran. She and Simon bet on whether or not I would show and he'll shit if she doesn't see me. Do you have a guess?"

Boots shook her head and a look of annoyance crossed her face. "Same old Matthew Jacob. Come on, we'll find her. She's probably in the solarium. Too many people downstairs."

"What do you mean 'same old' me?"

She shook her head again. "Forget it." She started for the hallway and I followed. At least I didn't have to negotiate the party alone. "What's with the cast of thousands?" I tapped Boots on the shoulder as we entered the foyer. "I have trouble believing all these people are Simon and Fran's friends."

The good humor returned to her eyes. "Haven't you been to a party here before?"

"Nothing like this."

"Alex Hirsh isn't going to celebrate his daughter without inviting every important person he can think of. Don't you recognize anyone?"

"I don't know. Some of them seem familiar."

"They ought to be. Enough of them are on television."

"These folk don't guest on reruns."

We were on the stairs leading to the solarium when she stopped and looked at me. "You're an infuriating man, Matthew Jacob. You know exactly how to separate the wheat from the chaff but half the time you can't find the damn bushel."

What she said sounded right so I looked like I understood. I didn't want it to seem like I couldn't find the wheat.

—19—

We found the entire family, plus, right where Boots thought they would be. Alex stood by the immense curved windows that ran across the front of the room and down the entire southern face of the house. Fran and Simon were sitting on top of a pool table with Lena perched like a bird on a wing chair off in the corner. A number of vaguely recognizable personalities were spread throughout the room listening as Alex extolled the virtues of fatherhood. We entered and slid our way toward Simon and Fran.

"We have had nothing but *nachas*. Don't get me wrong. You can't have kids without worry, but it's not the worry you remember."

One of the jeweled blue-haired women couldn't resist. "Alex my friend, if children are such a pleasure, why did you stop at one?"

But Alex was feeling too good to be disturbed by the catty remark. "I couldn't tolerate the idea of dividing my affections. Also, Netti, we didn't start with all this and I wanted Frances to have everything."

A few people in the room turned toward Fran and smiled. She gave a slight wave acknowledging them as Alex relinquished center stage and the room began to buzz with independent conversations. Fran glanced at Boots and gave her a questioning look. Boots shrugged back. I began to feel uncomfortable, but Simon seemed oblivious to the interchange and said to Fran, "You owe me some money, hon."

Fran turned toward me. "You're full of surprises, Matt."

95

I threw my hands up, palms out. "How can you say that? I told you I was coming."

She laughed. "I've won a lot more of these bets than I've lost."

Simon interrupted. "You're going to drive him out of here before I get a chance to visit." He leaned over and kissed her on the cheek, then told Boots, "I'm going to steal him for a few minutes if you can bear it."

"Only on the condition you bring him back before he sneaks away."

The three of them laughed. I managed a smile before Simon hopped off the table, grabbed my arm, and led me to the door. I could feel eyes on the back of my neck and I found myself hoping it was Boots. When I turned back to look, however, I was surprised to see Alex looking at the two of us intently. I guess I really was underdressed. Simon and I walked up another flight of stairs and entered a room that could have passed for a public library. "How'd I end up on Alex's shit list?" I asked.

Simon looked at me with surprise. "What are you talking about?"

"I noticed him staring at me and it didn't exactly look friendly."

"You're your usual paranoid self. He's just interested in whether you've discovered anything."

"He knows I agreed to spy on Fran?"

"Damn it, Matt, stop calling it 'spying.' All that does is make me feel guilty."

I spoke without thinking, "You have nothing to feel guilty about, Simon."

He looked at me sharply. "What's that supposed to mean? Have you found anything out?"

"Nah, I told you there's nothing to find out."

"You're holding something back, man. Don't fuck with me."

I thought about butchering my tongue while another part of my mind raced for something to say. I flashed on the Lincoln with the scraggly beard and used it for a life raft.

"Okay, I happened to notice a sleazy kid sitting in a Lincoln and the match didn't seem right. It's not going to amount to anything, and I didn't want to encourage your fantasies." It seemed lame to me; but Simon looked like he'd stumbled into a judgeship.

"All right! See, maybe I'm not crazy. Way to go!"

I shook my head. "No, man, this is why I didn't want to say

anything. It's just more fodder for your delusions." I felt badly, but better to feed his imagination than ruin his life. "Why does Alex know about all this?"

Simon rolled his eyes toward the molded tin ceiling. "He knows because I told him. I don't think you understand how badly Fran is doing."

"She doesn't show it."

"Yeah, she's impressive that way. But listen, if you doubt me, ask Boots." He looked at me slyly. "Still something there, huh?"

"Don't be an asshole. I just ran into her, remember."

He banged his forehead with his hand. "Right. I'm crazy about this too. If nothing's there, why get angry?"

"I'm not angry."

"Right. Anyhow, Alex is taking your search seriously."

I was relieved to change the topic. "Well, Alex isn't thinking any better than you. What I noticed is probably a kid with a rich father."

Simon looked at his watch. "Well, you don't know that yet. Do you have a way of tracing this kid?"

If I weren't careful he'd have me hit the street now. "I'll check, Simon, I'll check."

"Okay, Matt man, I knew you would deliver."

"All I'm going to deliver is a busted inside straight."

He clapped his hands. "Well, in that case, we better celebrate now. You wait here and I'll get the girls."

"Get the 'girls'? Simon, you've lost it. Get the girls! You're too happy about something that's going to be nothing. And I don't want to drink."

"You just keep working. Also I know better than to try to keep you at a party with booze. Sit tight and prepare your nose."

I didn't need a second invitation. "I'll wait, but you better ask one of the 'girls' whether she wants to come. I'm not exactly her best friend."

Simon didn't hear anything I said. He was intent on his celebration. While he was gone I walked around the room and tried to admire the appointments. I liked the smell of leather and wood but the atmosphere of white male supremacy was overbearing. It bothered me that Simon had spoken with Alex. It bothered me more that Alex had taken him seriously. Maybe I was missing something.

I was getting around to trying some drawers when Simon and Fran returned. I was glad Boots was with them.

Simon bustled over to the desk and removed a matte black cigarette case from his inside jacket pocket and opened it. From his other pocket he pulled a small glass bottle the size of his thumb, three-quarters full of coke. The three of us stood around the desk and silently watched him dump a quarter of the bottle on the case's flat interior and spread it into lines. Hispanics just dumped it into their hand and snorted, but Anglos liked their tools. I loved the show. I loved cocaine. But I had always steered clear of leaning on it. My kind of love cost too much.

We took turns with the metal straw. I enjoyed the way Boots snorted. Nothing loud or protracted but she got every bit of her lines. The drug was coming on and I thought of sex with her. I forced my attention back to the desk and took my turn tooting until the case was empty. Everyone agreed that we'd had enough, but I still felt pangs of regret when Simon snapped the black case shut.

We made small talk while the drug did its damage and pushed my discomfort at being in the same room with Fran into a low murmur. After fifteen minutes of talking and laughing, Fran began to look like she was late for a meeting. "Simon, we have to go back downstairs. Dad is probably wondering where we are."

I looked at Fran. "Who are all those people?"

She shrugged. "Dad can't help himself. If he's inviting more than four people over he invites the world. He says he can't afford to offend anyone." A bleak look crossed her face. "Mom hates these things. It's hard on her. She's not very social." She looked at me and smiled. "You can relate to that."

I could and, as the thought of going downstairs took shape, began to. Simon came over and handed me the small bottle.

"You don't have to come downstairs now; just turn the lights out when you leave. But say goodbye before you split."

A reward for pretense. I shoved the bottle into my pocket. "You got it, boss."

Before they were out of the room Boots was sitting behind the desk with her feet up. Her dress was flounced around her legs, and she should have looked ridiculous. Should have, but didn't. She looked like she belonged so when she told me to have a seat I did. I took a

chair and moved it to where I could see her on a slant. I didn't want
to look up her dress.

The coke pumped words out of my mouth. "Why didn't you go
downstairs with them?"

"Your self-pity is tired."

"No, I mean it. Why the interest? I thought we were doing okay,
then I didn't exist." Sometimes I surprised myself. Coke balls. I
squeezed my hands shut. Sweaty palms.

"You sound angry." She leaned forward and her dress rode a couple
of inches higher. Like hell I didn't want to look.

"Nah, not angry, but my rule is one slum ride to a customer."

She swung her legs off the desk and swiveled her chair until she
was looking right at me. Her eyes were flashing. "You stupid son of
a bitch. You always thought I was slumming."

Coke or not, I was suddenly less sure of myself. "I don't get it then.
Why the stiffing?"

"I didn't want to be friends with you." Her voice had lost a little
of her anger.

"You're not making sense. Okay, we weren't going to stroll off into
the sunset hand in hand. So? We hung out okay together." For a
moment the memory of that period of my life flooded back. "There
wasn't much else in those days that was fun. Why shouldn't I figure
slumming when you cut me cold?"

"You thought I was slumming long before I refused to see you."
The anger in her voice was replaced by tears in her eyes. "I was falling
for you."

I felt like I was on a foundering raft in a schizophrenic ocean. "I
was a wreck. You knew that."

"Logic wasn't running the show. If I had continued to spend time
with you I'd have landed in an all too familiar swamp." She looked
at me directly, her eyes clear as she unconsciously pulled at her dress.
"I landed there anyway."

I sat back from the edge of the chair and lit a cigarette. I needed
time to regroup. I felt embarrassed, foolish, guilty, and relieved. All
at once.

"And what makes you think I'm interested in you now? I knew he
had cocaine, bigshot." Her voice was easy and light. I was back on
land. I pulled the little glass bottle out of my pocket, poured some

on the back of my hand, and snorted. Poured some more and offered it to her. She leaned forward and got every granule. I stood, then pulled her onto her feet. "I don't care whether you're interested or not. It's just good to see you."

"It's good to see you, even if you are a broken-down fool."

"Does that mean we can go back to being friends?"

"I don't know, but I can't believe Simon never told you why I wouldn't see you."

"He might have tried. But I wasn't too willing to talk or listen."

"And you are now?"

I smiled and pulled her toward the door. "Nah, not really. That's why it's time to get out of this dump."

—20—

We left without saying goodbye. I wasn't prepared to socialize in enemy territory with my synapses on fire. Boots wasn't surprised when I led us past another tuxedoed usher and out the side door. She just looked at me with a faint smile and shook her head.

"Who are the bulls in black?" I wondered out loud.

Boots tugged at my arm. "Shhh! He'll hear you. Alex is a stickler about security for his guests, so he gets off-duty policemen to chaperone. I think he's afraid of terrorists. It helps with his delusions of grandeur."

We walked around the corner of the brightly lit plantation porch and down the front steps without anyone biting at our heels. We turned and moved slowly toward the general direction of the parked cars. Boots kept her hand on my arm and I was aware of each of her fingers.

"I didn't think a town like this had cops like that. I always thought they'd be slender blond guys with designer uniforms. Not prime beef."

"You are a bitch, aren't you?" she laughed. "They're not from town. The city's chief is friends with Alex. You could say he caters all Alex's large affairs." She glanced at me sideways as the word "affair" hung between us. Boots pushed it away. "I can't believe Alex hasn't bombarded you with his important connections."

"He may have. I probably didn't pay any attention."

We were in the makeshift parking lot and I felt myself slow down and stop. She looked at me, smiled, and dropped her hand. My arm, where her fingers had been resting, suddenly felt cold.

"You don't talk, you don't listen. What kind of a detective are you?"

"A reluctant one. But I'll listen to you; where do you want to go?" The night had grown overcast and the surrounding grounds had taken on a moorlike quality. Boots stood in the midst of a swirling mist with her back to the mansion's reflected light. She looked lovely and cold.

"We forgot your coat."

She shook her head and grabbed my hand. "I don't need it; I'm going back inside."

"What are you talking about? Let's go to Chinatown and eat. I haven't felt human in a while."

"Can't do, Matthew." She looked up into my eyes. "If I go to Chinatown we'll end up in bed. Don't shake your head, you can tolerate a bit of truth." She dared me with her eyes.

I looked down toward the ground. "I haven't thought that far ahead. I've been enjoying this."

She stood on her toes and kissed me on the cheek. "So have I. I'm glad we ran into each other and talked. I want to spend some time with you but I have to make sure I'm on solid ground before I luxuriate in a night of cocaine and sex."

She was right about bed. Just listening to her excited me. As we walked to my car I told myself she was being smart, since I wasn't any more eligible now than I was in the old days. Unfortunately the thought lacked conviction. We were silent when I got into the car but she tapped on the window, and after I opened it, leaned in and kissed me on the mouth. Before she pulled away she asked me to save some of the coke. I watched as she skipped up the stairs and turned to wave. I waved back. Though disappointed about driving home alone, I found myself listening to music rather than my typical all news and sports.

————

When the telephone sounded I slapped at the alarm in a desperate attempt to shut it up before I realized what was happening. I lurched out of bed and grabbed the receiver.

"Mr. Jacob, Matthew? Is that you?"

I recognized the voice and reacted automatically. "Dr. James, I'm sorry if I'm late. I must have overslept. What time is it? I know it's Thursday. I get the same stomach ache every Thursday morning."

"What are you talking about? We weren't going to meet today. Are you drunk? Damn it, I hired someone who is drunk or high at seven-thirty in the morning?"

Maybe it was hearing that it was seven-thirty, or maybe it was hearing that I wasn't expected to be shrunk, or maybe it was the disappearance of the naked Boots I'd been caressing throughout the night, but suddenly I was wide awake.

She sounded an awful lot like Simon. "Slow down, slow down. I'm not drunk and I'm not high. I woke up confused." And defensive. "What can I do for you?"

"How much drugs and alcohol did you take last night?"

"What the hell is this? You have nothing better to do than to call ex-clients and question their drug usage? Next you're going to want me to do urine tests. Let's go back to the old way. At least I got to sleep later, even on Thursdays."

Her voice was apologetic. "I didn't call to check up on you. Last night more offices in the building were broken into, and one of them was mine. I hoped you might come over. The police were already here. They say it's more proof that a drug addict is working the area." Her voice went up an octave. "They stole my files. What would a drug addict want with my files?"

"Was anything else taken?"

"The other offices may have had files stolen as well."

"Listen, don't touch anything and I'll be right over. I have to get dressed and stop for some coffee . . ."

"Don't stop. I'll have coffee here." Some of the earlier shrillness had returned to her voice.

"Hang tough, I'll see you soon."

By the time I hung up the phone the shock of being awake was settling into a drugover. Or maybe the fatigue came from listening to someone—into whom I had poured years of fears and desperations—call back in a similar plight. I thought about having a hair of the dog but was sure Dr. James would notice, and I wanted to save the coke for Boots. I settled on a pipeful of grass.

It struck me on the drive to her office that I didn't know what I was doing. I thought about returning the deuce, but the memory of the beating was still too fresh. Also, quitting now would be quitting forever and that felt worse than my ignorance.

I parked around the block from the office and tried to spot stakeouts. I thought I saw one, possibly two. Neither car contained the other night's entertainment, but I didn't doubt they would hear about my visit.

I could smell the coffee as I walked down the corridor to Gloria's office. Her door was ajar and there were no busted doorjambs or visible scratches on the lock. She stood as I entered, looked at me, and without a word walked over to the coffee machine and poured me a cup. I was relieved that she had used a real mug, I wouldn't have to suck Styrofoam.

"Just black, please."

She nodded and handed me the cup. She seemed to have regained her usual composure.

"I'm sorry about the call. I seem all too willing to take my anxieties out on you."

I shrugged and felt the caffeine diffuse through my body. "That's okay, I can handle it. It comes with the work." I tried to smile.

"You seem to handle it too well, I'm afraid," she said dourly.

"Can't stop shrinking, can you?"

"I guess not." She sat down in her chair. "It's not easy to turn off."

"Fair enough."

I walked over to the couch, thought about looking out the window, but just sat down. "Now what happened?"

"I came in this morning and found the door to my office unlocked. The room looked okay, so at first I thought I might have forgotten to lock up when I left."

"Does that happen often?"

"Never." She shrugged. "But you know these haven't been typical days for me and, when the office seemed undisturbed, I thought it possible. Why do you ask?"

"If you didn't leave the door unlocked it was very cleanly picked. Does anyone clean your office at night? Could they have left it un-locked?"

"No, only the common areas are maintained. Each of us is responsible for our own office. That's why I was here so early. I needed to put my garbage out. In the confusion of last week I forgot, and it was beginning to overflow.

"So at first I just thought the unlocked door was my fault. After I took care of the garbage I decided to catch up on my paperwork. That's when I realized something was wrong. Very wrong."

"Your files were gone."

"Not all of them. Maybe a dozen."

"Where?" She pointed to a four-drawer file cabinet in the far corner of the room. It amazed me that I'd never noticed it before. I stood and walked over. "Is this the only one you have?"

"No, I have a file drawer in my desk."

I was looking at the lock. You didn't need to be a master thief to get in, but whoever had been here was carrying tools.

"Was your desk broken into as well?"

"No."

I pulled on the cabinet drawer but it wouldn't open. It had been a nice, neat job. Reminded me of Julius. I turned toward Dr. James and stretched out my hand.

"Flip me the keys, please."

"Why?"

"I want to look inside."

"Don't be ridiculous."

"What do you mean?"

"These are private records. I wouldn't let the police look at them, and I'm certainly not going to let you." Her jaw was set as she shook her head from side to side. "I would think you would understand that."

I ground my teeth deep into my annoyance, turned, and walked behind the couch. I looked out the window and was perversely satisfied to see one of the cars I had made still sitting there. I half-looked for the Lincoln but it wasn't there. I turned and glanced at the clock. I wanted to stay within a fifty-minute time frame.

"What about the other offices? Same procedure?"

She seemed relieved by the topic change. Sometimes a straight line is not the fastest way to get somewhere.

Her mouth lost some of its stiffness. "It was the same for the other office on this floor, but the two offices on the first floor were pigstys.

That's why they don't know if anything was taken. Also, both doors were kicked in. Do you want to go look?"

It wouldn't have mattered if I had all day. There was no need to look. "No."

She looked puzzled.

I walked to the front of the couch and sat back down heavily. It was the first time today that I had noticed my body. The thought fortified me. "I have a strong idea that the downstairs offices were an afterthought. Why kick in a door and make all that racket when he could pick the lock with no trouble? I'll check later if there were special locks, but I doubt it."

She sat down behind her desk, frowned and leaned forward on her arms. "The implication of what you're suggesting . . ."

"No implications. I think he finally found what he was looking for and he found it on this floor."

"You have no proof of that."

"That's right." I nodded agreeably. "But look, since neither of us believes the junkie bullshit, think of it this way. Someone comes looking for something, doesn't find it, then returns. The first time he hit he was neat—I know because I looked at the doors—and this time he starts off being neat and ends by trashing the remaining two offices. Let me guess, the two downstairs were next to each other, weren't they?"

Dr. James nodded. I was beginning to enjoy myself. "He found what he wanted and finished by adding confusion." A troubled thought crossed my mind and I got distracted.

"What's the matter, Matthew?"

I pulled my head back into the room. "Why doesn't our termite know that the police are covering for him? Unless of course they're not. But then, it all makes even less sense."

"I don't follow you."

"Like you figured before you came to visit, the most apparent reason to steal files is blackmail. It's not farfetched to imagine a cop or two in on the play. But the ferret wouldn't bother with an extensive cover." I didn't add that police involvement explained my beating, but then, the beating was going away.

She looked annoyed. "So you do or don't think it's possible that one of my patients might be blackmailed? Which is it?"

I grinned bleakly. "I don't know." I looked directly at her. "I need access to your files."

"Don't be absurd. I already said no."

"This is nuts. One or more of your patients might be in some deep shit. How am I supposed to help? Run a background check on each of your clients until I find something blackmailable? Why don't you ask them whether you ought to show me the records? I'm not talking Peeping Tom, Dr. James." I'd had too little sleep to keep the sarcasm out of my voice.

"And I'm not accusing you of voyeurism, Mr. Jacob. But perhaps even you might object if I handed your file over to the police, or even to a private investigator." She seemed ready to get angry again but added in a quiet voice, "We might disagree about this, Matthew, without me becoming a target of your hostility. Neither of us is forced to accept our therapeutic roles right now."

She was polite enough for me not to feel the knife until it was all the way in. I began to feel guilty but she interrupted the descent.

"Don't look so hurt. Just because I'm not going to let you read my files or kick me in my teeth doesn't mean you're fired. But I'm not going to give you names of people I work with." She suddenly smiled. "You're really invested in this, aren't you?"

"I suppose."

"It's not just the beating, is it?"

I was reminded to look at the clock. I had a couple minutes left. "Not entirely." I thought I saw her nod. "I'm not sure where to go from here. Reading the files would have given me a starting point." I shrugged.

Dr. James sat back in her chair. "You'll figure out something. At least there is a real reason for you to keep on with it." She paused, "For real money. Not television money."

"Doesn't it bother you that one of your clients might be in trouble? Or that you might be?"

"Of course it does. It scares the hell out of me. But if it's one of my patients I hope they'll bring it to me. Then I can talk to them about you. But I can't alarm a dozen people with no hard facts. That's why you have to stay on it. I want those files back."

I stood up. My therapeutic hour was about up.

"Where are you going?"

"I want the cops to think I was here for therapy."

"There are police outside?"

"Plainclothes."

"Will you keep after this?"

I smiled. "Have I solved the beating yet?"

"We need to establish a rate of pay."

"Pay me what you get."

"That's too much."

"Per day. Your hourly, my daily."

"That's too little."

I was already out the door. What a trashing will do for punctuality.

21

The stakeout was gone when I left the building. I was trying to light a cigarette when, out the corner of my eye, I saw a flash of cream. Without thinking I raced toward Boylston hoping the car would catch a red. I got within hailing distance and watched it run a yellow. Standing there breathing like a bull in heavy heat, I wondered what the hell I was doing. I had hoofed a block and a half and couldn't be certain it was the same car or driver. I manufacture a suspicion, then act as if it were true. Despite feeling idiotic, I tried to see the plate number but just caught a piece of it; at least I'd have something to tell Simon.

The slow walk back to my car was spent trying to breathe. Sitting in the seat, I was too busy catching my breath to react to the opening of the passenger door. By the time I turned, the black body-by-Gold was sitting next to me, pushing me against the back of the seat, his elbow rudely probing my chest, his tricep pinning my arm to my side. Though I couldn't have gotten to my gun, I cursed myself for having left it home. If I was going to be a fucking detective I ought to remember the uniform. Of course wearing it increased the probability of being shot with it.

"Are you here to talk or to hurt me?"

His grin wasn't reassuring. He dug his elbow in a little deeper by way of emphasis. "At least one of us is going to talk."

And one of us was going to hurt.

"Why the fuck do you keep bothering me?"

The corkscrew motion of his arm and elbow brought tears to my eyes. "That's not what I want to hear, Mouth. I told you to stay away; and lo and behold, you are back again after another robbery."

"I had a fucking appointment. It's Thursday. I'm here every Thursday. Can you leave my chest alone? I don't plan on running and leaving you my car. Shit, you know where I live."

He didn't take his arm away but did let up on some of the pressure. "Your appointment time is later than this. Why do you want to lie?"

"I'm not lying. The damn office was broken into and she called and asked if I could come early. She wanted to leave early today. What's with you? This is the second time you've used your hands. What the fuck is all this about?"

I slowly moved my body into a more comfortable position. He didn't stop me. I figured it might pay to stay on the offensive. "At least you didn't bring your oversized pit bull."

I figured wrong. A slight movement with his arm made me gasp for air. "Okay, I'm sorry. Leave a rib, will you?"

He showed me teeth again, but backed off my chest.

I had pretty much run out of things to say. I still had plenty of questions but, given the givens, this was not the time or place. We sat there quietly for a moment or two before he took out a cigarette pack and offered me one.

Both of us sat there smoking. I wasn't getting high but I wasn't getting hit either. "Can I open a window? I won't scream, I promise."

He nodded his assent, "Always a smartass, aren't you? You don't want to run your mouth when I'm with my partner. He always figures it's directed at him and he's usually right. Explains his disposition."

"Look, man, I don't ever want to see your partner again. I don't know what you want or who you are."

He turned toward his window and opened it. I thought about bolting but liberated the butt instead. He got rid of his and turned back to me. "Same as the other night. Why are you hanging around this building?"

"You're ignoring my other question."

"Yes I am. But you better stop ignoring mine." He reached into his coat pocket. I thought about rolling out of the car if he pulled a gun, but all he produced was a piece of paper.

"I found this in your apartment. It's time to explain yourself. No more smartass, no more lies."

His voice hadn't changed, but I knew my copy of the police report hanging from his massive fist meant I wasn't going to be able to nurse any new wounds. "Dr. James got scared when the first burglary occurred. She didn't believe the junkie story. She couldn't figure why an addict would skip medical offices. She knows I have a ticket and asked me to check it out. I didn't think much of her worries, but you don't turn your shrink down when she asks a favor."

"A little unusual, isn't it, a shrink asking a client for a favor?"

"Yeah, but I'm almost done anyway. Maybe she thought it was a good way to terminate." I looked at him. "Her idea might be more terminal than she realized." He didn't smile. "Like I said, I don't think much of her worries."

He shook the copy of the police report at me. "Then what's this?"

"I had to do something after I walked around the hall, looked at the locks and nodded."

"For a cherry P.I. you got long arms into the law."

"Nah, the thing fell through the cracks."

"Whose cracks?"

I looked at him and grimaced. "I'm gonna have to take the beating. If I tell you what you want to know, I'm done as an investigator. I don't see getting rich off this gig, but I want to be able to work."

"You don't know whether you'll be able to work after I get done with you."

"I told you everything I know. You wanted to know why I was around, now you know. You wanted to know how I got involved, now you know. Leave me alone. I don't give a shit about the robberies. Christ, I still believe it was a junkie."

He twisted his body a little more in my direction and I braced myself for a blow. "Can I have another cigarette before I die?" I couldn't help myself. Physical intimidation loosened my tongue.

"You can relax, Jacob," he paused, "without an s. I'm not going to hurt you anymore today. I don't believe you're as innocent as you sound, but I don't think you're lying about how you got involved.

It's too pathetic. Like play therapy for a kid. Only, Jacobs," he leaned on the s, "you are not a kid."

No wisecrack now. I just sat there.

"What did the two of you talk about today? Your problems?"

He made the last word feel like a gob of spit. I answered evenly. "Mostly. We also talked about the break-in."

"She tell you that her files were stolen?"

I thought about lying but my chest still hurt. "Yes."

"What else?"

"Nothing else."

His eyes were all over me. I couldn't feel innocent even if I had been. I hoped he factored that into his study. "What about copies?"

"I didn't ask."

He didn't try to hide his disdain. "And the rest of her files?"

"What about the rest of her files?"

He grabbed me up by my throat. Mostly shirt but a little goes a long way when someone has ham hocks for hands. I moved in the direction he wanted. "I want to know if she showed you her files."

I pointed to his hand and he reluctantly released me. "When she said she was still uneasy about the police analysis I asked to look through the file cabinet."

"What for?"

"To look like I was helping out. Same as marching around the hall."

He shook his head in disgust. "They'll give that license to anyone who can walk, won't they." It wasn't a question. He looked at me sideways. "What did you see when you went through the cabinet?"

"Through it? I didn't get near it. She was like a fucking tiger with her cubs."

He was sitting back in the seat and there was a smile on his face that seemed almost genuine. "She was like that with you too?" He began to laugh. It wasn't a pleasant sound but I caught it and began to laugh as well. Probably for different reasons. All of a sudden he tightened up as if the momentary camaraderie was distasteful. He leaned toward me and I prepared for new pain, but he just tapped me lightly on my arm and said, "Don't be in my face, Jacobs. The next time I bring back my friend."

He got out of the car as quietly and gracefully as he got in. I didn't look nearly as elegant as I fumbled for my cigarettes, put my head on the steering wheel and wrestled with the shakes.

It was a long while before I started the engine. I didn't think there was any need to make sure Dr. James substantiated my story. She'd just claim client confidentiality. I didn't think they would try to beat it out of her. Body-by-Gold finally seemed to have lost his interest in me. Most of me was relieved. Some of me wondered why.

I wanted to ask Phil for specifics about my police visitors but was reluctant to chance being followed, and too anxious to shake a tail. No need to hang Phil out on a line. Better to talk to Julius.

I drove home fully intending to see him first, but when I arrived I detoured to my apartment. It felt strange not to have Mrs. Sullivan's light flash. I looked for a long moment at the lifeless bulb and felt a serious yen for my pre-detective days. Though it had been only a week since everything began, the week had eclipsed much of my prior life.

I went into the alley and retrieved the newspaper. I dug out my stash, sat at the kitchen table, and rolled a joint. Although I had the paper opened to sports, I didn't do much reading. I just sat getting high, wondering what I was doing and why. Eventually thoughts of Boots began to creep in and with them another whole set of concerns. My anxieties were becoming unbearable. I decided to delay my search for Julius and visit Mrs. Sullivan instead. I also wanted to find Charles and see if he would mind tending store for a few more days. I didn't know how to spend them but, however much a part of me wanted to return to my normal routine, I wasn't yet ready to let go. I couldn't answer the why of that one either.

The visits took longer than I expected. It was passing strange to discover how much I liked these people. Mrs. Sullivan greeted me like a returning hero. Charles, I suspected, had neglected to tell her who had won the fight. It thrilled her, she said, to have a "private dick" in the building. She ignored my protests by insisting that I was "playing my cards close to my vest." We both watched too much television.

When she heard that I planned to go downstairs and talk to Charles she demanded to come. I tried to explain that I'd just be repeating my story but she insisted. There might be a "tidbit" I'd neglected to tell her. I suggested that we invite him to her place so she wouldn't have to walk, but she shrugged off my idea claiming she hadn't felt as energetic in years. Who was I to argue since neither had I?

Rich was back from his trip and the four of us sat around their apartment drinking tea while I ran my rap. After I finished Richard said quietly, "It surprises me that you intend to continue with this."

"Me too. But right now I can't let go."

"That's good. Despite the beating, the work seems to suit you."

I was oddly pleased by his remarks. "I sure don't feel great."

"I don't think it matters. It's much better than you sitting around in your place getting," he interrupted himself and looked at Mrs. Sullivan, "getting stupid."

The conversation was making me nervous. "I didn't know you cared, kind man."

Mrs. Sullivan cackled and Richard smiled. Charles, who up to now had been quiet, burst in. "He better not care too much," he said with mock jealousy.

I stood up. "Not to worry, Charles, I'm too fat for Richard." This time Mrs. Sullivan laughed so hard she had to wipe tears from her eyes.

After I finished the arrangements with Charles and Richard I walked Mrs. Sullivan back to her place. She was in no rush and I realized when I walked through my apartment door that just getting out of her apartment had given her real pleasure. I sat on the couch smoking a fresh joint and began thinking about Boots when I admitted the obvious. Getting out of the apartment was a pleasure for me as well.

—22—

"You might have left a note."

I laughed. The day had turned April-nasty. Gray, windy, and damp, as usual too cold for my spring jacket. I detested spring in the Northeast, although we were walking because I wanted to. Simon hadn't been shy about his preference for more civilized surroundings, but I had been insistent. I didn't want to be inside with him right now.

"Simon, you nag more than my first wife."

"Why don't you ever use her name? Don't you think I'd know who you meant if you said 'Megan'?"

"Why don't you go back to school and become a psychiatrist? You could become a twentieth century knight—Simon the shyster/shrink."

He smiled and showed me his middle finger. He had a relaxed stride working as he looked around the community gardens. I was glad someone was enjoying this walk. I pulled my coat tighter against the raw.

He slowed his pace a bit. "It's funny how some things bother you and others don't. A couple of days ago when we were at the El Rancho you said the place stirred memories, remember? I used to have a garden right here. Shit, it was a long time ago. I was working for Legal Aid, kicking government ass. I used to come here at lunch to grow my vegetables. Tomatoes. If Earl Weaver could grow tomatoes in a Baltimore bullpen, I could grow them here."

"How did they come out?"

"Lousy. He had the grounds crew get him special dirt. I read that in *The Sporting News*. No matter how broke I was, I always had a subscription to *The Sporting News*. Now it's *The Wall Street Journal*." He looked around the area slowly as if he were sipping at his past.

He stopped walking and turned to look at me. "Do you get *The Sporting News*?"

"Nah. I can't stand the way the print comes off in my hands. Same thing keeps me away from the *New York Times*." I didn't think he'd ask about the *Christian Science Monitor*.

Simon seemed relieved by my answer and started to walk again. We came to the edge of the gardens. He didn't seem to care and continued on the path that led to the bushes. Kneejerk homophobia nodded its head and I nodded back. The bushes would at least give us some protection from the fucking wind.

We were parading around between the tree-height ferns and bullrushes before I said anything. "How long do you intend to keep us out in this shit?" I led us to one of the naturally protected cubbyholes that formed at the base of the giant bullrushes. It usually served as an after-hours meeting place for men who wished anonymous sex. The area was deserted, since the weather wasn't conducive to afternoon love. When the night came the weather wouldn't matter.

"You're the one who wanted to be outside. Here we are outside."

"Aren't we in a cheerful accommodating mood? Did you get laid for lunch?" The words were hardly out of my mouth before I was choking back the Aquarium image that flooded my mind. Simon didn't seem to notice. He just shrugged.

"No, but things are a little better at home."

"Really? The nightmares are easing?" God, I hoped so. An easy way out.

"No, damn it." He shook his head. I watched him button his coat. "No, but at least we are back in the same room. I like it better even though I lose sleep. Better to feel tired than useless." His face brightened as if he had remembered something. He had.

"What about you and Boots?"

"What do you mean?"

"You guys looked so good I was sure you would leave together, but then I saw her back at the party. What happened?"

"Nothing happened, and nothing will. Why didn't you tell me that she stopped seeing me 'cause the relationship was a dead end?"

"I did tell you. You wouldn't listen. You would only believe she was slumming. You were an asshole. Worse than usual."

I didn't have the slightest memory of the conversation. "She's a good lady. I don't want to fuck with her head."

"How can you fuck with her head?"

"Come on, Simon. She wants long-term."

"So?"

"What's the matter with you? Back off, will you? First you want to be a shrink, now a *shadkin*?"

He put his hands up. "Whoa. I'm not sure what I just walked into, but sorry."

"So what are we out here for?"

"Look, I didn't mean to hurt your feelings. I know that Boots cheers you up. Nothing terrible about that."

The wind had died but the drizzle was thickening as I lit a cigarette. I felt impatient yet another part of me felt ridiculous. Here I was sulking because there was someone who could cheer me up and I didn't want to admit it. I finished the cigarette and stuck my head out from under the branches and let the rain fall flat on my face. Two men walked down the path in front of us and graciously made sure not to look in our direction.

Simon lifted his arm and leaned it against the twisted trunk of a bush. I pulled my head in and asked, "What do you want to talk about?" My voice sounded quiet underneath the drops of rain tapping on the leaves.

"I wanted to follow up on the Lincoln lead you dug up."

"It really isn't a lead."

Simon looked at me anxiously. "What do you mean?"

I looked at him standing there. Water was still running down my face. All the years of his concern and friendship washed over me. I was asked to guard his wife but my job was to protect him.

"We go back a long time Simon. After your divorce you said you weren't ever going to let yourself get beat up again, especially by your own hand. Well, I'm an expert in punching myself out. That's why you have to listen. What you're doing here is wrong. However you term it, you have me spying on Fran. It's lousy for you because it's a wild goose chase that's going to leave you disappointed. It's lousy for Fran because she hasn't done anything to deserve being followed. And it's lousy for me because of the position I'm in when she finds out. And she will. Everyone finds out everything eventually. The point is to do as little as you can to hurt your people when the truth finally does come out. And when this comes out, it will hurt her."

He thought about it. He thought about it for a while. We stood there as the rain slackened and watched a small bird peck in the weeds alongside the rutted path. Simon leaned back against the gnarled trunk oblivious to the shower of water his action produced. He rubbed his face with his hands and when he pulled his hands away his relaxed look went with them. Taking its place was tired resignation.

"I think you're half right. I have been getting carried away and not keeping things in perspective. But I still think you're wrong about labeling it spying. I don't think anything terrible will happen between me and Fran if she does find out about it. I'm not prying, I'm trying to protect her in whatever way I can." He shook his head. "I just want to make sure that all the angles are covered."

He meant it. But how do you tell someone that he was covering too many angles already without telling him why? I wasn't going to change his mind and I knew I was being drawn into something that wasn't going to leave anyone dancing.

Simon kept on talking. "The other thing you're right about. It does put you right in the middle. Since you think this puts your relationship with Fran in jeopardy, let's pull you off. I can find a more neutral party. Give me what you've got. It wasn't right to push you into this and I'm sorry."

A part of me lunged toward the door Simon had just opened, but the friendship side didn't budge. I couldn't let Simon walk wide-eyed into another gumshoe's incriminating information about Fran. I owed him more than that. "Look, if you're convinced that this is the right way to go then I should do it."

He looked at me carefully. "Why? What about being in the middle?"

"I don't want a stranger poking around in your life. Especially since I don't think there's any reason to."

He still looked tired, but a little less resigned. No worry, I had resignation covered for the two of us.

"That's been my feeling, but I hadn't really thought about you in all this. I suppose I've been pretty self-centered. I would like you to continue if you really can see your way clear."

I shrugged. Clarity was the problem, but there was no choice. If I kept seeing things I didn't like I would just add them to the mound of crap I already lived with.

He smiled and a little of his earlier humor returned. "So what about the Lincoln?"

"I don't know yet. I have the plate number and now I need a way to check it out."

He ran his hand through his hair. "What's the problem? Call Motor Vehicle, they'll give you the name and address."

"It's not that easy, I only have a fragment. Don't worry about it, I'll think of something. In other words, you take your mind off this shit and I take care of it for you."

"Aren't you getting carried away? I can find a way to check this easier than you. What's the big deal?"

"It is a big deal. If I do this I want to do it my way. You can't keep this stuff in perspective. Just let me do my job and leave me alone about it."

He looked at me like he was about to argue but only said, "It's frustrating to telephone and get no answer. Are you sure you won't get a machine?"

I shook my head. "Just give me a little breathing room."

He rubbed his face again. "You know, the stuff I said about you owing me and all, that was bullshit. There was no call for that; you don't have anything to repay me for."

But I did. "Of course I do, but this isn't a favor. I'm going to charge. Between you and the other case I can almost think of myself as working."

He didn't seem too interested in my sudden industry. He started out from under the bullrushes and walked absently toward the path. After a step or two he looked back at me with a determined look on his face. "I'm happy to pay. How are you going to trace the fragment? As your client I think I'm entitled to that much."

The rain had stopped, though every time the wind blew the branches shook their moisture loose. But Simon was planted pretty firmly. It was no time for invention.

"I'm not sure yet. I told you, I would figure it out."

"What about Boots?"

"What about her?"

"She's probably got access to government mainframes."

"Why?"

His face broke into a big grin. "Everyone knows that Uncle Sam sleeps with Ma Bell. I'm not sure she can get the information but she would know how." He paused for a moment and looked at me. "If you don't want to see her I can."

"No thanks, I'll do my own talking. But leave me alone about the fucking Lincoln. Please Simon, this ain't gonna turn up anything that will help you. You got to remember that."

He started to walk up the path and back into the park. I caught up with him and could see the tightness of his jaw and the obstinacy in his eyes.

"It's difficult to leave it alone."

I nodded and, as I walked him back to his car, we talked ball. Although the weather seemed a brighter shade of gray and the wind had regained hints of summer breeze, neither of us supplied the conversation with much zip. Lately, all we had managed to spark in each other were our problems. It didn't make for good baseball talk.

23

I stripped off my wet clothes and settled down, exhausted, in front of Charles Laughton playing Henry VIII. I jacked the heat high enough to loll around in my underwear; if I couldn't have sunlit warmth at least I could use technology. I was still waiting for it to feel like summer when the phone rang. For someone who disliked the telephone, I was spending an awful lot of time answering it. I made a mental note to pull the plug after the call.

"Matthew Jacob? Alex Hirsh here."

I stood up. His voice sounded distant, as if he were talking on a speaker phone. It conjured up an image of him, spare, ramrod-straight, standing in a penthouse office overlooking the city.

"Hello, Alex. This is a surprise. What can I do for you?"

"Matthew, I'll get right to the point. Simon informed me about your work concerning Fran and I think it's time we talked."

I don't know why I was surprised. I really should have anticipated this once I'd heard that he knew. Important people don't get important by ignoring what's going on around them.

"How can I help?"

"I think it would be a good idea if we met." Unlike the other night there was no trace of Jewish in his voice.

Laughton was just getting ready to rid himself of his first Anne. If

121

we quickly set a time I could get back without missing much. "Where and when?"

"How about your place now?"

"My place? Now?"

"Is there a problem? Are you occupied?"

I had previously seen old Henry hang 'em high and I had a hunch that even if I hadn't Hirsh would have trouble accepting the four o'clock movie as a substantial barrier to our meeting.

"Are you sure you don't want me to come to you?" I looked around the house and calculated the length of time it would take to make it presentable.

"No need, Matthew. I would prefer it this way."

His tone made it clear that we were going to meet here. What the hell, it isn't often that money and power walks through my door.

"Could you give me twenty minutes?"

"Of course. See you then." The connection was abruptly severed and I was left with a dial tone in my ear as I wondered how he knew my address. I looked at the clock and hurried to get dressed and neaten the apartment. I felt like a college kid ready for a visit from his parents. I guess I was smiling at myself when Alex knocked and walked through my front door.

"What's so amusing, Matthew?" He stood just inside the doorway and surveyed my living room decor. I stifled my grin. Alex could look imperial anywhere.

"How did you find your way down here? I was waiting for the buzzer."

"It wasn't that difficult." He looked away from me and walked around to the shelf where I kept my radios. "Quite a collection you have here. Brings back memories. I'm surprised you don't have any wooden ones."

"I started with wood but the more enamored I became with Deco, the more I got into Bakelite designs."

He walked around the room and inspected some of my other stuff. "Is this romance with the Forties the reason you are a private detective?"

I smiled. "Maybe. I get the romance without the danger since I don't really have a practice."

He had his eyes on me. They seemed friendly enough, but contained a hardness I never before noticed. Social was different from business, and right now I was business. Being in my apartment certainly couldn't be a pleasure.

"Why don't you have a practice?" His tone was polite and he had walked over to the picture of the Chrysler Building that hung by the radios. I walked into the kitchen and shook the thermos. Empty. I went back to the other room.

"Mostly I take care of the building."

"Do you own it?"

It was funny how you could relate to someone in what seems like a variety of situations, over years, and still not know shit about them. His questions were just verifying the lack of knowledge we had about each other. I lit a cigarette. He didn't like cigarettes, that much I knew, but we were in my house. "No, my father-in-law does. I manage it."

Maybe my touchiness showed.

"And you do investigations part time, is that it?"

"If you want to call legal research for Simon 'investigations.' "

He looked at me and nodded toward the kitchen table. "Do you mind if we sit over there? In this atmosphere I feel I should be sitting in the kitchen drinking tea from a glass." He smiled. "I mean that as a compliment. There aren't many places that could throw me so completely back to my past."

I didn't know if that was a compliment or not. "Would you like some tea? Or something else?"

"No, I'm fine." He glanced at his watch as we both sat down. He looked at my cigarette but didn't say anything for a moment. I reached for an ashtray and stubbed the cigarette out.

"I know you didn't come here to visit; what's going on?"

"I'm here to ask you that."

"Nothing really. Simon asked me to keep an eye on Fran and I have."

He looked at me steadily. "Knowing my daughter I find it unlikely that nothing is going on."

There was enough ambiguity in his statement to make me nervous. "Well, you must know that she has been bothered by nightmares and

Simon has a crazy idea that maybe someone real is bothering her."

He shook his head. "That's not exactly what I meant. You are of the opinion that Simon's idea has no merit?"

I flopped my hand onto the table. "It's a long jump from nightmare to reality. I'm an expert in the field."

"Oh? Well, Simon isn't one to leave any stone unturned." I couldn't tell whether that was a compliment either.

He looked at me earnestly. "It's very difficult to stand idly by watching someone you love feel so troubled. Simon told me your view of this matter and I agree with your logic. Still, he also mentioned something about a young man with a Cadillac?"

I was instantly guarded but saw no reason to respect my paranoia. In fact, I felt embarrassed about my caution. Alex, while aloof, had always been gracious in his dealings with me.

"A Lincoln, but it's nothing." I shook my head and forced myself to tell the truth. This was quite a different Alex from the man who'd held center stage the other night. I wasn't going to bullshit him. "I told that to Simon to keep him off my back."

"But there was a someone, wasn't there?"

"Yeah, but what's the difference? There were a lot of cars there. I just picked it out of my head."

He looked at me carefully. "So you really don't have any concerns about this person?"

"Of course not. Like I say, I was just throwing Simon a bone."

He seemed satisfied with my answer. At least he didn't push me to track the shmuck down.

"Look, Alex, I'll tell you what I told Simon. Nightmares are inside problems. There isn't going to be an outside solution."

He stared at me for a long moment and said, "I agree with you. I'm not a person given to chasing illusions. But as far as I can tell, Simon is adamant." A tired expression crossed his face. "And since you will be keeping an eye on Fran, there are some things you should know. If you don't already."

I started to protest but he cut me off with a wave of his hand. Or maybe the flash of diamonds when he moved his hand silenced me.

"No, let me finish. Since her teenage years Fran has been extraordinarily insecure about her attractiveness to men." He shook his head sadly. "No amount of reality mattered. Or therapy for that matter.

You see, although Fran is very much in love with Simon she relieves her insecurity with occasional encounters. I would not like to see her marriage with Simon disintegrate. And not just for my daughter's well-being. I would not like to see my son-in-law hurt over something that has so little meaning or importance."

For a moment I wondered how protective he was being of his own reputation, but I thought my idea a reflection of my discomfort with the conversation. Reputation was irrelevant to an Alex Hirsh at this point in his life. My silence pushed him to underscore.

"What I'm asking for, I suppose, is discretion."

I thought of my encounter with Fran at 290. "What if one of these men is a source of difficulty?"

"Difficulty?"

"What if someone got her pregnant?"

He looked directly into my eyes, "Frances has handled complications before without their becoming disastrous."

Enough was enough, and I'd heard more than I wanted to. As far as I was concerned I'd trust Alex's assessment of Fran's competency. I kept my mouth shut and nodded my understanding.

His smile wrapped around me like an embrace. I resisted at first but slowly felt myself drawn into his paternal warmth. "Your tact goes a long way to relieving my worry. If you discover something specific, perhaps we could talk before any action is taken? Or before you spoke with Simon?"

The idea seemed deceitful. It also seemed wise. I'd been doing detective work for only a week, and I was already discovering personality qualities in myself that up till now I'd barely acknowledged. At this rate of discovery it would take another week before I'd know whether I'd take a bribe. "It seems okay to me. I really don't think it will come to that."

He stood. I struggled to my feet. It had been a long time since I last noticed the aches in my body. Alex watched but didn't say anything. Instead he asked, "What are you planning to do about the Cadillac?"

"Lincoln. I don't know. Maybe track it down."

He shook his head. "I worry about feeding Simon's desperation. The longer he thinks something is possible, the longer he'll keep up this charade."

I didn't like hearing myself called a charade, but I knew what he meant. The less I'm out there looking, the less I was going to see.

"I sort of agree with you, Alex."

"So you'll drop the Lincoln hoax?"

"I wouldn't call it a hoax, exactly."

Hirsh was instantly apologetic. "You are absolutely right. I'm sure you are doing your best to calm Simon and I do understand his capacity to be overly enthusiastic." We both smiled in silent acknowledgment of Alex's understatement.

"Okay, Alex, I suppose you're right about the Lincoln. It probably would just fan the fire." I felt a pang of regret about losing a lunch with Boots, but it wasn't enough of an argument to hurt Simon or fuel my own delusions about detecting.

He stood by the front door and took a long lingering look at me. "I appreciate both your time and sensitivity, Matthew. This was an extremely difficult visit for a parent to make, and you have made it as painless as possible. Please, let me know if you need anything. I will try to be of help. And please contact me if you do see anything at all untoward."

"Thank you, sir. That's very nice of you." He bowed slightly and walked out the door. I walked after him and stood in the hall as he surefootedly navigated his way to the stairs. I heard the first floor door shut before I walked back into the living room. I sat down on the couch and didn't bother to get the dope or turn on the television. I looked around the tidy apartment and wondered what the fuck just happened.

— 24 —

I woke the next morning drenched in sweat. Dreams of an undertow I'd wrestled during the night kept trying to insinuate themselves into my wakefulness but I fought them off. I didn't need the details. Awake, I already felt pulled into the underside of people's lives, and it made me uncomfortable to remember Richard's comment that the work suited.

I showered off the frights and dug around in my dresser for clothes. Most of them were dirty. I stood naked and transfixed in front of two almost empty drawers.

I yanked myself away from the bureau and grabbed yesterday's pants. I walked into the alley to get the paper and was hit with a strong smell of ocean. It was going to be another chilly day. I sat at the kitchen table drinking coffee, smoking cigarettes and guarding my rolled-up paper. The clothes seemed symbolic. When I had nowhere to go I had plenty of clothes. Now I had places to go but I didn't know where, or what to wear. In a perverse way the idea gave me pleasure. I prepared to do a wash.

After the changeover from washer to dryer I pulled on a tee shirt and sweats and marched barefoot through the building to Julius' apartment. If I got there early enough he might still be around. I banged on the door and waited. I heard him rustle and then call out.

"Who's there?"

"Me. Matt."

"Well, pick the lock. No need to get me on my feet in the middle of the fucking night."

"If I do, the landlord will evict."

The door opened and I stood staring at Julius' saggy face. His eyes were red and blurry and his breath smelled like he had just used bourbon for mouthwash. For a moment I thought about leaving him alone but he was already grunting me through the entrance. All the blinds in the apartment were down but there was enough light from the bathroom fixture to make finding the kitchen possible.

"Jesus, Julie, you ain't a bat."

He walked over and put the stove's hood light on. "I don't like light when I'm sleeping. Or when I'm supposed to be sleeping."

"It's not that early."

He just looked at me.

"Okay, it is that early. But hell, you woke me up the other night."

"I brought you shit when I came over." He looked at my hands. "Your arms are empty." He looked down at my bare feet. "Damn, even your feet are empty." He walked into the bathroom and came back with a bottle of bourbon. He sat across the table from me and took a drink. Or was it a rinse? He offered but I just made a face. I didn't want to swallow and it wasn't polite to spit on the floor. My refusal made him smile. Or grimace. I wasn't sure.

"Are you doing rent collecting, s'lord?"

"Look, I'm sorry about disturbing you. If you want we can meet another time." I put my hands up. I'd been party to Julie's bad moods before and I wasn't about to instigate another.

He took another swallow from the bottle, stood, walked into the bedroom and returned with a fat joint. He sat back down, snuffed out his cigarette, and lit the joint. I watched as he smoked. Eyes closed, settling back in his chair. I could almost see the smoke work its way through his body. I wanted some.

As if he could read my mind, Julie opened his eyes and offered me the joint but I didn't want to get high until I made a final decision about calling Boots. I shook my head and lit a cigarette instead. Julius continued to focus on the joint. I didn't see the percentage in rushing him.

When he finally spoke the edge of hostility was gone. "Doesn't seem like you're here about the building."

"I'm not."

He carefully put the joint on the rim of the ashtray and watched as it slowly burned itself out. He took another drink of the bourbon and lit a cigarette. Everything seemed to be moving in three-quarters time.

"How is your body?"

"You heard, huh?"

"Be hard not to."

"It seems like people around here have been confusing humiliation with heroism. I'm all right. Down to twice a day reminders. Couple more days it'll be normal."

"Nothing's ever normal with you. Why did it go down?"

"I don't know. The closest I come has the police protecting whoever's been breaking into the building I'm interested in."

He raised his eyebrows underneath a cloud of smoke. "Police. Why police?"

I summarized the beating and yesterday's discussion with the black guy. "Neither of them showed a badge or warrant but something inside of me is certain." I lit another cigarette. Talk of the beating had gotten me angry. The glowing tip of the joint in the brown glass ashtray was fading. I wanted some before it extinguished but pushed the feeling away. Julius just sat there with his fucking eyes closed. At least he didn't go for another toke. I'd a had my hand out if he had.

He opened his eyes. "What do you suppose I can do?"

"You can think. And you know what to think about. See, I can't get it to add. Whoever is busting in doesn't seem to realize the cops are buffering him. He keeps trying to cover his tracks."

"Or making it look that way."

"Maybe. But why twice? He could have spent the entire night there if he knew he was protected.

"Maybe he had to git home to his momma."

"No curfew in this town, Boss. Why would police cover for someone who isn't a cop?"

"Did you describe the meat to Phil?"

"No. The guy in the car tried to squeeze me about where I got the report. I managed to talk my way out of answering and I haven't wanted to chance leading anyone to Phil. Hell, he did me a favor; I don't want to get him fucked."

Julius relit the joint. "This time give me a detailed painting of the situation and the tag team."

I did the best I could. When I was studying for the ticket I spent most of the time with the gun. I had imagined that little things, like detecting, came with common sense. Of course back then I didn't have any. Now it was on-the-job training. Julius just sat there and listened to my account of Dr. James' case and the beating. I figured Simon was personal business.

The only questions he asked were about the pit bull's shoes. At first I wondered whether he was ribbing me about kissing floor, but he stayed serious and so did I. When I finished, a good chunk of my anger had dissipated. I hoped he would light the joint. He did. We passed the dope back and forth. It almost seemed like the other night when we smoked together at my place. But it wasn't. The beating, my deepening involvement with the cases—I was starting to think of them as cases—added a somber note nonexistent the last time.

"Your jokes are missing."

"I'm not used to being trashed in my own house."

"What do you want to do about it?"

I took a deep inhale on the roach and held my breath. I exhaled slowly. "I don't know. Right now I want to know what it's about. Later I can think about what to do."

"If you keep on with this you got to be ready to do it all."

"What's 'all'?"

"Everything, I mean everything." His voice had grown even softer. It sent a chill through me. "Jail, Mr. Jacob. How's that for starters? You be fucking with cops that's where you got a good chance of getting."

He opened his eyes a little wider. "This is a very grownup game, slumlord. You don't get a little bit pregnant." His voice became a sarcastic hiss that stung like the spray from a riot hose. "So you got hit. You still got all your parts and most of your blood. Let it go. Violence is like this, man. You are involved or you are not. There's plenty of crossover but, if you are going to live on my side of the fence, you best be ready to do it all. You got to give a beating as well as take one."

His voice lost all traces of sarcasm. It was almost tender. "Are you ready, Matthew, to give a beating? Feel your hands break someone else's bone? See a piece of skin rip off a body? Crush an eye with your boot? You don't even wear boots, do you? The guy that kicked you was wearing a boot. Are you ready to shoot someone and watch the life drip out of him? Let it go. You are a housekeeper, slumlord, not an asskicker."

I felt stunned. Julie wasn't the first to tell me not to get involved, everyone was doing that. But he was the first to give me good reasons. Real good reasons. I sat there for a long time thinking. Every once in a while Julius would lean forward and nip from the bottle or light a cigarette. I sat there thinking for a long time. He didn't rush me.

"You know, I've been giving a friend of mine similar advice about a problem and all he keeps telling me is he can't help it."

Julius leaned back in his chair and gave me his best lizard imitation. "Sounds like your friend has woman trouble."

I grinned. "That's the trouble with advice from you. You're too fucking smart to ignore."

"But ignore me you will."

"I can't help it." I lit a cigarette. "When I was growing up, the house was a free-fire zone. Anything went. I spent my time trying to figure out what was going on and stay ahead of it. It kept me alive, but didn't prevent me from running my own life into the ground once I got out. I caught a reprieve, had my guts torn out again, and I'm back here hiding in a basement. I haven't been interested in much of anything and that's the way I thought I was going to play out the string. Only this shit interests me." I let out a long breath. For a moment I wondered if I had just hired a new shrink.

"The shit that interests you might also kill you."

"Probably not."

"And the practicalities?"

"Practicalities? Julius, from you? Please, get us more dope."

He smiled but didn't move.

"The practicalities worry me. There are serious limitations to my learn-as-I-go method so I'm trying to ease into it."

"Ease might not be slow enough."

"It's got to be. The violence scares me and jail worse. I intend to avoid both."

"You do this detective work for real, not just in your mind, sooner or later you can't avoid nothing. That's what I been trying to tell you and what you spent all this time ignoring."

"I'm not ignoring it. I just don't know what to do with it. I'm not thinking beyond this situation and I don't think I'm involved with something that's going to get me killed or thrown in jail. Right now all I want to know is what the hell is going on." I shrugged. "Later is later. It'll take care of itself. Will you please roar the damn pipe?"

"You waited this long you can wait a little longer. You didn't come marching down here with your naked feet to ask permission to do something you were going to do anyway."

"I want to stay away from Phil, but I want to find out whether the Bobbsey twins are freelancing, or if there is something going on in the Department. You know, there could be a simple explanation for all of this."

It was Julius' turn to think. I drank a little bourbon to quench my thirst. It didn't work but it felt good going down so I had another. I lit a cigarette and waited.

"I'm comfortable with you, slumlord. We ain't what I'd call friends, but there's not too many people I'll share a high with. When you first got here you be like something out of a crazy house. Like they did surgery on your head. I seen you recover, but you're still one tired dude.

"I thought you must be some kind of outlaw for me to feel easy with you, but my only clue was that dead license. Hearing that you're waking up that license, that's good and bad. Makes me feel more comfortable sharing my high. But it's gonna change you. And you're too green to know it."

I wasn't too green to know he was telling the truth, just too green to let it stop me. I waited for him to say something about my request.

"I liked what you told me about Phil. The way I see outlaws is you got two types. Decent ones and assholes. Has to do with character, not something you learn. Doesn't matter which side of the law you're on either. Your attitude about covering Phil is good character."

For a moment I was hurtled back in time to my elementary school where they talked a lot about character. But they never talked about it as part of an outlaw's makeup. Nor did they divide the world into decents and assholes.

Coming from anyone else the idea might have been funny, but sitting across the table from me was a man I believed did all the things he asked me if I could do. I just sat still and smoked.

He spoke in a clipped, unaccented, business tone. "I will ask around and see if I can find anything out. I doubt I can, but I will try. If I do hear about something there won't be any simple answers. Prepare yourself for that. If you want more dope I will be happy to get some. If not, will you go the fuck away and let me sleep?"

25

"I can't go out for dinner, I already have an engagement."

I knew it was a dumb idea but when I got home from Julius' the rest of the day and night stretched out before me like a Nebraska highway. I hadn't wanted to do the ride alone. As soon as she turned me down I tried to remember where I'd put the coke.

"Well?"

I was ready with a snappy rejoinder. "Well what?"

"You are an oaf. You ask me out for dinner a couple of hours from now and because I have an engagement you act like a Turkish prison guard ripped out your tongue."

"Yeah, you're right. It was a bad idea."

"No, it was a good idea. I'm not looking for apologies, I want a little more insistence."

I could lose my breath trying to keep up with her. "I'm not sure I understand you."

"Boy, you can say that again! What about 'How long is your engagement supposed to last?' Or, 'Break the engagement.' Anything but dead air. Were you really only looking for company while you ate?"

A shaft of sunlight through the clouds. "Okay, I'll bite. How long will your engagement last?"

"Until my after-dinner headache. Where do you want to meet?"

She seemed to have lost a lot of caution between Wednesday and Friday. So had I. "I don't know. Where are you going to dinner?"

The place she named was the kind that, no matter how old I was, always made me feel like a kid. I suggested we meet at Amalfi's at nine.

There was a long pause. When she spoke her tone sounded guarded. "I'll be overdressed."

"I'll even it out."

She started to speak then stopped. There was another long pause during which I thought she was going to change her mind about the evening. I went back to thinking about the coke, but before I made any headway she said, "See you later," and was gone.

I was left holding a dead telephone and reaching for my subsiding excitement. It had been a long time since I'd slept with anyone. I lit a cigarette, and remembered where I had hidden the cocaine. I thought about doing a line, but didn't want to add to the crash I was already experiencing from the bourbon and dope. At least this way I'd be in better shape to start over again later.

I tinkered with one of my radios to kill time, and even managed to finish the laundry. There were no notes under the door from any of the tenants so I guessed there were no complaints. It felt like not being missed. I thought about dropping in on Mrs. Sullivan but I couldn't face more questions about the cases. I decided to nap. I was hoping for a long night.

Sleep came and went in between thinking about my morning with Julius. I wondered about my stubbornness. A series of unwanted requests from Simon and Dr. James, requests which I resisted and resented, had become a lifeline. Julius' prophecies of external violence and horror notwithstanding, it was an unknown interior edge I was flirting with. I guessed I would wait and see what happened.

What happened was a call from Dr. James. "Have you discovered anything yet?" There was excitement in her voice.

"I'm working on it, Dr. James."

"Come on Matthew, I thought we were on a first-name basis."

"Okay, Gloria. Do you want to tell me what you're excited about?"

"What did you say?"

"What is it, Gloria?" It was eight o'clock, and I wanted to walk to Amalfi's. Dr. James was a case, and tonight I didn't want to work.

She was also my shrink and it almost felt like my mother calling right before a big date.

"You were wrong about the other offices." Her voice sounded triumphant.

"What about the other offices?"

"They had records stolen as well. You said the thief got what he was looking for in my office and just used the others to throw off the police. Now that we know he took other people's records we don't have to believe it was mine he wanted."

I wasn't going to argue with her; she might be right. "I'm not sure what you're trying to tell me."

"I'm telling you that we don't have to be frantic about this."

"Were we?"

She laughed. "I was. Heck, I even considered letting you look at my files. Thank god I didn't."

"You seem pretty sure that you are out of the woods."

"I'm not positive, but I hope so."

"So now that you figure you're off the hook you don't think I should continue, is that it?"

She laughed again. The other offices' stolen records certainly cheered her up. "No, I want you to continue. I'm not sure I'm off the hook; it's just not certain that I'm on it."

Sometimes inspiration hits in the oddest moments. "Is the decision to continue one you made yourself, or was it a collective one?"

"What do you mean collective?"

"I mean Holmes. Eban Holmes. Was the decision for me to continue to work the case made during some therapeutic consultation with Eban Holmes?"

Her voice grew less cheerful. "I did talk with Dr. Holmes about it, yes, but I don't see what that has to do with anything."

I couldn't really blame her but I hadn't wanted to be a case tonight either. I felt deflated. "Look, I gotta go. I'm meeting somebody. I'll call you after I have a chance to think about what you've said."

"What's the matter? You suddenly sound very tired. It's a tone I recognize."

"The drugs are coming on."

"What? What is it that you're using now?"

"Nothing." I forced some enthusiasm into my voice. "I was just kidding. I have to meet someone and I'm running late. Really. I'll call you."

"I don't trust what you're telling me. I know you are upset that I spoke with Dr. Holmes. Are you uneasy about continuing the investigation under these circumstances?"

"Don't be silly, Gloria, nothing's bothering me. I want to continue." I couldn't help myself. "It'll be nice to have the check roll in the opposite direction."

"Mr. Jacob."

"Matt, Gloria, Matt. Hey, I gotta be able to joke with my clients. Look, I'm really late. I'll call you."

The phone rang a moment or two after I hung up. If it was Dr. James as I suspected, fuck her. If it was Boots I didn't want to know about it.

I finished getting dressed with a fair amount of slammed doors and drawers. The image of Dr. James and Eban Holmes huddled, strategizing about the health and well-being of a patient in an awkward moment of his patienthood, infuriated me. For a moment I wondered whether the two of them might have plotted the burglaries as some avant-garde therapeutic approach.

That's when I knew I needed to relax. I smoked half a joint, put it down, and rolled three more. The dope burned itself out before I finished, so I relit it and had a couple more hits. I debated about doing a line of the coke and compromised by pouring a bit onto the side of my hand and taking a little toot. I put the coke and dope into my jacket pocket, lit a cigarette, and went out the kitchen door into the alley.

The cool, early morning ocean breeze had long since faded. The night air hung thick and heavy. Air to walk through, not in. I had spare time to get to Amalfi's so I wandered over to the park to find a basketball game. The lights were on and so were the players. Roberto Clemente Park could legitimately boast having the best street ball in the city. The same could not be said of the court itself. One basket was twisted on a downward angle and the other rattled anytime someone ran near it. The secondary courts were unusable. It made me angry.

During a pretty fast break the coke hit. I had been thirty years old before I saw a lead guard do a between the legs crossover dribble. A decade later eighth graders had it down cold. Maybe Western civilization really did boil down to Jesus, Marx, Einstein, Freud, and Julius Irving.

I decided to move on. I had taken the right amount of drugs. My body didn't hurt and my sweat felt comfortable. I promised myself that I'd start working out again tomorrow. Or at least soon.

I got to the Arch and stood there. The hookers stood in small clusters on the Boylston side of the structure. Symphony nights they huddled on the park side. Since they began cleaning up lower downtown the Arch had become a comfortable place to work. Word was out that drugs and ripoffs would be dealt with harshly. Word was also out that discreet hustling would be permitted as long as it remained discreet. A simple service for the suburban rich.

Right after the accident, when I spent a lot of time walking around town, I'd sometimes pick a Symphony night to sit on a stoop by the Arch and watch the women work. After a while I even learned some names.

I was reminded that those nights were long ago the minute I walked into the tavern. Instead of the huge oval mahogany bar that had dominated the front, the place had turned into a restaurant. In front of me was an array of tables with clean-cut people sitting at them. I stood there for a moment, sweating and wondering where to go when a dark gloved hand waved from the rear. I looked at the clock on the wall with surprise. I was late.

I threaded my way between the tables and silver wine buckets and glanced at the food. Despite the coke, I was starving. Boots had secured a booth back in the corner. She and I used to hang out here occasionally and we often wound up in the back. I felt awkward sliding onto my bench but managed it without meeting her eyes. I mumbled my apologies and looked at her. She was wearing a midnight blue cape with matching gloves. Her hair hung straight down and was held close to her head with a gypsy cloth wrapped around her forehead. She looked like Amalfi's felt; same place but very different. "You look terrific. I'm surprised the other place let you in."

"I haven't been anywhere else tonight."

I felt my forehead scrunch. "I thought you had a date?"

"I lied." Her eyes sparkled. I felt a dime short, a step slow. She smiled and said, "At least you showed up. Is that why you picked Amalfi's? To make up for the last time?"

For a moment I didn't know what she was talking about, then it registered. I had been pretty erratic during the time we spent together. Especially about time. I was always late, sometimes outrageously so. Occasionally I didn't show at all. I was always contrite, she was usually forgiving. What I had forgotten was the last time I didn't show we were supposed to meet at Amalfi's. She wasn't unforgiving; we just never saw each other again.

I remembered the night. I was in the process of renovating the building and we were going to meet for late-night drinks. On the way over I sat down on the stoop by the Arch and watched the street begin its nighttime undulations. Every twenty minutes or so I'd think about leaving, but something held me to the spot. I didn't want to talk about Boots' civilized world. I wanted to watch the street's primitive, sweaty transactions. It was remarkable—I had completely repressed the memory, but still chose Amalfi's for tonight. It was the kind of thing I would tell Dr. James—if I still had a Dr. James.

"I had forgotten."

For a moment she looked annoyed but it quickly passed. "The sad part of it all is that I believe you."

"I remember now." I tried to smile but it wouldn't work.

The waitress came by and I wanted to ask her to join us. Instead I ordered Amalfi's version of the seven-dollar hamburger, and a Bass. Boots ordered the exact same thing, then turned her attention to her hands. The way she stripped off her gloves turned me on despite my embarrassment. I changed my mind about the waitress.

The interruption eased the tension between us. I lit a cigarette. She sat back in her seat and put her feet between my legs on my bench.

"I'm glad you remember now."

"When we talked on the phone after that miss you said you understood."

"At the time we both said a lot of things that seem different now." She waved her arm toward the rest of the room. "Look," she challenged, "we're at Amalfi's again; does it seem the same? Do I?"

—26—

The food arrived quickly and tasted like it. I lost my appetite, but Boots tunneled into her plate and barely came up for air. When she finished I wondered whether she was going to ask for mine. Instead, she put her feet back up, this time without shoes. I knew because one of her feet rested on the inside of my thigh. She rummaged through an oversized bag and withdrew a pack of cigarettes.

I leaned forward to light our cigarettes. When I did, her foot pressed against my crotch. I felt myself get hard and nervous at the same time. "I didn't think you smoked."

"I don't," she said and inhaled deeply. She kept her foot where it was.

"Why do I keep thinking that you're fucking with my head?" But I didn't ask her to move.

She looked directly at me. "You keep thinking it's a couple of years ago. It's not." She moved her foot back to my leg. "Even you are different."

I was spared hearing how while the table was cleared and coffee poured. I took the opportunity to go to the john and snort more coke. When I returned I found Boots had removed her bandana, her hair falling loosely around her head. I slid back into the booth and drank some coffee.

The snow was starting to work its way to the back of my throat when she lit another cigarette and asked, "Did you use up the last of the coke in the bathroom?"

"No," I paused, "just a little." We both laughed.

She signaled for the waitress. "We better leave before it's all gone."

"Fine." I finished the rest of my coffee, then stood by the side of the booth and watched her slip into her shoes. I wondered what she was wearing under her cape and felt a rush of desire. Maybe it was the coke or the length of time since I last had sex, but the intensity of feeling was unlike anything I'd felt for Boots before, or ever imagined I would.

She grabbed my arm and aimed us toward the exit. Walking through Amalfi's that wasn't really Amalfi's with Boots who didn't seem like Boots was the answer to the Firesign Theater's question: "How can you be in two places at once when you're not anywhere at all?" I was glad to get out the door.

Once outside I looked at her with less desire and more jumpiness. "Where to?"

She took my hand and silently headed toward Symphony Hall. We walked all the way up Mass Ave. to Commonwealth, then strolled in the direction of the Gardens. When we passed 290 I had the uneasy feeling that Dr. James was at her office window. I repressed a desire to peek but carefully looked around the area. All I saw was a Friday night.

Boots' voice interrupted my concentration. "What's the matter? All of a sudden you seemed to disappear."

"It showed?"

"Not very much." A hint of a smile flashed across her face. "At least I hope not. I like to think I can see you more clearly than most."

We were off the block and the fantasy of being watched receded with it. "I just got distracted for a moment. I'm working on something back there, that's all."

Boots kept her steady pace. The humidity had, if possible, increased, and our joined hands felt bathed in a warm salt sea of sweat. "Fran told me that she saw you at her doctor's building. Were you working then?"

I dropped her hand and shrugged. I almost asked whether Fran was pregnant but I didn't really want to work tonight. "What's the difference?"

"Working as a detective gives you an excuse not to talk?"

I grinned. "No, it just gives me something to do. I'd take your hand but I don't know where we're going."

"We're going to bed."

"I don't remember you as this forward."

"You still can't get out of the past. I change. Even your work changed. You're not just a social worker anymore."

"Just a social worker? Your nose is starting to tilt again. Some things don't change, huh?"

She didn't say anything until we turned down Exeter toward the river. "I live here now. Don't say it; it goes with my nose, right?"

I didn't say it.

We walked to Back Street, turned right and continued silently to the rear of a tall modern building squeezed between the traditional brownstones. At the service door she pulled a plastic card out of her bag and stuck it in a slot. The door clicked and opened, and we went inside. I stood at the back of the service elevator and sweated while she pushed the uppermost button. Halfway up the row of floor markers I wondered why we came through the back, but before I had a chance to ask, the doors opened. Boots led us through a spacious corridor painted a handsome gray with pale lavender accents. We stopped in front of a doorway with no handle, knob, or number— just a box of lettered squares to push. Something like this would give Julie fits.

The door opened with pneumatic ease. I followed Boots inside and was stunned by the panorama spread out before me. The entire wall facing the river was glass, extending a third of the way across the side walls like a pair of wrap-around sunglasses. For a moment, standing there with the city's light pouring in from the right, I felt like an explorer with a sea of flickering jewels at my feet.

"This is gorgeous."

"Not too rich for your blood?"

I grinned and looked at the minimalist furnishings in the room. "Maybe too high for my vertigo."

She pointed to a cabinet in the kitchen alcove. "The liquor is in there. Why don't you find something for us to drink. I'll be right back."

She went through another door on the right while I dug through the bottles to find bourbon for me and wine for her. I was about to pour her wine when she returned and said, "I'll drink what you're drinking." I didn't remember her as a liquor drinker. I poured the bourbon and walked over to the unrolled futon where Boots was sitting. I put the drinks on the low glass table in front of the mattress.

The zipper on her cape was lower and it was clear that she was wearing only a black slip underneath. She smiled and said, "I couldn't count on your saving any so I got some more." I pulled out the little bottle in my pocket and put it down between her open legs alongside the flat rectangular piece of glass she was chopping on.

"See, everyone changes. Two years ago there wouldn't be a chance that you'd have any left."

"Don't be so idealistic, doll, I haven't had the time."

She looked up at me and fingered the zipper on her cape. "Two years ago you wouldn't have had the time for anything else." Her hands played with her zipper. In the old days sex had been more friendly than hot. I told myself to believe in her theory of change. That was then.

I waited and watched as she finished spreading the coke into four ripe lines. When she finished she positioned herself on her knees and swiveled gently until she sat with her feet tucked under. As she leaned forward to snort the dope with a metal straw I looked down the front of her cape at the swell of her breasts. As usual, the minute I finished my lines and put the tool down, I wanted more.

Before I had a chance to say anything she reached for her drink, took a long swallow, and put the glass back down. I felt the hairs on my legs grow damp and it wasn't the humidity.

She lifted her arms and stretched. With one movement she stood— I watched the muscles on her legs tighten and release—then she walked over to the console of buttons by the door, and pushed one. The light in the room, already dim, disappeared entirely and we were suddenly awash in a kaleidoscope of urban night sky. The bare walls became screens upon which the city lights danced with patternless abandon. Boots moved softly around the room as neither of us spoke. She unzipped the cape, let it drop, and turned to face the river. She was framed in the graffiti of light and shadow as she ran her hands down the front of her slip. I began to unbutton my shirt.

"No," she said, "let it be." She walked to the futon, dropped to her knees, and pressed my hands against the front of her face. She drew my hands down and licked where they crossed her mouth, then she dragged my hands across her chest and belly. She began to unbutton my shirt and scrape her teeth along my chest. I could feel the coke hit the back of my throat as my skin came alive wherever she touched. She was pulling the tails of my shirt out of my pants when I said, "I need a cigarette." She nodded but kept her face pressed up against my belly.

I reached over her head to the table and fished for my cigarettes and lighter. While I fumbled, Boots rubbed her face against my pants and began to undo them. I stayed still until she had them open, then I sat back down and lit the cigarette. She got up and brought back a couple of oversized pillows and an ashtray. I finished taking off my pants and sat yoga-legged, smoking.

"I was going to do that," she said. "Give me a cigarette."

I lit another smoke and passed it to her. She put the pillows behind her and leaned her back and head against them. She put her feet on the front of my legs and spread her knees. She wasn't wearing any underpants and even in the shadowdance of light her pubic hair glistened with dampness. I felt myself harden as she watched me look at her.

I reached into my pants pocket for the joints, lit one, and turned to pass it. She was lying on the pillow with her legs spread, caressing herself. Her eyes were open, looking directly at me. I offered her the marijuana but she shook her head and kept rubbing. She put both her feet on my legs while I smoked and watched. I took a couple more hits of the dope then put it in the ashtray next to my burned out cigarette.

When I stretched out beside her she kept her hands where they were but turned her face toward me. I pulled her head next to mine and began to kiss her. My fingers ran lightly over her body until they rested on the hand that was moving between her legs. Squeezing her upper thighs, she pressed both our hands hard into her wetness.

I slid my body down toward her feet, while she lifted her buttocks and pulled her slip off. I tongued the brownish pink sides of her lower lips while she cupped her breasts. Her eyes were closed and she had her fingers around her nipples, pinching them. Hard. The sight sent a surge of excitement through me and, as I lowered my head, I had to restrain myself from biting. I felt her body shift, and suddenly her hands were pulling at the hair on the back of my head.

She ground her groin into my face and hissed, "Harder, dammit, harder." Her hands pulled my hair until I was looking right at her. Her mouth was drawn wide across her face and through clenched teeth she said, "Fuck me, Matt, fuck me!" I moved up her body and slid inside.

Her hands were back on her breasts, pulling at her nipples. I was both excited and angry; part of me felt like a dildo. I closed my eyes and concentrated on moving rhythmically but suddenly her hands were pummeling me on my back.

"Stop holding back, you bastard!" I opened my eyes in surprise; there was genuine hostility in her voice. "You pick Amalfi's and now you pretend to be sweet and gentle." I felt my own anger grow but tried to push it away. "I'm not interested in your phony niceness, you prick. Just fuck me. You don't have to bullshit, I'm not your dead wife."

I slapped her across the face. Almost instantly I felt her shudder. She gritted her teeth and looked at me triumphantly. I hit her again, her words still ringing in my ears. She wound her legs around me, pushing me in deeper and trapping me. I tried to peel her off and felt her whole body twist with excitement underneath me.

The walls in the room were diving at me. I pushed her shoulders into the mattress, broke her grip on my back, and pulled out to keep from coming. Her hand was back at her breast. It made me angrier. I bit hard into her other nipple. I heard her groan and felt her clench her legs. She scratched at my face with her hand. I yanked my head away and grabbed her around the throat.

I crawled up her body until I was hunched over her chest. She lifted her head but I pushed her down. I didn't want to be blown; I wanted to fuck her face. I stabbed at her mouth. We stayed like that for awhile, me angry and humping, sweat flying off both of us. Then she jammed her finger in my ass and I instinctively tried to pull away, but she felt me move and sucked harder and dug her finger in deeper.

I saw myself raise my hand and ball my fingers into a fist. She saw it too and loosened her mouth but there was no fear in her eyes. I pulled my dick from her mouth and twisted away from her finger. I forced her onto her stomach as she reached back and struck at my face with her fists, trying to claw me with her nails. Part of me was sorry that she missed. I teased her vagina from the rear and listened to her moan. It only made me harder. She got up on her knees and tried to back into me, but I pushed her flat on her belly and pulled her legs wide apart. I spit in my hand, wet my cock, and pushed inside her small opening. She was biting on the pillow by her face. I closed my eyes and pushed in deeper. The inside of her ass seemed to open just ahead of me. I heard her crying and I opened my eyes. She was on her elbows looking back at me. Her eyes were streaming and the light spun off her tears and our sweat, and her hair spun wildly in the carnival of strobe lights. Her body was trembling and coming and shaking, and her mouth opened and she spat, "Who's slumming now?" as I exploded inside her.

There was more. More coke. More sex. Little talk. The night was filled with shadows that played along the walls in a dance of clawing hands and hungry mouths and aching genitals. All of my violence drove me to mount her again, or suck her again, or just cling to her and rub a soft and empty dick against her. Boots matched me need for need, hate for hate. By the time the walls began to look plain and unadorned, but before the morning light completely canceled the nighttime's trail, I discovered why we had used the service route. The boyfriend who paid for this place wouldn't like the concierge laughing behind his back.

I left the building depleted and depressed. The images of hitting, hating and loving it, choked me. The morning was unseasonably hot, but my perspiration was cold and clammy. I stayed inside the Emerald Necklace and ran panic-stricken with a pounding heart and sick stomach. Finally I was there. I stood and panted and felt my body shake with fatigue. But it was all right now. I was in my alley. I was home.

— 27 —

The rest of the weekend passed in a walking nightmare. Awake, I was sick with myself as images of my misogyny burned across my eyes. Asleep, I loathed everyone else. I would sit on my bed sweating and shaking, but with rage, not fear. Then shock, when faces of those whose spirits I tortured and murdered flooded my initial wakefulness. There were no sacred cows. Not even my dead wife. My stomach would turn with shame, humiliation, and guilt, then the whole cycle would repeat. Julius's Friday morning lecture sang like Muzak, awake and asleep.

By Sunday night my upheaval slowed enough for me to think as well as ride. It was sad and ironic; Boots wasn't one of my dream victims. I couldn't allow myself the idleness of the damned, I had to face her and face her honestly. And not just her. I had too much spinning to pull an ostrich now. Julie had been pretty accurate. Although I might not have to do it all, I sure had to do a fuck of a lot more than I was accustomed to. Only I wasn't going to do it the way I did Friday night. Out of control, to people who didn't deserve it.

When the phone rang early Monday morning I didn't mistake it for an alarm, doorbell, or institutional siren. I knew it was the telephone and I woke instantly. I groped for my cigarettes, and realized my sleep hadn't been littered with other bodies. The ringing phone had provided relief because the few corpses there were resembled me.

147

The relief was short-lived. Boots' voice was flat and businesslike. "I tried to reach you during the weekend."

"I wasn't answering the phone."

"No surprise."

There was a long silence. It was my turn and I knew it. "I would like to talk."

"So talk." Her tone stayed flat.

"Not on the phone. I would like to see you. Breakfast, lunch, dinner, or anything between."

"Maybe a between." There was a note of hesitancy in her voice.

"Today?"

"Today?" Now there was genuine surprise.

"Yes. I don't want this to sit. Of course if you want to wait, I'll respect that."

"Please, let's not talk about respect. I can make it today. I'm just surprised by your sudden interest in talking."

I ignored the sarcasm that replaced her uncertainty. I was due a lot worse than sarcasm. "Where would you like to meet?"

"My choice this time, is it?"

I kept quiet.

"Okay Matt, why don't we meet at the wharf at four."

"That's fine. Where at the wharf?"

"I don't know. What's big down there? We can just meet in front of the Aquarium."

My stomach jerked and I grunted.

"What's the matter, changing your mind?"

"No. The Aquarium reminded me of something, that's all."

"What?"

"I'll tell you later." Our meeting place also reminded me of the favor I never got around to asking for on Friday.

Her voice interrupted my thoughts. "Why are you so quiet?"

"I don't know," I lied, "just spacing out."

Her voice suddenly got harsh. "You better fucking show up." Before I could reply I heard the line go dead.

I felt impatient to get on with the day but the time limped by until I could reach Simon at work. I barely coughed before I got his, "Where the hell have you been? Are you working for me, or what?"

"I thought you were going to leave me alone and I was going to call you. Well, I'm calling."

His voice did a 180. "You have new information?"

"It sounds as though you had a rough weekend."

Simon sounded very far away. "I'm in Siberia again. Do you have something?"

"Not yet and probably never will. Why are you in the other room?"

"Her nightmares are getting worse and she's ashamed for me to see her like that." His voice was flat and empty of any emotion. I wondered if Fran was afraid of volunteering something she didn't want Simon to hear. Maybe her affairs were finally catching up with her.

Simon broke into my thoughts. "I know I'm supposed to keep my hands off, but are you working?"

"I didn't this weekend but I will this week. That's what I want to talk to you about." I was surprised at my honesty.

Simon's voice was strained. "Nothing over the weekend?"

"I was busy."

"Busy? With what, a house repair?"

"No. I spent some time with Boots. Why didn't you tell me about her sugar daddy?"

His voice lost a little of its bite. "What's to tell? He's old and harmless and she lives good. Does it matter?"

"Probably not. But what was all the matchmaking shit about?"

"I don't think Boots' friend poses an insurmountable obstacle."

"Think or hope?"

He chuckled. "Look, according to you, all this is irrelevant."

I knew what he wanted but I wasn't going to give it to him. "I just don't like surprises."

"Was it a good weekend?" He sounded curious. At least his annoyance was disappearing.

"Sure." No amount of reformation was going to make me completely honest.

"Great." I could hear the topic hit the floor. "You said you wanted to talk business, Matt man, what is it?"

I took a deep breath. "I want to talk money."

"Money?"

I took another breath. "Yeah. I need money for this work."

"I don't see the problem. Keep track and charge me."

"I want to charge more than our usual rate."

"Why?" He didn't sound antagonistic.

"Because I have to pay Charles to cover the house for me." The weekend had left me too aware of my tendency to exploit those around me. Mrs. Sullivan's quiet light was testimony that Charles had done enough unpaid labor. "The research work is different. I can set my own timetable. Now I don't have that luxury."

"It sure seems like you do."

I chuckled politely. "What do you charge an hour?"

His laugh sounded more genuine than mine. "Get serious. I'm not going to pay you that."

"Why not?"

"It's way too much."

The same thing Dr. James told me. Apparently professional identities come equipped with full commitment to financial superiority. "The usual is too little." I could feel myself grow stubborn unnecessarily.

"That I accept. It's the amount we're negotiating."

"Don't lawyer me, Simon. I don't want to negotiate. I don't have a clue about what a real private investigator makes. You would know that better than I."

"Why do you think I hire you?"

"Funny guy. I'm serious; what's the real going rate?" He named a figure higher than I had imagined. Maybe he did hire me to save money. If the rate he quoted was significantly less than what he made, Simon was pulling in a bundle. At least I didn't need to feel guilty about my request. "That seems okay to me if it is to you."

There was a moment's hesitation before he said, "I'm not worried about the money. That's fine, but I am worried about whether you'll do the work. Did you ask Boots if she could trace the car?"

"Simon, we had other things to discuss."

I thought he was going to get angry but he just laughed and said, "That's okay this time, but only this time." The laughter left his voice, "I want that information. Do you need any money up front?"

"No. I'll let you know."

He began to say something but I recognized what was coming and cut him off. "I will let you know if anything is worth knowing. But what's really going to happen is you'll pay more for the same results."

"You just do the work. That's what I'm paying for. I know you can't guarantee results." He stopped and let out a long sigh, "Jesus, Matt, sometimes I really miss the old days. Things seemed so much easier."

I kept bringing out the Sixties in Simon. "They weren't any easier, Simon, we just knew less."

I promised to keep in touch and we hung up. Two down, one to go. I expected the answering machine but got a human. "This is Dr. James, who's calling, please?"

"It's Matthew Jacob, Gloria. I'm calling to apologize for making an ass of myself on the phone the other night. I was wondering if we might have lunch?" Spontaneous me, I hadn't expected to ask her out.

"When are you thinking of?" She sounded amenable.

"I don't know. Today?" I certainly hadn't planned that.

"I can't make a regular lunch but I could do a late breakfast." She paused, then asked, "Isn't it a little early for you to be up?"

"You don't forget much, do you?"

"As you're quite aware."

For a moment I wasn't quite sure what my mouth had gotten me into. I pulled myself back into the conversation. "Sure, a late breakfast will be fine. Where and when?"

She told me and we rang off. I had an hour to kill. Plenty of time for a little dope and a chat with Charles.

—28—

⸻

"Somehow I never expected us to terminate in a pizzeria."

"Nor I. I'm much more comfortable sitting behind my desk working through a rehearsed treatment plan, but you insisted that we meet." She looked around the cafeteria, then returned her eyes to mine. "It seems a little late to rely on comfort."

"This wasn't what I had in mind when I suggested lunch." I checked my vital signs and, except for a lump of facsimile veal working in my belly, I felt numb but alive.

"What did you have in mind?"

I tried not to spill any of the red tomato sauce from the roll as I bit into my sub. "A couple of things became clear over the weekend. Especially my capacity to mistreat people. Like I said on the phone, I wanted to apologize for the way I sounded the other night."

Dr. James looked at me strangely. "What happened this weekend?"

"Nothing in particular. Look, I'm not saying termination is wrong, I'm just surprised that you beat me to the punch, that's all." I could hear the petulance in my voice.

Dr. James shrugged. "It's impossible to get you to be specific if you don't want to. I'm glad we're in a pizzeria; if we were in my office I'd feel compelled to work through your resistance."

Gloria might not be in her office but she hadn't left her jargon behind. "I don't know about my resistance, but my appetite is gone.

152

Anyway, now that we're terminating, you can be spared the bother."

"You were the one to initiate termination, Matthew.. My weekend was spent thinking and talking about our relationship. I discovered that you were right about ending our work, but that doesn't mean we can't talk."

"You spent the weekend with Holmes?" An unexpected moment of jealousy filtered through my sullen shock.

She looked startled. "I spent time talking with Eban, yes. I didn't consider it a betrayal of confidence. We spoke mostly about me."

"That's nice." The image of the two of them huddled discussing my therapeutic fate flashed before me.

"I don't understand your annoyance about terminating or my discussions with Eban. You weren't reticent when the three of us met."

I pushed the tray with my half-eaten sub to the side of the table, felt exposed, and pulled it back. "I'm not sure I understand it either." Some feeling was returning to my body, and I realized that my panic might not last indefinitely. "A lot has happened in a short amount of time."

She nodded. "A lot *has* happened, but the time hasn't been all that short."

"What do you mean?" As the numbness faded I found myself becoming curious about what she had to say.

Gloria took a deep breath and plunged into her words. "When we first met you were unable to see beyond your self-pity and rage. You were either violently self-loathing or completely despondent. There was no middle ground. My work was to help you create that middle." Her voice was tense but her eyes resolute. "I thought I did a good job."

"So did I."

She waved off my interruption. "Until the past year, that is, when I found myself frustrated by your passivity." A small tight smile flashed across her face. "Like every good therapist I blamed my frustration on you. You were no longer out of control or immobilized by depression; why wouldn't you take the next step? Why weren't you even thinking about something more creative than managing a building?"

"So you did use the burglaries as work therapy?"

"Not consciously." She played with the salad in front of her.

"But I was right. Conscious or not, it was therapy."

"It's not that simple. Some of my motivation certainly had to do with your passivity, most was due to my frustration. Also the break-ins really worried me. I didn't lie to you about that."

"I thought your frustration was about my passivity."

"My frustration was an unfair projection. It isn't your passivity that's been the problem, it's my attraction to the intensity you brought with you when we first met. Heaping expectations onto a client can't be considered good work. If you are going to be angry you might as well start there."

There was something about Dr. James' vulnerability, however discrete, that shattered my hostility. I leaned back in my chair, rubbed my face, and spoke through my hands. "The truth is I'm not angry at you, especially about our work. I'm scared. Now that it's official, I'm scared."

She shook her head ruefully. "What I'm saying probably just makes it more difficult for you, but it's too late for me to cloak honesty under a veneer of professionalism."

I smiled. Although my anger and fear were disappearing, the sub still felt like a cannonball in my gut. "That last part sounds straight out of 'the world according to Eban Holmes.' "

Gloria wasn't finished being earnest. "In most instances it is Eban. This time it's me. I'm trying hard not to hide from myself and I don't want to fabricate to you. I haven't had so many crises like this one not to realize its importance."

I leaned forward and spoke through the noise of the burgeoning lunchtime crowd. I tried to match her honesty. "You might have been attracted to the intensity that originally walked into your office, but I couldn't live with it. At least not the way it was. My insides were on fire and I was consumed by what I saw as the injustice of my entire life. The fight with the bartender was suicidal. Even I could recognize that. I don't know how, but you pulled me out of it."

I looked at her. Lines of worry tugged at her eyes. She had pushed her salad to the side, creating an ocean of formica for me to cross.

"Regardless of my fears I think I'm ready to do without therapy. How many times have you reminded me that fears aren't the same as reality? If I'm wrong, I'll find another shrink; hell, the town's filthy with 'em. I bitched and moaned all during our work together.

But the truth is you've given me gifts I'll never be able to repay."

There was a tinge of rose on her cheeks. "Gifts?"

"Gifts. I've had a long, sorry set of relationships with women—even the good one turned into a disaster. You and me worked. Beginning, middle and end. Yeah, I'm shocked by the suddenness, the suddenness of everything these days, and I might even get angry again later about this. But I want you to know that you saved my ass when we first met, and your unconscious may have done it again."

"My unconscious?"

"The work therapy. The case has put me on my feet. That's some of why I wanted to meet. To tell you."

"The case has gotten you beaten up."

"Since my body has stopped hurting it seems like a small price. I'm not going to become another Sam Spade, but there's something about this sort of puzzle I enjoy. There is a niche here, some kind of crack I may fit into. No matter how I've acted or what I've said, pulling me into it has been good."

"You sound so sure. I know it's the right thing, but a part of me sits here wondering what the hell I'm doing. I'm still terribly worried about your drug usage. Only I don't think there is anything I can do about it." She looked around the room and lifted her arms in a gesture of helplessness.

I nodded at the remains of our lunch. "You could have picked a greasy spoon with better food. Look, I'm not a junkie but you're right, there's nothing you can do about it. Maybe since our counseling relationship is officially over, it will be easier to trust what we say to each other. At least the case will go smoother."

She started to reply but stopped. Some of the anxiety seemed to clear from her eyes. "Do you really think there is a case? I've been so focused on our therapy that the burglaries seem almost beside the point."

"That's the weak link in psychotherapy. Yes Virginia, there is a real world. Of course I think there is a case. My body might not hurt but it remembers."

"You're still concerned that I might be involved though other doctors' records were also taken?"

"I believe it's a good possibility."

"Eban said you would think that."

"It's nice to know that all three of us agree. So it's clear about my continuing?"

Gloria nodded.

"Good, but I want to be paid."

"I have no idea what a private investigator makes. We went through that once before."

"You won't feel so happy when I tell you."

"Try me." Her relief was evident. She hadn't even tried to dissuade me from pursuing the break-ins. I didn't want to guess about her motivations. I thought of the figure that Simon quoted and gave her a number that was considerably less. There was no complaint and for a moment I wondered why I lied about the price. Then I realized I didn't want to question my motivation either.

29

I sat in the car smoking a cigarette while I thought about the conversation with Gloria. I felt stirred but not shaken. Although plenty of ambiguity remained, the animosity I usually experienced after a Thursday session was absent. I was oddly satisfied though a little lonely.

The satisfaction lessened and the loneliness grew when I looked at my watch and focused on my next piece of business. I pulled a joint from the ashtray and smoked, but the call of my living room couch grew insistent so I stubbed the dope out. In no rush to move, I still wasn't ready to retreat.

I got to the Aquarium in time to see Fran's shock of blonde hair blowing in the ocean breeze as she walked the ramp onto the dolphin boat. I quickly crossed the courtyard to the ticket booth and knelt to avoid being seen if she should suddenly turn around. The ticket collector admonished me to stop holding up the line. It pissed me off because there was no one behind me, so I untied my shoe and stayed hunched over until I felt too stupid to continue. I stood, apologized, and bought a ticket. I hung around the huge glass doors of the main building until there was a cluster of people at the kiosk, gritted my teeth, and ambled over to the boat. I didn't have my gun, regretted it, but no one stopped me so there was no call to shoot.

Everything here seemed the same as last week except me. New

insights didn't improve my vision any, and I cracked my skull against an unexpected girder. I gave myself a moment—no blood or sounds of anyone running to investigate the noise. Cautiously, I felt my way over to the door I had used last week and nudged it open.

It was no wonder I hadn't remembered the girder. I was nowhere close to where I thought I was. Instead of being across the auditorium, I was about a dozen rows behind Fran and friend. I had planned to get closer than last time but not this close.

After my heart quieted and the hammer in my head eased into a dull ache, I was rewarded with the eternal truth of trade-offs. While I couldn't see faces, if I controlled my anxiety I could clearly hear what they were saying.

Twenty minutes later I prayed my way back outside. I was relieved to find my illegally parked car ticketed but untowed. I left the red swatch on the windshield and slid inside, smoking a cigarette and thinking about what I'd heard. Fran had solved Simon's case herself. She had apparently reached the same conclusion I had about her troubles. Although she never mentioned nightmares, she told her friend she "couldn't handle it" enough times for the message to sink a piling into the harbor. Which it hadn't by the time I left. The guy didn't sound big and bad so learning his identity seemed like a needless precaution, but I had plenty of time to kill before meeting Boots. Plus, it would neatly round off my pay from Simon, though he wasn't going to get an itemized bill.

I had a feeling the nightmares were soon to be history.

Ten more minutes passed before I saw Fran on the boat's platform. I watched as she threaded through the line of people waiting on the ramp for the show. She crossed the courtyard toward the parking garage and out of my line of vision. I kept shifting my eyes toward the top of the ramp and the garage until Fran's Mercedes pulled up to the attendant's booth. I watched long enough to make sure she wasn't going to drive in my direction, then returned my attention to the boat.

A man with the general appearance of Fran's lover slipped onto the ramp as the waiting crowd surged forward. I still couldn't get a decent look so I hopped out of the car and hurried across the street. Halfway there I glanced toward the garage and saw the rear of a cream-colored

Lincoln heading in the same direction as Fran. I thought about returning to my car to give chase. As a motorist blasted his horn at my indecision I realized I'd never catch the Lincoln, so I ran the rest of the way to the Aquarium's main door. It was too late to remain unobtrusive.

It was too late, period. My man was nowhere to be seen. I stomped back to the car, got in and slammed the door before I saw the second ticket on the window. I jumped out, grabbed those red fuckers, and ripped the shit out of them. Too late I noticed a meter maid three cars up staring at me strangely.

I stood there with the shredded tickets in my hand while she walked briskly toward me.

"Not only am I going to rewrite each of your tickets, but I'm going to give you a third for ripping up the other two." She looked pointedly at my hand. "And, if I see one scrap of those tickets on the street, I'm going to cite you for littering."

I ground my teeth. "What do I get for more than one scrap?" and opened my hand wide as the garbage floated south.

I found out when I added the numbers on the red slips after I parked in a legal spot about three yards from where I'd been. I stared at the tickets. I was going to do the last work on Simon's case for the city.

I sat in the car and stewed. I wanted the rest of the joint but was afraid the meter maid was hiding behind a nearby parked car. I looked around and surreptitiously lit the joint. Still nervous about the fucking meter maid, I took a couple of quick hits and stubbed it out. I finally let some of my mad go. I couldn't find the Lincoln now anyway, but I was still too pissed to check on Fran's beef.

It took a while but I managed to shake enough change for dollars from passersby to replenish the sinking parking needle. I had plenty of time before meeting Boots and, without thinking, began to walk toward the North End.

As I strode up Commercial toward Hanover, years of reading about the city's development leaped off the printed page. If you liked big buildings and brick plazas and renovated piers, the city was big-time. Personally, I missed the dowdiness. I marched into the heart of the North End, thought about eating, but settled on groceries instead. I walked into a hole-in-the-wall pasta store for fresh noodles and home-made pesto. I bought enough for two. It didn't take a weatherman to guess what was blowing around my brain.

I killed the remaining time in a bar drinking Becks' Dark and watching well-dressed men and women relate. They worked hard at it. It was something that apparently didn't come easy to anyone. I luxuriated in my generosity. Eventually I looked at the clock behind the bar and confirmed the bad news with my watch. I paid for the beer, gathered my bundles, and walked outside into the afternoon sunlight. It took a moment for my eyes to adjust, then I hustled to the car and stashed the groceries.

The concrete and brick courtyard in front of the Aquarium was swarming with people. I angled over to the harbor seals and sat on the lip of the viewing wall. Although there were plenty of families milling about, the area seemed like an outdoor convention for midtown business people. I turned my head and watched a seal lying on its back catching rays. I wasn't absolutely sure but I thought it winked. I looked back into the crowd and worried about missing Boots.

I didn't notice anything until I felt a hand on my shoulder. "You were early."

I looked up but was blinded by the sun. "Can you move around to this side? I can't see shit this way."

"Were you intending to stay?"

I stood up. "Where would you like to go?"

I felt rather than saw her move away. I rushed to catch up before she melded with the crowd. Something was telling me this wasn't going to be an easy conversation. I followed her out the concourse and down the street to a red brick building. She walked purposefully through the door and led us into a large bar with a number of rooms. She grabbed my hand and pulled me toward one in the back.

"Hurry, I see something open." She skillfully sliced her way through the jostling crowd as I tried to keep up. Although she wasn't a drop-your-jaw looker, she garnered a fair share of male appreciation. I didn't feel nearly as accepting of humanity's struggle to relate as I had in the first bar. I kept my eyes straight ahead and followed. It wasn't until we were in our seats—two small easy chairs intimately connected by a small wooden table—that I really saw my surroundings.

I was in the belly of the whale. Not one workshirt or pair of dungarees. The closest thing I saw to informality was a blazer. "I'm not going to pass the dress code."

"They don't have one."

I nodded toward the rest of the room. "You mean they dress like this voluntarily?"

"Who do you think you're sitting with, a prisoner?"

I waved for the waitress. This morning's speeches seemed far away. And Boots wasn't bringing them any closer. I ordered German, she ordered tonic with a twist of lime. We waited quietly until the waitress returned with our order. The crowd of people in the room seemed to fade as I grew used to the decibel level and I began to focus on the woman I had abused the other night.

— 30 —

"You wanted to talk, so talk." Her voice was brittle and her lips were drawn in a tight line across her face.

I took a long swallow of my beer and lit a cigarette. "I don't blame you for being hostile. I don't imagine it makes much of a difference, but I'm ashamed of my behavior the other night. Not just the, the physical stuff. I'm pretty embarrassed about choosing Amalfi's to meet."

"And why is that?" Her voice challenged, but her eyes showed interest.

"Too close to the crap of a couple of years ago."

"So why do you do it?"

I finished my drink and waved for another. She hadn't touched hers.

"I don't have any single answer. Somehow treating me decent was something to take advantage of. I seem to have trouble belonging to clubs that'll take me."

She drank from her glass. "Give me one of your cigarettes, will you?"

I lit and handed her one.

"You think you took advantage of me the other night?"

I offered a grim smile. "What would you call it? I had an explosion coming for a hell of a long time and I had just enough balls to explode on you. Not exactly what I'd call 'real man' material."

She started to say something and I leaned over and put my finger on her lips. "Wait a second." I was gratified that she didn't pull away from my touch. I took a deep breath and willed myself to keep talking. "I spent the rest of the weekend full of hate. During the day I hated myself, at night, everyone else. But, at no time over the weekend did I hate you."

Her eyes flashed the rest of the way alive. "Why should you? We did Friday night."

I shook my head. "I don't hate you, Boots, never have. I hated me and couldn't stand the fact that you didn't." I felt my words starting to run out. "I don't know, I don't have any brilliant interpretations about Friday night. I'm just sorry. You've always been good to me and I've always been rotten to you. I'm just sorry about it."

All the words from this morning were gone. I felt stripped down to my beer and cigarettes. I couldn't explain myself to anyone else; I couldn't explain myself to me.

I heard her voice and looked up. Much of the tautness was gone from her face. "You didn't take any more advantage of me Friday night than I took of you. You weren't there by yourself. This idea that you weren't some sort of 'real man' the other night is part of the bullshit. You were as real as it gets. And so was I. You didn't control what happened, we agreed. I put my face where it met your hand; to think otherwise is macho bullshit."

I watched as she picked at the cigarette's filter with her free hand. After a moment she stopped and looked back at me and continued, "Toward the end of our relationship I realized that your backhanded treatment of me was a turn-on. Your hostility attracted me. In that respect you were right about the slumming, though not because of class. You were a piece of me I wouldn't admit to. I stopped seeing you because I fell in love with you, but I was beginning to despise myself."

She smiled and touched my hand. "I didn't come here expecting to say this, but you've been so damn honest. I had planned to take the self-righteous high road. To make you pay."

She stubbed her cigarette hard into the ashtray. "I wanted us to be together like that. I wanted it like that since we met."

Her eyes narrowed and grew hard. "Wanted it. Past tense. No more losers, no more abusers for me." She smiled again, only a bit more ruefully. "If we're different as a result of Friday, maybe we ought to thank each other."

The rest of the people in the bar had long since disappeared. There were just the two of us. Or maybe just her. "What's the matter with us, Boots? It's not as if we're bimbos."

She finished her drink. I lit two more cigarettes and passed her one. She took a deep drag, "You once told me that people play the hands they're dealt. I guess we're helping each other see our cards."

"I'm not sure I like what I see."

"You never did."

"Then I couldn't see the cards. Now I can."

She grinned, waved to the waitress, and signaled for the check. "It's a start."

"I wish I knew to what."

She didn't say anything and, as we sat there, the room began to slowly reemerge. I leaned forward. "Where does all of this leave us?"

She looked at me and shook her head. "Sometimes you really surprise me. That's the last question I imagined you would ask." She pushed her half-smoked cigarette into the ashtray and sucked on the ice in her glass. "Give me another one, will you?"

I lit one and handed it to her. On my way I pushed the still smoldering cigarette deeper into the ashtray.

"I don't know where this leaves us, Matt. I don't have many friends."

Before I could think of what to say I heard words pop out of my mouth. "Well, what about sex?" My voice dropped with the last word. It didn't matter; she heard.

Her eyes widened and she burst out laughing, "I'm sorry, I'm not laughing at you, you're just amazing today. I don't know any more about sex than you do. Less, if our last encounter is any indication."

Her attitude about Friday was a relief. I felt my cheeks grow hot. "I didn't mean that, exactly. I, uh, meant . . ."

"I know what you meant and I don't know. We'll see what happens. If we are going to be friends we'll talk things over. We'll wait and see."

The operative word was wait. I decided to forego my dinner invitation, I felt disappointed and relieved. "Can I ask a favor?"

"Why not?"

"It's a work thing. I'm not sure what your job is exactly, but Simon thinks you can trace things."

"Are you kidding? I'm Ma Bell. Information Ma can't get isn't worth having."

"I have a partial license plate I need matched with a cream-colored Lincoln. I want the name and address."

"A day."

I fished what I had out of my head, told her and added, "It'd be a real help to have it."

"You're doing repo work?"

I laughed. "No. Nothing like that."

The bill came but we ignored it. "What then?" she teased. "You have to give some information to get some. Anyway, why didn't you just have Simon check? He certainly can."

"I don't want him involved. This is a tricky situation."

"Don't tell me you care about confidentiality. Not when you ask me to jack into the matrix."

"What the hell is 'jack into the matrix'?"

She tossed her head. "It's information mining. What's this about?"

"I'm not sure you really want to know."

"You don't want Simon involved and now you're protecting me?"

"Maybe you should be the detective."

My words fell on deaf ears. Boots was staring straight ahead. I knew I was back in focus. "This has something to do with Fran. That's what you were doing at that building? You were following her?" Tension and suspicion filled her voice. "Whatever you are working on better not hurt her. She is one of the few real friends I have."

I thought about denying it all. Telling her that her imagination was overheating. Or relating the car to Dr. James' case. But I had been too honest for too much of the day; it was a variation of Newton's third law. "I'm not trying to hurt her. That's why I don't want Simon involved. The trace is an attempt to get Simon to stop prying into Fran's private life. Nothing else."

She looked into me. "You know about her affairs, don't you?"

I nodded. "I know about one."

She didn't blink. "What's this about?"

I told her. I suppose I wanted to. It was a relief to talk about it with someone other than Simon. Someone I didn't have to lie to. She changed her order to rum and coke and we added a couple more drinks to the tallied check as I detailed Simon's request and my thinking. I didn't leave anything out. I even managed to weave in the James case. By the time I finished she had smoked more of my cigarettes and I was feeling lighter. It was in moments like these I appreciated the rite of confession.

Unfortunately my relief was short-lived. I hoped Catholics had it better. She slowly shook her head. "I don't buy it."

"Of course not. Simon's idea was crazy from the jump."

"I don't mean Simon's idea. I just don't believe that Fran's affairs have very much to do with her problem."

"Nightmares."

"I think it's more than nightmares."

"You sound like Simon."

"So what? Maybe he's onto something."

I didn't buy that. "Do you know anything about her dreams?" For a moment I felt like a gossip. I had to remind myself that this was work.

"She won't tell me."

I still thought the reason for her problem wore pants. "I don't see why you are so sure the pressure from her affair"—I wasn't comfortable surrendering to the plural—"couldn't be the reason for her breakdown."

"It isn't a breakdown." Boots' voice flared with protective anger.

I moved my fingers in a gesture of peace. "Could Fran be pregnant?"

"I don't know. It's not something she'd tell me. But even if she were I don't think it would get to her like this."

I shrugged. "If it means anything, Alex agrees with you."

She took a deep breath, tucked her head into her shoulders, and leaned forward. "How close did you get to the guy Fran is seeing?"

"Pretty close."

She bobbed her head upward. "God, I feel like a shit talking this way. What did you think of him?"

"Not much. Why?"

"If you know Fran it's obvious. I don't even know which one you saw, but no guy she sleeps with is much. They're a tension release, not a cause for concern. None of them has the capacity to cause her any anxiety. That's how she picks them."

I felt uncomfortable about Boots' attitude. "You seem pretty confident about Fran's judgment. It seems possible that she could have made a mistake along the way."

"Her judgment about anything else might be questionable, not men." Boots shook her head in her characteristic manner and grinned. "Some of us don't travel blind when it comes to sex."

I lifted my bottle in her direction, then took a swallow. "If her act is so together why is she breaking it off? How long has she been doing this to become so good at it?"

I caught Boots eyeing me with a mixture of annoyance and pity. "This bothers you, doesn't it?"

"Not in the abstract, but Simon is my friend."

"Does my relationship with Hal bother you?"

"Hal?"

"The man who pays my rent."

"Some," I admitted.

She kept her eyes on me until I grew uncomfortable. "Maybe you're the one who needs protection?"

"I don't do so good with mothers." I kept talking through my discomfort. "I never thought Fran was getting any real harassment, just bothered by her guilt."

"That's what she says."

"You don't believe it?"

"No I don't. I'm not saying there's no connection, only that guilt about affairs isn't causing this amount of panic."

I wondered whether her certainty had more to do with herself than Fran. "How can you be so sure?"

"Intuition."

"Well, we'll see. If I'm right we may have to question your intuition."

"Don't patronize. My intuition has been plenty right about our relationship."

I smiled and raised my arms in mock surrender. "Okay, okay." I began to gather the social debris strewn on the table. "Are you going to help with the license plate?"

She stood and looked at me with surprise. "Don't worry, I'll get your information."

I rose and left plenty of money to cover a revised bill and tip, followed her through the thinning crowd to the door, and stepped outside. I was surprised to see it was dark into the evening.

We stood outside the doorway and talked. "Since I opened a possibility in Simon's mind, I want to close it down. Also, at this point I'm curious."

She took my hand and walked toward the trains. "It's nice to hear about your curiosity."

I shrugged and matched her pace. "You don't need to take the train, I'll drive you home."

"No thanks. Was it your curiosity that got you beaten up?" We were standing at the top of the subway station steps.

"Not mine, my client's. Why won't you let me take you home?" I paused. "A friend thing."

She started down the stairs and I watched as she turned back toward me and held the rail as a train shook the station below. She had a wide grin stretched across her face and she had to shout to make herself heard above the sound. "If I stay with you for another ten minutes I'll want to be best friends and neither of us is ready for that."

She blew me a kiss which I caught. I stood watching until she disappeared into the station. I lit a cigarette and strolled back to my car relaxed and pleasantly hungry. Relaxed, that is, until I saw my windshield. I couldn't believe it. I pulled the red ticket out from under the wiper to decipher the coded violation and a small scrap of paper fell onto the hood. I picked it up, read it, then stuffed it and the ticket into my pocket. I opened the car, got in, and started home. I didn't even feel angry. Just deflated. The note read, "For the hell of it."

—31—

I had originally planned to see Julie when I got home, but convinced myself I was too hungry to spare the time. After I unloaded the groceries I was too lethargic to cook. There was no going back outside, which left corn chips, dope, nicotine, and alcohol for supper; the day had taken more out of me than I realized.

The last thing I remember watching was *Honeymooner* reruns. What I really remember was how frightened I became when I awoke to someone picking the lock. A legacy from the beating. I jumped to remember where I had left my gun, while part of my head told me to relax, it was probably Julie. Another part urged me to off the white noise coming from the TV. Instead, my body just protested the position I had slept in and the speed which which I had yanked it vertical. When the door opened I was sitting back down expecting the worst. I was able to reach the remote control, but Julius was inside before I used it. Quick-draw Jacob.

Julie looked slowly around the room, then moved to the chair across from me. I nodded toward the smorgasbord on the coffee table.

"No thanks." He made a face at my dinner. "You eating like a drugged-out Rockford." He motioned toward the test pattern, "If you're watching that, then you're watching too much television."

"Thanks for the advice, Dad." I touched the switch on the remote and the light and white noise disappeared. We were left sitting in the dark. I put the tube back on and hit the mute. "What time is it?"

"Three-thirty."

I rubbed my eyes and pulled at my twisted tee shirt. "What the hell do you do this time of night? The damn town closes at two and you're not a night watchman."

"What you see is what you get, Sonny."

"I don't see anything. That's why I'm asking."

He just grunted and reached across for my pack of cigarettes. After he finished lighting his, I lit one for myself. I had a little trouble lining up the flame with the end of the cigarette. I hadn't fully digested dinner.

Julius watched quietly until I finished my act. "Sometimes you are a sad case. You be smart to stop using your head for a toilet."

I waited for more lecture, but he just sat there smoking. I grew impatient, he hadn't broken in to hand out gratuitous advice. "You found something out?"

He raised his eyebrows. "Yes."

"You going to tell me?"

"Rather not."

I waited for my usual knots of foreboding but there were none. My system was working too hard to stay awake to have room for much else. I suppose I should have been grateful. "You didn't truck in here to bum a smoke."

"Slumlord, you are involved with a pair of very big balls. The Irish one could be any one of a hundred, but the black works for the Man."

"What's new? I figured they were cops."

"The black's name is Washington Clifford and he works on the Commissioner's Squad. That's different than working for the police." He sat deeper in the chair.

I felt confused. "What do you mean 'Commissioner's Squad'? I never heard of it. Is it a special unit?"

"Nothing official. Just a few very special Blues who work for the Chief. Won't find it written anywhere. Especially official."

Michael Devlin had been Police Chief for as far back as I could remember. Like they say, "Men live and die, but institutions try to last forever." About Devlin it was said with equal amounts of affection and hate. But ties go to the incumbent and no recent mayor had the clout to remove him.

"I'm in the shit with this unofficial posse that works for Devlin? What's he need them for?"

"Don't know who you are in trouble with. I only know that Clifford was the man who slapped you around and he works for the Chief. The Man has 'em to help him stay the Man."

"The whole idea of a secret squad seems pretty amazing."

He heard my disbelief because he sat forward, opened his eyes and let them glitter for a moment before he lowered his lids down to their usual half-mast. "You best believe, slumlord. All cities have their version. If you doubt me ask your father-in-law about the Red Squad in Chi-town."

"How do you know about Chicago?"

"I did some time there."

I knew better than to ask what kind of time. "What else should I know?"

Julius was almost out the door before he answered, "You should know enough to close down your operation."

I was left sitting on the couch watching a soundless test pattern. Questions swarmed in my mind but I wasn't coherent enough to clarify them. I thought about flicking the remote to see what was on, but Julie was right about watching too much television. I turned it off and lay back down on the couch. Supper was still working so sleep returned, only this time it wasn't the sleep of the dead, it was the sleep of the anxious.

I was relieved as my eyes opened to scraps of morning light. The feeling passed quickly, however, when I remembered Julie's visit. I couldn't imagine why the Commissioner or his office might be interested in the burglaries or in me. Of course Clifford might be freelancing. Somehow that idea made me feel better.

Despite my body's protests I tried to get organized. I had poured more inebriants into the infrastructure than I had realized, and three aspirin didn't even rip the cotton in my head. I took two more and hoped for the best. I didn't want to spend the day rewiring.

The pills helped and the coffee helped. I considered working out but that thought didn't help. I rolled a slim joint instead. At least it cured some of the trembling. I decided to find out more about Washington Clifford, so I looked up Alex Hirsh's office number and smoked and read the paper until I could call. When I did I was surprised to be put through without a third degree.

"Matthew, Alex here. What can I do for you?" His voice seemed friendly, if a little distant.

"I'm sorry to disturb you but I have a big favor to ask."

"No disturbance at all. What's the request?"

"There were robberies in Fran's doctor's building and I've been trying to tie something together."

"How did you become involved with that?"

"It's a long story, but I thought since there was a loose connection to Fran you might be willing to help."

"Quite a loose connection, Matthew. What can I do to help?"

"There is a rumor that the Police Commissioner has an unofficial unit working just for him. Supposedly one of the guys who paid me an unfriendly visit is on it. I want to find out what's going on and I know that you know the Chief so I thought . . ."

"That I could speak to him about it."

"Something like that."

"I heard about your beating from Simon. I wondered about the sunglasses the other night. I hope it wasn't too serious. However, the rumor about a private unit is unfounded. It's terribly difficult for people to imagine that someone could be as powerful as Michael, for so many years, without some nefarious method. These rumors have been around for a long while. I can assure you the information is totally inaccurate."

I didn't know if it was stubbornness or loyalty but, despite Alex's assurances, I still believed Julie. Alex was sincere, just wrong. That is, probably wrong.

"I'm sure you're right, Alex, but I wonder if I might ask you the favor anyway. I have a name to go with the animal who visited me and I hoped you might set up a meeting between me and Devlin to ask about him."

"What's the name that you have?"

I didn't think there was any harm in telling him. "Washington Clifford."

"I never heard of him."

"I didn't think you had. That's why I want to talk to Devlin."

There was a long pause. "I don't think he'll meet with you, Matthew. Certainly not to talk about a working policeman."

"Couldn't try, huh?"

"This beating is what you are interested in?"

"Very. I also want to know why the police, or at least this Clifford, want to protect whoever keeps breaking into that building."

"This is very confusing. What makes you think it was the police?"

"Sources."

There was another long pause. "Sources?" Alex sounded dubious. "I'll need more information than that if I'm going to talk to Michael."

I understood his dilemma but I wasn't going to compromise Julie. I didn't care if Alex and Devlin slept together, I didn't trust any cop with a name.

"Alex, I understand your position and appreciate your willingness to go out of your way, but I can't do that. If I start naming names, I won't get another case."

He chuckled. "Protecting your sources, eh? Perhaps you've been watching too much television. I thought you were a researcher, not a detective."

"Right now I don't know what I am; I just want information about the beating." I remembered last night and smiled to myself. "My friends have warned me about TV, you can join the line."

"Perhaps you should listen to your friends." He sounded grim. "Well, Matthew, if I have an opportunity to approach Michael informally and do find anything out, I will let you know. You have no idea why this Clifford beat you up?"

"Only what he said. He wants me to stay away from the burglaries I told you about."

"And you don't want to?"

"I don't now."

"I see."

There was more silence as he thought about what I said. Just when it seemed like he was no longer there his voice boomed into my ear, "I thought you were going to end Simon's suspicions about that kid with the car. When I last spoke to him he was still hanging on to your story." He emphasized his last two words.

"To tell you the truth, I was going to, only I caught another glimpse of him and he might have been following Fran. I thought I'd check for the hell of it."

"Why are you still following Fran? I thought we both agreed it was a waste of time?" He was starting to sound angry and I didn't want to give it an opportunity to gain momentum.

"Wait a second, Alex. I was closing out the job, that's all. I actually believe her nightmares are about to end."

"Why is that, Matthew?" He had regained his composure.

"She's stopped seeing her friend."

"So why are you still chasing that young man?"

You would think he might have shown some relief about my information. I suppose he shared Boots' opinion. "I'm not, he just bothers me."

"You seem to grow obsessed when things bother you."

His words annoyed me. Maybe because they were true. "I wouldn't exactly call it an obsession, Alex. You seem more concerned about Simon's hopes than Fran's nightmares."

"I think it's time to get Simon's feet back on the ground, don't you? If I offended you by the use of the word 'obsession,' I apologize." His voice held out an olive branch.

I was still riled but took it. "You're right. I was out of line, I'm sorry."

"No apology is necessary. We are both under considerable stress. I am concerned about my daughter, Matthew, but her demons reside in a world I can't influence. I deal in reality and the reality is that Simon has to stop chasing a dream. He must be prepared to come to grips with the situation. To take over my work. His marriage needs attention, and he's not going to face that by hiring you."

I realized it was too late for Alex to groom anyone else. That meant going with Simon, whether he was a son-in-law or not. Alex wanted to be spared the "or not." I'd bet rent he knew something about their marriage I didn't. I thought about asking, then came to my senses. My nosing around in Simon and Fran's marriage was over. Almost.

"I think you're right, Alex, and I will shut the door."

"Thank you, Matthew. If there is some information that might be helpful in regard to the other situation I will let you know, but please keep in mind what I said earlier. This has no connection to Fran, and I know the information about Michael's private police is false."

"Maybe so, Alex, maybe so, but I appreciate the help."

32

I poured myself more coffee and lit a cigarette. Everyone watched their own goddamn ass. Alex was a father who seemed more concerned about his successor than his daughter's mental health. I wondered whether mortality made that inevitable and, in a perverse way, was almost glad my own daughter hadn't lived long enough for me to find out.

But Alex didn't deal in reality, he dealt in deals. Somehow, he and I had just cut another one. The unspoken sense of commitment that lingered after a conversation with him must work pretty well with honorable men; me, I was impatient for Boots' call so I could track the damn kid down.

I shook myself out of the kitchen and upstairs to Mrs. S. Cold coffee wasn't making it; maybe tea would help my hangover and impatience.

It did, at least for a while. Charles joined us, catching me up on news of the house. Although they questioned me thoroughly, little remained of my prior hero status. I got the distinct impression they thought there were no real cases. If I hadn't a few leftover aches and pains I might have thought the same. As it was, by the time I wrote some checks, the cotton returned, only this time with a thrasher; I needed more grass.

I stayed clear of the couch and settled into the easy chair. That lasted long enough to roll a joint. I smoked and prowled around the apartment. Meeting with Charles and Mrs. Sullivan had been unsettling. Not them, actually; more my disinterest with the building and its goings-on. A couple of weeks ago it had been my entire life.

The dope changed the rhythm of my pacing, but was no help settling me down. It had been a long time since I'd waited for a call.

Somewhere between the walking and the ring of the telephone I had fallen asleep. I jolted awake, fought off a chocolate lust, and lunged for the phone. Praise the lord for machine memory.

"I'm here. Don't hang up, please." Where were my fucking cigarettes?

"Who is this?" A hoarse, scratchy man's voice parted my hair.

"Matt Jacob. Who is this?"

"The wrong goddamn number."

I couldn't put the phone down. I pulled the dead receiver into the kitchen where I retrieved my cigarettes, and looked through the drawer until I found Boots' card.

"Elizabeth Stuart. Who's calling?"

"How is it that a VIP answers her own phone? I forgot to ask you yesterday."

She chuckled. "Something everybody asks and always remembers. Did you call to learn about my meteoric rise to the top or is there some ulterior motive behind your newfound initiative?"

"Funny lady. Is this Ma Bell's new advertising campaign? A happy worker is a productive worker? Or does your office use nitrous oxide," I glanced at the clock and read 2 P.M., "for a mid-afternoon break?"

"Actually, I'm happy you called. Are you home?"

"Yes."

"Well sit tight and I'll call you back in a couple of minutes."

What choice? "Okay." I must have sounded disappointed.

"I'll explain when I call."

By the time she called she didn't need to explain. "Are you in a pay phone?"

"Yes."

"So it's a little like, 'Who's making love to your old lady while you're out making love?' "

"I suppose, though the analogy makes me think you have more than one ulterior motive. You do want the name and the address?"

"Right. And you wanted to be out of the building when you told me."

"Right, we work well together, don't we?"

"You just stepped on my line."

"Fuck you," she said with a slight giggle. "Here it is." Name and address. "Actually not much information. Must be a newcomer to our wonderful state. I could play computer games and trace interstate, but since the breakup there is much less professional courtesy. It would probably take a couple of days and I thought you wanted this sooner."

"Boots, this is mindblowing. Are you sure it's the right car?"

"Only Lincoln in town with the number and letter you gave me."

"Christ, you're not even Government."

"It would have taken the government six weeks to get this," she said sarcastically. "Do you want me to work on their schedule?"

"Of course not. I don't know if I'll need more, can I let you know?"

"Of course."

I wrote the name and address she gave me on the back of an envelope. "You don't mind doing this?"

"I'm not the one fretting about Big Brother, am I?"

"Thanks, Boots. When do you want to go out?"

"I don't know my time yet. Call me in a couple of days."

I resisted an urge to ask who made her schedule. It would be mean and she'd just finished doing me a favor. Also, I didn't want to confirm what I suspected.

I put the phone down and looked at the envelope. Joe Starring, 27 Gardner, 555-3449. I pulled a map out of my junk drawer and looked up Gardner. It was in Brighton, right behind Brighton Avenue. I wouldn't have any difficulty finding it.

If I wanted to. Faced with actually finding this kid, the uselessness of my interest struck me. There was no reason to track him down. I stuffed the envelope in my pocket and trudged around the house

gathering my stuff. I felt especially foolish when I strapped on the
gun and slipped into a loose-fitting sports jacket. If it hadn't been for
the image of his car driving in the same direction as Fran's, I probably
would have dropped the whole thing there and then. But he did and
I couldn't, so I stopped thinking and called the number on the envelope. No answer. I had stepped out the door into the alley when I
remembered the lock pick. When I went back inside I put my dope
away. If I ended up busted, I might as well make it as easy for Simon
as I could.

33

Despite the angry gray clouds that served as the city's late afternoon ceiling, there was still light when I got to Gardner Street. I drove around the block to let my nerves settle. I was planning to break into a stranger's apartment for no reason other than my own curiosity. I couldn't stop smiling. It seemed like the best idea I'd had in years. I kept driving; if I did run into trouble I didn't want to be caught laughing.

I found a deserted parking lot tucked across the street and down the block from the apartment building that housed my mysterious Mr. Starring. The lot could be used as a cut-through to Brighton Avenue. I was having fantasies about quick getaways.

The building itself was plug-ugly. Patched onto a block of tree-shaded converted three-flats, it was an imitation red brick lowrider, containing maybe twenty or twenty-five units. Not garish or terribly overbearing, just ugly. The bleached red clashed with the three double-sized orange dumpsters hulking at the building's side. I drove past one last time and parked in the lot. I lit another cigarette and stayed in the car until I finished. I didn't intend to leave a butt in the kid's ashtray.

When I left the car I debated locking it. If I needed to leave rapidly, it would help to have the door unlocked. On the other hand, it would be nice to have the car there, period. Since it was a "Live free or die," day, I left the door unlocked and walked expeditiously toward the building. I didn't want to change my mind; it would spoil the mood.

I marched through the entrance but had the composure to ring the apartment number that Boots gave me. The little slot for a name under the bell was empty, so I rang twice. Risk was different from stupidity. There was no answer, so I flattened my palm against a row of buttons and hoped. Along with the squawk of a few voiceboxes came a buzz. I opened the door and called in a muffled voice, "Okay, sorry," hoping my response would discourage people from thinking thief.

I took the stairs two at a time. I didn't want to attract attention, but wanted to get in and get out. That was the way I used to feel as a kid when my cousin and I stole from local stores. I was always impatient to get out; he always insisted on staying longer. I felt he was just flirting with danger; he thought I tended toward panic. I tried compromise as I took the stairs.

There was no one in the hall and the lock was a snap. Know one building, know them all. I thought of the computerized contraption on Boots' door but pushed the image from my head. I needed to pay attention to what I was doing. I looked at the leather driving gloves on my hands and wondered whether I should be holding my gun. I decided I'd be too dangerous. I peered around the apartment and tried to see through the gloominess of the approaching evening.

There wasn't much to see. I stood in the living room and, from there, the only furniture I saw was a cot over in the bedroom. I looked in another direction and saw a refrigerator in the walk-through kitchen. I didn't see a table or chair. As far as I could tell the boy ate off the floor. And the floor wasn't too clean. Some kind of vomit-green astroturf. It wasn't a place you'd invite parents. It also didn't look like the apartment of a Lincoln owner.

I started to tour but heard footsteps in the hall so I stopped and tried to think of a reason for being there. I couldn't, my heart pounded and I broke out with the sweats, but the feet kept going until I was left, again, with the silent gloom. I headed straight for the bedroom.

There was nothing in the room except the cot and an oversized suitcase with a pile of clothes strewn haphazardly around it. I pawed through and looked, without luck, for an identification tag. The clothes were mostly underwear with a couple of pairs of jeans and tee shirts. Here was someone *really* ready for a quick getaway.

I retraced my steps back into the living room and considered turning on the light but couldn't see the percentage in illuminating dirt. I walked into the kitchen and opened the refrigerator. The interior light didn't work, and the contents resembled Lenny Bruce's description of a whore's fridge: a couple of onions and a carton of milk. There might have been more but I wasn't going to stick my hand inside. I closed the door, looked into some empty cabinets, and stood there stumped. If this was Joe Starring's apartment he didn't seem to have much to hide. He didn't seem to have much of anything. Except a Lincoln.

I felt along the top of the refrigerator and was rewarded with a torn piece of a receipt from Towne Lincoln and Mercury. I searched for other information but all I got for my trouble was carbon smudges on my gloves. I couldn't even find a date. I replaced the scrap and did another futile round of the apartment.

My internal clock was sounding. I placed my ear against the door and listened for noise. It was quiet, so I let myself out and walked into an empty hall. I gave my eyes a moment to adjust to the fluorescence, then walked slowly down the stairs with the look of someone deep in thought. At least I hoped that's what I looked like. I was really just listening to my cousin's voice.

When I hit the street the sky had grown even nastier but I felt like a summer day. My nerves were firing and my adrenaline was in overdrive. It was all I could do to keep from dancing. That I hadn't discovered anything seemed unimportant. I almost didn't care.

By the time I returned to the car I was quiet enough to light a cigarette. Without thinking I started driving to the address on the receipt. At the third light and second cigarette I wondered why. How far was I going to carry this? So what if the kid didn't fall into traditional Lincoln demographics? There could be a hundred reasons why someone without furniture, food, or clothing could buy a luxury car. And none of the hundred had to do with me.

I pulled into a vacant parking spot and felt myself come down the rest of the way. I thought about driving home and crashing on the couch, but it seemed like only a few minutes since I'd left. I wanted dope, remembered I hadn't brought any, and thought about a bar instead. My stomach rebelled. Last night's binge was still too close. I lit another cigarette and admonished myself for smoking. I pointed out to my conscience my ability to refrain from even thinking of a cigarette while I was in Starring's apartment, but my conscience just laughed. There was another long night coming.

Some of my delight was refreshed by the thought of my escapade, so I decided to delay the night by stopping at the car dealer. I didn't have the slightest rationalization other than, perhaps, the best one. Fun. Which turned real sour, real fast.

A pinstripe suit about thirty watched me from the other side of the door as I walked through. While he eyed me carefully I tried to reassure him by pulling off my gloves. He didn't seem relieved. Even without the gloves I didn't look like easy money.

"I'm sorry, sir, I'm about to lock up." He looked pointedly at the clock on the wall behind a blue convertible. "We've been closed for a while."

"I'd like to talk to you for a moment."

"If you come back tomorrow one of our salesmen will be available to help." Almost as an afterthought he added, "I'm the manager here."

I didn't want to wait until tomorrow. I wanted something to think about tonight.

"This will just take a minute."

"Which I don't have. Now if you will just come this way." He leaned lightly against me, but drew back when he felt the bulge under my jacket.

"Sir, I must ask you to leave." His impatience had taken on a tinge of nervousness. It was one thing to match a three-game-a-week racquetball body against mine, another to match it against metal.

"Look, I'm not here to buy a car. I'm a detective and I need some information." It sounded strange to me also.

"You're with the police?"

"No, private."

"Then please return during business hours. I'm in a rush and don't want to waste time with you."

His tone exceeded his authority and I was sorry that I hadn't introduced myself as Perry Smith. I let myself be pushed out the door but waited as he locked up. When he turned around he acted surprised to see me.

"I want your name for when I return." I heard what he said and immediately forgot everything but the George.

"Well, George, I just want to thank you for the time and effort." I tried to sound sincere and stuck out my hand.

He looked as though it were a dead fish but reluctantly clasped it. I squeezed down hard; then squeezed harder. I saw his eyes widen, then fill. Finally I let go and turned away just as he was about to speak. He wasn't going to need my name to remember me.

-34-

I went to sleep as depressed as I had been the night before. I managed to avoid wholesale annihilation of my physiology, but I wasn't sure if that was maturation or the weakness of age. When I awoke the next morning my body felt better but my spirits weren't any brighter. It was time to punch the clock for Simon and put the meter on hold with Dr. James. Starring and Clifford were dead ends. I even had to wait for Boots' call to find out when I could see her. This wasn't how I'd hoped things would turn out.

When the phone rang I gratefully answered.

"Matty, how are you?"

"Lou. Good to hear your voice. How's Martha?"

His voice lowered. "The same." Then louder. "She is great. She can't come to the phone right now, but she told me to send you her love."

The words were familiar but, where they once conjured up the image of a beaming Lou and Martha, today the image was different. "And how are you, Lou, really?"

His tone took on an amused note. "You know what they say. Good things come to those who wait."

"Are you being sarcastic?"

He laughed, "No, not at all. I'm not talking about your kind of waiting, Matty. I have to unload money, actually as much as possible, into the building."

"As much as possible?" I was baffled.

"I'm not talking Rockefeller. But a substantial amount. No jokes, please. A few things came home, and tax laws being what they are, it makes sense to spruce up and expand."

"Expand?"

"I thought it might be nice to add the twin next door."

"Are you kidding?"

"Not at all. Attaching and renovating would be the right scale of expenditure." His voice grew a little more somber. "Of course you might have to *schmere* the local people. We can talk about alternatives if you're reluctant."

I coughed my way through a hesitation. "Don't be silly. I wouldn't be reluctant to bribe an official. It would give me pleasure."

"Don't be smart. Sometimes you do what you have to do. You don't have to enjoy it."

"So I'll hate it."

"Always a wiseguy. What's the matter, boychik? You don't like my idea?"

"I don't know. Are you sure it's good business?"

"Look who's talking about business! What do you care about business? Now what's bothering you?" He sounded kindly.

"Remember I told you about this detective work?"

"Do I remember? You almost gave me a coronary when you crashed through the door playing cops and robbers. How is it coming?"

"There were two cases. One solved itself and the other's going nowhere. But the specific cases aren't the problem."

"What is?" He sounded interested.

"Well, I think I like the work."

"Mazel tov."

I chuckled. "Now who's the wiseguy?" I lit a cigarette and stopped. I didn't know what else to say. We were both quiet and I could hear him wheezing across the connection. After a time he said, "I think I understand."

"I'm glad someone does."

"You are worried about doing the detective work and also coordinating the project."

"I guess. But it seems silly. I really don't have much to do. Especially with the cases I'm working on."

"You've managed to work and cover the building up to now?"

"Not really. This detective stuff pays well so I've arranged for Charles to cover."

"Charles?"

"You know, Charles from Charles and Richard."

Lou chuckled and said, "Who would have thought you could live without Mrs. Sullivan's light? How is she? I didn't stop upstairs when I was in town. I hope she wasn't offended."

"I don't think she knew you were in. Hell, it was so brief I barely knew it. Lou, I feel bad about my lack of enthusiasm. I'm sure I'll perk up once the project gets started."

"And your detective work?"

"I'm trying to tell you, I don't have any work to do."

"Don't be a shmuck. It's not what you have that's important. It's what you want. If I saddle you with this project you won't be able to develop the business."

"Lou, I'm not going to screw you up because I have fantasies."

"Fantasies shmantasies. Who's talking screwed? We'll use both of them."

"Both of who?"

"We can use your friend Richard. From Charles and Richard." His needle made me smile. "We'll use both," he continued.

"What are you talking about? Are you on pot?"

"Mr. Joker. Please, don't be so loose-mouthed over the phone. It's simple. Richard's an architect, so we'll hire him to develop the project. Charles, if you think he can do the job, will do the day-to-day. It's not that big a deal and you, as part owner, will oversee."

"You are on drugs."

"Enough with the drugs already. Richard and Charles won't do?"

"It's not that. They'd do fine if they decided to take the job."

"You don't think they will?"

"They might."

"So what's so crazy?"

"This part owner talk—all this talk. Do you know if the building is available?"

"It's already ours."

"Ours? What the hell . . ."

"I didn't want to tell you when I was there because I didn't have time for your arguments." He paused, then continued, "Also you were focused on your cases and I didn't want to disturb you. While I was in town I closed on the six-flat and rearranged the present building."

"Rearranged?"

"Put the buildings in both our names. Those papers I sent you a couple of months ago that you signed and sent back. I didn't think you would read them."

He was right. I thought they were insurance forms.

"Look, boychik, before you say anything, use your head. I'm no spring chicken. This way no matter what happens, everything is covered."

"Is that what this is all about? Age anxieties?"

He laughed. "Maybe a little." He lowered his voice. "In my situation it would be unwise not to take care of things." His voice returned to conversation level. "But much to my delight, the windfall is real."

"Lou, is there something I should know about Martha?" I felt a sudden rush of panic. "Or you?"

"No, no, I'm fine. I swear it. Just came back from a physical. I'm a horse. Martha's Martha."

"Lou, why don't I come out there? The rest of this can wait."

"I want you to stay put. It's better that way."

"It sounds terrible. Why won't you let me help?"

"I do want you to help. I want you to stay home and get the project off the ground. With the purchase of the second building there is enough money coming in to pay you out of profit. If Richard and Charles aren't good, pick someone else. From where I sit, you should be able to do the project *and* your detective work. Though from the sound of it you'll do more project than detecting." He sounded disgruntled.

"Probably."

"You should hear yourself. One case solved itself, the other is stuck. Boychik, it's time to wake up—nothing solves itself. The stuck one means you're stuck, not the case. I know *gornisht* from detecting, but I know you don't build a business sitting on your *tuchas* thinking cases solve themselves."

I usually reacted badly to a kick in the ass, but Lou was at least half-right. I was the one stuck about the robberies.

"Lou, you are right, I don't know the first thing about building a business. That's what makes this whole thing seem ludicrous."

"It's not ridiculous, you're ridiculous. You've *pished* away more time than you realize. You've got to have a track record and contacts. With your friend Simon you might have the contacts, but you've got no record. And you won't if you keep thinking this way."

I smiled. It was nice to be treated like a son. Never really felt it before I met Lou. Probably why it had taken me so long to recognize what our relationship was.

"I don't get it. I thought kingmakers grew nasty when they got old."

He laughed. "I used up all my nasties becoming a kingmaker, bub-belah."

We spent the next few minutes talking about the project and how to proceed. Lou was correct when he said I knew nothing about business. I grabbed a pen and paper and wrote as fast as I could. I wanted to get it right.

My head was swimming when I hung up the phone. I looked at my list. From what I could gather I had authority over a ton of money in a local business account. I could hire someone to caretake as soon as I wanted. Even if we didn't get the proper variance from the city we were going to create a project. I felt lightheaded and wanted to tell someone. By the time I thought of Boots and Simon, I was already deep into the details with Charles and Richard.

35

They loved the idea. Richard welcomed a hands-on project and Charles was delighted by a paying job that kept him home. Richard took the morning off, and we spent the next few hours discussing my good fortune. I would have my basketball court after all. Despite the avalanche of details, I still had very little to do. Charles promised to let me know if he needed any help, but for the time being everything was covered.

I thought about a celebratory joint but passed. I didn't want to sit around the house and think about what had just happened. I would manage to find the fly in the ice cube. I wanted to go outside, get back to the cases. But there was one thing I had to do first for the project; I had to talk to Money.

When I arrived at the bank I relearned a basic truth: an owner is not an outlaw. I was treated with the utmost respect. Apparently Lou had laid some heavy tracks. I could have worn my gun without being accused of attempted robbery after they heard his name. It was a basic truth I couldn't integrate right away since, despite the money palace's treatment, I still felt like a withdrawal, not a deposit. It was a relief to be back in my car headed for Towne Lincoln and Mercury, though I wasn't thrilled about kissing the car manager's ass.

I didn't have to. He wasn't there. I asked around, but no one seemed too eager to spend any time with me. It was a letdown after the bank. Maybe I was integrating my new status better than I thought, though clearly I still didn't look like multiple-dealer options. I finally bothered a salesman into listening. I used a James Garner rap about providing Starring with inheritance money. It went over so well I began to consider buying polyester clothes. The salesman left to retrieve Starring's paperwork and, returning, loped toward me with a smile and a sheet of paper.

"I thought the name sounded familiar." He held up the single sheet. "Not much paper, huh?" He almost guffawed.

"What's so funny?"

"Have you met this guy?"

"No. Why?"

"Listen. The reason there is so little paper is this joker bought the fucking car with cash. We're not talking low end here. We're talking top shelf, loaded. When you walk in with that much green there's not too much to write down." He looked at me and his grin grew bigger. "You just say thanks."

Looking at a showroom full of new metal drove home the bleakness of Starring's apartment. "I understand about the paperwork but I still don't see the humor. Were you the salesman?" I glanced at the clock. I didn't want to run into the manager.

"No salesmen for this deal. The manager handled it, but everybody knew. First of all it rarely happens, and second, this guy looked like he crawled out from under a rock. Most of us thought he scored big on a drug deal. I guess not, though?"

I fought the sinking sensation in my stomach. "You guess not?"

"I mean, with you here to give him money and all?"

"Mr. Starring's looks belie his means." But not much different from your stereotyped drug dealer.

"No shit. Is he going to get a lot of money?"

I did a professional number and ignored what he said. "I assume your manager checked on the legitimacy of the currency."

He took a turn at being professional while I reached for the paper. The only thing new it gave me was a date and an address in New Jersey. I pointed toward it. "Out of state residence."

He looked up from the document suspiciously. "Don't you recognize that address?"

I avoided his question. "Was this address confirmed or was it another 'just say thanks'?"

He puzzled over that for a moment but the suspicion never really left his face.

"You'll have to ask the manager. I thought you worked for his family?"

"I don't remember saying who I worked for."

"Well, who do you work for?"

Again I pretended deafness, gave him back his papers, and thanked him before he could continue his questioning. I was just out the large glass door when, in my haste, I nearly collided with the manager. His eyes opened wide when he recognized me. Before he could speak I stuck out my tongue and skipped to my car.

I wasn't so in love with myself after I scribbled down the Jersey address and thought about what the car salesman said. With all the television I watched, I hadn't really considered drug money. On top of that, the date on the paperwork preceded the burglaries. Another case starting to solve itself. I'd end up a fucking squire yet. I thought of Lou's disbelief in magical fixes. At least this one was an easy check. If it was drugs it had to have been big enough for Julie to know about.

I started the car, wondering whether Boots had tried to get in touch. For a moment I regretted not having a machine. It was only a momentary lapse. I really didn't want to go back home and sit around to wait for a telephone call and contemplate my new wealth. I drove toward Brighton. The skinny beard with his fancy cash car bit at me like a bad case of crabs. A simple conversation with Julie, regardless of what I discovered, was not going to be a strong enough shampoo. If the kid was just a lowlife drug dealer, I still wanted to know what he'd been doing hanging around 290 and the Aquarium. Let the fucker convince me of coincidence.

Also, visiting Starring meant a reprieve from returning home.

I pulled into the cut-though and was surprised to see the cream-colored Lincoln parked sedately under a tree in the far corner. I pulled in next to it, got out of my car, and walked around kicking its tires. The Lincoln was empty and locked. I thought about busting in, but I walked over to Starring's building instead. The only noticeable change was the orange dumpsters had more shit in them.

I walked into the hallway and rang his buzzer. There was no answer.

I rang it again. A long one, but there was still no answer. I would have left but someone hadn't locked the downstairs door properly and it was too open to ignore. I walked up the stairs and finished concocting a story. Somehow I still expected to speak with Joe Starring.

I hammered on his door, frustrated when he still didn't answer. Although I didn't figure he had left his Lincoln behind, I let myself into the apartment prepared to wait for his return. Inside, I stared through the glare of the naked, one-bulb overhead that illuminated the emptiness Starring called home. Only it wasn't empty. When I realized the tie-dyed mural on the far wall was a mixture of face, brain, skull, and blood, I held on to my stomach, backed out of the room, and ran like hell.

I sat in the car and tried to regain control of my gut. Television hadn't prepared me for this. I smoked furiously, trying to rid my nostrils of the smell of blood. Then I tried to remember if anyone had seen me.

I started the car and thought about racing home, but instead shut the engine off and lit another cigarette. I should have looked more closely at the body. But the moment I thought of returning, the abstract blood picture on the wall snapped the idea in half. Still, I didn't feel right about just walking away.

I hopped out of the car and jogged across the lot to Brighton Avenue. The first bar I entered had one of those exposed phone booths so, after a very quick boilermaker, I kept going. You couldn't make a fucking private call these days, not even in a ginmill. In a drug store I spotted a real booth back in the corner; I walked in and dropped an anonymous tip to the police. Then I ran back to my car and drove it to another spot in the parking lot where I could see the building but remain fairly well hidden. I wished I had my gun.

I couldn't sit still so I trotted over to the Lincoln and let myself in. There was nothing, not even a garbage bag, or half-smoked butts. The trunk was different. Its floor was littered with paper, and there was a battered blue gym bag shoved into the corner. It looked as if someone had dumped the contents of the bag onto the trunk floor and pawed his way through. When I noticed Eban Holmes' name at the top of beige stationery I knew I'd struck gold.

Sirens in the distance; after a moment of indecision I stuffed all the records into the bag, and wiped down the trunk with my handkerchief.

I slammed the lid and walked back to my car, where I wedged the gym bag underneath my spare tire. I got back in, lit a cigarette, and waited for the police to show. The case wasn't solving itself.

None of the police assigned to the scene were interested in anything but the scene. No flashing lights, and they even canned the siren before they turned onto the block. No big red ribbons or sawhorses. Just one ambulance and a few cops. I was impressed that they had brought the ambulance before they confirmed the call. When I was a caseworker and law was needed, police were a lot more aggressive and hostile than they appeared to be here. Maybe they were more comfortable confronting the dead. If I stayed in this business would it be the same for me?

I pushed the image of the dead kid out of my mind and watched the cops go upstairs. After a moment one of the uniformed officers reappeared and used the radio in his car. I felt a little better when I saw him get out of the car, go to the side of the dumpsters, and puke. I hoped he wasn't a rookie.

He leaned up against the side of the building and lit a cigarette; I grimaced and lit one myself. His heave had bonded us. We were about halfway through our smokes when a gray nondescript sedan pulled up in front of the building, double-parking on the wrong side of the street.

At first all I could see was a hand snake out the window. Suddenly there was a blue light flashing from the roof. I looked back at the uniformed officer and noticed his cigarette was gone. When I saw who he was looking at I drew on mine harder. Every inch of Washington Clifford was neatly crossing the street.

— 36 —

My body reflexively slouched low in the seat as my free hand groped for the ignition. I forced my fingers away from the keys, and peeked out the window. It wasn't easy. Washington Clifford scared the hell out of me.

He stood next to the uniform, registering no surprise at whatever the man was saying. I prayed I hadn't left a trail. Dealing with Clifford officially would be no more pleasant than it had been unofficially. I figured it would only be a matter of time before he went upstairs and I could leave. My body hadn't hurt for a couple of days, but watching Clifford rock lightly back and forth revived all the bruises he and his mastiff had inflicted. The pain felt so real I looked at my palms expecting blood to spurt, but nothing happened. It was comforting to discover limits to his power.

Clifford didn't go upstairs. Instead, he walked back to his car, leaned up against it, and stared vacantly ahead. In the far distance I heard the multiple squeals of a siren working an intersection. The sound began to close in. Clifford also seemed to hear it. He pulled out of his reverie, took the light off the roof, and burned rubber as he jack-rabbited his car.

Momentarily I wished I could question the cop about Clifford, but sanity prevailed. The sirens became police cars, and suddenly the scene looked a lot more like *Quincy*. I started my engine and drove

195

toward the Brighton Avenue exit. I had just pulled the car into traffic when I realized what I'd seen—a criminal returning to the scene of the crime.

Just like I knew Clifford was a cop when I first saw him, just like I knew that Starring was connected to the burglaries at 290, I knew that Clifford had murdered Starring. It was easy to picture him blowing Starring's head onto the wall. The thought piled dread on top of the panic already lodged in my gut. I jerked the car over to the side of the street. I didn't have time to think. It was all I could do to roll down the window and stick my head out. The horror in the apartment, the fear of Clifford, and the new knowledge that I was mixed up in something that I didn't understand came pouring out in a bucket of sick. When I stopped throwing up I looked guiltily up and down the block to see if anyone was watching. With my luck I'd run into a meter maid.

My hands were shaking but I got them working well enough to light a cigarette. I inhaled and held my breath to regain some control. I sat there for a couple of moments and finished the smoke. I knew it was time to leave when I relaxed enough to smell the foul odor of my puke wafting through the open window. Nursing the car home like I was sixty-five and the car had 140,000 took some time, but I couldn't afford more surprises.

I went straight for the alley. If I went through the front Charles or Richard would buttonhole me. Thinking of them reminded me of how the day began, of Lou, only it seemed so much longer than a few hours ago. I didn't feel much like a squire. I unlocked the door, started inside, and stopped when I remembered the gym bag.

I dropped everything on the kitchen table but didn't stop moving until I dug out my stash and rolled a fat doobie, returned to the table, and sucked on the joint. After I dumped the records on the table I organized them into neat piles. There were no papers with Dr. James' name on them. I got up and prowled from window to window, though I didn't know what I was so anxious about. No one had seen me and I could, if I had to, explain my prints at Starring's. Couldn't I? Jesus, I hadn't shot him.

Suddenly panicked about my gun, I walked quickly to the bedroom. I dropped to my knees, grabbed the strap of the holster, and yanked it toward me. The gun was there, which brought an audible cry of relief. At least I wasn't being framed.

Framed by whom, for what? I flopped down on my ass and tried to steady my nerves. It was all right to be overwhelmed. This was my first time out of the box. Any more todays and it would be my last.

I grimly strapped the holster on my shoulder. It made me feel safer. Calmer. But I didn't like it. Guns. Vigilantism. Suspicion. Not the kind of world I'd spent much of my life advocating.

I felt myself get angry. When the mental image of Starring's wall wriggled in its brainfold I didn't feel my stomach rise. Only a rotten taste in my mouth and the growlings of starvation.

In the refrigerator I saw the food I had bought in the North End. I stood there with the door ajar, then closed the fridge and turned toward the table covered with office records. I wanted them out of my house, so I postponed eating until I had called Dr. James. While I stood there I checked again to be certain there were no records with Gloria's letterhead.

I was in deep shit and I didn't know how I got there. Worse, I didn't know the way to shore.

I went to the bathroom intending to shower but was reluctant to remove the gun, so I brushed my teeth and rinsed my mouth instead. I didn't have many memories of my old man. One I did have was watching him rinse his mouth in the morning. He'd make a big production of it, cupping his hands rather than using a glass, and gargling loudly. I looked at myself in the mirror and used a glass. Quietly. The older you get the more appreciative you become of nuances.

When I finished I walked to the phone. On the third ring I was answered with a recorded message informing me that Dr. James was away for a couple of days but I could most certainly leave a message. If it was an absolute emergency I could call the number left on the tape at the end of the message. I grabbed a piece of paper and scribbled the emergency number. I didn't want to leave a fucking message and it was an absolute emergency.

I had barely finished dialing when I heard a gruff male voice.

"Holmes here. Who is it please?"

"Matt Jacob, Dr. Holmes."

"Oh, Matthew, please call me Eban. I was just on my way out."

"This shouldn't take long. I'm looking for Dr. James. She left this number on her machine."

"Yes, yes, I know. That was in case any of her clients were in crisis. I really don't know how to get in touch with her until she calls."

"Who does?"

"I don't think anyone. She wanted to be alone for a few days."

"Bullshit. She may have wanted to get away, but I don't believe she didn't leave her number with *someone*."

"I'm sorry you don't believe me, but I don't think I can help you. If you want to leave a message I can pass it along if she calls."

"Goddamnit, I don't want to leave a message." My voice rose a decibel level. "I want to speak to her."

"I'll leave your number for her." He paused then continued, "As I said, I was just on my way out."

"Listen, motherfucker, I want to speak with her. Stop playing gargoyle. I recovered the stolen records from 290 and we need to talk."

His voice never changed inflection, nonetheless there was no mistaking his abrupt detachment. "That sounds wonderful, Matt. I'm sure Gloria will be pleased to hear that. I'll be sure to tell her if she calls."

"And you're not guarding the door?"

He chuckled. "You are very stubborn."

I didn't find anything amusing. "I'm standing here looking at a bunch of yours."

"Mine?"

"Records. Your office records."

He never skipped a beat. "Of course. If you'd like I'd be happy to pick them up. No reason to make you run."

I wanted to wrap the telephone cord around his neck. If I told him I'd spent the day discovering gory murals he might relent, but I didn't want to tell him anything, much less beg.

"Fuck you." I slammed the receiver down so hard I had to check to see if I had cracked it. It was a '40s phone that I'd found in a junk store and resurrected. If I had broken it I would have found Holmes and beaten Gloria's whereabouts out of him. As it was the phone was intact.

I reopened the refrigerator door and remembered standing in front of Starring's yesterday. That settled the question of cooking and I slammed the door shut. When I called the neighborhood sub shop, the guy swore he'd have the pizza at my door in fifteen minutes. That gave me about forty-five, so I decided to shower and change.

I had just finished strapping the holster over my clean tee shirt when I heard someone rap on the door. "Wait a second," I called while I fumbled with my wallet to get the money. The delivery was surprisingly quick. It was a relief because I was starved.

I pulled the door with one hand and held the money in the other when suddenly the door flew open and Simon came streaming through. His action pushed me aside and knocked the money from my grasp. I knelt down on the floor to pick it up. It was a good way to ease the panic that hit when the door swung open.

I looked up. "What the fuck are you doing?"

He slammed his hand on the table and glared at me. "That's my question. What the fuck are you doing?"

"What the hell are you talking about?" I stood up and closed the door.

He didn't have a chance to answer because there was another loud knock. This time I took the gun out of my holster and waved at Simon to move to the side. I wasn't going to be caught looking again. At least not today. I grabbed the door handle and yanked it open. I'm glad I had the gun facing down; the pizza boy was scared enough. I was still a dime short and a dollar wide with everything. I reholstered the .38 and paid for the pizza. I gave him a big tip. Then I turned around and placed the pie on the table.

"You eat yet? It's Greek, but edible."

"I don't want to eat." He didn't sound any friendlier.

"Suit yourself." I feigned mellow and sat down to eat. Some of my anxiety showed. The tape on the box took me three rounds. All the while Simon stood, glowered, and breathed. Loudly. I finally got the box open and he began to speak.

"I told you I didn't mind paying you, I only wanted you to work. 'Sure I'll work,' you said. Look at you. You disappeared again. Only this time you're fucking dangerous. Who the hell are you imitating? Hunter Thompson?"

I tried to interrupt but he kept ranting, "Are you shooting up now? Or is it the DTs? You can't even get a goddamn pizza box open. Christ!"

"Wait a minute. That tape was tough."

"Fuck you and your jokes. I got a wife who is close to a breakdown, a marriage that's falling apart, and you can't follow one fucking lead. I've been calling regularly and you've been too stoned to hear it ring."

I was getting tired of being thought of as a junkie or a lush. I didn't think of myself that way. "My dope isn't that good, Simon. If I'da been here I would have heard the phone. I'm surprised to hear that Fran is doing worse. I was sure things would turn around."

"Come on, Matt. You haven't been out of the house for three consecutive hours since the accident. And I'm sorry if I'm not up to date on the substance you're abusing."

The pizza looked like an overhead camera shot of open heart surgery. I stuffed the top of the box into the uneaten pie and rose to my feet. "Look, you asshole, I said I was out."

"Out where? Another pleasure jaunt with Boots? On my dime?"

"Pleasure jaunt? If looking at a head splattered against a naked wall gets you off, I suppose you could call it pleasure. You ever see human brains, Simon? You know what a big fat bullet does to a face? Spend the day with me, asshole. On your fucking dime? Your dime bought me admission to a very ugly death. You're damn right it's your dime. That corpse was the kid I've been looking for, for you. And before you get self-centered about it, his fucking murder has nothing to do with you. He was into some shit, but it wasn't yours. Let me tell you again what I been trying to tell you all along. Alive or dead, the kid don't have nothing to do with your problems. Get it?"

I suddenly ran out of steam. "I'm sorry things aren't improving with you guys. I truly thought they might."

"What the hell are you mixed up in?"

"I don't know."

"You don't know what you're involved with, but you know things were going to improve for me. If what you're telling me is true, why, goddamnit, did you think anything was going to change?"

"I don't know. Time, I guess." I scratched around for something to say. All I felt was fatigue and I wanted him to leave.

He walked over to where I was standing. "Time, my ass. You're holding out. What the fuck do you know that I don't? If it isn't information about this kid, what is it?"

I wanted to escape. I shrugged helplessly and could feel my face flush. Though the heat from both our tempers was gone, the tension in the room was electric. He kept staring and I kept trying to hide. Neither of us moved a muscle.

Suddenly his eyes flashed and I knew he had it figured out.

"You son of a bitch. I don't believe it."

I didn't move. Or say a thing. Or ask what he didn't believe. I didn't have to. He looked around the apartment like he had lost something and shook his head. He started to talk, but stopped. He turned away and walked slowly to the door. From the rear he looked like another Willy Loman. Before he got there he turned back toward me and showed his teeth. I suppose it was a grin.

"You could have said it wasn't so. You know, like Shoeless Joe."

I looked at him. I didn't know what to say. Shoeless Joe hadn't. All I could do was shrug. He turned back toward the door and walked out. I didn't want him to leave but I didn't follow. I still had nothing to say. I heard his car squeal out of the alley before I locked the door.

I lit a cigarette and wound up on the couch. I was too exhausted and too miserable to watch TV. I stuffed the cigarette but kept the gun. It made me feel better, despite the delivery boy fiasco. It was too early to sleep but no one told my eyes. Even with my eyes shut I couldn't shake the image of Simon frantically glancing around the apartment like a trapped animal.

Somehow that image transformed itself into another . . . Simon had my gun and was pointing it at me and Fran who were naked in bed. I kept trying to explain that I wasn't the one, but he wouldn't listen. Fran kept telling him that it was all over, but he wouldn't believe that either. He kept looking at the gun and back at us. Then he put the gun to his own head in front of a blank wall. I knew the way the wall was going to look and I heard myself pleading with him to put the gun down, but he just stared with the same look he'd worn when he left my apartment.

I saw his finger squeeze the trigger and I braced for the explosion. But instead of the roar of the gun I heard the bell of the phone and the picture of Fran, Simon, and myself began to fade, and I was confused about whether I was awake or asleep.

The telephone kept ringing. I shook myself alert and glanced at the clock. It was 3 A.M. and the phone was ringing, but the sound was a relief: I didn't have to watch Simon paint the wall.

The ring refused to play itself out. I struggled to my feet and padded across the floor and stabbed at the receiver. "It better be good!"

"Excuse me?"

The voice was familiar but I couldn't place it.

"Who is this?"

"It's Eban Holmes. I'm sorry to disturb you at this time of morning, but something happened and I think you ought to be involved."

Although his voice was quiet I could hear the raggedness around the edges. "What's going on?"

"Gloria was assaulted and her house ransacked."

I felt my stomach lurch and my hands begin to sweat. "Is she all right?"

"Not really. Nothing fatal or long-term, but serious." His voice cracked, but he took a deep breath and continued, "Look, I can't talk about this on the phone. Will you come over to her house? I know this is quite an inconvenience . . .?"

He was winding up to go into a sell. "You don't have to convince me, Eban. I'll be there as soon as I can. I take it you're with her?"

"Yes, yes, of course." He sounded friendlier now than he had this afternoon.

"Where is it?"

He gave me an address in Brookline. "I'll be there as soon as possible."

"Thank you, Matthew. It's a relief."

"Right."

I put the phone down and tried to regroup. Despite the change in calendar, yesterday continued. I tried to push the thought of Eban comforting Dr. James from my mind. This really wasn't the time to pander to weird jealousies. Hell, she had been my shrink until a couple of weeks ago.

I pushed myself toward the bedroom and quickly dressed, gathered my things, and headed into the dark alley for the car. Someone was sleeping by the rear wheel and I was met with a drunken protest. When he saw the gun in my hand he stopped talking and pulled himself to his feet. I slipped the gun back into the holster and climbed into the car. I wasn't in a coddling mood.

37

I was halfway down the alley before realizing I'd left without cigarettes or dope. Nothing was going to be open this time of the morning, so I jammed on the brakes and threw the car into reverse. You couldn't buy dope from a convenience store anyhow, this wasn't New York. While I sat at the table rolling, Simon's words rattled in my head. It took a moment to decide whether I'd use a cigarette or joint to get rid of them. I took a toke of grass, held my breath, exhaled, and did another.

I was conscious of the time but still delayed leaving. My initial intensity was dissipating, something was telling me I'd seen too much and done too much to do any more. It didn't matter; an image of Gloria attacked kicked me out the door.

The drunk looked at me reproachfully. Rather than feeling guilt for moving him, I moved him again. I was beginning to lose my lethargy.

The overnight parking ban meant I had Dr. James' block to myself. I walked up the brown concrete steps. There was only one mailbox. Only one bell. The door opened and Holmes stood there looking like shit, and somehow that calmed my own tight nerves. He waved me inside, signaling for silence.

"She's dozing."

He must have seen something in my face because he rushed to

reassure me. "I'll wake her, I didn't ask you out in the middle of the night for no reason."

"What do you mean you asked me out? Doesn't Dr. James know you called?" I was annoyed by his authoritative tone though I found myself whispering. "Is there a room where we can talk? The place looks big enough."

"Of course, please excuse my manners. I'm not doing my best thinking. As far as Gloria knowing that I called, frankly, she doesn't. She wouldn't even allow me to call the police." He shrugged his shoulders, indicating he had fought the good fight but lost. I believed him.

"I didn't want to mention you." He didn't want to lose again.

"Well, I'm here."

For a moment he stood there confused. He really wasn't doing his best thinking. Just then Dr. James called from another room. "Eban, who are you talking to? I wasn't knocked deaf, you know."

Holmes looked trapped. It pleased me but hearing Dr. James' voice rekindled my anxiety, so there wasn't much room to gloat. I listened as he ripped the words from his throat. "I called Matthew Jacob, Gloria, and he's just arrived."

Her groan was clear and unmistakable. "I told you that I wanted nobody to know, goddammit." She paused for an instant. "That's no reflection on you, Matthew."

I walked across the hall toward the sound of her voice. "Matt, Gloria, Matt. Informality for those bonded by blood." Holmes dragged after me.

I walked into the room at the tail end of her laugh, and heard myself gasp. I was sorry I'd made the joke. It must have hurt to open her mouth. Gloria's face was swollen and already turning a blotchy purple. She looked like a late-night public service announcement about wife abuse.

Gloria moved the arm that rested over the bedspread. "It looks worse than it is."

She was lying. It was as bad as it looked. "What's the matter with your other arm?"

She moved her free hand and pulled aside the blanket. She was wearing a sweatsuit and her arm was bandaged and set in a sling.

"They broke your arm."

She was wearing a giddy smile. "Not they, Matthew, he."

I looked at Holmes. "She has to get to a doctor. If her arm is broken it has to be set correctly."

Holmes looked at me and some of the color returned to his face. "It's set right. I did it."

Gloria chipped in, "Eban studied medicine, tell him, Eban." She smiled, "Eban studied lots of things, didn't you, Eban?"

I turned toward Holmes. "I didn't know you were a doctor. I thought your Dr. meant Ph.D."

"You almost have it right, Matthew." She was blinking. "*I'm* the Ph.D. Fid."

I smiled at her and nodded to Holmes. "What's she on?"

"A little Demerol."

"Is there such a thing as a little Demerol?" I tried to keep the anger out of my voice. I didn't want to fight the only coherent person in the room.

He nodded. "I know what you mean. No, I'm not a licensed doctor but I've studied a great deal of medicine, and we'll go to her own physician in the morning." He looked at her. "As soon as the painkiller wears off."

I couldn't stop myself. He was a little hard to believe. "Are you nuts? Aren't you taking this anti-professional thing too far? You want to wait for the fucking Demerol to wear off so you don't get busted?"

He coughed and glanced away. "Perhaps. I'm not sure this is the time and place to discuss it, do you?" He met my eyes and smiled. "Don't you think it's interesting that you object to my setting a broken bone, but said nothing about my work in psychology?"

He abruptly changed topics. "It was a clean break. All I did was some advanced first aid and shake a few tablets from a bottle. Nonetheless, if it had been up to me, we would have gone directly to the emergency room."

I had a couple of rejoinders but they weren't going to help the situation. I pushed my misgivings away. Hell, after Starring's painted wall, what was a broken arm? I turned my attention back to Dr. James. She was lying quietly, looking a little more sober but no better for wear.

I felt my theory of relativity slipping away. "Look, Holmes was right to call. This is too serious for heroics. If you're too tired to talk I'll just wait until you're ready."

Gloria's eyes opened a little wider. "Why would you wait? Eban is here." At the sound of Eban's name the corners of her lips trembled and her pupils began to dilate. I didn't say anything and waited quietly for her to come down.

She was so hostile toward Holmes I wondered if he had beaten her. I turned toward Holmes. "When did you get here?"

His face grew puzzled. "Why do you ask?"

"Let me see your hands."

It was his turn to be incredulous. "What are you suggesting?" But even as he became indignant his hands drifted out in front of his body. He hadn't hit anyone.

Gloria muttered from the bed, "You are very suspicious, Matthew. Eban's torture is of a less tangible nature."

Holmes had had it. "Gloria, please! I know you've been through hell and the drugs are still affecting you, but enough already. I don't blame you for being angry but, despite Mr. Jacob's accusation, it was me you called from the floor. I was not your assailant. I am not a thug. I relented when you refused to go to the police and the hospital, but you have been assaulted and it was no damn accident. You can talk to Matthew now, or I can, or," he gave a brusque nod to me, "we can wait. But I am not going to sit and listen to a drug-induced history of relational recriminations."

With his speech he grew more like the powerful dynamo he was when we first met. I liked him better this way, but his relationship with Gloria less. Her eyes seemed clearer and frowns of physical discomfort were starting to flash across her face.

"I understand, Eban. We will have to talk about these things later." She shifted her body slightly in my direction. I wanted to look away from her face but didn't. "Not too pretty to look at today, huh?" She tried to smile but the effort was overtly painful. "I'll tell you what happened but first you answer one question." I was going to argue but decided to take the path of least resistance and nodded instead.

"What's going on? If you know something, please tell me."

Just her effort to ask the question deserved an honest answer. "I don't know what's going on. I found the office records today . . . not today, yesterday. I found them in the car of someone who was murdered."

Dr. James blinked and seemed to sink into her pillows. Out of the corner of my eye I could see Holmes' jaw drop. I didn't want to say anything about Clifford. Some suspicions are better kept unsaid.

Holmes was the first to speak. "My God, you said nothing about this on the telephone. Are you certain?"

"If seeing a corpse is certain, I'm certain. Look, if I've shocked you, good. We're involved in something that's gotten two of us beaten and someone else dead and we don't understand shit about what's going on. Now tell me what happened."

"I was in bed reading," Gloria took a deep breath and shuddered, "when I heard the back door being kicked in."

I involuntarily looked around and Holmes interjected, "I've already rigged something up."

Dr. James had a vacant look in her eyes and I realized she was still in shock. I felt another jolt of anger toward Holmes for not getting her to a hospital.

Her voice was a monotone. "I couldn't react. In some ways that first instant was the worst. All the years of dread coming true. It felt inevitable, but I couldn't respond." She frowned. "He was clumsy. By the time he ran into the chair I could move. I have a fraternity paddle and when he came into my room I hit him with it. I aimed for his groin but hit too high. That's when he grabbed me and punched. I fought him as best I could; he wasn't very big, but he was strong and out of control. I guess he didn't expect to be hit." She winced at the next set of memories. "After he calmed down some he told me I was lucky, that I should be glad he was on the clock or he'd rape me."

She drifted away as she recalled the moments. Finally, in the same flat voice, "He said some other things too. He was very aware of the time. He seemed upset that I was home. He asked me where my office was. I told him 290 Commonwealth but he kept slapping me and saying 'not 290, the one at home.' I tried to tell him that I didn't have an office at home. I thought he was looking for drugs. Eventually he grabbed me around my throat and demanded to see my files. I only had a few . . ."

"Duplicates of the stolen ones," I guessed.

"Yes."

"All this has something to do with one of your clients." I expected her to resist the obvious but it was too obvious for her to resist.

"The files were all he wanted. He didn't take the stereo or the TV."

"What happened to your arm?"

She looked at me and tried to focus. "He tried to change his mind about sex. We wound up on the landing and he pushed or I fell down the steps. I guess I blacked out because the next thing I remember is calling Eban."

I looked at her purple face and felt another wave of anger and helplessness. "Why wouldn't you go to the police or the hospital?"

"The hospital would report it to the police. I don't want them poking around my clients."

"You know this has to do with one of them, don't you? You have to make me a list of the names on the files that were stolen."

"I can't."

I could feel the measure of impotent rage that was ready to run its course. "No more of that shit, Gloria. Someone is dead now. There is no more grandstanding on this one."

"It has nothing to do with grandstanding. I haven't glanced at those files in weeks. I need an hour in my office." She closed her eyes and sank deeper into the bed. "I'm sorry. I know it's important and I'm not trying to be difficult."

"Goddammit . . ."

"I'm sorry but I'm telling the truth." She kept her eyes closed.

She seemed so frail and wounded. "I'm not mad at you, I'm frustrated, that's all. Can you describe what he looked like?"

"Small, wiry, but I couldn't see his face. He was wearing a dark stocking over his head."

"Did you see his hands?"

"No, he was wearing gloves."

"So we don't know if he was black or white?"

"We know. He was white. He had his penis out for a while."

I drew a deep breath. "*Were* you raped?"

She opened her eyes. "No. I guess he got nervous when I fell down the stairs. Maybe necrophilia wasn't exciting to him. Or whatever you call sex with an unconscious woman."

Holmes interrupted. "How much more information do you need? She's in pain and it might be helpful if she slept."

I looked back at Gloria. She was starting to breathe in a regular pattern. I turned toward Eban. "I have to get something from my car. Keep her awake for a few more minutes."

Before he could answer I walked out of the room and retraced my steps to the door. I thought about checking Holmes' jerryrig but decided to let it go. I felt for the gun under my jacket. I wanted the opportunity to use it.

The sky was beginning to lighten with the first faint hints of daylight. It made it easy to spot the parking ticket from the porch. For an instant I thought of making Holmes pay, then shook my distemper off his back. He hadn't created this situation; he was just caught in it. Like me. I pocketed the ticket; Eban wasn't getting paid, I was. I reached into the back seat, pulled out the pile of records, and walked back into the house. I found the two of them talking quietly, Holmes sitting on the bed, their heads close together. I felt like I was intruding.

I dropped the pile of files down on the bed. "Are yours there?"

They shuffled through the records. Holmes pulled his from the stack but Gloria shook her head. "None of these are mine."

·I nodded and sat in the easy chair next to the bed.

Holmes looked at me. "You don't seem surprised."

"I'm not. They wanted her records, right? Well, they got them."

Gloria looked like she was going to fall back to sleep.

"What time can she see her doctor?"

Holmes glanced at his watch. "We could call in a couple of hours."

"Is it possible to meet him at a hospital?"

Dr. James' eyes flickered open. "*She* works out of Beth Israel," Gloria said.

I stood up and looked directly at Holmes. "I want you to wake the doctor and set up an early meeting here. I don't want the police informed if we can help it. See what you can do to convince the doctor."

"Are you sure it's wise not to inform the authorities? From what you've indicated Gloria might still be in danger."

"I don't think she is but I want to be cautious." I could hear a feeble protest from the bed. It was feeble because she was gritting her teeth against unmasked pain. I lit a cigarette before I realized there was no ashtray. I stood and began to look around. Eban signaled for me to sit back down and walked over to a china cabinet to get one.

"Why don't you think she's in any more danger?" he asked.

"They wanted her records and they got them."

"But you aren't sure about all this?"

"I'm not sure of anything. But I'm not so far removed from my own beating to simply trust the police." I didn't want to get started on Clifford's connection with Starring. I didn't want to get started on Starring.

"What do you suggest?" Holmes' tone made it clear that I'd better come up with a good one.

"We have to stash her somewhere safe."

Holmes thought about what I'd said, then stuck out his jaw. "Gloria, you'll stay with me."

She opened her eyes and almost began to laugh. "What will you say to Yvonne? Will the three of us share a bed?"

"Yvonne will understand. She has to."

I interrupted. "No, she doesn't. Gloria can't stay there."

He stared at me. "Why not?"

It was perversely gratifying to hear the resentment in his voice. "Gloria's attacker figured her to be away because of the message on the machine. That message has your number on it. Fact is, you should play it safe. Go with Yvonne on a trip out of state."

He looked at me while the implications of what I said began to sink in. "You're serious about this?"

I nodded. Then pointed to Gloria on the bed. "I'm deadly serious."

Holmes began to stomp around the room. "I can't go running off and leave her alone. Not now. Not after this."

"You won't do her any good if you're hurt."

Gloria suddenly pushed herself up on her good elbow. "I am tired of you talking as if I weren't here." She looked at Holmes. "It would be a cold day in hell before I'd stay with you and Yvonne." She almost spat the name out.

Holmes barked at me, "What is your plan?"

"I'm going to contact a friend of mine. Gloria will stay with her. I want you to bring her back to my place after you've seen the doctor, and I'll take it from there."

"What makes your place safer than mine?"

He was a competitive fucker. "We can't wait for a cold day in hell."

Gloria spoke up. "Do you really think these precautions necessary?"

I looked at her swollen face. "Yes."

Holmes kept licking his wounds. "I still don't see . . ."

I didn't want to continue the debate. "Yes you do. I don't know if you are in any danger, but it's not a bet I'd take. We don't need stubborn heroes."

"I don't like running."

"Keeping yourself intact is not the same as cowardice."

Dr. James had her teeth clenched. "I'm too tired to fight anymore, Eban. We'll do what he wants. Please call Carol for me. It's time for some legal medication."

Eban nodded. It wasn't his night for victories. He left the room, then poked his head back through the door. "Where are you off to?"

I took a deep breath. "First I'm going to get some breakfast. Then, after I get Gloria safely placed, I'm going to New Jersey."

—38—

Ashes to ashes. I decided to have breakfast at Charley's. I wasn't sure why I felt like I was going in a circle, but then, I wasn't sure I was going anywhere at all. Except south. To New Jersey. I drove my car through streaks of gray light. Like the window in Starring's apartment.

Either I got there before the morning rush, or Phil was living off past success. Other than a bread truck parked in the no-parking zone in front of the restaurant, there were no cars on the block. As I walked through the door Phil and his redheaded waitress looked up with curiosity from a corner table. For an instant they seemed bothered by the disruption, but I didn't think it was personal. More likely they were comfortable with the deserted atmosphere. It was a shame; the place seemed more seasoned than dingy, but failure has a way of rushing things. The man in a slate-blue Wonder Bread uniform sat in the corner, his plate piled high with corned beef hash. It had been ages since I had hash. Of any kind. The deliveryman kept his head buried in his newspaper and didn't bother to look up.

By the time I settled at the counter the waitress had her face two inches above her black and white enamel table. She seemed to be wrestling with her eyes. I couldn't tell if the problem was makeup or contacts. Phil slowly left his seat and leaned his body in my direction.

I nodded my hello. "Can't make up my mind yet. Trying to choose between ham and eggs and hash."

STILL AMONG THE LIVING

He pushed himself away from the counter and wiped his hands on a towel hung nearby. He shook his head. "No choice." He turned his back and cut two thick slices from an honestly cooked ham enthroned next to the stove. This pig wasn't shook out of a can. "What kind of eggs?"

"Over medium."

He turned around and looked at me. "This is why I don't carry a cook." He pointed with the spatula toward a door off the far end of the counter. "No way to tell a cook what someone means by 'over medium.' "

Before I could explain the redhead interrupted. "You don't keep a cook because there is nothing for a cook to do. Just like there is nothing for me to do."

She was finished snorting the table and held a small square mirror an arm's length from her face. Her very pretty face. It almost made up for the carping tone in her voice, but not quite. I'd heard enough of that between Gloria and Holmes. I hoped the lady would knock it off. I turned back toward the grill where both my eggs and ham were making some nice smells and sounds. "Hey, if it tastes as good as it looks, why would you let anyone else cook?"

He looked into the mirror that ran directly across from my seat and spoke to the waitress, "Don't be an ass. If I started to cook quiche you'd have plenty to do. What the hell, I got no complaint. This joint had a good long run. Long enough to take me to my last stop."

"Jesus, Phil, cut that out! I hate it when you talk like that." Her voice sounded sincere. It surprised me. After a moment, though, she settled back into a more comfortable role. "How come I never saw any of this so-called run?"

I could see him lift an eyebrow. "You're living off it, sweetheart." She didn't bother to answer and I kept staring at the grill. He added home fries and slipped two pieces of rye into the toaster. I was starving. He turned and reached behind the large institutional coffee urns and pulled out a small glass pot from an electric drip model. I didn't know if I was a special customer or he just didn't use the big one. He poured coffee into a thick china mug. I considered leaping across the counter but didn't have to. He handed it to me and seemed pleased to see me drink it black. The coffee was tremendous.

I talked to him while he assembled my meal. "If you served this," I lifted the mug, "you'd fill the place."

"You wanna do a commercial?" Phil said as he placed the plate in front of me.

I grabbed my knife and fork and ignored the napkin. "I'll tell you in a minute," and dived into the food. Phil disappeared and I didn't notice him again until he slipped another slice of ham onto my plate. I lifted my face and saw him staring at me. I nodded my thanks and put my head back down. I finished with another mug of coffee and a smoke. It had been a long time since I treated myself to a good meal. To any meal.

I flashed back to the pizza, then Amalfi's. I stubbed out the first cigarette then lit another as the memories lopped a hunk off my well-being.

"You eat like you haven't eaten for a while," Phil said as he refilled the mug. "You in some kind of trouble?"

"Is it that apparent?"

"It's pretty early in the morning for a private cop to be out unless something was going down." He dragged his stool over to my section of the counter when he saw I wasn't going to shoo him away. " 'Course I don't know if you're still a private cop. For all I know you could be a social worker again, doing some early morning job."

"Jesus, Phil, no one could answer anything with you slobbering in their face like that," the redhead said. "Sorry, Mister, my Phil likes you and he don't get to talk much with people he likes."

Her tone seemed almost caring by the time she finished. Another lady full of surprises.

Phil said, "I tell her everything. A man's got to talk to someone, you know."

I did know; but it felt odd to hear it from Phil. Since I began this romp, shields were sliding off everything and everyone. I wanted to smoke my joint but I doubted Phil liked me that much. "Well," I looked right at him, "I'm still a private cop. But at the rate I'm going I'll need that social work job."

He grinned sympathetically. "Having trouble, huh?"

"Yeah."

"No surprise." He leaned in over my plate. "Not if you're working on the one with the cop."

"That's the one."

"You're looking at real heavy. I never told you, did I? Julius, I told Julius. He got you the message, right?"

"Yeah. He didn't elaborate, though."

He looked past my head to the table where the redhead sat. I saw her face in the mirror. She seemed interested, there was nothing else for her to do. The deliveryman had left while I had been buried in my food.

"You hear that, Red? Julius didn't elaborate." The three of us smiled conspiratorially. Phil continued, " 'Course, there wasn't much e-lab-or-ating anybody would do, including some real Blarney Stone kissers." I could see Red begin to shift focus to her fingernails. I pulled my eyes off the mirror and paid attention to Phil. He had lowered his voice, "I'm telling you it was tighter than the Virgin Mary's ass-hole. This squad ain't supposed to exist, so the people on it don't exist neither."

"But they do?"

"They sure do."

"Why can't it be traced through Personnel?"

"They don't pick them from the force. Most people think the squad's recruited out of state. Out of state, believe it or not." He shook his head as if it would be only a moment before the Fascists arrived. "Sometimes even the regulars recruit that way."

"What do you mean?"

"When they put stripes on a black guy they hire him from some-where else. Definitely don't want him from too close to home. This Washington Clifford is an exception."

"So people know him?"

"People used to know him. Dropped out of view a couple years ago. People were more relieved than curious."

"Why?"

"Too independent for most people's taste."

I thought of Starring's head. I didn't think "independence" was the right term for what Clifford had going.

"Why do people think he's attached to Devlin's special squad?"

"Nothing hard. Occasionally shows up at scenes and shows tin. That sort of thing. Nothing for the bank, but good enough for me."

"So there was no information?"

"Let's put it this way. I been nosing around the cops and City Hall for forty years. Either the lid is clamped tighter than a rich man holds Ben Franklins, or people don't know anything offside about those burglaries. So far, all that's interesting is Clifford." Phil made sure to grab my eye. "But he makes it *very* interesting."

I had a hunch that Clifford was more interesting than even Phil knew. I lit another cigarette and offered him one. He took it but quickly tucked it in a pocket of his apron. He nodded toward the redhead and moved his hand back and forth. I got the message. I wasn't to talk about smoking, and I didn't want to talk about Clifford.

"What do you think of someone who breaks into a house to get something specific? Says he is *on* a clock? Then can't make up his mind whether to rape the woman he's surprised to find there?"

"Kills her?"

"No. Whacks her around."

"I'd say he wasn't very good at his job."

"Neither fish nor foul. Sounds like a quick hire, doesn't it?"

"He really say that about a clock?" He had a bemused expression on his face and was shaking his head.

"Yep."

"I'd say a very quick hire. And dumb. Shit, all you got to do is ask Julius. He'll get you the name."

I didn't want to ask Julius. Somehow I began to feel suspicious of the little dregs of information Phil kept feeding me. "You give me just enough material to keep me in the dark."

Before he answered I heard a peal of laughter from behind my head. I knew who it was coming from.

"I know why he likes you, private cop. You're as suspicious as he is. Do you have a name?"

I swiveled around to look at her directly. "Matt. And you?"

"Red will do."

I nodded my agreement, then turned back to Phil and his slight smile. "She's right. That's some of why I like you. Also, Julius told me you didn't run my name. It wouldn't matter, but that was thought-ful."

My suspiciousness evaporated before he finished. Too many ugly hours, too little sleep. I rubbed my eyes. "I'm sorry, Phil. I'm not wrapped very tight these days. I'm lost in this fucking case. I can put faces into roles and names to the faces, but I don't know what the hell is going on or why. It all feels ass-backwards."

He sat back down on the stool. "I wish I could help you. I seen this plenty. That's why it's an open case and not closed." He bobbed his head. "Sounds like you're working on one that's not even open. Look, there's no right way to figure things out. You just grab at whatever's flapping and hope it takes you somewheres. Ass-backwards is a state of mind."

He sounded like Lou. His words gave voice to a buried optimism, and I smiled and thanked him. He told me what I owed for breakfast, and I thanked him again. The terrific coffee was free.

So was the outdoors, but the java was the better deal. The dirty sky had turned up the brightness notch, which made it just possible to see the drizzle. It was cold and clammy and made me wonder about the climate in New Jersey. Probably the same, only a little warmer. I pulled my jacket tighter against the chill. This wasn't going to be a vacation. I thought back to the times my first wife and I used to go to Jersey. Her family lived there; those were supposed to be vacations.

I started the car and pulled slowly into traffic. I was tired but fought the urge to rush. I doubted Holmes and Dr. James could get there before the light amped up a little more. I pointed the car in the direction of my house and hoped it knew the way home.

The idea made me chuckle. My house. The one next door was mine too. I tried to remember what the front of it looked like. I couldn't, so when I got to my block I parked on the street instead of in the alley. I was standing on the sidewalk comparing the different facades when Charles came flying out the front door, his green plaid flannel nightshirt flapping in the wind and rain. He was wearing matching plaid slipper socks that wrapped around his partially exposed calves. I immediately decided to spend some money on Charles this Christmas.

"Matthew, I'm glad you decided to park in front. I would have met you in the back but sometimes it's difficult to hear over the noise from the parking lot." He was breathless from his run.

"Slow down. What's so important?"

His head drooped and his shoulders sagged. I almost reached out to keep him from slumping to the ground. He looked back up at me. "I blew it. I fucked up."

"Charles. Stop the operetta. What's going on?"

He looked at me with Mastroianni eyes. "I let them into your apartment."

"Let who in?" I didn't know whether I sounded scared or angry; but Charles had just lost his Christmas gift.

"It was a short hairy man and a lady who looked injured. She looked familiar, but I couldn't place her."

I was relieved. "No problem. I'm glad you let them in, but be careful now. I'm still in the shit and it feels closer to the fan."

"Sounds like you are in trouble?"

I started toward the front door. "Come with me to the apartment, will you? I might need your help."

—39—

Holmes was eyeballing the Bakelite when Charles and I entered. Gloria was sitting on one of the two chairs that my grandfather had happily salvaged from Dutch Schultz's bar. She'd pulled the chair over to the kitchen table and looked uncomfortable and distracted.

"Why don't you sit in the living room? The chairs are more comfortable. You might want to lie on the couch."

She smiled gratefully but stayed where she was. Holmes walked into the kitchen and motioned impatiently toward Charles. "Your friend let us in. If he hadn't we would be standing in the rain." His head was tilted up and he was glowering.

"Gee, I'd have thought you'd get back into your car." Breakfast began to bunch in my belly.

He snorted and looked at me with annoyance. Absence hadn't made his heart grow fonder.

I turned back to Dr. James. "What did the doctor say?"

"She said that by the looks of it I was in serious trouble. But no permanent injuries. A slight concussion, a broken arm . . ."

"Set correctly, Matt. Just want to reassure you." Holmes' sarcasm irritated me and I wished I had a muzzle.

"Set correctly," Gloria agreed. She ignored Holmes' belligerence. "She also hoped you know what you are doing."

"Me?"

219

"She was concerned that I didn't want it reported to the police." She looked away. "Among other things."

I looked at Dr. James with more confidence than I felt. "I hope you didn't tell her how you decided to hire me."

She smiled painfully through her bruised lips. "That seems so long ago. Why did I decide to hire you?"

Holmes reached out and grabbed the edge of the table. "Don't we have better things to do than flirt?"

"Jesus, Holmes, what the hell is up your ass?"

"Nothing. A couple of hours ago you sounded like Chicken Little. Glo is in danger, I'm in danger, and now we've been cooling our heels while you are off doing god knows what."

"Eating breakfast." I could hear Charles swallow from the corner of the living room where he'd gone to be clear of the fray.

"Was it good?" Holmes sneered.

"Great. What is the matter with you?"

"He's scared." Gloria's voice was quiet but firm.

I told him, "Look, I didn't mean to imply that you were on a hit list. It's pretty unlikely that you are in any serious danger. They wanted those records and they got what they wanted." I looked over at Dr. James. "There are no more copies, are there?"

"No."

I turned back to Holmes. "No one has to panic. Just be careful."

"It isn't that." Gloria spoke before Holmes had a chance to. "He isn't afraid of getting hurt. Or of our getting hurt. He just can't tolerate this much helplessness. As long as Eban is in control everything is fine. Only now I won't let him make the decisions."

She stared at Holmes and tears started down her raw cheeks.

They were in my home, but I felt like an intruder. Their relationship was shifting, sliding into a lacuna of unexplored feelings. I'd spent too many Thursday mornings avoiding this sensation not to notice the signs.

"Again I have to deal with your displaced anger?" Holmes tried to maintain his sarcasm but now there was a wariness, a caution in his voice that wasn't there before. "We have discussed this in the past and I am sure we will discuss it again. But why are you so damn angry with me now?"

"I'm angry at me, Eban. For ten years I've deferred to your brilliance and control. I know we've talked about this, but it always seemed so abstract or loaded with jealousy toward Yvonne." She shook her head. "All of this," she waved her good arm wearily including everything in the room, including me, "changes things. I really don't want it the old way anymore."

"I don't understand . . ."

Although I couldn't fill in the details, I knew what she meant. And Holmes did too.

Dr. James grimaced as a jolt of pain flashed across her face. I wondered what her doctor gave her. The look passed and was replaced by a flat coldness. "Nothing more needs to be said now." There was a finality in her tone that brooked no argument.

She looked toward me. "I need to sleep. I don't like the idea of not going home, but if you think I shouldn't, I won't. But please, can we get organized now?"

Charles excused himself to get dressed, saying he'd return shortly. I nodded my thanks, then reached over to the phone and dialed Boots' number. Holmes kept trying to meet Gloria's eyes and avoid mine, but Gloria kept her eyes closed.

The line was busy. I cursed and lit a cigarette. Although I no longer felt like a stranger, the tension in the room was still high. Everyone remained quiet while I picked the phone up and dialed again. The line was clear now, and I waited expectantly.

What I heard was another recorded message on another fucking machine. "Sorry, blah, blah, blah, will be away for just a day or two at most, please leave a message." I thought of the busy signal and wondered if she was in the apartment and just screening calls. I thought about hollering into the machine, but before the message signed off, she dated it. It had been left yesterday. The busy signal was just someone else trying to get through.

I sat down in the chair closest to the phone. Holmes was on me like a lousy smell. "What's the matter? Has something gone wrong?"

I had enough problems without his voice cutting across my brain like a Philip Glass composition. Over his shoulder I could see the wallboard where Mrs. Sullivan's bulb was mounted. I lit another cigarette to keep from grabbing Holmes by the throat. I wanted Gloria and her doctor to have faith in my ability to deal with the situation. I looked at the light again and caught an idea.

"Listen, Eban, you've been at me all night. I don't really know what's happening between you and Dr. James. But it ain't me." There wasn't a trace of anger in my voice. Just a quiet man-to-man. At the sound of my words Gloria opened her eyes. Holmes glared but I kept my eyes steady.

"I wouldn't be too certain of that." His voice contained a healthy chunk of hostility, but the rest of it began to drain from his body. Hell, he was tired too.

I inadvertently glanced toward Gloria but she had her eyes closed again. I kept my voice soft. "Look, Eban, we've been thrown together by something that's dangerous. Two beatings and a murder's worth. When all this began you talked about dealing with first things first. We got to do that now."

He rubbed some exhaustion from his face and said in a neutral tone, "What exactly are you thinking?"

"I'm thinking two things. First, it makes more sense if you don't know where Gloria is. In the unlikely event someone does locate you, you'll have nothing to hide."

He was already shaking his head before I finished my last sentence. "Absolutely not. And frankly, I think it's time to inform the police. I don't want you to misunderstand—it's clear that you have Gloria's well-being in mind, but you are extremely inexperienced. Supposedly someone is dead. I think it's probably time to involve professionals."

I tried to leave the "supposedly" alone, but couldn't. "I know what you mean. I felt that way earlier about Gloria's arm." I gritted my teeth, then forced myself to continue. "I was wrong then, and you're wrong now."

I looked at him evenly. "I don't intend to try to sell you on anything. I'm especially not going to sell myself. Gloria will have to determine whether she wants to trust me or not. And, in some ways, so will you. But even if neither of you do, I still wouldn't go to the police. They are up to their necks in this nightmare. I'm sure of it. You won't be doing anyone any favor if you go to them." I shrugged in the general direction of Dr. James. Her eyes were wide open.

I turned my palms up toward Holmes. "I'd like to think your suspicions of authority extend beyond psychiatrists." I waved my arm around the room. "We know that some police have been involved with this from the beginning. I don't think now is the time to imagine any of them our allies. Take a week off and go somewhere. If you want to stay in touch I can work something out with Charles. He has a machine. But for Christ's sake, keep it minimal. The more noise you make the more potential risk it creates for Gloria. The cops' involvement makes everything incredibly complicated."

I didn't have much fight left. If he kept up his resistance I was going to throw him out and cope with whatever happened. But he turned toward Dr. James and waited.

Gloria kept her eyes on me and thought for a long moment. In the quiet, looking at the woman's battered face, Holmes' point about my inexperience didn't seem far-fetched.

"Do what he says." Her voice was as opaque as the look in her eyes.

"Why?" His voice was cold.

"If he says not to go to the police we shouldn't. I hired him to clear this up. Matthew's a lot of things but he isn't stupid."

I was too tired to figure out whether I was pleased or insulted. Holmes seemed to be rousing himself for another skirmish, but Gloria cut him off. "I want you to do what he says. I want him to finish this. I want you to be safe." She shook her head ruefully. "Even Yvonne. Please, Eban, just do what he says." Her voice was so utterly sapped of strength that if Holmes offered one more note of obstinacy I would see that the talking stopped.

Charles tapped on the door and let himself in. It broke the strained silence.

Holmes turned toward me and nodded toward Charles. "What about his number?"

I looked at Charles. "I want to give Eban your phone number as a message drop." I'd tell Charles where to drop the messages later. Right now I wanted to ease Holmes out the door. "Eban may need to get in touch." I hoped his ego would keep him from calling, but I also wanted him available to discuss Gloria's cases. If I had to.

"Also, Eban, please call with a number. I might need your help and should know where to reach you." He didn't look like he believed me. "I may need your perspective on the cases in the missing records."

He was partially mollified. Appealing to his expertise was something he liked. We sat silently and allowed fatigue an opportunity to replace the tension. Charles watched for a moment, then found a piece of paper and scribbled his phone number.

"I'll keep the machine on so there will be no possibility of missing your call," he said to Holmes.

Holmes nodded stiffly and rose. He walked into the living room and retrieved his coat. "I don't suppose there is any need for me to stay around." The words were spoken more to himself than anyone else. No one responded. Gloria had her eyes closed; I wasn't sure whether she was sleeping. Holmes didn't care. He bent down and murmured something in her ear. She nodded but kept her eyes closed. A look of frustration passed across his face, but he just stood upright and asked, "How do I get out?" Charles signaled that he would show Holmes the way and, after another awkward moment, they were both out the door.

Dr. James' eyes opened after she heard the door close. "That was very difficult."

I stayed silent.

"It was nice of you to find a way Eban could save face. His pride is important to him."

"I noticed."

She looked at me sideways. "It's not all false pride, you know."

I shrugged and waited quietly until Charles returned.

"What now, Matthew?"

"Mrs. Sullivan's. I want to keep Gloria with Mrs. Sullivan. I don't think anyone will roust the building looking for her. Maybe my place, but that's all. I'll take down the light. Do you think she'll mind?"

Charles began his high-pitched laugh but caught himself when he saw Gloria wince. "Mind? It will make her day."

Gloria spoke through her exhaustion. "Who is Mrs. Sullivan? Is she nearby? I have to sleep."

"She lives upstairs."

Gloria's eyes opened. "Oh, that Mrs. Sullivan. I know all about her." She smiled weakly, "It will be fun to meet her after all these years."

Charles looked perplexed, then remembered my relationship with Gloria and arched his eyebrows. "This really is quite a scene, isn't it?" He looked at me. "There is nothing simple about you, is there?"

"Did you bring extra clothes?" I asked Gloria.

"Yes. I packed a small overnight case. I think Eban brought it inside with him." Charles walked over to the couch, reached behind, and pulled it up and over. "Do you want me to come upstairs with you?" he asked.

"I'd like you to see if Julius is home first and, if he is, bring him up there."

I grabbed Gloria's bag and helped her to her feet. The movement brought tears to her eyes. We made our way carefully to Mrs. Sullivan's apartment. By the time we arrived, Charles was there with Julius, and Mrs. S. was clucking as energetically as I'd ever seen her. My new occupation continued to suit her.

I didn't want to keep Gloria awake any longer than necessary. "Mrs. S., I need . . ."

"I already know what you need." She took Dr. James by the hand, and eased her toward the back of the apartment. "I think if you change you'll be more comfortable. Then sleep, you need sleep, child." Charles followed with the bag.

I took out my cigarettes and offered one to Julius. I nodded him into the outer hall and lit the two of them. "Julie, I'll explain what little I know, but I really need a favor." He opened his bloodshot eyes a little wider. "Sometime tonight or tomorrow, whenever she can stand it, Dr. James has to go to her office to work on her files so we can find out what's missing. She's going to need an hour or so, and she is going to need protection."

Julie's voice was a low rumble. "By the looks of it she already needed protection."

His remark was a slap, and it stung. "Well, whoever it was got what he wanted so I don't think it'll happen again. But I don't want to take any chances. Will you help?"

Julius didn't say anything, just nodded. Slap and all, I felt relieved.

"Phil says if I give you a composite you'd be able to make him."

His tight nasty grin gave me my answer.

We went back inside, ran water over the cigarettes while Charles watched, then threw the soggy butts away. The two women had returned to the kitchen, Mrs. Sullivan looking motherly and Gloria looking relaxed. I wondered whether Gloria had any family.

Julie was staring at Dr. James. "What did the mugger look like, girl?" His lips barely moved.

She looked at me. "You tell him. I can't give anyone a description of anything right now." She looked at Mrs. Sullivan who was hovering around her shoulder. "I need to take some pills."

Julie kept his eyes on her. "Rather have it firsthand."

"I'm worn out now. I can't stand being awake."

Mrs. Sullivan snapped, "You know better than this, Julius," and wrapped her arm around Gloria. Without another word, the two of them worked their way back down the hall toward the bedrooms.

I shifted my attention and described Gloria's assailant and behavior. "I want to know who the hired help was. First because of that," I pointed to the back of the apartment, "and I want it so there'll still be something to do if everything else goes down the drain." I grinned tightly. "You know how it is when you're paid by the hour."

Julius didn't return the grin.

I shrugged. "The important thing is to get her to the office. She may get hesitant about going or getting the information I want. Be velvet, but please get it."

Julius reached into my pocket, withdrew my cigarettes, and placed one behind his ear. He put the pack back in my pocket and shook his head disgustedly.

Charles had retreated to the far side of the room, almost forgotten. "Please, Charles, keep alert," I said. "I don't think anyone will show up here, but I didn't imagine Gloria getting assaulted either."

Julie murmured, "Not to worry, slumlord."

Charles looked at me. "Where will you be?"

"New Jersey. I won't be there long."

Charles nodded, but Julius was looking at me out of the side of his eyes.

"There is a stiff involved with all of this and I'm going to get some background. Isn't that the way all good detectives work?"

Julius and Charles exchanged glances.

I looked hard at Julius. "Can I count on the two of you?"

Charles nodded. Julius' mouth twisted into another mean smile. "I wouldn't want anything to happen to your shrink, man. You need one."

—40—

I returned to the apartment and thought I could get a few hours of sleep. It was impossible. I just lay flattened and frustrated by my inability to understand what was happening around me. I was tightening a noose—and more information about Starring and the case records would help cinch it further—but I had no idea who would hang. I hoped it wasn't Gloria and me.

I kept trying to sleep, and kept failing, so I finally gave it up and took a long shower. When I finished I dug through my stash, found the coke and snorted; there were things to do, places to go.

I pulled the phone, cigarettes, grass, and gun to the kitchen table and sat down. I didn't have a reason for bringing the gun. Maybe I was getting superstitious. I stared at the phone and tried to decide who to call first. It wasn't an easy choice.

Looking up at the wall I remembered that I wanted to remove Mrs. Sullivan's light. If someone came hunting for Gloria, I didn't want them to wonder about the flasher. The momentary relief I felt about delaying the calls was quickly replaced by a vague sense of loss as I dismantled the equipment. I told myself that it was only temporary, but part of me wondered.

When I finished I returned to the table. It took two cigarettes and a hit of dope to compose the message I wanted to leave on Boots' machine; it took two words of her recorded distorted voice for me to

228

shred the entire idea and replace the receiver. I'd talk to her when I got back.

After I got my answer from New Jersey Information I stared hard at the telephone. This time it wasn't going to be fun playing Rockford. The phone was answered on the fourth ring.

"Who is it?" A man, his tone brusque and defensive.

"This is Detective Jacob calling from . . ."

"I know where the hell you're calling from," he interrupted. "For crying out loud, how many times are you people going to call? We told you a dozen times that we'll go along with delaying the autopsy. Can't you leave us alone?"

Despite the surly greeting I was glad someone was home, not up here looking after the body. I heard a woman's voice saying something in the background, but couldn't make out the words. The sound of the receiver twisting in Starring senior's hand suggested attention to what she was saying. He finally returned to me and growled, "My wife says I oughta shut up and listen. What do you want?"

"I would like to come down to Perth Amboy and talk to you about your son."

"Not my son. Her son. How many times do I got to tell you people before it sinks in? Her son. I let him use the name, that's all."

I tried not to blink. "I apologize, Mr. Starring. The more paperwork there is, the less accurate the important information seems to be. That's why I want to visit and speak directly with you and your wife."

"What the hell is there to talk about? You want to know what kind of people raise an asshole who could get himself in that kind of trouble?"

I wanted him to continue but he stopped and just breathed heavily into the phone. He didn't want an answer to his question. I heard the sound of a hand slapping over the mouthpiece and muffled voices. I waited patiently and wondered what kind of trouble Mr. Starring referred to, and whether that trouble had been real or something the police up here were telling him. The questions slipped from my mind when a woman came on the other end of the line.

"Can I help you?" She sounded tired and resigned. It was a tone I was familiar with.

I skipped an introduction, the fewer lies the better. "I would like to visit you and your husband to talk about Joe."

"Must you?"

I decided to take a chance. "Not absolutely. But I think it would help." It would be nice to have her on my side.

She gave a rueful laugh. "No one has sounded very interested in helping so far." Her voice grew closed and protective. "One lousy thing after another. It's just been something for Ernie to hurt me with. Now you want to come down and tell me more."

"No ma'am, not at all. I don't want to tell you anything about your son. I want to learn about him." I thought hard for a moment and swallowed. "I don't think it's possible to get an idea of someone unless you speak to the people closest to them. As far as I'm concerned, I don't know him at all." I felt like a real estate agent poring over obituaries in a hunt for choice property.

"I'm afraid you'll only get one point of view. Ernie won't talk to anyone about Joe. And what he says to me isn't really talking. I'm sure it's much too far for you to come just to speak with me."

"Not really. It seems to me that you could talk about your husband's perspective. You've been quite honest and I would learn a great deal about Joe."

"You really are interested in talking about him, aren't you?"

"Yes I am."

She grew quiet. I closed my eyes and hoped that talking about Joe to someone other than Ernie might give her some relief. Bullshit—I hoped it might give *me* relief.

Almost as if she were whispering to herself she said, "They said we wouldn't be needed until sometime next week."

"You mean up here?"

"Yes. Can't your questions wait?"

"I don't think that's wise. The quicker we act, the faster everything will be resolved."

"Everything is resolved," she choked. Then she drifted off and added absently, "Ernie will probably drink 'til then. What is your name?"

It took me a second to realize that she had asked a question. "Matthew Jacob."

"Officer Jacob, if you insist on coming it will have to be tomorrow. And I must warn you that Ernie will not talk about Joe. Tomorrow he probably won't be able to talk at all."

"Is there a particular time that is good for you?"

She hesitated, then said, "About eleven, if you would like."

"That would be fine."

There was a moment of strained silence that magnified the background hiss of the long-distance connection. I grew uncomfortable and moved to fill the gap. "I'm grateful for your cooperation, Mrs. Starring."

"Thank you for your respect, Officer Jacob."

I was still uncomfortable when I got off the phone. Like I'd just conned Mrs. Sullivan. I still had one more call to make, but I couldn't do it feeling like this. I got up and packed for the trip.

It had been a long time since I went anywhere that demanded packing, and by the time I'd finished, less of the sleaze and more of the hunt was back in my system. I returned to the kitchen table and dialed Simon's number. I knew the call would bring me down, but now at least I had somewhere to drop.

"Roth here." He sounded tired.

"It's Matt."

"Just send your bill." The receiver crashed in my ear. I redialed his number. The line was busy. I got annoyed, then admitted to some relief. I smoked more dope, went over a checklist, then tried his number again. As soon as I identified myself he said in a hard, chilled tone, "I apologize for hanging up on you, it was juvenile. But I still don't want to talk to you."

"Look . . ."

"There is nothing to say."

"Okay, you need more time. I can understand that."

"No, you don't understand. Time hasn't anything to do with this. Call today, call tomorrow, but all you're going to hear is the same."

"Simon."

"Don't 'Simon' me. Just send your bill."

It was just like his last walk out of here, only this time I was looking at a dead telephone instead of his back. I wasn't guilty of anything except failing to protect him, but his words drove home the magnitude of that failure. I felt like doing some slamming of my own, but I gently hung the receiver back and sank down into the chair.

I looked at the clock and knew it was time to leave. If I kept sitting, I wouldn't get up. I finished gathering my things and forced myself out the door. I thought about saying goodbye to Mrs. Sullivan, Gloria, even Charles, but I just pushed my bag into the back seat and drove to Manuel's. When I got there he was surprised that I asked him to do a trip check but immediately agreed. It had been a long time since I'd made a similar request.

I met Manuel the first time I moved into the neighborhood. I was a young social worker learning Spanish, he was a young mechanic learning English. I spoke to him in his language, he in mine. Over the years we kept up our dialogue; his English became impeccable, my Spanish passable. He did the maintenance on the different cars I'd owned and, since I never bought retail, he did plenty of it. Before trips I always came in for a Dominican blessing and due to Manuel's mechanical creativity, I always got it.

And I got it today, though it took a while. It was night by the time I got out of town, and the dark brought on a fatigued restlessness. I wished it were a faster car to give me something to do with my time. Since it wasn't, I stayed pretty legal and only occasionally played tag when memories of other trips to Jersey made me too uncomfortable to simply cruise. Too many first wife fights along these roads, too many bitter attacks, defenses, and painful silences to be alone with my thoughts. Megan was from the Garden State, but between her, her family, and me, there was no garden.

Route 95 wasn't an easy highway to hardnose so, with a mixture of relief and dread, I finally pulled onto the Turnpike and headed south. I stopped at a motel just outside Elizabeth. It advertised cable television and was far enough from Perth Amboy to give me time in the morning to think about my meeting. I was too fucked up to think now.

The room was a room and the TV worked. I lay on the bed, smoked, and watched the tube while images of life with Megan danced past my eyes. . . . thrust back into the jagged shards of one lousy marriage, my inner eyes riveted on the still-open wounds in my heart. A grammar school air raid jingle, "Duck and Cover," chorused nonstop in my ears until a part of me wished the bomb would drop.

When I awoke the next morning the television was still on, but mercifully my life with Megan, at least for now, was gone.

—41—

The Starring home was on a sliver of a street off a dead end. I had
to circle the area a couple of times before I noticed it. None of the
houses on the street looked as if they'd been noticed for a long time.
Actually, calling them houses stretched the point: they were more
cottage than house, workers' housing of another era. I wondered which
factory made its bones on the people who lived here.

The door was opened halfway by a woman who looked like she
had seen too many difficult years, and stared at me like I just brought
another. Maybe I had.

"Officer Jacobs?"

"Detective, ma'am, and it's Jacob, without an s." I smiled, "Everybody adds the s."

Her mouth returned the smile and she opened the door the rest of
the way. We walked through a small, dim living room cluttered with
stacks of clothes, N.R.A. magazines, and other signs of indoor life.
Mostly male. Somehow I didn't think it was Ernie who kept it neat.
I didn't spot baskets of flowers or cards or anything else suggesting a
recent death in the family.

There was very little daylight throughout the house and I almost
tripped on a small, frayed throw rug that lay just before the kitchen
entrance. I followed her into the kitchen over to a gray formica table

surrounded by three unmatched chairs. When she turned and faced me in the lamplit kitchen, I got my first real look at her.

She was a tall gray-haired woman who looked sixty-five but might have been a decade younger. The hard-knocks impression I'd had at the door was reinforced by deeply etched wrinkles crisscrossing her face. In another economic bracket her face and bearing might have become elegant and wise; here she just looked tired and old.

"Please sit down. We can talk here, Ernie won't disturb us."

I didn't ask why.

"He's not a terrible man, really," she launched into a practiced monologue. "He just doesn't relate to strangers. His retirement has not gone well."

"Has he retired recently?" I asked politely.

She waved her hand in reply. "I'm sure you don't want our entire history." She turned away. "Would you like some tea, Detective Jacob?" She recaptured my eyes and smiled wearily.

Watching her stand there, friendly, almost open, in a kitchen that catapulted me back to my own youth, left me unable to lie. "Mrs. Starring, I'm not from the police."

She looked at me warily and put her hands in her neat gray housecoat. "Aren't you Detective Jacob?"

"Yes I am, but I'm not with the police. I'm a private detective, licensed by the State of Massachusetts. The police don't know I'm here," I finished lamely.

She pulled her hands from her pockets and dropped them to her side. She clenched and unclenched her fists. Her eyes alternated between fear and anger.

"I'm not here to bring you more trouble, I'm really not. I meant what I said on the phone."

"Why do you want to know about Joe?" She put her hands in front of her body and rubbed them together anxiously. They looked red and raw, as if she'd done too many dishes or spent too much of her life worrying. Both were probably true.

"I'm working on something that might be related to his death. It's unlikely, but if I didn't check, I'd be cheating the woman who hired me."

"You don't want to cheat her, so you lie to me." Her voice sounded bitter and resigned. She'd heard my story, or some variation, too many times to be impressed with it now. "I'm not surprised. She is paying you, and I'm not."

"It isn't the money. She's a friend. I'm sorry about the lie. If I told Ernie or you the truth, I was afraid you wouldn't see me."

"If you had told Ernie the truth he would have hung up on you. He almost did anyway."

Before I could answer the tea kettle whistled and she turned her attention to fixing our tea. I had a cupful of time to plead my case.

Her graciousness overcame her hostility and, when she turned back to me with the cups in her hands, she nodded for me to sit. "You came a long way. I suppose there is no harm in having tea with you."

I smiled in return. "Thank you."

We sat down and she pointed to the sugar on the table. I helped myself.

"Is Detective Jacob your real name?"

"Yes. My name is Matthew Jacob. Please call me Matt."

"You have two first names."

"They thought it would be easier to get me coming and going."

She chuckled and some of her tension seemed to ease. "I think I prefer to call you Mr. Jacob."

I swallowed some Red Rose and nodded. "That's fine."

"Mr. Jacob, what is this visit about?"

"Pretty much what I said. Do you mind if I smoke?"

She stood and walked to a cabinet over the sink and returned with an ashtray. I offered her a cigarette and was surprised when she accepted. I lit the two of them and said, "I'm really only doing a background check."

Her eyes welled up with tears. "Why do you need a background check? He's dead, Mr. Jacob. Joe is dead." She extracted an oversized handkerchief from her pocket and pushed at her eyes.

I waited until she finished before I continued, "That's just it, Mrs. Starring. I don't understand why he died."

Suspicion replaced the tears. "The police said it was a drug deal. Joe was killed in a drug war. What is it you don't understand?"

I sidestepped the question. "You don't seem shocked by what they told you."

She looked at me for a long moment. "I don't know if I should talk to you. How do I know what I say won't come back to haunt me?"

I pulled my wallet from my pocket and showed her a copy of my license. "Mrs. Starring, what you tell me is confidential. That's why I can't be more specific about my client and my work."

"What about talking to the police? Does your confidentiality extend that far?"

She surprised me again but I had a sudden idea. The lie lined up right behind it. "It might relieve you to give me a dollar."

She looked confused.

"If you give me a dollar I would be working for you. What we say would be completely protected. If I talked to the police it would be the end of my career." I told myself that some of what I'd said was true, and that she really wanted to talk. Then I told myself the truth; I really wanted her to talk.

She shifted gears. "Do you work for criminals, Mr. Jacob?"

I looked into her eyes. "I don't understand."

She stood and walked toward the door. For an instant I thought she was going to show me out, but she kept walking into the hall. She returned a moment later with a dollar bill in her hand. She handed it to me and sat back down. I stuffed the money into my pocket.

"Sometimes to survive you have to look the other way." Her eyes stared down at the table top as she struggled with herself. "I'm really more worried about Ernie finding out than the police." She glanced up at me. "All they could do is put me in jail. Sometimes I think that would be a relief."

She wanted to talk to someone who wouldn't beat up on her or Joe. I wasn't going to do either.

"Mrs. Starring, the police are often correct but, from what I understand, Joe was a recent arrival in Massachusetts. I'd be surprised if he could make contacts quickly enough to be involved in a drug war."

I was shoveling, but I hoped I was on target. I flashed on Clifford pulling up to Starring's apartment building, then knew I was right. Unfortunately, Mrs. Starring wasn't ready to give her blessings to my instinct.

"Mr. Jacob, Joe sold drugs in Perth Amboy."

I managed to keep the disappointment out of my voice. "How do you know?" I asked gently.

She didn't meet my eyes, but she began to talk in a hushed, shaky voice. "Amboy has been hit pretty hard for quite a while." She looked at me, "There's a story that back in Colonial days they flipped a coin to see whether New York City or Perth Amboy would be used as the major dock." A small smile stole across her face. "New York won." The smile vanished into a frown and her eyes went back to the table. "It's been hard times for a long time around here."

She was talking about the town and her family.

"Ernie was forced to retire. For a long time I worked, but it drove him crazy. That's when he started on Joe."

"Started on?"

"Picked on Joe, unmercifully, Mr. Jacob. Ernie never had much affection in him, but when Joe couldn't find work, Ernie really let him have it." She grimaced as a flood of memories crossed her eyes. "It was terrible. He would say anything, even call him a bastard. If Ernie was in the wrong kind of mood or was angry drunk, he'd beat on Joe."

I thought of the tight row of bungalows that lined the block. "The neighbors never intervened?"

She deflected the question. "We don't see much of the neighbors, people mind their own business around here."

I didn't think she meant it as a jab. "This began after Ernie lost his job?"

"That's when it got really bad." She looked at me as if I could help her forgive Ernie. "He couldn't accept retirement. Ernie was never a perfect husband but without work he was a nothing in his own eyes. He took it all out on Joe." She shook her head sadly. "It's hard to understand."

Not really. I was the Joe in my family. I kept quiet, though, and gave her room to continue.

"I asked Joe to move out many times, but he wouldn't leave me alone with Ernie." She stared at her hands in front of her. "If I had made him, all this might not have happened." Her voice had the hoarse whispered tone of the guilty.

"Why, Mrs. Starring? Why wouldn't this have happened?"

There were hints of desperation in the way her hands rubbed each other. "You see, Mr. Jacob, Joe couldn't find a job but the only way he could get Ernie off his back was to bring home money. He said he had a job, but I knew better, and Ernie never bothered to check. Joe knew he wouldn't."

"How did you know it was drug money? Did Joe tell you?"

"I just knew."

I persisted. "But he never told you?"

She looked back up at me with some annoyance. "He didn't have to tell me." She watched her hands as though they belonged to someone else and blurted, "I made him swear he would never sell to children or sell hard drugs."

"And he agreed?"

She bowed her head. "Yes."

The word hung there like a lighthouse beacon mocking my detective instincts. I wanted to get up and leave the woman alone. But the thought of driving home with nothing more than the salted wounds of a lonely, grieving old lady forced me to continue. I asked if there was any more tea. Mine had grown cold in the cup.

The request and the familiar tasks associated with it seemed to ease her ache. She stood at the stove while the water reheated and fished two new teabags from the box. She gathered our cups and poured the water just as the kettle was ready to sound.

When she returned to the table she asked me for another cigarette. "Ernie complains about money for tobacco, so he never buys the kind I like." I could hear the frayed edges of the "Ernie is a good man" routine.

After we both had a sip of our tea and smoked a little, I asked, "Why did Joe finally leave?" But before she could answer I stepped on my question with another. "Mrs. Starring, did you ever see any equipment that Joe might have used to, uh, do his work?"

She looked at me dourly. "You are being polite. You mean drug paraphernalia, don't you?"

I nodded. She looked like she was trying to remember but she just shook her head. "The only thing I can think of is, he once asked me where I bought my scale."

"What kind of scale?"

"Just a regular baking scale."

It wasn't much but it breathed a spark into my seriously sagging hopes. Maybe the boy kept his promise to his mother. If he had, it would be pretty damn unusual to get dead in a drug war over pot.

"Why did Joe leave? What changed his mind?"

"I didn't know he had rented an apartment up there until the police called. I thought he was going on a short trip."

"So you didn't think he'd be gone too long."

"No I didn't." She glanced away.

"But you thought something?"

She nodded. I remained quiet.

"I thought he was going away to do something illegal."

"More drugs?"

"Yes."

"You thought he went back on his word. You believed he was selling more than pot."

Her hands gripped the edge of the table. "No! That's not it at all. He didn't want to tell me that he was going to sell marijuana in another state, that's all. He didn't leave here to sell hard drugs, Joe wouldn't go back on his promise. He *swore*."

It was all the faith she had, and I wasn't going to take it from her. Or me. "What did he tell you? What reason did he give for leaving?"

She shook her head rapidly, really wanting me to like her kid. To think differently of him than Ernie had.

"You're afraid he lied to you. Well, maybe he didn't, Mrs. Starring. Can you remember what it was that he told you about leaving?"

It was an idea she hadn't really believed, despite her love. A life like hers lent itself to harsh limits on optimism. "Not really, Mr. Jacob. Joe talked mostly nonsense when he told me he was going."

"Even the nonsense might help."

"He said he had a deal that would get both of us away from Ernie. But that he had to go out of state. That's when I asked him if it had to do with drugs. He just laughed. He said he was done making just enough money to keep us here." A shadow crossed her face.

"What is it, Mrs. Starring?"

She seemed reluctant, but talking to me helped so she continued, "That's when he began to talk nonsense."

"What did he say?" I asked softly.

"He started talking about how Ernie finally gave him something useful."

"Do you know what he meant? Was it a car?"

She looked completely puzzled. "A car? What car?" She shook her head impatiently. "I don't know anything about a car. Joe was talking about a fight he and Ernie had. Ernie always had a story about how if he had a kid of his own the kid would be a somebody. He used to scream that at Joe all the time."

"What was Joe like during Ernie's tantrums?"

"Tantrums. That's a good word for it. Joe was always quiet. That's what made this fight different. Joe was baiting him. Like kidding Ernie about not having a kid of his own, questioning his, uh . . ."

"Virility?"

"Yes. I thought Ernie would kill him. Ernie was so mad he was shaking." Mrs. Starring was beginning to tremble at the memory. "Finally Ernie started screaming that he did have a child. That it was the same age as Joe and a hell of a lot better than Joe would ever be."

"What did Joe say? Did he laugh at him?" Somehow I had an image of a bully yelling "I can too, I can too."

"No, Joe didn't say anything."

"Nothing?"

"No."

"What did Joe look like when Ernie was yelling that?"

She looked bewildered as she recalled, "He looked pleased."

My head was spinning and my system felt like I'd just mainlined adrenaline. I knew I'd just gotten what I came for, even if I didn't yet understand it. I forced myself to settle down. "What did you think about what Ernie said?"

"I thought it was hysterical garbage," she said flatly. "Some foolish way to save face."

I could see she had already rejected the other possibility and I wasn't going to rub her face in it. But if I couldn't bite into the steak, I could cut away at the fat. "Mrs. Starring, did Joe sell drugs by himself or was there someone else he worked with?"

She squared her jaw. "I can't believe I've talked this much. I'm not going to involve anyone else."

"I'm not asking you to. Look, like I said, the police are probably right about all this. I just want to make sure. I have no intention of doing anyone damage. I only want to talk to them."

"You are asking me to trust you quite a bit, Mr. Jacob."

"Yes I am."

She worked it over in her mind. "Joe had a close friend named Toby Rudnow." She stopped, troubled by her disclosure. "I don't know if he was involved or not, but they were close."

I began to gather up the social debris. Mrs. Starring looked relieved.

"Leave everything, please. It will give me something to do."

I put my cup back on the table and pushed my luck. "Is there any place I might find this boy?"

"He's not a boy," she said with a scowl. Mrs. Starring did not like Rudnow but that still didn't make it easy. "He spends his time downtown at Warren's Tavern."

I stood up to leave. She remained seated, eyes on the table.

"Mrs. Starring, I have just a couple more questions."

She met my eyes. "Isn't it enough already?"

"Almost. Did Joe say anything else to you before he left?"

She shook her head. "Just what I've told you. That he was going to New England, and was going to get even for the abuse he'd taken from Ernie." Something new crossed her face.

"What is it, Mrs. Starring?"

"A few days before he left he pulled something out of his pocket. It looked like some official paper, like a birth certificate, and he laughed." She paused and I could almost see her looking at her Joe. The room was filling up with an unbearably sad emptiness. Mrs. Starring didn't want to know from birth certificates, but I did.

"Did he say anything about this paper?" I was pushing her further into her depression and felt ashamed of myself. Her face twisted and she spat, "Only that Ernie was too stupid and too drunk to remember he even had it." She sat there stuck to her seat.

"Had what?"

"The paper. Now this is enough, Mr. Jacob."

"One last thing. What year was Joe born?"

"1953." Her hands were twisting and squeezing, "Mr. Jacob, I must get ready for Ernie. Please, would you mind leaving now?" She didn't rise and I started down the hall. I was about halfway to the door when I heard a loud whisper.

"Mr. Jacob."

I turned and walked back to the kitchen door. She was still sitting stiffly, tears filling the creases in her face, her hands wringing furiously. "Even though I gave you that dollar I don't ever want to hear from you." She bit her lip. "No matter what you discover."

I started to say something about keeping our conversations private but she shook her head. "No matter what you discover. It's better that way."

I nodded, turned, and stumbled the rest of the way out.

42

The light outside was as gloomy as the bleakness inside, and the clouds were bunched as black and tight as my mood. Rain slapped my windshield, making good the sky's promise. Wind gusts smacked the side of the car. I thought about heading home, but decided on thoroughness instead. If I found Rudnow it wouldn't take long to get what I wanted; I was in no mood for play.

I found a street that looked like it went somewhere and followed it straight downtown. Or what passed for downtown. Small rundown hardware, sundries stores, and convenience markets lined both sides of the street. Toward the end of the road a faded green sign marked the municipal parking lot before the wharf. The weather had emptied the streets, but I had doubts whether the sun would have made much difference. From where I parked the car you could see the harbor that lost the bet. The desolation reminded me of the billboard just outside Seattle during the early Seventies: WILL THE LAST ONE TO LEAVE PLEASE TURN OUT THE LIGHTS. Mrs. Starring hadn't lied; around here the lights had been out a long time.

I saw Warren's Tavern about a half block back, so I pulled my jacket around me and trotted through the escalating rain and wind to the door. As dark as it was outside it still took a couple of moments for my eyes to adjust, though I could smell the universal stench of every working class bar: alcohol, bad breath, traces of urine, and the clammy sweat of forbidden lust and barely controlled violence. Ammonia and urinal deodorant just added to the mix.

By the smell of it Warren didn't use much ammonia.

I walked over to the bartender. About a half a dozen men sat around the large oval bar with enough distance between them to make hollering a must. No one seemed inclined to raise his voice. They showed none of the reputed smalltown curiosity when a stranger walked into their midst. No one even bothered to look up.

I leaned over the bar and tried to catch the bartender's attention. He saw me but didn't seem too impressed. When he finally arrived I ordered a Miller and gulped at it to dilute the ghost of a forlorn Mrs. Starring alone at her table braced for her husband's appearance. I put the glass down and signaled again. This time the man looked annoyed as he lumbered over. I thought the neatly folded ten-spot under the glass might lift his mood.

"I'm looking for Toby Rudnow." I expected some negotiation, but all he did was take the money and nod toward the booths in the back. I saw only one head so I grabbed my bottle and headed that way. I passed the booth, swung around, then slid onto the bench across from a praying mantis wearing a peacoat. His long skinny face was covered with the remains of a lost war with acne. His hands had a slight tremor as he grabbed his drink in surprise.

"What is this? Who are you?" He started to pull his slouched body upright.

"Stay still." The menace in my voice froze him. "I know who you are and I know you sell dope. I don't want to know who you sell it to, or who you buy it from. I only want to know what you sell."

A cunning smile crept across his ugly face. "Fuck you. Buy your shit somewhere else."

I grabbed his hand and twisted it onto the table. "I wasn't clear, I guess. You are going to tell me what you sell."

I dug my fingers into the cartilage and twisted a little more. Seeing his tiny close-set eyes still trying to figure an angle, despite the pain, enraged me. I had to bite my own lip to keep from breaking his wrist. I leaned forward and, with my free hand, opened my jacket and showed him my gun.

"We can talk now where I probably won't shoot you, or we can talk later where I probably will. There's nothing in the middle, moon-face."

The tears brought on by my grip wiped the defiance off his face. He was back to looking like who he was: an overage grifter who'd probably never been out of Perth Amboy. I let go of his hand. He pulled it and the rest of his body way back into the corner of the booth. Maybe he thought he was out of reach.

"Who are you?" he asked plaintively.

"None of your fucking business. Now, what do you sell?"

"I don't sell anything. Someone was bullshitting you."

"Have it your way." I hooked my leg around his and yanked. Caught by surprise, he slid lower in the booth. His head was only a couple inches higher than the table and I reached over, grabbed his hair, and cracked his chin hard on the solid wood table top. For a moment he was too astonished to respond but I could see him getting ready to yelp so, as much as it disgusted me, I leaned forward and covered his bleeding mouth with my other hand. I stayed like that until he began to choke on his blood. I let go of his hair and put a finger to my lips. He nodded and looked frightened enough for me to believe him. I let go of his mouth and while he gasped for air, I poured beer over my hand and wiped it on his coat.

"Now, asshole, right now. What did you and Starring sell?"

He blanched whiter than he already was when he heard Starring's name. He stopped breathing heavily and pulled a dirty handkerchief out of his pants, wiping at the blood. I regretted using his coat to wipe my hand. I started to get ready to hit him again when he finally got wise and slumped in his seat.

"We sold dope, man."

"What kind of dope?"

He whispered, "Grass, mostly grass."

"What else?"

"Sometimes hash. But hash is hard to get."

He was holding something back. "You sold more than that, didn't you? You sold coke, and crack, and horse and if you don't tell me that truth real quick, I might kill you here." I half-meant it. When he saw me put my hand inside my jacket he bought the other half.

"No, no, we didn't sell that. I wanted to, but Joe wouldn't go for it. He said the risk was too big, that we couldn't get high enough up the food chain. I wanted to, Mister, but I swear, he wouldn't let us."

"Then what are you holding back, Rudnow? You didn't just sell grass."

He looked away as if he hoped that when he looked back I'd be gone. I wasn't.

"Every once in a while we would do a job on a drugstore. He'd take the cash, I'd take the goods. He said it kept me off his back." Rudnow poked inside his mouth with his finger. "Jesus man, you messed up my teeth."

I kept looking ugly. "You did this shit in Perth Amboy?"

"No way. We'd cork our faces and hands and wear masks and drive to Newark. Hell, we didn't even need to do that. You rob a drugstore in Newark, everybody figures it's gotta be a junkie spade."

He was proud of their ingenuity. I had underestimated him. He had been outside Perth Amboy. If you can call Newark outside of anywhere.

"You do this often?"

"Every few months. We were good at it." His greasy pride made me sick, though his information pleased me. Now that he'd begun, he enjoyed talking. I knew if I let him continue I would hit him again. I lifted my hand to signal him quiet and watched him cringe. I held my position longer than necessary, and let the silence sit there ominously.

"Who did the actual entry work?"

His eyes tightened and his tongue ran lightly over his lips as he checked the bleeding.

"Don't lie to me now."

"Joe got us in, Mister." He didn't know whether to be relieved or ashamed. "He was good at it."

I stood. "I'd watch your back, Sonny, if I were you." He nodded while I almost laughed out loud. The encounter was straight Grade B, but I got what I came for no matter how ridiculous the style. I was finished with this slimeball. Next stop home.

But first a storm. It had gone from bad to worse while I'd been in the tavern. The sewers were backed up and the wind was pushing the rain with cutting force. I sloshed back to the car and sat dripping as I watched the harbor's water roil, and white-tipped peaks on an angry, hostile ocean.

I thought about returning to the motel to wait it out, but the idea felt more claustrophobic than driving through the gray sheet of wet. I checked the map and plotted my way to 95. The Pike was bumper-to-bumper with the shoulder of the road under water. I was clammy with sweat from the amount of concentration needed to drive safely.

Route 95 was better. Instead of 15 mph I could do 30. Visibility improved and, although the storm continued, conditions were good enough to think about things other than driving.

It took me 'til New Haven to weave the information into a tapestry that made sense. Although I still couldn't get the dates to fit, I understood what triggered the burglaries, but specific conclusions were fainter than an unremembered dream. No matter how I turned it over, I couldn't figure Clifford, or why Starring was dead. From where I sat, this was some serious overkill.

It was almost midnight when I finally pulled into the alley behind my building, bone tired. I thought about rushing up the stairs and collecting the records, but I figured everyone to be asleep. Driving and thinking had left me numb and needing a long hot shower. Everything else could wait until the morning. Including me.

In bed I thought about how much I had wanted to hurt Rudnow. Between the street of cottages and the bar, too much of my own early life had been jolted loose. I felt guilty about picking on the little prick, and resolved to keep better control. My resolve lasted until I fell asleep and saw myself slamming Rudnow's head into the table and felt myself laugh out loud. Then it wasn't just Rudnow. A cast of familiar characters all had their chance to chin the table.

The next morning I felt fresh and eager. Curious to learn, if I could, why Starring was dead.

43

I was busy rolling my morning joint when the phone rang. Without thinking I reached out to touch someone.

"You fucking prick," Boots' voice hissed.

"What's the matter, Boots?"

"It's just like old times; I call, you don't answer. What drug stupor have you been in now?"

What was left of my good mood evaporated. "None, Boots. I've been away working." I grew sullen thinking about the taped message on her machine. "Alone."

"What does that mean?"

"Nothing, forget it."

"Am I supposed to forget that you ruined Fran's marriage?"

"Whoa, Boots, wait a minute . . ."

"I'm not waiting for anything. I told you that if you did anything to hurt Fran I'd have nothing to do with you. And I won't."

The receiver crashed and for an instant I was flooded with angry rejoinders, but I just pushed the telephone away. It didn't matter that I hadn't told Simon anything, or that Fran's ruined marriage had more to do with libido than me. My nasty remarks went the way of the day's pleasure and I lit the joint; innocence had nothing over my guilt.

Gloria's records had stopped burning a hole in my ceiling and became just another chore, so I moved to the living room and stretched out on the couch. I puffed at the dope and watched my two closest friends go up in smoke. I tried to push their faces outside of my head but just succeeded in creating more taunting versions.

I decided to call on Julius. At least I could find out if they got the fucking files. I debated wearing the gun. It was becoming a little too comfortable. Rudnow's bleeding face flickered across my eyes and I decided to leave the gun home. Half out the door, I changed my mind. I pretended the house was under siege by Gloria's assailant.

I rapped on Julie's door and waited while he grumbled it open. He didn't seem surprised or displeased to see me. I followed his back and thought about commenting on the darkness but let it pass. I wasn't gonna look for trouble. Too much had already found me.

Julie led me into the living room and motioned toward the couch. He walked over to the windows and drew the shades up a quarter. I was reaching into my pockets looking for my Kools when he returned to the chair across from me. I didn't have anything with me but the gun.

Julius pointed to the Camels on the end table. "Help yourself." He sat down and nodded toward the shoulder holster as I leaned across the table to get the smokes. "You trying to be Al Capone, slumlord? Now that you've added to your empire you think you got to shoot the tax collectors?"

"Nah. Just feels good. You heard about the thing with Lou?"

He looked at me balefully. "Hard not to with Charles strutting like a rooster. You still haven't explained the gun. You here to hold me up?"

I lifted my palms. "No shit today, I can't take it. I've had too much already."

He raised his eyelids. "You find what you were looking for on your sojourn?"

"Some. I'm pretty sure that the kid who turned up dead broke into 290. He came up here with something out of his stepfather's past and parlayed it with what he got in the building. The information was worth a brand new Lincoln."

"What information?"

"Good question. I'm hoping the records that Dr. James reconstructed will tumble the specifics."

"You working like a real shamus."

I shrugged, "What I can't figure is why Clifford did him."

That got his eyes three-quarters of the way up. "You think Clifford killed him?"

"Yeah. First covered for him, then killed him, but I don't have any proof." The conversation was pushing Boots' phone call further away and I could feel my interest returning.

Julius reached across the coffee table and tapped me on the holster. "If what you say is true, you best stay geared. You're not chalk against Clifford."

I got annoyed. "You make book too? Did you get James to her office?"

"Lighten up, shamuslord. No insult intended. Yes, we went to the office and yes, she did her work." He lit a cigarette and offered me another. "She's a tough cookie, that one."

I looked at him through the smoke of our cigarettes. "How so?"

"It was a lot of work, and she wasn't feeling too good from the jump."

"Did she finish?"

He stared at me. "You have a jones about this, don't you?"

"It takes my mind off my new tax status."

He almost smiled and pulled a joint out of his shirt pocket. "Here. This will help."

I reached over, took it, and lit it. "Did she?"

"Did she what?"

"Finish the damn work?"

"Yes, she finished the work. I told you she was a tough one. Hell, if I believed in head shrinkers I'd almost figure her a good one."

"Why do you say that?"

"While we were in her office she took a call. From what I could hear she did good."

"Man of a thousand trades, are you? Did you have any hassle with the transport?"

"No eyes anywhere."

"You're sure?"

He didn't say anything and I grew uncomfortable with the silence. "I'm sorry. If you say there was no one around, there was no one around."

"That's right. One more thing."

"What?"

"The honkie that broke into her house and broke her arm was a loser who works for Armour Security Company. Way down the ladder. Him and the company. Rent collectors."

Julie must have seen my eyes light up. "There's no way to squeeze him. Long gone."

"You did some work."

"Like I said, she's a good one."

I sat there smoking the dope. Extortion or blackmail I could figure, but cops, corpses, and security guards left me underwater.

"Matt."

I looked up. Julius didn't call me Matt very often.

"I don't want you to take this wrong, but you are in way over your head."

I grimaced. "What else is new?"

"No bullshit now. Somebody be beaten, somebody got their arm broke and almost raped, and somebody be dead. If you're half-right about Clifford, the town's wrapped up."

His words went in one ear and out the other. "Look, I can't go to the police and I'm not going to hire someone else. That leaves me, don't it?"

We smoked and sat there quietly while I waited for inspiration to shatter the dull drone in my head. None came and after another Camel, I accepted that all I had left was the perspiration side of the creative equation. I thanked Julie for his help and found my way back to my apartment.

But not before Charles found me. "You're back!" He reached his arms out wide as though welcoming the return of a long-lost relative.

"I was only gone for a day, Charles. How are things around here?"

He ignored my sarcasm. "Very exciting, Matthew. Richard spoke with Lou and they got along famously. Richard said that underneath his tough Chicago exterior, Lou's a sweetie."

It surprised me someone thought of Lou as having a tough exterior, but I might be too close to tell. "Lou's homophobia didn't act up?"

"Darling, after living with yours for as long as we have, who cares if someone's homophobia shows?"

"Fuck you too."

He batted his eyes. "Promises, promises."

I had to laugh.

"Seriously, Matthew, we are determined to start this project. Richard is crucial to the renovations, but if my job is to be as you said, what will you do for work? I just want you to consider things, Matthew. Knowing you, you won't want to fire me. I know you are doing these cases now, but when you solve them . . ."

"If I solve them."

He tilted his head. "When you solve them, what will you do? Are you certain you want to do detective work?"

"Charles, I'm not sure I even know what detective work is, much less that I want to do it. But I'm sure I don't want to do the building." I watched as I slammed the door on another part of my life. Charles put his hands on my shoulders, neatly avoiding any direct contact with the gun, and kissed me on the cheek.

When I got to my apartment I picked up my cigarettes and had one before I went upstairs: I knew it upset Mrs. S. that I smoked. I sat down and looked at the phone. I had a sudden longing to call Boots, and Simon. I thought of how nice Julius and Charles had been to me, and wondered why the ones who got away were always the ones you want.

—44—

I stubbed out the cigarette and unstrapped the holster. If I looked like Big Al to Julius, I'd look like Attila the Hun to Mrs. Sullivan. And I didn't need any psychological interpretations from Dr. James. I tried to remember what it felt like being the client. It was surprising how quickly a four-year role could disappear, though it was hardly the first piece of my life that had vaporized. I pushed myself away from myself and headed upstairs. Time to look for someone else.

The women were pleased to see me. Mrs. Sullivan was dressed in her usual flowered housecoat, Gloria wrapped in a huge terrycloth robe. She rested in the living room with her feet on a hassock. Her bruises were midnight blue and her eyes looked tired behind her tortoiseshell reading glasses. It wasn't any easier to look at her.

"Still not very pretty, am I?" she asked. Her lips were puffy and her words slightly slurred. "Carol told me this would happen. The healing process and all that."

"You look all right," I lied. "But don't speak. Take it easy."

"Now you worry about her taking it easy?" Mrs. Sullivan stood beside me. "She was out all yesterday afternoon on that bloody errand of yours. It didn't help her mend, I'll tell you."

I felt pushed out of the nest. "Seems like the two of you are hitting it off."

Mrs. Sullivan started to say something but Gloria interrupted,

"Now, Mary, stop. I had to go yesterday. Matthew knows what he is doing."

At least someone thought I did. In any event it seemed to mollify Mrs. S. She offered tea and I readily accepted, though it stirred images of Mrs. Starring. I looked at Gloria's face and jerked back to the present. While Mrs. Sullivan was out of the room preparing the refreshments I moved to the couch, sat down, and forced myself to keep my eyes on Gloria's face. I didn't want to hurt her feelings. "Julius said it took a long time."

She nodded. "I hadn't realized how disorganized my session notes were."

"Session notes?"

"Yes. After each session I scribble information which I use when I develop my formal records. They just contain raw data."

"And you save the session notes?"

"Yes. Not very orderly though. I basically stuff them in boxes and cart them down to the basement. I have a storage area there. Didn't Julius tell you about his schlepping?"

"No." I'd have to buy him a bottle. Or something.

"He's a good person. The people in your life care about you."

I felt uncomfortable. "Yeah." Her comment made me think of Boots and Simon, so my tone was a little sharper than I intended. "Isn't saving all those things a little compulsive?"

She didn't notice the edge. Instead she started to giggle but tears quickly filled her eyes. "Please don't make me laugh, it hurts too much. I'm a packrat when it comes to records. Eban pokes fun at me all the time.

"Of course he hardly writes anything down." She looked at me. "Anyway, don't complain, be thankful for small favors."

I stood. "Where are the notes?"

She pointed toward the bedrooms with her good arm. "In there is a huge cardboard box. I'd get them but . . ."

"Nobody is getting anything before a cup of hot tea," Mrs. Sullivan announced from the living room doorway. "I've a mind to force the two of you to drop all this until Gloria recovers, but both of you will gang up on me."

I walked over and put my arm around her shoulders. "Nobody is going to gang up on you, Mrs. S. From the smell of it, you've got more brewing than tea." I was rewarded with a cracked-lipped smile from Gloria and a sigh of resignation from Mrs. Sullivan. "Well, at least help her into the kitchen, will you?"

"Gladly, ma'am, gladly."

I scooped Gloria off the couch and paraded down the hall. She started to protest then went silent and put her arms around my neck. I was aware of her body pressed against my chest. I was both relieved and disappointed when we got to the kitchen.

It looked like Mrs. Sullivan had been baking since I'd left for New Jersey. Despite breakfast I wolfed down two pieces of Irish soda bread with great pleasure. Gloria sipped at her cup and began to slip into a funk as the pleasure of my arrival wore away. I wished I could buoy her spirits but I couldn't think of anything to say—a familiar form of helplessness. I forced my thoughts back to Starring and the cardboard box in the bedroom. "Can I get the files?"

Before Gloria could respond Mrs. Sullivan interjected, "Let her finish the tea."

Gloria waved her hand wearily, "That's all right, Mary, the sooner we deal with this the better." She looked at me warily. "Is this a fishing expedition? I'm not excited about letting you nose around in my clients' business. I don't care how long it took me to resurrect these things."

"It's not a fishing trip in the way you mean it."

"What does that mean?"

Mrs. Sullivan busied herself at the stove.

"I don't know exactly what I'm looking for but I'll recognize it when I find it."

"That sounds like a fishing expedition to me."

I bit back my impatience. She was my client and entitled to know what was happening. I flashed on Boots, then Eban. This case had cost both of us something. Somehow that made it easier to talk.

"Let me tell you what I found out. The murdered kid's name was Joe Starring, a minor-league dope dealer from a small town in Jersey. From what I could gather he wasn't a bad kid, just one with no future. He lived with a depressed mother and an alcoholic stepfather who never took to him. After Ernie, the stepfather, was laid off on his job, it went from bad to worse. The mother wanted Joe to move out for his own good, but Joe didn't want to leave her alone with the stepfather. The old man used force to drive points home. Mrs. Starring never said it, but I don't think Ernie limited his violence to Joe. The kid dealt grass and broke into drugstores for spending money. Believe it or not, Joe contributed money to the home.

"So far, fact. What comes next is speculation. The stepfather had a natural kid some time in his past. While he never came out and said as much, there was a constant theme of comparison which Joe and his mother took for flights of fantasy. But Joe discovered that Ernie wasn't lying. He came up here in order to turn his information into money."

Dr. James was listening intently. The story I was spinning pushed her pain into the background. "Why do you think so?"

"Because he told his mother he would return with enough bread to cut her loose from the old man."

She looked at me skeptically. "You think he meant it because he told his mother? Aren't you being a little naive? He probably came here to sell his drugs. I never thought of you as quite that romantic."

I shook off her doubts and mine. Mrs. Sullivan had stopped fiddling at the stove and moved to the end of the kitchen table to listen raptly to our conversation.

"Listen, the kid was devoted to his mother, what can I tell you? I was able to confirm that he didn't lie to her." I had a momentary memory of Rudnow's chin cracking against the table. "He didn't have the kind of contacts that make hard-drug dealing a reasonable assumption. Also, New York would have been an easier do. He came up here with something else in mind."

"Don't forget the drugstores. He might have gotten the drugs from his robberies."

"He kept the money, his partner kept the drugs. It also doesn't fit with coming up here. I'm not trying to put a halo over his head, but I don't think he lied to his mother and she said he wasn't dealing anything harder than pot. Coming here is a long way to travel for a very small profit."

Her professional curiosity began to show. "Do you think she would have left if Joe had returned with enough money?"

"I don't know. Probably not. But I don't think the kid believed that."

"You sound like you identify with this Starring."

"Not the mother part." I looked toward Mrs. Sullivan and smiled, "Until we met, that is."

I continued, "I'm telling you the kid came to score and did. He bought himself a loaded Lincoln and paid for it with cash. We're talking at least twenty-five grand that he didn't have when he left New Jersey. One of the people in your stolen files was his John."

Mrs. Sullivan broke in excitedly, "So he blackmailed one of Gloria's clients who killed him." The tone in her voice brought smiles to both Gloria and myself. "Almost as good as TV, eh, Mrs. S.?"

"Better!" She heard herself, then began to smile. Suddenly the three of us were sitting around the table laughing. I stopped when I refocused on Gloria's battered face. She pushed her glasses onto her hair and wiped her eyes with a napkin from the table. "You never had this kind of imagination in therapy, Matthew."

I looked at her as she continued, "It's impossible for me to imagine that one of my clients could commit a murder and I not have a hint of it. And I needn't look through any records to assure you there is no hint."

"Well I wouldn't necessarily disagree with you."

"But you said . . ."

"No, Mrs. Sullivan said. I'm not that far along in my thinking."

"What do you mean?"

"I believe that Starring's hustle connects to one of your clients, but I don't know how directly. For some unfathomable reason, the police covered for Starring's burglary, then killed him."

"No!" Mrs. Sullivan rose from her chair, then sat back down. "First you say police protected him, then you say they killed him." She shook her head. "You are the one who watches too much television."

I wanted to smile but I could see Gloria staring at me with anxious disbelief. "Gloria, when you first came to me about the burglaries you were suspicious of the police. We also know I was beaten up by a cop who wanted me off the case." I needed a closer. "The same cop was there when Starring was killed."

Gloria shook her head. "I don't understand it."

"Neither do I. That's why I want to look at the files. If we can find the John we'll unravel the connection to the police."

"I wish you would stop calling my clients 'Johns.' "

"I'm sorry." Everyone sat there quietly engulfed in confusion; at least I finally had company.

I rubbed my face. "I wish I could be clearer about all the convolutions, but I'll be a lot closer after I read the files."

"And if you don't get any closer?"

"I'll think of something else." It didn't sound like much, even to me. Gloria started to talk, then changed her mind. I quickly moved to take the spotlight off the holes and onto the cheese. "I can limit the search if you give me the records of clients who were born around 1953. And who have money."

She did some mental arithmetic and started to chuckle, "That leaves just about everyone. Most of my clients are between thirty and forty. Their financial business is their own. There are a few insurance forms mixed in with the session notes for some of the people. Not all."

"You have extra copies of insurance forms?"

"Some." Her face started to sag. She hadn't eaten any meds since I'd been there. I decided not to push her or my own credibility any further.

"Look, just let me take the box and you rest. If I need any help I'll write the questions down and we can go over them later."

She wasn't happy but all she did was shrug. Mrs. Sullivan asked me if I wanted to take any of her good bread with me and I nodded gratefully. I stood and walked into the back bedroom to a large box stuffed with paper. I lifted the carton and returned to the kitchen. Gloria sat with her eyes closed. Mrs. Sullivan put her finger to her lips and shoved a bag on top of the box. I whispered my thanks and staggered home.

—45—

I slogged my way through Gloria's carton, the excitement of the hunt matched only by my fear of discovering nothing. She had separated each patient's file with a large piece of red construction paper, so I put them into individual piles on the table. After I covered the table I used the floor.

The last file I pulled out of the box was Fran's. Her name scrawled in black marker hit me like a kick in the face. She hadn't visited a gynecologist at 290, she'd been there to see Gloria. I felt like a fool. Although Simon had referred me to Dr. James, I had no recollection of Fran being mentioned. He might have; my memories of that period were hazy at best.

Standing immobilized in the middle of my kitchen, surrounded by the urgent pleadings of battered lives, I remained oblivious to the obvious connection. I suppose Starring alarms should have sounded, but I just wanted to stuff Fran's records back into the box. I was too close to the fissure in my relationship with Simon to stomach any more of his wife's emotional reality, no matter how compelling. Later, I realized that I had lied so frequently to Simon about Starring, it was almost impossible for me to believe it could be anything but a lie. I left her shit on the floor and went back to my original search strategy. I eliminated a few due to age and a couple because of money, but the majority of Gloria's clients were thirty- to forty-year-old burghers.

During the shakedown I kept being drawn to Fran's file. I thought it was just perversity, an opportunity to see for myself what her dreams were about. To see how badly I had misunderstood. To somehow atone for the damage I had done.

But I didn't think Ernie Starring would brag about a girl so I started with the boys. Dr. James' notion of scribblings must have referred to her handwriting; the notes detailed the anguish she listened to all day, every day. By the time I eliminated the first person from suspicion, I felt grateful my own records hadn't been among those stolen. There was enough material in a person's session notes to learn the worst.

A couple hours later, deep into somebody's heartache, I closed the file, lit a cigarette, and retrieved Fran's voluminous folder from the floor. A half-formed idea tugged at me. Since the beginning I had steadfastly kept the two cases parallel. Separate but equal. Holding Fran's folder, I saw the possibility of their intersection. As uneasy as I felt diving into Fran's psyche, something new began to drive me. Something more than guilty voyeurism.

It took almost two hours to read and reread the file. If I obscured the line between fantasy, dreams, and reality, I had my answers. I tried to think of what to do, but there was no divine guidance. As if by rote I stood, slowly walked to where I'd hung my holster, and strapped it on. It was almost evening and I felt like I was floating, suspended in an opium cloud. I shook myself, searching for other feelings, but found nothing except the urge to keep moving.

I reached for the phone and dialed Mrs. Sullivan's number. "Mrs. S., I have to talk with Gloria. I don't care if she is resting. Please." She grumbled but responded to the tenaciousness of my tone.

"Hello, Matthew?" Gloria's voice sounded furry. She had been sleeping.

"What do you know about Alex Hirsh?"

"Alex Hirsh? You mean Fran Roth's father? I know quite a bit, actually." The drift in her voice was replaced by an undercurrent of tension.

"Tell me."

"Tell you what? What does he have to do with you?"

"Please, Gloria, just tell me about him. If you were talking to Eban what would you say? I'll explain later."

"From what I'm given to understand he's had a difficult life. His father, Fran's grandfather, died when Alex was quite young and his mother was unable or unwilling to parent him. He was dragged in and out of orphanages depending on whether relatives were in a position to care for him. According to Fran, he won't talk about his mother with anyone."

"Then how did Fran learn about his childhood?"

"From *her* mother. What is this about?"

"Why did you assume Fran's dreams weren't a reflection of reality?"

"What are you saying?" A note of defensiveness crept into her tone.

"I'm saying that her dreams may have related to actual experiences."

"What makes you think I disagree with that?"

"Do you?"

"I don't like your tone. Why are you asking about this? What are you trying to suggest?"

I brushed aside her feelings and her question. "Do you think Fran's dreams were fact or fantasy?" It was work to keep from shouting.

When she spoke she sounded overwhelmed. "I've gone around in circles about that. When I first heard the dreams I leaned toward the idea of actual events and circumstances. But there were no memories. None. No matter how I investigated, questioned, or confronted, there were no specific memories. That still didn't exclude a connection to reality but, with dreamwork, I have to stay openminded. By insisting that it had to be reality I would only negate exploring other alternatives."

"What did Fran think?"

"She was absolutely adamant against the reality of it. Almost all her feelings about her father are positive. The few exceptions are in the notes."

"The notes don't give me the sound of her voice. They don't let me know if she's running from reality or discovering something new about it."

"The few negative instances she spoke of were ambiguous. There might have been some cruelty surfacing, or simply overaggressiveness on the part of a father who didn't understand when to stop. You sound so high and mighty. Don't you think I've been concerned about this? What should I have done? We are talking about the past, you know."

I heard myself sound flat and dull. "I don't think you're irresponsible. If anyone has been irresponsible it's me. I've had the luxury of investigating the present and I've been blind."

I shrugged off my guilt and honed in on the specific. "What you are telling me is: *you* may not be sure, but *Fran* is certain her nightmares have nothing to do with Alex?"

"No. That's what I would have told you last week."

"Huh?" I felt my face curl.

"Yesterday, while I was at the office, I got a call from Fran. Although she wouldn't discuss it, she said she had realized that her dreams were based in fact. She acted terribly withdrawn and I worked just to make contact. Apparently she had been trying to get in touch for a couple of days without success. She never left a message or called Eban. She had been so absolute in her belief that the dreams sprang from her own sexual ambivalence that what she discovered just added more pain rather than any relief."

The dread of my suspicions was replaced by a germinating anger. "Did she say why she changed her mind?"

"She refused. It was not the time to push but to settle her down and reassure her that, real or imagined, we would work it through. I know she is a friend of yours, so talking like this is terribly complicated. I've broken so many professional canons with you." She paused. "I'm worried about her, Matthew. I gave her this number and she promised to call, but she hasn't."

I registered the information as if it came through the wrong end of a telescope, clear but distant. "Well, it's too late to sweat the ethics." I tried to be light but the words hung like an overdose of carbohydrates.

"This has to do with the robbery and murder, doesn't it?" Her voice was small and almost plaintive. "Have I bungled so badly that it cost a life?"

I answered carefully. "I don't see either of us responsible, Gloria. We did the best we could with what we knew." I hoped my words worked better for her than they did for me.

"Are you saying that out of kindness?"

"I'm not feeling kind."

"I don't understand how all this fits together."

I was impatient to get off the phone. "You will, but I can't explain now. I have to go."

"You can't leave me floating like this. Are you going to find Fran? I've called her a number of times today but all I get is the damn answering machine."

I avoided her questions. "There is nothing you can do now except be there if Fran needs you. When Fran needs you. After this is over you are going to be her rock, but right now you need to recuperate."

"You sound strange, Matthew. You've got something in mind. I know you well enough to sense when you're keeping something to yourself. It scares me."

"Don't be scared. Just get well." When she started to say something I pushed the button and disconnected. I held onto the receiver and dialed Simon's home number. No one there. I hung up without leaving a message. I called his office where, after listening to that machine, I did the same.

It didn't really bother me that I couldn't find them. There were other people I needed to see. I unholstered the gun, flicked open the cylinder, and checked that the chambers were loaded. I was reminded of my grandmother who nosed the stove three times a night to make sure there was no leaking gas.

I had no real plan; no idea of what I wanted to say. But I knew I was going. I had spent too much time crawling around in the gutters of people's lives, and my own, to act like a social worker unrolling red tape.

I finished the last of the cocaine, hoping to loosen my frozen anger. The image of friends' lives lurching toward shambles rekindled my intensity. I gathered my stuff, shoved the gun back into the holster, and made my way to the car. The weather was unusually cold; I could see steam rise from my naked hands. When the car refused to start I felt the anger coil just under my skin. I would have walked if necessary, but it turned over on the second try. Too many lives were careening out of control to sit still now.

— 46 —

This night I found the driveway without pause. Even before I got to the circle I could see that, except for the solarium, the mansion was dark. The cold bleakness offered me an ominous greeting intensified by Fran's Mercedes parked in the circle, its red shrillness smothered by the dark. I remembered the last time I was here, and instinctively looked for guards. No shadowy figures punctuated the night. Except for me. The only light was the dim glow from high above, the only sound the soft crunch of my own feet on the finely cut shells of the path through the rolling lawn.

I got to the entrance and almost rang the bell before I thought to try the door. It opened, and I stepped into the moonlit foyer. I stood dead still and waited for an alarm or servants, but all that met me was silence. I walked quietly through the ballroom until I got to the circular steps that led to the promise of light. I could hear voices but I couldn't make out their words.

Halfway up the spiral I heard somebody scream and something shatter on the floor. Quietly I ran the rest of the way to the conservatory, then tiptoed behind one of the two white Roman pillars that braced the glass door archway.

Although rows of hanging plants obscured my view, I could see everyone reflected in the mirrored wall framed by greens and flowers.

Lena Hirsh was shrunk into the same wing chair she had been in at the party. Only now she wasn't made up, so the thinness of her body was accentuated, her face pinched, her eyes staring at Hirsh with fear. Fran, sprawled on the floor in front of the pool table, looked bewildered but unharmed. A vase lay splintered on the rim of the table, its flowers strewn across the elegant white Chinese rug. Alex stood on the far side of a small glass and chrome desk holding a .22. He wasn't pointing it, just looking at it.

"You come here to accuse me of unspeakable behavior and you bring a gun?" The door was open a couple of inches but it needn't have been. It was easy to hear.

Fran picked herself slowly off the floor. Her eyes were red and puffy.

"Were you going to shoot me with this?" Alex sounded amazed.

"I don't know what I was going to do with it."

"This is very difficult to understand. Do you hear your daughter, Lena?"

Lena seemed beyond hearing. Her mouth open, she was breathing with shallow panting breaths. She looked from Hirsh to Fran and back again.

"That's right, Father." The word oozed off Fran's tongue like foul-tasting oil. "Another thing you spent your life hiding, lying about. I'm not even your fucking daughter."

Hirsh's eyes narrowed and, for a moment, his hand trembled. "So you met him."

"A while ago. And paid him. Up to the very end protecting my Daddy. Or maybe I was protecting Mom, or me, I don't know. Only now I'm done protecting anyone. My sick dreams had to do with you, not me. Had to do with our midnight walks.

"I don't know what's more amazing—that I could forget or that I can remember. I even remember your forgetting game too, Daddy." Her voice parodied a child's tone as she accented "Daddy," then the rage began to spill. "You bastard, you loved me all right"—tears started a silent journey down her face and I thought about rushing into the room, but I was rooted to my spot by the intensity of the moment and the horror in Fran's voice. Hirsh stood rigid.

"You loved me so well that I couldn't stay faithful for more than five minutes, despite marrying someone I adored. I had to debase and abuse myself. You loved me well." Her tears had stopped and she stood breathing convulsively.

I was shocked to hear the raw hatred in Alex's response.

"No, Fran, the whore that you are comes from the whore who birthed you. An apple doesn't roll far from its tree. If you became a slut, thank her." He nodded derisively toward Lena and lifted the gun. "The one you came to shoot is the one you should be thanking." He leaned toward Fran and I prepared to rush in again, but he placed the gun on the desk and spat, "You should be on the damn ground kissing my feet with thanks. I took care of you even though you are the living reminder of the fool that bitch made of me." He snarled his last words at Lena, but Lena didn't notice, she had her eyes closed.

"I worked every minute of the day to make her life decent, while she whored with scum. Do you know how hard it is for someone to make all this from nothing? My parents didn't help me, my mother hated that I was born." He looked at Fran. "What have you ever begged for? Nothing!" His voice sank to a hoarse whisper. "And now you come here with this disgusting story about *incest*."

Fran said in a flat monotone, "You really hate me. You always have. Every compliment was a lie. Every gift a smokescreen for what you really felt.

"And Mom, you must have known what he really felt. If not toward me, then toward you." She shook her head and I could see the rush of truth wash over her. She shivered, despite the heat and humidity of the indoor Eden.

"You're right about your mother. She deserves everything she got." His contempt was palpable but just as quickly his distaste dissipated and he looked puzzled. His voice filled with wonder, his words a singsong. "Hate you, you don't understand, I love you. You were my doll. It didn't matter to me that you weren't my child. I was free to love you more than if you were. You make my love into filth. You insult all my work, all my love. You were all I loved. I worked for you, Fran. For you."

"And killed for yourself, Alex." I opened the door the rest of the way and stepped into the room. Three pairs of eyes turned and stared at me. Only one pair was my concern.

I looked directly at Fran and tried to be as gentle as I could, though it made me nervous to take my eyes off Hirsh. "Gloria James asked me to find you. We are concerned for your safety. Alex has killed someone. I think you know who Joe Starring was."

I heard a moan escape from Lena's lips. She seemed so comatose I was startled she had a voice.

Fran said to me, "I'm surprised to see you here." The words were automatic, and her eyes darted anxiously around the room while she struggled to compose herself. "How much of our conversation did you overhear?"

"I already knew everything."

"You seem to know more than everyone else," Alex said, his voice calm and relaxed. I turned toward him and was relieved to find his hands empty. My presence relaxed him. Put him, once again, a man among men.

"No, Alex, you know as much as me. Except you don't know how crazy you are."

Fran interrupted. "How do you know he killed Joe?"

"Because Alex has a bigshot policeman working for him who, since this began, has done nothing but make certain Dr. James' records would never be read again. And that included the person who'd already read them. Starring."

"Starring didn't show me any records when we met. He didn't say anything about records."

I was curious about her encounters with Starring. I wondered what her meeting with him felt like, but this was no time to press on raw hurts. "You were just the appetizer." I wanted to cement Fran's and my alliance. "How much did you give him?"

"Twenty-five thousand." She didn't sound angry about it. "He had information about my real father. The information was worth the cost. At least the financial cost." She jerked her head toward Hirsh.

Alex intervened. The conversation between Fran and me had allowed him to regain some of his authority. "I really don't know what you are doing here." He looked pointedly from me to Fran. "Either of you."

"Let me be clear, pervert." My voice was a growl; I felt like hurting him. I started to use my words as if they were rocks. To wipe away his corporate smugness. "Starring blackmailed Fran about her parentage, then got hold of Gloria's records and blackmailed you about your perversions. The kid was just smart and greedy enough to get himself killed. Abused himself, maybe it was easy for him to spot an abuser. And you are an abuser, aren't you? Well, you killed the kid for nothing. Everyone is going to know just how sick you are."

His eyes glittered with hatred and the mask dropped a little further. His voice trembled along with his upper body. "Who are you calling sick? I didn't kill anyone. Why should I? I could buy off ten blackmailers. You are the sick one. *You* break into my house and eavesdrop on private conversations. *You* rub your face in the soiled underwear of peoples' lives, smelling for the worst. Your own friends, no less."

I moved slowly across the room, away from Fran. Alex rocked back and forth on his feet. It reminded me of old religious Jews in prayer.

"Goddamnit, don't move!" he shouted. I stood still, about a foot away from a heavy mahogany chair. Illogically, I thought it looked out of place in a flower room. Alex's hand gripped the side of the desk.

I kept badgering him. "How far would you have gone, Alex? Would you have killed Dr. James? You moved too quickly on that one, didn't you? You or your bull. I think it was you, though, who had James beaten, the bull would have done a better job. The hack you hired was very sloppy. It's not going to take long to trace the connection between you and the security firm, is it?"

Fran looked at Alex like he had just crawled out of the sewer. He was sweating so profusely I could smell him. The humidity was stifling even with the door open. I was sweating too. There was a wet shimmer to my vision.

Fran turned to me. "Did he really kill Joe and hurt Gloria?" There was little question in her tone, certainly no surprise. Nothing Hirsh did was unbelievable. She was past caring.

"Him or his hired hands."

Hirsh exploded. "I killed no one, Jacob, no one. You little nobody, I wipe my ass with shits like you. You know nothing about me or my life or what it takes to be somebody." The veneer was gone. Fran and I talking as if he weren't there was the insult that pulled the plug on his kind of civilized. He turned to her. "You don't know anything either, you take my love and sacrifice and turn them into a dirty word . . ."

I stayed on him like a tick. "How many people would Alex Hirsh kill to keep his good name intact? That's all you killed for, your fucking reputation. Did you know that it wasn't even Starring's kid that you killed? It was Starring's stepkid. What were you going to do when Fran finally remembered? Were you going to kill her too? Or maybe you hoped she would think that fooling with a five-year-old wasn't slime but beauty, pageantry, ecstasy. You sick fuck."

I finished my words in a rush as a torrent of hatred and anger blew out of me. When I wiped the water from my eyes I was looking into the mouth of his gun.

"She was a living timebomb for me." Alex waved the gun in Fran's direction. "Her very existence left me open to shame and humiliation, and I lived with it my whole life." His eyes burned into mine. "Of course I was worried that she might remember. She had pigshit in her blood, her genes." He wiped his sweaty face. "But I never hurt her, Matthew. Yes, I touched her. I wanted to kill her, to close a breathing wound, but instead I touched her. I was gentle, and I would whisper to her all the while, and the hatred would seep out of me when I held her. Seep out of me like this sweat."

The surge of feeling in me made everything seem wet and slow. Hirsh looked like he was in a trance, and I went for my gun. I thought I heard a woman scream but it sounded far away. All I saw was Alex's gun sneer, his trembling hand jerk, then felt the hot sear of a bullet snake across the top of my head.

The blood exploded in front of my eyes, and my slow wet world suddenly accelerated like a knife slash. While the red washed my eyes I felt myself fall forward and crack my head on the arm of the chair. I finally squeezed the metal trigger, heard the roar next to my ear, and squeezed again. I wiped blood from my face. Hirsh's body wobbled but remained upright. At the same time I felt something pierce the top of my thigh. My leg was on fire, but I squeezed the trigger again. I tried to sit up and smashed my head on the leg of the chair.

The next time I opened my eyes I was on a rolling stretcher in the hall. I could see a crowd in the conservatory, but all I could hear was a roar in my head. I shut my eyes and concentrated on hearing the voices but I couldn't get past the roar. I reopened my eyes but everything was starting to blur, when into my field of vision walked Washington Clifford. Staring right at me. I tried to scream but all I did was push myself back into a world peopled by everyone who had ever frightened me.

—47—

Nearly a week later I was discharged from City Hospital. The doctors had explained that the head wound would leave just a hidden scar. The most discomforting aspect—the itch and tightness as my hair and scalp grew back. There were too many bad jokes about barbershop quartets. The doctors also explained why they left the bullet in my leg and what I might expect over the course of my unnatural life.

But everyone refused to discuss what had occurred after I was shot, other than to say that no one else had been hurt and, unfortunately, I hadn't been able to prevent Hirsh's suicide.

The head shot hadn't scrambled my brains, so I thought it prudent not to confess to a murder no one accused me of.

I might have left sooner but fear of Washington Clifford, who I assumed was responsible for the cover-up, was the only feeling that penetrated my depression. It didn't help my nerves that the gun and holster were absent from my pile of personal possessions. I was in no rush to go anywhere.

I had refused all visitors while I was in the hospital, so I wasn't entirely surprised to see a welcome party after I struggled out of the cab and gimped into my apartment. Charles, Richard, Mrs. Sullivan, and Gloria were sitting around the kitchen table with a bottle of champagne resting in a silver bucket. I figured they knew my release time before I did.

It was pleasant to see everyone, especially since most of Gloria's face had returned to normal. After a quiet drink, though, people accurately read my mood and left. No one brought up the shooting and neither did I, though I had to convince Mrs. S. I could stay in my apartment and care for myself. I wasn't in the mood to be a returning hero. I didn't feel like one. I just wanted to be alone.

After everyone left I noticed a stack of newspapers piled neatly in the corner. I rolled a joint, smoked, and leafed through them, though I didn't learn anything new or revealing. I was a friend of the Roth/Hirsh family who valiantly tried to prevent Alex's suicide. There was no mention of anyone else getting hurt. For a moment I was sorry that I hadn't heard from Simon or Fran. I felt forlorn and thought about calling Boots—but I had nothing to say.

I ransacked my stash, swallowed some codeine, and flicked on the tube. It felt comfortable to be home. I lay on the couch and reviewed for the thousandth time how blind I had been, and another thousand times how it felt squeezing the trigger. At least I had been spared seeing anyone's blood other than my own. I kept wondering why I'd taunted Alex, pushing him past his breaking point. Who did I want dead? Him or me? It wasn't a question I could answer.

Sleep mercifully arrived and, though I rocked with dreams of fire in my leg and head, I didn't wake up screaming. I slept for almost twenty-four hours, though I didn't feel very rested when I finally dragged myself awake.

On my way through the house I had found a package on the table. It contained a large and varied supply of dope. There wasn't a note, and I left it while I retreated to the bathroom to change my dressings. It was difficult to do myself and took all of my concentration. When I finished I looked in the mirror, didn't like what I saw, and limped toward my package, then pulled up short. Washington Clifford sat at the table rummaging through the bag. He looked up when he noticed me standing in the hall.

"I didn't hear you leave the bathroom."

I forced myself to speak. "If I'd known you were here I wouldn't have come out."

A tight smile skipped across his face. "Why is that?"

"We both know why." My leg hurt and the part in my head throbbed.

"Why don't you explain it to me?"

A rush of anger found a path through my fear. I walked over to the other side of the table. "Fuck you," I waved toward the dope. "Go ahead and bust me, or are you going to do me too?"

He ignored my intensity. "Do you? Why would I want to do you?"

The anger and fear merged. "Look, cut the crap. We both know you worked for Hirsh and tried to protect him. It just happened that protecting him included killing Joe Starring. Why the fuck do you need to lie now? You worked for him, beat me up for him, and killed Starring for him."

Clifford's lips barely moved. "Hirsh is dead."

"And I'm next, right?"

"You are a living fool, shamus. Why don't you sit down and take the weight off your leg? Maybe it will help you think."

"Are you going to cook me a Last Supper?" But I pulled the chair out and sat down. Might as well be killed in a comfortable position; I couldn't run anywhere. I dumped the contents of Julie's package on the table, found some painkillers, and dry-mouthed them.

Clifford shook his head and wore a disgusted look. "Didn't the hospital give you any legal ones?"

"I'm like you. Why be legal when there are other alternatives?"

He didn't say anything so I reached over to the shelf, grabbed my rolling papers, and rolled a joint. I couldn't think of a reason not to. I lit it and offered it to him.

He waved it off. "I didn't kill Starring."

"Right. And I didn't kill Alex."

Another humorless smile flashed across his face. "As far as people are concerned, you didn't."

"But I did. And you know that too."

He nodded. "Yes, I know that but, between me and your buddy Simon, it's all been arranged."

I was caught off-guard to hear him mention Simon, but it didn't stop me. "You're good at arranging things, aren't you?"

He surprised me again. "Yes. I'm real good at it and so is he. His wife called him immediately following the incident and it was a good thing she did." He reached under the table and pulled up my holster and gun. I must have shrunk in my seat because he put it on the table and took both his hands away.

"Are you going to shoot me with my own gun?" My words sounded lame, the last sputtering of fear and anger.

"I told you I didn't kill Starring. If you try to be a little less stupid you might learn something." He shook his head. "You are a hard-headed son of a bitch, but I already knew that."

I sat there, confused and quiet.

"According to the story I heard from the daughter and wife, you put most of it together. Most, but not all. I was hired to protect Hirsh by containing the records, though I had no idea what was in them. I created a buffer around Starring to prevent any incidental leaking of the shrink's files, but I wasn't going to cover for a murder. You just beat me to the punch. I was going to do it legally. There is a difference between a rogue cop and a bad one."

"Sounds like a pretty thin line."

"No thinner than between a suicide and murder."

Stalemate. It didn't matter whether I believed him or not. The message was clear; he was going to leave me alone and I was going to return the favor. For an instant I felt the same burning rage I had felt in Hirsh's house. I thought about grabbing my gun, but I'd used up my quotient of self-destructiveness for the week. At least I didn't have to be afraid. Who knew, Clifford might even be telling the truth.

He read my mind, because he took a deep breath and rose. "We understand each other, don't we, shamus?"

"Unfortunately, too well."

"Good. If it eases you any, I didn't kill Starring."

"So you keep telling me."

He grimaced and shrugged. "Maybe this will help"—he reached inside his jacket pocket, and I wondered whether he'd set me up and was about to shoot me. It bothered me that I didn't seem to care, but all he did was pull out a fat envelope and toss it on the table. While I reached for it he let himself out the kitchen door.

The letter was from Simon, typewritten and businesslike. He thanked me for my work, and expressed appreciation for my dogged-ness. He was aware of the medical report and was relieved that I'd be all right. He regretted he wouldn't be around during my recuperation.

He and Fran were going away right after the funeral and didn't know when they would return. Although he knew the house project would keep me busy, he had taken the liberty of doing the paperwork for my detective license's renewal. He was sure I would receive it in the mail in due course. He assured me that Lieutenant Clifford would return my gun and fill in any missing details, and that Clifford had been a huge help in organizing the mess.

He was also sorry that I wouldn't have an opportunity to be much of a hero, given the cover, but he was sure that I would understand. Both he and Fran appreciated my flexibility and hoped I could live with the story they and Clifford had arranged.

On the back was a handwritten postscript. "I know things are lousy between us and I'm sorry we can't talk face to face. But right now I need to be with Fran. I know it's irrational but Fran, and to some extent I, can't let go of the feeling that you torpedoed our marriage. You were right about the costs of spying. Of course it was Alex and I who wreaked the havoc, but Fran needs time to rearrange her heart. It's difficult to imagine that someone clinging to a sentimental souvenir of a child that he had no interest in could ignite such a wholesale disaster.

"I'm hopeful that when Fran and I have an opportunity to work things out, the three of us will return to normal. I really do appreciate all that you've done, I just haven't been able to get over my shock. Before we left, Fran and I met with Boots to explain things. Although she understands why you did what you did, she is so protective toward Fran I'd leave her alone if I were you. I'm sorry. Simon."

-48-

===

I might have gotten it without the letter, but I doubt it. A few days to realize and another couple to believe, but it finally sank in. Maybe he wanted me to know. Less than a week later I finally reached him at his office. He wasn't prepared to drop everything to visit a friend.

"Look, I'm sorry I haven't checked in, but I've been swamped. Believe me, I know what I owe you. I want to see you but I won't be out of here until late tonight. Can't we wait for a better time?"

"No. I'm tired of waiting. I don't care how late you show, just let yourself in the alley door."

There was a silence, then, "I don't like being away from home right now."

"Don't worry, there won't be much of a delay. I'm not planning a party."

"Matt man, you're angry and you have reason. Hell, first I wouldn't speak with you and then I'm out of town during your recovery, but you've never held a grudge before . . ."

I chuckled and hung the receiver gently on its hook.

———

I was sitting at the kitchen table when I heard the crunch of tires on the alley's gravel. The apartment was dark, but my bottle of Wild Turkey and the single-shot glass glistened in the amber anti-crime

276

security light seeping through my window from the grocery store's parking lot. My gun lay in the gloom next to the bourbon.

I heard the rattle of the knob and watched as he quietly pushed the door open.

"Matt, Matt, are you awake?" His voice was low. I didn't think he wanted to disturb me if I were sleeping. He was out of luck—I was already plenty disturbed.

"Right in front of you, Simon."

"Oh, there you are." He sounded disappointed. "What's with the dark? The doctors never mentioned vision problems."

"I don't have any problem with my sight. I just don't like what I'm seeing."

He started to open his mouth, shut it, and dropped into the chair across from me. He pointed toward the middle of the table, "You have another glass for that stuff?"

"That one is for you."

"Since when do I drink alone when we're together?"

"Since your letter. Check that, since I understood your letter."

He pulled his already loose tie a little further from his neck. "I just needed a little time to be alone with Fran. I told you that." He reached for the bottle and glass, poured, drank, and poured again. He stuck his hand inside a pocket and pulled out a cigar. "You have a light?"

I flipped the matches across the table and watched him fire up. I held on to the mad that had kept me afloat the past week. "I thought really smoking those interfered with your climb to the top, Simon."

He stared at me. "What's wrong, Matt?"

"The little things, buddy, the little things. See, Alex was right when he said he could afford Starring. Why kill when all you have to do is pay? Then there's the guy who whacked Gloria around. Why would Alex hire scum when he had someone good like Clifford in his pocket? Fact was, he didn't hire him. You did. My guess is Dr. James mentioned her duplicate record to Fran and you found out. It was easy enough to gild Alex's lily by adding them to his collection.

"The lock was the line about 'sentimental souvenir' in your letter. I never talked about the birth certificate with anyone. *Anyone.* I figured Alex had it destroyed, until I understood your letter. I had Alex and Clifford figured wrong, didn't I, buddy? You were jerking me around from the start."

Simon shook his head, drained his drink, and poured another. "You're still figuring wrong."

I felt my anger begin to crackle. "Don't lie to me, you bastard. You wanted Alex out of your way and found an almost foolproof way of accomplishing it. You were tired of being 'Simon the second fiddle.' Tired of being the boss's son-in-law. Tired of waiting. You wanted it all."

He sucked furiously on his cigar, his other hand trembling. "That's not it, Matt. What do you take me for?"

"Since I realized you killed Starring, I haven't known what to take you for."

Simon pulled a handkerchief from his pocket and wiped his face. "You have an ashtray?"

I got up, walked to the counter, then slammed one down in front of him. The headlights of a car in the parking lot shone through the window momentarily, adding a milky paste to the amber. I went back to my chair and pulled it deeper into the shadows.

"I wasn't jerking you around. My marriage was coming apart, I just didn't know why. When I discovered that Fran had withdrawn a large amount from her account, I guessed blackmail." His voice dropped lower. "I just didn't know who, or why. As soon as I got Starring's name and address from Boots I went to his dump to get him off Fran's back. I wanted him to stop, I wanted the bleeding to end. He just laughed and waved that fucking birth certificate in my face . . ."

Simon's face contorted. "But that wasn't enough for him. Blackmailing Fran wasn't enough, blackmailing Alex wasn't enough. He rubbed my face in Fran's adultery, and then tried to get money from *me* to keep quiet." He shook his head in disbelief. "Money from *me*."

Simon breathed deeply. "Matt, he had pictures. He showed them to me and I exploded. All the torture he'd already put us through wasn't enough. He wanted to put us through more. I didn't think there would ever be a way to stop his leeching. I didn't know what I was doing. All I could see were the damn pictures, the damn birth certificate. I lost it, Matt. When I first got there he waved a gun in my face, then put it down. I grabbed it and . . ."

Even in the dark I could see the tears run down his face. "So you shot him and decided to frame Alex."

"Matt man," his voice begged for understanding, "nothing was going to happen to Alex. Bad P.R., that's all, a law student could get him off. Ten million don't do time." He ran his handkerchief across his face, breathed deeply and said, "Fran hasn't been the only one with nightmares."

My fingers snaked out and rubbed the cold metal of my gun. I could feel electricity where I touched it. "You used me to bloodhound the kid and you used Fran's dreams to point me toward Alex. I saved you a lot of worry, didn't I?"

"Damn it, no one asked you to kill Alex, you did that on your own!"

The night in the solarium flooded my head, and the crease in my scalp felt raw. I gritted my teeth, and closed my eyes. Somewhere I'd harbored a secret hope that I had gotten it wrong, that it had been Alex after all who was responsible for Starring's death. Desperately I had wanted to wash some of the blood from my own conscience.

When I opened my eyes Simon was staring at my hand, the one pointing the gun.

"Are you planning to turn me in?"

I shook my head. "Like you said, Simon, ten million don't do time, and right now you are the one with the ten."

"You're going to kill me, aren't you?"

For a very long moment the idea seemed appealing. My unnecessary slaughter of Alex had shoved me out further than I'd ever been from civilization. My finger began to tighten, then stopped. I placed the gun back down on the table. "No, I'm not going to kill you, Simon."

"Then what?"

"Then nothing."

For a second relief flooded his face. It almost made me change my mind. He stood up and held his hands apart. "I don't know what to say."

"Don't say anything."

He took me at my word. He gulped the last of his drink and turned toward the door. Before he was out he looked back and opened his mouth, but I shook my head. He shrugged and was gone.

I listened as the sound of his car's engine grew faint, then disappeared. Still I didn't move. I wasn't mad, didn't want a drink or any dope; my belly was full of betrayal, and there just wasn't room for anything else. I sat deep in the dark and waited for the depression to hit. But all I felt was the tug of disappointment. I didn't know if more of me was dead or I was just older.

I sat until gray cracked the pale amber and erased the room of shadows. I stood, stretched, and felt the pain in my leg and the tightness of my muscles as I walked to the sink. I splashed water on my face and stared at my reflection in the kitchen window. The glass needed a good spring cleaning. I wandered into the living room and lowered myself down on the couch. I hoped there was a decent dawn movie—I had time to kill before I could explain things to Boots.